CW00872351

The Witch And The Watcher

The Witch And The Watcher

The Forsaken Series Book 3

Phil Price

Copyright (C) 2018 Phil Price
Layout design and Copyright (C) 2020 by Next Chapter
Published 2020 by Evenfall – A Next Chapter Imprint
Cover art by Cover Mint
This book is a work of fiction. Names, characters, places, and incidents are the product
of the author's imagination or are used fictitiously. Any resemblance to actual events,
locales, or persons, living or dead, is purely coincidental.
All rights reserved. No part of this book may be reproduced or transmitted in any form
or by any means, electronic or mechanical, including photocopying, recording, or by
any information storage and retrieval system, without the author's permission.

To Joanne Barnes
From stranger
To reader
To good friend.

Book I – The Witch

Prologue

Another Plane
The Island of Tenta

The witch sat in a large vat of snakes. Her milky white eyes staring blankly at the ceiling. A small blue and red snake fastened its mouth onto one of her scarred nipples, gently working the hard flesh with its jaws. The room was decorated with severed heads, slowly decaying, coating the space in a thick cloying stench. Animal bones hung from the ceiling, gently rattled by the numerous drafts that worked their way inside. A large black rook with milky eyes flew in through the open shutters, landing on a lifeless head. Its large jagged beak stabbed at an empty eye socket, pulling a slither of flesh out, gulping it down greedily.

"What news, Kowl?" the witch asked impatiently. Her mouth remained closed. Their communication was on a different level.

"Giant dead," Kowl answered.

"Dead? How?"

"Big man in black kill him. He kill big man too." The rook stabbed the solitary eyeball, pulling it from its socket, consuming it greedily.

"The others?" she asked.

"Gone. Through cave. Then bang. Cave collapse. Man, woman, and baby escape. Two left. Man and creature."

"Creature?" she asked curiously.

"Yes. Smaller than man. Eyes of fire."

"Tamatan! The demon with many names. He's not been here for a long time. Where did they go?"

"They take lonely road, away from town."

"Very foolish if you ask me. That road is not the place for men or demons." She chuckled, coughing up a black ball of phlegm. Spitting it into the vat of snakes, she addressed the bird. "Take the sunken road. Find Valkan. Tell him that Lenga is calling in her favour. Tell him to come here with his gang and beasts."

"Will take time to get here."

"No matter. They will find them out there soon enough. Then I will have two more heads for my collection."

The bird hopped across the room, flying out through the shutters. Lenga lay still, her expression clouded. *Elias was here with a woman and child. A half-breed, part vampire. It got Elias killed. But who are they? And what place did they come from?* Lenga pulled the snake from her breast, its fangs snapping off in her flesh. She threw the reptile across the room, pulling the teeth from her nipple with gnarled fingers. *Whoever they are, they are from lands beyond the forest. They were far from home.* She smiled, her blackened teeth poking out through her cracked lips. "Man flesh. I cannot wait to taste you, whoever you are."

* * *

Far away, in another place, a force stirred. Deep below a red crypt where a recent battle had raged, the force began pulsing. It had been contained in the lifeless pit, devoid of light and air for hundreds of moons. The force took shape, trying to find a weakness in the red stone walls. It could feel similar energy far off. The entity called to it, pulling it towards the red land, where a constant wind battered anything exposed to its wrath. It sensed a weakness in the confines, a hairline crack that led to the surface. The misty apparition waited patiently for its allies, focusing its energy on breaking through. It needed to escape, craving a new purpose. Chaos.

* * *

The scorched forest lay in darkness, low clouds blocking out the moon's glow. Wisps and tendrils of long dead beings writhed and twisted around the blackened trees, which were showing the first signs of recovery after the recent fires. In between two trees, a black doorway, framed in a blue glow, disappeared for the night. The forest lay quiet. No animals dwelt there, choosing to leave Amatoll for safer climbs. It was a graveyard of trees. Morbid and still. A whisper on the wind, caused the spirits to stir. They felt the call from far away, a voice echoing through the land. As one, the entities began to move, gliding through the forest towards another doorway. A doorway to another place. A red place, with howling winds and dark forces.

One

Vicky lay on the kitchen floor, her makeup streaked with tears. Her reddened-eyes, tightly closed. She lay in a ball, a silent scream escaping her ragged mouth. She was dressed in black. Her once immaculate hair was as unruly as her attire. A loud sob echoed around the kitchen as the crying intensified. "Why? Why us? Why God why?" She flipped onto her back, her stockinged feet banging the quarry-tiled floor. The woman's hands were pressed to her face, trying to block out the cruel world around her.

"Mummy," a voice said. The boy ran over, his socks skidding on the smooth floor. He sat next to his mother, lifting her head into his lap. Dark brown eyes framed by wavy dark hair looked down at his beloved mother. A mother that he'd watched fall apart over the last few weeks. "Don't cry, Mummy. Please," he said as his voice cracked with emotion.

Vicky looked up, seeing the angelic face of her youngest child, contorted in grief and pain. "Oh, Jasper. I'm sorry. Don't cry, baby bear." She got up, pulling her son into her embrace. "Mummy's just upset. But I will be okay. I have to be. I have to take care of my boy." She kissed the top of his head, drinking in his smell. She closed her eyes, blocking out the pain for a brief moment.

"I need to look after you too, Mummy. It's just the two of us now. I'll help you as much as I can. I will even tidy my room before bedtime. Well, most nights anyway."

Vicky laughed, squeezing her only remaining child to her chest. "I love you, baby bear. More than you'll ever know."

"I love you too, Mummy." Tears fell freely from her eyes. "I'm so sad that Daddy, Lucy, and Brett are up in the stars. I really miss them. I miss Daddy's beard, tickling my face. I miss Lucy's lame music and Brett's bad guitar playing. I wish they were still here." Jasper's emotions boiled over as he wept in his mother's arms.

"It's going to be alright, Son. Really, it will be." Her empty promise died away, leaving them sitting on the kitchen floor, holding onto each other. Clinging to hope, when hope had deserted them.

* * *

"No, I'm not the account holder. My husband, Steve Evans was the account holder. He recently passed away. I want to become the account holder. Can you help me?" Vicky sat on the settee, her feet propped on the coffee table as she looked out of her bay window. Spring was starting to show in her garden. The first shoots of green could be seen appearing, alongside the already green holly bushes and conifers that surrounded the cottage. "Death certificate? Do you really need me to send you that?" she said, her emotions starting to rise. The voice on the other end of the line paused as Vicky began to cry. The person, who was sitting four thousand miles away on another continent, decided to wave the rules. The change in tack calmed Vicky somewhat, her tears wiped away with the back of her hand. She thanked the person on the other end of the line, telling them quickly that she didn't require any more help. Vicky ended the call, dropping the phone on the settee next to her. She laid her head back on the cushion and closed her eyes. She breathed deeply, trying to remember what her old yoga teacher had told her. The window was open a few inches, allowing the sounds of her front garden to filter inside. Birds could be heard in the trees, the sounds of bushes rustling in the gentle breeze. For a brief moment, all the pain of the last few weeks ebbed away. She stretched her feet, pointing her toes to the ceiling. The phone's ring tone shattered the silence. Vicky's eyes fluttered open as her hand reached for the offending object. She pressed the green button.

"Victoria. Are you okay?" a female voice asked.

"Hi, Mum. I'm fine. Just having five minutes."

"Oh! Sorry, love. Shall I call back later?"

"It's fine. Are you and Dad okay?"

"We're alright," the voice lied smoothly. "Your Father is out in the garden, attempting to cut wet grass. I was wondering if you and Jasper would like to pop over for a bit of supper this evening?"

"He's got football after school. That should finish by five. What time do you want us?"

"After that is fine. I'm cooking your favourite."

"Chorizo and butterbean stew. Sounds just what I need."

"That's why I'm cooking it. We'll see you later then. I'll let you get back to your five minutes. Love you."

"Love you both too," Vicky said before ending the call. Five minutes later her toes, encased in black socks, were pointing to the ceiling once more. Her chest rose and fell gently as Vicky tried mentally to slow her heartbeat. Gradually it started to decrease. The woman was about to fall asleep when the phone rang once more. *Shit!* She snatched the ever-offending object off the sofa and pressed the green button again. "Hello?"

"Mrs Evans?" a male voice said.

"Yes."

"Sorry to bother you. It's Mr Wellings, from Jasper's school. There has been a bit of an incident here. Would you be able to pop down and pick him up?" Vicky's lessening heartbeat was now hammering in her chest. The solitude shattered.

* * *

Jasper sat in his grandparent's conservatory wrapped in a blanket. His head was propped on two cushions, headphones plugged into his tablet. He was oblivious to the rest of the world as he lay playing his favourite game. In the lounge, Vicky sat on a large brown sofa, her legs tucked underneath her. In one hand she held a steaming mug of Cappuccino. Her other arm rested on the side of the sofa. She faced her parents across the cosy room. It had recently been re-decorated, with an ochre feature wall behind a real brick fire surround and wood burner. The other walls were painted a deep cream, canvases and family pictures adorning the walls. A large mango wood coffee table sat in the centre of the room on a thick rug, adding to the showroom feeling. The rest of the floor was wooden, polished with love and care. Every item of furniture was either oak or mango wood. All individual, giving the room a premium quality. Vicky thought it was the kind of lounge you would see in a glossy magazine in a doctor's waiting room. She felt at home. Safe and warm. Karen and Mike Tucker sat opposite her, mugs in hands. Their expressions were sombre.

Mike placed his mug on a cork coaster on the coffee table, picking up the piece of paper that lay folded on the wooden top. He opened it, tears stinging his eyes as he looked at the crude drawing. In the middle of the page, a burning car lay on its side, three stick figures lay around it, all on fire. He balled the paper in his fist, tossing it back onto the table. "Little bastards! How can kids be so horrible?"

"Beats me, Dad. The boy that did this is a right little bleeder. He's the class bully. Well, he was, until Jaspy punched him one. He'll think twice about doing that kind of thing again."

"How is Jasper?" Karen Tucker said. Her closely cropped grey hair framed an attractive face. A face used to laughter and mirth. However, the last few weeks had already taken their toll on her. She was a youthful sixty-four, full of vigour and zest. She sat looking at her daughter, feeling ten years older than she should.

"He seems okay. More angry than upset. The Head Master hasn't exactly suspended him. Rather sent him home until the dust has settled. I'm sure the parents of the boy who did this will get involved. They'll probably rock up at the school tomorrow. So, I've been told to bring him back on Monday."

"Oh well, at least he gets a long weekend," Mike said as he reached for his coffee mug once more. The threesome all looked into the dimly lit conservatory, their collective hearts reaching out to the young boy, who seemed oblivious to their stares.

"So young," Karen said, shaking her head. "Lucy and Brett too." Her voice trailed off as Mike placed a weathered hand on her black trousers, squeezing gently. The older woman melted into her husband, crying openly. Vicky was over a second later, wrapping her arms around her parents. They all wept together, sharing their pain. The closeness that had formed over the course of their lives solidified and hardened even more-so as their tears and sorrow mingled. Mike held his wife and daughter, wishing that his son-in-law had taken a different route that day. Wishing that they'd stopped off for a burger at a motorway service station, instead of being run off the road by a drunk driver. He'd closed his eyes tightly when he recounted what the news reporter had said a few weeks before. He'd been sitting with his wife, watching the early evening news, unaware that the three people who had burned to death in a wrecked car, had been his son-in-law and two grandchildren. He cast the memory aside as his daughter broke the embrace.

"Oh, Mum!" Vicky started. "It'll be okay. We'll get through this." Her words ended as sobs wracked her body. They sat there, clinging onto each other as Jasper sank a birdie on his favourite golf game. Thoughts of death and pain, a million miles away.

Two

As the hills slept, a faint blue glow appeared between two trees. It barely illuminated the night, blinking out a few minutes later. A yellow mist lay dormant on the forest floor. Nearby animals woke from their slumber, taking flight in the darkness. The mist started moving slowly, clockwise around the trees. It sensed something far off, gliding through the forest towards the unknown beacon. It skirted a golf course to its right, gradually climbing as the pull became stronger. It made its way ever upwards, through thick undergrowth until it broke out onto a deserted road. The mist crossed the black tarmac, heading back into trees and undergrowth until it came to rest a few hundred yards later. It settled on the wet grass, gently swirling in the blackness of night. Across the lawn, a small cottage sat, framed by trees and holly bushes. Two people inside, one sleeping soundly, the other, restless.

* * *

"Do you want a sausage sandwich, Jaspy?" Vicky asked across the kitchen. Spring light spilled into the room, bathing the kitchen in crisp sunlight. On the stove, a deep frying pan held sizzling sausages, their aroma flowing through the cottage. A digital radio sat on the windowsill, gently playing Take it easy, by *The Eagles*.

Jasper glanced up from his comic, looking at his mother. "Yes please, Mummy. Could you dip the bread like Nanny does?"

"It's not very healthy, baby bear. But just this once I'll do it for you. Sauce?"

"Brown please," Jasper said as his eyes dipped back to his comic. Talk of sausages was replaced by *Captain America* and *Tony Stark*.

Vicky walked over to the double fridge, pulling a pack of Lincolnshire sausages from the middle shelf. As the door clicked shut, she expertly grabbed an egg from the door compartment. Her bare feet moved soundlessly over to the Range-master, where she deposited two plump sausages in the black pan. Fresh sizzles echoed through the kitchen as The Eagles were replaced by *R.E.M.* Two minutes later, Vicky placed a plate in front of Jasper, ruffling his bed hair as he tucked into his breakfast. She walked back over to the cooker, rattling the pink sausages around in the pan. Picking up her coffee mug up from the counter, she took a sip as she watched her son. She smiled as he sucked egg yolk from his thumb, before taking another hearty bite. Vicky would never have admitted it to anyone, but Jasper had always been her favourite. Lucy and Brett, she'd loved to bits. When her daughter was born, Vicky had been in her early twenties. Brett had come along a year later, taking over her world whilst her husband Steve, had worked all hours to grow his I.T consultancy business. He was six years her senior, already attracting attention from local companies, who'd needed his skills. Vicky was quite happy to have played full-time mum, her life spent at playgroups, coffee mornings, and children's parties. When Brett had finally started school, Vicky decided to resurrect her career in graphic design, securing a part time position with a local company in the nearby town of Redditch in North Worcestershire. For five years, Vicky had enjoyed the flexibility of being a graphic designer and a mum, whilst Steve worked seventy-hour weeks, coming home most nights when the children were in bed. It had worked perfectly for them though, enjoying and appreciating the time they had together. Her parents would regularly babysit, allowing the young couple to share quality time at fine restaurants, pubs, and concert venues. Vicky knew that her parents had tried doubly hard, filling the void that Steve's parents had left when they'd both succumbed to cancer within a few years of each other. Just when life had settled into a steady rhythm, Vicky had fallen pregnant once more. Steve had reacted swiftly, buying a four bedroomed cottage on the fringes of the Lickey Hills, not far from their Alvechurch home. Vicky had instantly fallen for the cottage, loving the secluded, secure feeling it gave the family. She gave up work again, devoting her time to looking after her new arrival, Jasper. She'd been besotted by his dark looks, a trademark inherited from her half Spanish husband. Vicky herself had a faintly Mediterranean look. Her brown hair and naturally tanned skin melding well with the rest of her clan. Jasper had grown into a fine young boy. Lovable but sensitive. His elder siblings tended to do their own thing, the age gap becoming apparent as they'd ventured into their teenage years. But they were close. They were a happy family, liking nothing more than spending time sat around the dining table, recounting their days, or listening to Steve's corny jokes. They had been the perfect family. Until six weeks before, when it had all changed. Vicky still felt numb to it all, not quite believing that her husband and two children could be taken away so cruelly and suddenly. The drunk driver had been arrested and charged. Vicky had been contacted by the police on numerous occasions over the following weeks, giving her updates. The trial was imminent. Vicky had told the authorities that she would not attend. She was not part of the accident and was content to let the system take over. She knew that the man who'd taken away her family would receive jail time. Probably a few years, which was nothing compared to the devastation he'd wreaked. Her focus was Jasper. The woman's eyes grew misty as she watched him polish off his breakfast, taking a glug of orange juice to wash it down. He was eight years old, and Vicky knew that she needed to provide a safe and loving haven for him. He'd suffered a cataclysmic shock, which if not treated properly, could send him off the rails as he became older. She was not short of money. Steve had ensured that in the event of his death, the remaining family members would be taken care of. At thirty-eight years old, Vicky had accepted that she would probably never work again. Or if she did, it would be in years to come when Jasper was ready to leave his teenage years behind. She finished her coffee, placing the mug in the dishwasher. "Do you want anything else, Son?"

"No thanks, Mummy. That was delish."

Vicky grinned, loving how her son had adopted one of her favourite words. "What do you want to do today? Shall we go for a walk?"

"Okay. Or I could play the *X-box* for a bit?"

Vicky sighed and smiled at the same time. "Alright then. We can go for a walk this afternoon. I'll pull a few weeds out this morning," she said, looking out at their rear garden, its manicured lawns leading to a post and rail wooden fence that drew the boundary with the Lickey Hills beyond.

"Mummy. Will I get in trouble for punching Sean?"

"No, Jaspy," Vicky said as she pulled up a chair. "I will make sure you don't. The boy that did this is very nasty and cruel. He did a horrible thing to you."

"Sorry I punched him, Mummy," Jasper said solemnly.

"That's okay, love. Normally I would not approve of violence. But that little boy deserved it."

"Why was he so nasty about Daddy, Lucy and Brett?" Jasper's eyes turned misty.

Vicky placed her hand over his, gently stroking it. "Some people are like that, Jaspy. Most people are nice, but sometimes, people do and say nasty things to hurt us."

"It's not nice."

"No, it's not," Vicky said as she looked into her son's deep brown eyes. "But you will just have to ignore people like that, Son. On this occasion, you did what you thought was right. I'm sure Sean will not be bothering you, or anyone else again."

"I hope not, Mummy. Can I play *X-box* now?"

Vicky smiled, ruffling her son's dark locks. "Of course you can, baby bear."

Jasper pulled his chair out, the wooden feet scraping the quarry-tiled floor. He embraced his mother, squeezing with all his strength. "Love you, Mummy. You are the best mummy ever."

I love you too, Jaspy. You are the best little boy ever," she said as tears peppered her eyes.

An hour later, Vicky was dressed for gardening. Khaki combat trousers, a blue fleece over a black top, and a pair of trainers were deemed appropriate for the balmy spring morning. Tying her hair back into a pony, she walked out to the shed at the side of the cottage, sliding the bolt. Two minutes later, Vicky was on her knees on a polystyrene mat, pulling weeds from the bare flower beds. Her mother had once told her what the weeds were called. *Hibiscus?* She thought as she stuffed a clump of greenery into the black bin liner. She worked her way methodically around the garden, half filling the black bag with various green things that she'd forgotten the names of. As she was about to walk back to the house, something caught her eye underneath a line of conifers that ran the length of the garden. She hunkered down, a cold feeling settling over her as she pulled a dead cat from the undergrowth. "Oh no!" she said, recognising Gracie, the cat from next door. Its lifeless eyes stared at Vicky, its body cold and stiff. She inspected the dead cat for signs of injury, finding nothing. *Strange. She's only a few years old*, Vicky thought as she ran her gloved hands over the animal's flank. *What happened to you, poor Gracie?* She walked back to the house, returning a minute later with a large brown box that had been sent from *Amazon*. Vicky gently laid the dead cat in the box, closing the flaps. The temperature and light dropped a few degrees as the sun was obscured by a large cloud. A stiff wind kicked up on the other side of the fence, rippling the lawn as it blew towards Vicky. The cardboard flaps opened and closed as the strong breeze buffeted them. A noise carried to Vicky's ears, making goosebumps stand proud on her neck. *What was that?* she thought as the wind whistled through the trees. Her bamboo chimes protested loudly, rapping against the tree trunk that they hung against. *Is it a far-off train?* Vicky thought as she walked over to the fence. She rested her elbows against the damp wood, trying to catch the noise once more. As her eyes dropped from the horizon Vicky's mouth fell open as she noticed several dark shapes on the grass beyond the fence. *Oh my God!* She ducked through the railings like a prize fighter, striding over towards the inert shapes. On the grass in front of her, lay several dead birds. All black. All large. Blank dead eyes staring up at the darkening skies.

"What the hell is going on?" The sound came again. Closer, more distinct. It set her teeth on edge, like nails drawn across a blackboard. Vicky whirled around as the wind intensified, feathers being plucked from the sad carcasses, flying towards the house. She was just about to head back to the house when something in a nearby hedgerow caught her eye. She walked over tentatively, stopping when a yellow mist spilled from the undergrowth. *What the-* she thought before the mist was lost on the breeze. As it dissipated, a low drone echoed around the Lickey Hills. The wind stopped dead, leaving Vicky stood there, her mind baffled as to what had just taken place. Her thoughts skipped back to the mist. *Was that gas? Could that have killed Gracie and the birds?* She slowly walked back to the house, opting to leave the birds for the foxes that would surely turn up later. Ducking back through the fence, Vicky spied the cardboard box, deciding with a leaden heart to ruin an old lady's day before she went for a walk with Jasper.

Three

Lenga crouched low over the crude tabletop, her withered breasts swishing against the rough planks. Stood before her was a giant of a man, his unkempt black hair almost touching the wooden ceiling. He stared at the witch through impenetrable black eyes. His swarthy skin pockmarked and scarred. An equally unkempt black beard almost reached his belt buckle. He stood watching the old hag patiently. At his side, an equally large man loomed. His shaven head covered in tattoos. His only eye surveying the snakes that writhed in the large vat. Over his empty eye socket, he wore a leather patch with a white spider stitched crudely across the front. At their side sat two large hounds. Huge heads in line with the men's chests. Their long grey tufted coats, bare in places, lesions adorning the skin. Their black eyes as dead as night.

The bearded giant cleared his throat. "What do you see, Lenga?"

The witch coughed up a ball of black phlegm, spitting it onto the table. She took an obsidian blade from her gown, slicing her wrist until it sprayed dark red blood across the table top. Her long fingers scored the surface, mixing the phlegm and blood into a grisly mosaic. "They have travelled far, in the time it took you to get here. They have entered the swamplands. How long will it take you to catch them, Valkan?"

The giant rubbed his face, his eyes not giving anything away. He turned to his brother. "Cranja. What say you?"

"Seven Moons," the other giant said, his light, lyrical voice out of place in the dreary cabin.

"Is that quick enough for you, Lenga? It will take at least another seven moons to get back, maybe longer."

"Fine, fine. I can wait. I've waited a long time for the taste of man flesh." She looked at the two men. "I know you are men. But you're diseased and riddled with pox and other nasties. This man is from another world. He'll surely taste like the sweetest nectar. It makes my quiver tingle just thinking about it." To emphasise her point, she rubbed herself between her thighs, cackling as she did so. Cranja's face wrinkled in disgust as she sniffed at her slick fingers, turning away to look at one of the severed heads on the wall.

"Well, we will begin the hunt immediately. The boys outside can forge on ahead, for they are faster of foot than us two ogres."

"You can do what you want with Tamatan. Eat him. Sodomize him. Feed him to your hounds for all I care. But bring the man to me, unmarked and unsullied."

"You have my word," Valkan said.

"Pah! Your word is as hollow as my dug's. Make sure you bring him unharmed. If you do, sweet treats will befall you. Now go. Make haste. I need to take my rest." She shuffled over to a rocking chair easing herself down, her bones protesting as loudly as the wood she sat against. "If you do eat the demon, bring his head all the same. It will look good on my wall."

The brothers made their way outside, the hounds shuffling after them. Twenty men stood, idly smoking crude pipes as the mist blew in from the sea. Valkan motioned them closer. "Listen up. They have taken the lonely road towards the swamps. A man and Tamatan the demon. The man is to be unharmed. Do you hear me?" A collective nod of heads. "Any man who harms him will taste my balls in his mouth." A low chuckle ran through the gang. "We will follow. Go. Get them." The men trotted off down the muddy slopes, towards the collapsed cave next to the sea. The two huge hounds following them. Valkan and Cranja walked slowly after them, lighting pipes of their own. As he blew out a breath, Valkan addressed his brother. "We said we'd not harm him. That doesn't mean that we can't have a bit of fun though."

The other man smiled, revealing blackened stumps. "I've not had sweet meat for a while. We can sample his backside a few times before we give him over to the old hag." They broke into a jog, their heavy boots thudding on the earth as they went. Both men held similar thoughts as they ran into the depths of night. Man flesh.

* * *

The two figures huddled together in the darkness. The moon above was shrouded in low clouds and mist, keeping the land cool. The glow from the demon's eyes cast a red hue on the tufted grass where they sat.

"How much further?" the man asked, massaging his thigh.

"I have no idea, Jake. This is an un-travelled road for Tamatan. The sea looks to have given way to swamps. We must carry on. There is no turning back. They will be coming for us."

"You still think that?" the man asked, wincing as his fingers probed a tender piece of muscle on his thigh.

"Without a doubt. I'd not visited that place for a long time. But there is darkness there. Darkness that will know we were there. The witch will send someone to take us back."

"Lenga."

"Yes, Lenga. She will want our heads on spikes, and not before she has had her fun. That's why there is no turning back. We must carry on if we're to find our way back to our loved ones. I do hope my family is safe."

"Mine too," Jake said solemnly. "Mine too."

* * *

The cottage was quiet. Around it, the forest lay still, no sounds of animals or far off traffic could be heard. Past the wooden fence that separated the cottage garden from the Lickey Hills, a mist appeared from a fir tree. It snaked its way down the trunk to the wet grass, slowly moving towards the cottage. As it reached the kitchen door, it wound its way around a drainpipe, slowly climbing until it reached the guttering. The yellow form slid its way across grey roof tiles, heading towards the window on the corner of the cottage. It pressed itself against the glass, swirling and pulsing as it located its quarry. The malevolent force sensed a life form beyond the glass. It swirled rapidly, pushing against the pane, trying to find a way in. Hitting the glass with more force, caused the sleeping life form inside to stir in their sleep. The mist sensed something to its right, a slither of its mass breaking away from the rest. It headed upwards, creeping through a vent built into the wall. Yellow tendrils seeped out of the other side of the vent into the bedroom beyond, curling their way down a light stand. It crawled over the carpet, climbing up the end of the bed, before making its way towards the life form. The vapour sat on its chest, feeling the rise and fall of its breathing, listening to a steady heartbeat. The mist outside enveloped the entire window, darkening the room further as the tendrils made their move. As Jasper breathed in steadily, the mist found its way in, snaking its way up his nostrils, vanishing from sight. Outside, the yellow cloud dispersed, heading away into the darkness. To wait. Jasper breathed deeply, his dark brows twitching slightly. He squeezed the brown bear that he'd always slept with, slowly wringing its neck with his hand. His eyes opened suddenly, the iris's yellow and blank. He blinked twice, clearing the yellow mist that quickly snaked its way into his mouth. Jasper sat up, his Captain America duvet falling away from him. Dark eyes fixed on the window as a word formed on his lips. "Reggan."

Four

The warm Mediterranean waters tickled Vicky's feet, her toes digging into the wet sand, as the surf washed over her ankles. The sun's strength was abating as the afternoon headed into early evening. The vast expanse of blue in front of her, turning pink as the sun dropped towards the horizon. Vicky smiled at the anticipation of a beautiful evening ahead, spent with the man she loved. She looked down at her tanned legs, smiling as she splashed sea water over them. The woman felt content.

"You look so beautiful, baby bear. I could stare at you forever. No one on this beach even comes close to you." Steve said next to her.

She looked at him, her breath catching in her throat. He was so beautiful to her. His dark hair and skin appearing full of life in the balmy afternoon sun. Steve's stone shorts and linen shirt completing the intoxicating ingredients. She was totally in love with him. "You give me butterflies, Steve Evans. I'm sure other girls on the beach are prettier than me. But thank you." She reached over, kissing his salty lips. He returned the kiss, holding her face in his hands. Goosebumps peppered her tanned flesh as he held her. She was tipsy. And he was her alcohol.

He broke the kiss, his eyes opening like it was the first time. "I love you, Vicky Tucker."

"I love you too, Steve Evans." The world around them melted away as they became lost in the moment.

Finally, Steve looked out to sea, the breeze ruffling his hair. "Are you hungry?"

"Starving, babe. Shall we grab a bite to eat? We could eat at the restaurant on the cliff, the one we walked past yesterday. La Plancha."

"Why not. I'm ravenous." He took her hand, kissing her palm gently. "I'm ravenous for you too, Señorita. I'll leave a little room for pudding later."

She blushed, drinking in his dark features.

Ding-dong!

Vicky looked around herself, trying to locate the noise that had invaded their moment. She shrugged it off, returning her gaze to her boyfriend. "Shall we go straight there? I don't want to go back to the hotel. Let's eat."

"Sounds good to me, babe. I'm gonna try the Cataplana tonight. It's-"

Ding-dong!

"Can you hear that noise, Steve?"

"Noise. No, babe?"

Knock, knock, knock. Steve's face evaporated from view as the banging continued.

Knock, knock, knock. Vicky sat up in bed, momentarily disoriented. She looked at the clock on the wall. Seven. *Who's knocking my door this early?* The knocking came again. Louder this time. She swung her feet off the bed, heading over to the bedroom door, grabbing her dressing gown as she padded downstairs. Before Vicky opened the door, she checked her reflection in the hall mirror. She tried in vain to smooth out her bed hair before seeing who was on her doorstep. A blast of cool air entered the house as she came face to face with two women stood on her doorstep. Two female police officers.

"Mrs Evans?" the one officer said. She looked to be roughly Vicky's age. Dark hair with a nondescript face.

"Yes," Vicky replied with a degree of trepidation.

"I'm Constable Jones. This is Constable Feasey."

Vicky nodded at the other officer, noticing that she was a good few years older. She also had dark hair, with dark smudges under her eyes. "Is everything okay?"

"Could we come in? Bit cold out here," Constable Feasey said softly.

"Sure. Come in." Vicky stood to one side, letting the two officers into the hallway. The cold wind and droplets of rain were left outside as the front door was closed. "Go through to the kitchen," Vicky said as she re-knotted her dressing gown. As she walked in behind them, she noticed that both officers had removed their hats, placing them on the kitchen table. "Would you like some tea or coffee?" Vicky enquired expectantly.

Constable Jones shook her head. "No thank you, Mrs Evans. We're both fine. Would you like to sit down?"

"What's happened?" Vicky said nervously as she took a seat, the chair legs grating on the tiled floor. The officers followed suit, Constable Feasey pulling a notepad from her breast pocket.

"Have you checked on your son this morning, Mrs Evans?"

A cold stone landed in Vicky's gut. "N-no, why?" she stumbled. Before the officers could respond, Vicky was heading upstairs. "Jaspy. Are you okay?" she called. Flinging the door open, her fears all hit home at once. The room was empty. She heard footsteps on the carpeted stairs behind her as tears broke from her eyes. "Where is he?" she cried as Constable Jones gently took her by the arm, leading her over to the single bed.

"Jasper was found this morning by one of your neighbours. A Mr Thomas, who I believe lives further down the road. He's fine, Mrs Evans," Jones said, squeezing Vicky's hand.

"I don't understand. Found him where?"

"On the Lickey Hills," Feasey answered. "Mr Thomas just so happened to be walking his dog early this morning. He found Jasper asleep on the floor. He'll be okay. He's been taken to the Alexandra Hospital in Redditch, where they are treating him for exposure." Vicky began weeping, collapsing into Jones's arms. The officer let her cry, rubbing her back gently as the woman's emotions boiled over. After a minute, Vicky pulled away, wiping her eyes. Constable Feasey handed her a tissue. "Here, Mrs Evans. Take this."

"Thanks," Vicky said, blowing her nose. She scrunched the tissue into her fist as she looked at the two officers. "I don't understand. How did he wind up at the Lickey's? How?"

"We've no idea. Your neighbour found him in the forest above the golf course, about a mile away from here. What time did he go to bed last night?"

"About nine. We'd been out walking, up the Lickey's as it happens. We came home about four, had hot dogs for tea, and just pottered about the house. I went up about ten. I was done in. We've suffered a bereavement recently. It's taken its toll on us."

"We know, Mrs Evans. And you have our condolences," Jones said patting her hand.

Vicky composed herself, swallowing back the tears that threatened to spill out. "I had a shower, checked on Jasper and was out like a light. I've no idea why he would get out of bed and leave the house in the middle of the night? He's never done anything like this before."

"Have you noticed anything unusual in the last few days?" Feasey asked.

Vicky immediately thought about the dead animals in her garden, quickly opting to keep that to herself. "Not that I'm aware of. We've just been trying to come to terms with what happened to Steve, Lucy and Brett." She stood up suddenly. "I have to go to him. Did you say he's in the Alex?"

"He is. Would you like us to take you, Mrs Evans?"

"No, it's fine. I'm fine to drive myself. I need to get ready."

"We understand. He's your son. He'll be wanting to see you too. We'll pop back later if that's okay? We may have a few more questions for you."

"Okay. I'll be here." Tears suddenly seeped from her eyes. She reached for the officers, hugging them both fiercely as she started sobbing once more. They returned the embrace clumsily. Looking away from each other as tears streamed down their own cheeks.

Five

Jasper smiled as his eyes focused on his mother. "Hello, Mummy. I'm sorry. I've been naughty."

Vicky smiled, tears of joy and relief streaming down her cheeks. She leaned over, hugging her son. Jasper returned her embrace, liking the smell of his mother's hair. It was a smell he associated with safety. With warmth. "Don't be silly, Jaspy. You've not been naughty. Mummy's just glad that you're okay. What happened?"

Jasper tried to recollect the previous night, his brow crinkling. "I'm not really sure Mummy. I remember dreaming. I was walking through a forest, but all the trees had been burnt. I kept hearing voices, Mummy. Someone was lost and they needed my help. I was trying to find them."

"Do you know who they were?" Vicky asked, her curiosity piqued.

"No. They were far away though. I couldn't see them. I could just hear their voices. Then I woke up here. What happened to me, Mummy?"

"You went sleepwalking, Son. Mr Thomas found you up the Lickey's, quite far away from the house. You were asleep on the forest floor. Oh, Jaspy. Don't ever scare your Mummy like that again!"

Jasper looked at his mother, seeing the anguish in her dark eyes. "I promise, Mummy." He looked around the small ward, noticing other children lay in similar beds. Nurses buzzed about the well-lit space, talking to children and loved ones. His eyes settled on the far corner, noticing a play area, equipped with a desk and various jigsaw puzzles. His thoughts were interrupted by a light female voice.

"How are you feeling, young man?" Jasper and Vicky looked up at the smiling nurse, standing at the end of the bed. Vicky instantly liked the face smiling back at her. The nurse was probably a few years her junior. Tall, with a girl next door look. Her dark hair was tied up in a ponytail, her smile infectious.

"I'm feeling okay," Jasper said, smiling.

"You okay, Mum?" the nurse said warmly.

"I think so. I got quite a fright this morning when the police turned up on my doorstep. This little man is quite the adventurer."

"Proper little explorer I've been told." She walked around the bed, ruffling Jasper's hair.

"What's your name?" he asked, enjoying the fleeting contact.

"Rachelle."

"Hello, Rachelle. I'm Jasper. This is my Mummy."

Rachelle smiled at Vicky. "He's adorable." Something caught her attention from across the ward. She nodded at the unseen person before turning back to Vicky. "We'll have Jasper in overnight, just to keep an eye on him. All being well, he'll be back home tomorrow."

"Okay," Vicky said, clearly relieved. She looked at the clock on the wall, noting that it was just after nine. She suddenly felt hungry.

The nurse seemed to sense this as she walked back to the end of the bed. "I can get some tea and toast for you, Mum? Or, there is a new café opened next to reception. They do a decent latte and croissants to die for."

"You read my mind," Vicky said smiling. The anxiety she had felt an hour ago was melting away in the spring sunshine.

Rachelle turned back to Jasper, tickling the exposed foot that poked out beyond the sheets. "If Mummy goes to get breakfast, do you promise not to have any more adventures?"

Jasper giggled as manicured nails grazed the bottom of his foot. "I promise, Nurse Rachelle. I've had enough adventures for today."

"Well, I'll be back in a bit. You go and get yourself some breakfast, Mum. We'll keep an eye on Jasper for you."

Vicky stood, stretching. She felt stiff and tired, but happy. "Thank you, Rachelle. You're a star."

The nurse smiled, wrapping her arm around Vicky's shoulder, squeezing her. "All part of the service. The doctor will be along shortly. I'll pop back in a bit too."

She walked off, leaving Vicky and Jasper alone. "She's nice, Mummy."

"Yes, she is." She looked at her son. "Mummy is just going to get some break-fast. Do you want anything?"

"A comic book please, Mummy."

"Okay. I'll see what I can do. Just don't go on any more adventures while Mummy's gone."

"Promise, Mummy. Love you."

"Love you too, Jaspy," Vicky said, before heading out of the ward.

* * *

"Oh my God! How did he manage that?" Karen said.

"No idea, Mum," was the brief reply. Mike walked into the lounge, placing two mugs of tea on the table. He motioned to his wife.

"Hang on, Vicky. Your Father wants you on speakerphone." The line crackled briefly.

"Hi, Dad," she said.

"Hi, love. What's going on?"

"I'm with Jasper at the hospital. Seems he went sleepwalking last night. He was found by Mr Thomas up the Lickey's early this morning."

"Bloody hell!" Mike exclaimed. How did he get out of the house?"

"Through the kitchen door. He's eight, Dad. He can reach the lock. I just never thought he'd do something like this."

Mike reached forward, taking a sip of his tea. "I'll pop by the ironmongers later and get a bolt for the door."

"No, Dad it's okay. I'll just put the key out of reach. It won't happen again."

"What have the doctors said?" Karen asked, her fingers drumming on the arm of the sofa. She felt tension building inside her. A rising anxiety that had plagued her recently.

"They said he's fine. They expected him to be in worse shape, being out all night. But it's been quite mild lately. They'll keep him for twenty-four hours, just as a precaution. He should be home tomorrow."

Karen and Mike looked at each other. The woman noticing tears in her husband's eyes. She patted his knee. "We had planned to go into Birmingham on the train. Your Father is watching the football later this afternoon, so that's him sorted." Mike smiled warmly, rubbing his wife's denim-clad thigh. "Do you want me to pop round? Do you need anything from the shops?"

"Jasper just wants his tablet. I'll be okay, Mum. Why don't you pop round tomorrow? About lunchtime. We should be home by then."

"Are you sure? We can visit him at the hospital if you like?"

"Honestly, Mum. I have a few things I need to get on with. I can just potter about the place. If you want to pop and see him, you can. He'd like that."

"Okay. We'll pop over to see him in a bit."

"Thanks, guys. Speak to you later. Love you."

"We love you too, Vicky. Send Jasper our love. Mind how you go."

* * *

Lenga stood on the rocky path, looking at the remains of the fallen cave. The sea was calm, its fury lessening as the false dawn broke. The witch knew that she would never feel the sun on her back in this land. That was her main reason for dwelling here. She liked the dark and the cold. She had seldom been to lands where the sun had tracked its way across the sky. But her curiosity was whetted. *Where had they come from?* She thought as she wrapped the fur shawl around her shoulders. Her boot kicked at a piece of black scree, knocking it off the path into the sea below. There was another reason for her foray out of her cabin. She'd felt something. Something far away, just out of her reach. *I can sense you, whatever you are. But I know not why you have entered my head. What are you searching for? Are you hunting for what I seek? Maybe we can share? Hmm. Maybe,* Lenga thought as she turned back towards the town.

Minutes later, she climbed into her crib, her milky eyes closing as sleep took her quickly. Her lips twitched, her blackened teeth tapping together as images swirled through her mind. *The man and beast, huddled in the darkness, embers from a small fire lighting the darkness around them. She recognised the vast swamps, mist rising from the black waters. They stood, heading off into the night, traversing the waters with care. Something else was close by, far above them. A boy, with dark hair and strange attire floated above the swamps. He sensed her, floating away into the blackness above. Lenga followed him, high up into the mountains beyond. From there, she tracked him through a void in a darkened forest. He flew through the trees, navigating with ease. Lenga lost sight of him, floating aimlessly for a few moments until she came across a small cottage surrounded by trees and bushes. She knew that the boy was inside, safe for now. The witch also sensed a darkness close by. It repelled her, driving her backwards, through the fence into the forest beyond. The evil had drawn its boundaries, repelling anything that came close to its prize. The boy. The boy was the prize. The darkness wanted him.*

Six

"Please, Mummy. I will put my coat on," Jasper said, pleading.

"You should be wrapped up warm on the sofa, Son," Vicky said as she cut crusty cobs on a wooden chopping board. The kitchen under-lighters bathed the room in a warm glow as the sun's rays began to lengthen.

"He'll be alright, love," Mike said calmly. "I'll make sure he's wrapped up. Twenty minutes, Jasper. Okay?"

"Okay, Grandad. I'll get the football." Jasper headed out of the kitchen, returning quickly with a leather ball and a blue fleece jacket.

Karen called him over. "Come here, young man," she said, taking the fleece off her grandson. She zipped the front up to the neck, pulling it down at the back. "Twenty minutes. Okay, buster?"

Jasper kissed her on the cheek. "Okay, Nanny. We promise, don't we, Grandad?"

"Scouts honour," Mike said with a mock salute.

The ball sailed into the blue sky, bouncing just before the fence. It careered off the railing, rolling back towards Mike, who was trying his best at being a goalkeeper. "Nice shot, Jasper. You put plenty of power behind that one."

Jasper ran towards the ball, his breath clouding in front of him. The tepid afternoon was quickly turning cool as the sun's rays left the garden for the evening. "Watch this, Grandad." He trapped the ball with his foot, flicking it up onto his knee. He kept his eye on the ball as it dropped, striking it cleanly. It sailed past Mike, over the fence, into the Lickey Hills beyond.

"Whoa. Easy, Ronaldo!" Mike said, clearly impressed. "You caught that one well too." Jasper scooted through the fence, running after the retreating ball. The older man rested his elbows on the fence rail, looking at the cottage. He could see his wife and daughter fussing over the soup. They were laughing at something, Karen, wrapping her arm around her daughter's shoulders. Mike smiled, enjoying the spectacle. His eldest daughter had always been close to her mother. His youngest daughter was too, just not quite as much as Vicky. Sarah, the younger sibling lived a few miles to the south, with her husband and son. He knew they had busy lives, but wished his daughters spent more time together. Mike knew why though. He remembered the drunken altercation between his two son-in-laws. *Bloody football,* he thought. *How can something so trivial cause so much division?*

"On your head, Grandad," Jasper shouted, untangling Mike from his thoughts. He turned around, just in time to see the ball sailing towards him. The man took two steps back, heading the ball back towards his grandson, a wet smear, plastered across his forehead. "Wow! That was great," the boy said as he changed direction deftly to retrieve the ball.

Mike smiled, wiping a hand across his hairline. A noise to his left caught his attention. He looked towards the conifers that separated Vicky's garden from her neighbours. The old man stood still, trying to catch the noise again. He didn't have to wait long. A low, distant drone drifted towards him. The sun's receding rays were suddenly blanketed by darkening clouds, the temperature dipping quickly. Mike walked over towards the tree line, his grandson momentarily forgotten. The noise came again, raising goosebumps across his arms. "Where the bloody hell is that coming from?" he said to himself as the ball bounced behind him.

"What's wrong, Grandad?" Jasper said as he jogged towards him.

"Not sure. I heard a funny noise. It sounded like, whale calls? Did you hear anything?"

"No, Grandad," the boy said, slightly confused.

A knocking noise from the cottage made Mike turn around. His wife was signalling that the food was ready. "It's probably nothing, Jasper. Come on. Grab your ball. Tea's ready." His grandson headed towards the cottage, dribbling his football expertly. Mike stood for a moment, listening. Above them, the sun broke through the clouds, bringing much-needed brightness to the darkening garden. He turned and headed for the cottage. His pace, slightly quicker than normal.

* * *

"Night, Mummy," Jasper said as he climbed into his bed. He gripped the *Marvel* duvet, pulling it up to his chin as Vicky walked into the room in a pink dressing gown and matching pyjamas.

"Ni ni, Jaspy," she said as she bent down, kissing him on the lips. "No adventures tonight. Okay?"

"Okay," Jasper said, drawing the word out slightly to emphasise his point.

She ruffled his hair before turning towards the window. The sky had darkened fully, plunging the rear garden into an inky blackness. Vicky suddenly felt a chill run through her, noticing how cold it felt. She reached down, grabbing the top of the radiator. *Hmm*, she thought. *Why's it so cold in here?* Vicky looked to her left, noticing the air vent set into the plaster. A cool breeze was permeating through it into the bedroom. Reaching up, she closed it before heading for the bedroom door. Jasper was curled up, his eyes closed as the main light was flicked off. The sundial clock on his chest-of-drawers offered limited illumination against the night. "Sweet dreams baby bear," she said, closing the door.

The light from the fridge spilled out into the dark kitchen as Vicky reached inside for a bottle of wine. A few minutes later she was sat on the sofa, a glass of ice-cold Sauvignon Blanc on the table in front of her. Beads of perspiration formed on the glass, heading slowly towards the stem. She picked up her iPad, scrolling through the various forms of social media that she had accounts for. After a few minutes, Vicky reached forward, taking a sip of the wine. Nodding in appreciation, the woman set the glass back onto its coaster. She clicked into the gallery, swiping through until she found the picture that she could not stop looking at. It had been taken the previous summer, during their family holiday to Majorca. Steve and Vicky sat in the middle, arms around each other. Jasper stood behind them, smiling serenely, a baseball cap hiding his curls. Lucy and Brett stood on either side, their hands resting on Jasper's shoulders. All five of them were smiling as the Mediterranean sun bathed them in warmth. Palm trees and the blue expanse of sea could be seen in the background. Tears spilled from Vicky's eyes, deep wounds inside her opening up once more, flowing freely. Barely a month had passed since the accident, with Vicky feeling a constant guilt at not being able to grieve properly. She wanted to, but Jasper needed her, and she him. She'd never been in this situation before, not knowing how to react. *I'll find my way through it*, Vicky thought as she took a large gulp of wine.

* * *

The bedroom was silent. Light shone through the windows, casting the moons glow onto the bed. Jasper lay still, the rise and fall of his chest, the only indication he was alive. His eyelids started flickering, a low murmur escaping his lips as he started to dream. The room became darker, the moon's glow obscured by a yellow cloud pulsating against the glass. Two tendrils of yellow mist appeared from the boy's nose, drifting over to the window. It writhed against the cool surface, mirroring the larger form outside. Jasper coughed in his sleep, causing the mist to shoot off towards the top of the window. It hung there before drifting back towards the bed. The boy opened his mouth, drawing in a deep breath. The yellow tendrils allowed themselves to be pulled into Jasper's body once more. Lying dormant. Waiting. Watching.

Seven

The mist from the swamps rose above their waists as they navigated the haphazard pathways. The moon was hidden beneath low-slung cloud that almost touched the rising fog.

"Up ahead," Tamatan said quietly. "Do you see it?"

"I do. Looks like a farmhouse," Jake said as he massaged his thigh. The duo came off the pathway onto a wide track that stretched far off into the distance. The man could see hills ahead. He could also hear what sounded like a river close by. A low rumble carried across the mists towards him as he made his way closer the stout wooden structure.

"Let us be careful, Jake. We know not, who dwells within."

Jake nodded, suddenly apprehensive. The building reminded him of Wilf's cabin. His mind wandered briefly, recalling how he'd first come across the cabin in the strange forest. A forest in another world, far different from his own. He'd visited the cabin numerous times before it was consumed by flames. A shiver ran through his body as he remembered the fight with a strange clan. Tall grizzled men, who'd wanted him for their dinner. It all seemed so bizarre to the man from Birmingham. He'd visited parallel dimensions, meeting and fighting monsters that he'd thought only existed in late night horror movies. And yet here he was, walking through a strange land with a demon. A demon that had saved his life on numerous occasions. A creature, known to his world as *Spring Heeled Jack*. "There are lights on. Someone is home," Jake said as he mounted the wooden steps that led onto a wide porch.

"Slowly, Jake. I can sense no evil here. But I may be wrong. Let us scout around first. See how the land lies." Tamatan turned to his right, about to head around the back of the farmhouse when a sharp point nudged his chest.

"Who are ya?" a female voice rang out. "What business do ya have on my property?"

Jake spun around, partially seeing a woman's form standing in front of his friend. He recognised the accent, a mixture of fear and curiosity washing over him. "We're not here to hurt you. We're lost."

"Don't move," she commanded, her voice harsh in the otherwise silent swamp.

"I'm not moving," Jake said, slowly sidestepping to his right so the woman could see him. "I'm Jake. This is Tamatan. We are trying to find our way home. We came across your cabin by chance."

The sharp point of the spear pressed into Tamatan's tunic, showing the demon that the woman would not hesitate to skewer him. "Jake speaks the truth. We are trying to find a way home. Maybe you could help us?"

"Stand against the railing. Any funny business and I'll tear you a new arsehole!"

Jake almost laughed at the threat, amazed by the language he was hearing. "Are you from Australia?"

The woman nodded, a surprised expression on her face. "Yes. Well, Tasmania. Are you a Brit?"

"Yes," Jake said. I'm from England. Tamatan is from the world in between this one and my one. How did you end up here?"

The spear was lowered to the ground as the woman leaned against the front door of the farmhouse. "I met a bloke. A bloke from your friend's world. He's called Kaiden. I'm Bea by the way. I would say pleased to meet you, but its early days yet. Anyway, he came through a doorway from his land into mine. I was camping at Lake Burbery with a mate. She'd gone off with some fella for a night of shagging. I was left alone in our tent when this strange guy appears out of the forest. He said that he was from another place. At first, I thought the bozo was high on drugs. But then I noticed that he looked different y'know? Like someone from a *Dark Tower* novel. I was staying at the campsite for a few days, so I hid him until he showed me the doorway."

Jake looked at the woman, noticing that she was probably a few years younger than he was. Probably just edging over the thirty mark he guessed. She was blond, almost as tall as he was, with a masculine, handsome face. She wore denim dungarees, her bare arms and feet exposed. "And then what happened?"

"He took me through the doorway to his world. A place called Kloofbai."

"I know that place well," Tamatan said. It's at the farthest point north of the land beyond. Jake has not ventured there yet. His travels were further south, around Amatoll and Korgan's Vale."

"Kaiden has mentioned Korgan's Vale. Said it's a place full of vamps." She looked at Jake. "Looks like we've both been through the whole 'another world' bombshell Jake."

"Tell me about it," Jake said absently rubbing at his thigh again. "How long have you been here?"

Bea placed the spear against the window of the farmhouse before answering. "About six months. Well, I think it's that about that long. Time doesn't exactly play along around here. I spent a few weeks in Kloofbai, falling in love with a man from another world. Then, we headed here."

"Where is here?" Tamatan said, looking around the porch.

"Kaiden call this place Vinka. He's travelled here a lot over the years. When I was getting to know him, he showed me a precious metal, found in the rivers to the south. Well, as soon as I saw it, I knew what it was."

"Gold?" Jake asked.

"Yeah. He showed me a lump, the size of an orange. I took it back to Tasmania to get it checked out. It was pukka. So, we hatched a plan. Come here and live in this dive until Kaiden can find as much as we'd need. Then, we head home to start a new life. My folks died a few years back. I have no brothers or sisters, and only a few friends. So, this will be our nest-egg."

"Where is Kaiden now?" Jake said, growing ever more curious.

"To the south, I think." She pointed out across the swamps. "He's got a cart and an ugly mule to pull it. He's been gone a few days. Should be back in a few more. He thinks another dozen or so trips, and we'll have enough. Already got a store full of gold." She suddenly became wary, realising her predicament. She looked at the spear, wondering if she would be needing it.

Jake saw Bea shift, seeing her eyes settle on the weapon. "We mean you no harm, Bea. And we're certainly not after your gold. We want to get home. Can you tell us where the doorway is to Kloofbai?"

Before she could answer, a low rumble of thunder drifted to their ears. A flash of lightning illuminating the dark horizon. They all turned, their eyes catching the remnants of the flash. "Storms heading our way. It rains like fuck here. I believe that you're not here to cause trouble. I will try and point you in the right direction, but for now, we'd better get inside and secure the doors and shutters. The weather is about to turn biblical!"

* * *

Jasper hung motionless over the land, the sound of thunder reaching his lofty perch. A flash of lightning strobed across the sky, lighting the ground beneath him. He could make out the two figures standing on the porch. They looked to be talking to someone. Someone that Jasper could not see. Rain began falling all around him, starting lightly, becoming fierce within minutes. He could hear and see it but the boy was protected from its cold fury. Only Jasper's essence floated above the land. His body was tucked up warm, on a different plane. He knew this, not dwelling on it too much. He was here to have fun. The young boy had discovered a new place to play, unaware that he was not just dreaming. Jasper was projecting. The two figures beneath him were lost from view as the storm increased. Keen eyes surveyed the land below, finding nothing of interest within the swampland. Turning around, Jasper propelled himself forward, dropping down until he almost skimmed the long grass. Laughter echoed inside his head as the lightning splintered the land around him. He flew on and on, leaving the swamps, heading along a solitary track, flanked by dark waters. The ground whizzed past as Jasper flew ever faster. The road ahead seemed to fatten, making him slow his journey. There were men ahead, huddled underneath a rocky formation. He edged closer, drawing snarls from the giant dogs that kept guard. The men noticed the growls, two of them heading out of the shelter. Jasper held his breath as two giants stood before him. They cannot see me, he thought as the men scanned the roadway for signs of danger. The dogs continued to snarl at him, teeth bared. Their black eyes could sense the boy close by, their matted coats bristling. The men said something to the dogs that Jasper could not quite hear. It was as if the sound was muffled by the wind, rain, and thunder. They all retreated underneath the rocky ledge, away from the fury of the downpour. The boy could feel that these men were dangerous. Do they live here? he thought, looking around for a house or cabin. Finding nothing on the blank featureless horizon, Jasper took off again, heading into the blackness. The roadway seemed to grow narrower as he climbed higher. Time seemed to become meaningless as Jasper floated ever further. After what seemed like hours, the track gave way to a large peninsular. A large settlement clung to the wet rocks, constantly battered by a roiling sea. A rocky path meandered from the town, clinging to the cliffs. It ended abruptly at what looked to

Jasper like a collapsed cave. He dropped down towards the entrance, noticing green tendrils of mist seeping from the rocks before rolling into the sea below. The green cloud unsettled Jasper, who turned towards the intimidating looking settlement. Tight windy streets played out before him as he drifted towards the summit of Tenta. He stopped at a small shack, a feeling of utter blackness blocking his path. A low hum seemed to shake the bubble that he hung in, threatening to break through. I don't like this, he thought as a small door opened. A figure emerged, smiling up at him. Her milky white eyes seemed to penetrate his skull. Jasper looked at her, frozen in fear.

Her mouth opened, revealing blackened teeth, decayed and fetid. "Hello, traveller. It looks like you've found your way to my door the way I found my way to yours. Come down. Step inside. Let Lenga refresh you. I bet you're hungry." Jasper hung there as the witch edged closer. He watched as a large snake slithered from her top, licking at her neck seductively. His mind began to float and swim. The witch sensed this, her hand extending out towards him, drawing Jasper towards the shack. "That's it. Come to Lenga. I have stories to tell. We could sit by the fire and become friends." She was about to speak further when the snake fastened its fangs into the withered flesh of her neck, breaking the spell. "Slithering shit!" she exclaimed, throwing the snake into the wet mud at her feet. Jasper broke from his trance, shaking his mind free. He turned and fled, low shacks and hovels passing him by. Suddenly, he was out over rocks once more, the sea to his right. His speed increased as he skimmed low over the black land, heading for the solitary road back to the swamps. We'll meet again soon, young man. Next time, I will visit your house. Lenga will be happy to see you. And your friends. The gravelly voice echoed through his head, causing him to veer from the road briefly. Jasper headed out over the dark sea as he tried to expel the words from his head. I need to get home to mummy, he thought. Enough adventures for one night.

After a while, Jasper came across the shack. He slowed his pace as the relentless rain pummelled the land around him. He passed by the cabin, rising up as he headed for the far mountains. Lightning lit the dark and forbidding peaks ahead of him. Craggy outcrops loomed over him as thunder rolled across the mountain range. The boy knew where he was heading. He'd used the cave a few times during his last few outings. Flashes behind him, lit the confines of the rocky tunnel before he passed through. Back to another land. A land with large forests, filled with strange mists. He knew where another doorway stood. One that led to the sanctuary of his home.

* * *

"How long will it rain for?" Jake said as he peered through the glass.

"Hard to say. Sometimes it rains for days. Can I get you fella's something to eat and drink? You're probably starving."

Jake suddenly felt his stomach contract, realising he'd not eaten properly for what seemed like weeks. "We don't want to put you out, Bea."

"It's no bother. I've not got a great selection of stuff. Dried fish, bread, and some of Kaiden's homebrew. It tastes like diesel, but you get used to it."

"Sounds just what I need. My tank is almost empty," Jake said smiling.

Bea returned his smile before heading through a doorway at the rear of the living quarters. Jake looked at Tamatan, who smiled wearily. The little demon walked across the room, planks squeaking under his bare feet. He sat down heavily at a gnarled table. The diminutive demon crossed his arms on the rough wooden top, laid his head sideways in the crook of his elbow and promptly fell asleep. "I hope this is enough to go around?" Bea said as she shuffled in through the door. "Your mate had enough?"

"I think we both have. We've been on the move for days. We're dead on our feet."

"How did you end up here?" Bea said, suddenly curious. She walked over, offering Jake a clay jug, filled with murky liquid.

He took a gulp, his face screwing up as though he'd sucked on a lemon. "God! You were not wrong." He took another swig, dark liquid running down his chin. Jake wiped his face, clearly refreshed. "It's not as bad the second time around?"

"You get used to it. It's strong mind. Better get some grub in your belly or else you'll be pissed as a rat." Jake walked over to the window, sitting down in a wooden chair next to a black barrel.

Bea walked over, placing the provisions on the black wooden top. "Help yourself. When you're done, you can fill me in on how you ended up in this shit hole."

A few minutes later, Jake was feeling almost human again. His leg still throbbed. He knew it was getting worse. Without holy water to keep the scar clean, Jake worried just what would happen to him. He'd even started rubbing his tongue over his canines, checking for fangs. "That did the trick, thank you so much."

"My pleasure," Bea said, draining her own jug. She reached for another two, handing one to Jake. He took is readily, placing it on his knee. "Go on then. I'm waiting."

"Oh right. Sorry. Err, here goes. It starts a few years ago. I was living back home with my wife and daughter, working as a policeman. They were killed in a hit-and-run."

"Oh shit! Sorry to hear that, Jake."

"It's okay. Well, my life changed as you can imagine. I quit the force and went travelling for a while. It helped me a lot. Travel does that. Grieving for lost loved ones get replaced by fasten your seatbelt signs and waiting in bus garages. Anyway, I ended up back home a year or so later. I started working as a Private Investigator. It was easy work, allowing me to pick and choose how I lived my life." Bea nodded before taking a swig. "Then one day, a double murder close to where I lived sent me on a wild goose chase. People started dying, along with my best friend. It was then that I discovered a doorway to another world. I also came face to face with vampires. Not the shiny variety that you see in the movies nowadays. These ones are vile. Really hideous." Bea's expression was grim as she heard the story unfold. "I followed the monster that killed my friend, into the world next to this one. It was there that I met Katherine. She lived in a village close to the doorway and she'd been shipped out to the coast to hide from the vampires."

"Why?" Bea said.

"Her blood. Basically, her blood was pure. Lots of the people in that land have tainted blood. The vampires won't feed on them. That's why so many people have gone missing from our world. A vampire called Elias, and his crew have been abducting humans for a long time to feed their master, Korgan."

"So that's who Korgan is!"

"Yes. Or was. He's no longer around. He was destroyed. So was his brother, Reggan. They've waged war against each other for ages, centuries probably. Anyway. I've gone off on a tangent. I met Katherine out on the coast. We were attacked by vampires and barely survived. Katherine was then snatched by Elias, but eventually, we got her back. After a few more encounters with them, we fled to Cornwall to start a new life. Things seemed to be going well. We have a daughter too, Alicia."

"So how did you end up here?" Bea said, the intrigue building.

"Elias found us again. He snatched them both and headed back to his world. I followed, of course, trying to hunt them down with Tamatan and Kath's Uncle Wilf. Elias also turned my mother into one of them. Eventually, we found them. It kicked off, with Katherine, Alicia and Wilf escaping back to their world. Mum and Dad were swept out to sea together. They're gone." Jake paused, trying to regain his composure. He swallowed back his emotions, focusing on the story. "We got stuck, in a place not too far from here, full of nutters. Tamatan over there thinks that they are following us. He says there is a witch in that place that will want our heads on spikes. So, you see, we really need to get the hell out of this place."

"Fuck me! And I thought my life was complicated." They both smiled, Jake's the weary smile of a man spent of life and energy. Something suddenly occurred to Bea, her body becoming tense. "So, there are people following you?"

"He thinks there is," Jake said, tipping his head towards the sleeping demon.

"Well, we need to get the hell out of here as soon as we can then. We need Kaiden home quick. He knows these lands well. Shit! Do you have any weapons?" Jake shook his head. "Shit! I have another spear out back, along with some knives. I suppose that's better than nothing." She walked over to the window, peering out into the storm. "Fuck! And here was me hoping for a quiet night."

"I'm sorry, Bea. If you want, we'll leave now and carry on walking."

"You can't do that. And anyway, if there are a bunch of headcases en-route, they may slit my throat anyway. At least if you're with me we stand a fighting chance. I just hope he gets back soon."

"Hmm," Jake said. "Me too."

Eight

Vicky walked into the kitchen, arms full of washing as Jasper sat at the kitchen table with a set of coloured pencils, drawing in his pad. "What do you want for breakfast, sunshine?" Vicky said.

"Toast please, Mummy," Jasper said as he picked up a green pencil.

"Okay. Just give us a minute. I'll pop this in the wash then do it."

"Thank you, Mummy."

She opened a side door at the far side of the kitchen, heading out into a cool utility room. She busied herself with putting the wash on, noting that the weather had taken a turn for the worse. A few cleaning products were put back in cupboards as the washing machine started its cycle. Vicky looked towards the window as the first pitter-patter of rain began to fall. A shudder ran through her body as she headed back into the kitchen. "Do you want some tea?"

"No thanks. Can I have orange juice?"

"Okay, baby bear," Vicky said as she began to prepare his breakfast. A few minutes later, she placed a plate and glass in front of Jasper, sitting down opposite.

"Thank you, Mummy," he said as he took a chunk out of the toasted white bloomer. A blob of butter was licked from the corner of his mouth as he reached for the orange juice.

Vicky took the pad, sliding it over to her side of the table. She looked at the drawing, her brow furrowing. On the page was a crudely drawn shack, brown in colour. A man and a green creature were standing next to it, rain falling all around them. At the top of the page, a smaller figure hung motionless, encased in a blue bubble. "What's all this, Jasper?" Vicky said, confused and slightly uncomfortable.

"It's from my dream, Mummy. I've been dreaming about those two," he said pointing at the pad. "They are lost, far away. That's me at the top of the page. I was floating high up in the sky watching them. They are trying to get home?"

"Home? Where is their home?"

"I don't know, Mummy. But I think it's far away."

"How long have you been having these dreams?"

"Erm, only a few nights. Since I was in hospital."

Another shudder ran through the woman's body. "Do you know their names?"

"The man's called Jake. Not sure about the other one. He looks like one of the *Marvel* mutants. He's a funny looking thing."

"Yes, he is," Vicky said, still uncomfortable.

Jasper continued to munch through his toast, wiping his mouth with his pyjama sleeve when he'd finished. "What shall we do today, Mummy?"

Vicky was about to answer when the phone on the wall started chiming. She walked over, her slippers scuffing the tiles. "Hello? Hi, Mum. Yeah not bad and you?" She listened for a few seconds. "Hang on I'll ask him. Jaspy. Do you fancy going to Nanny and Granddad's for dinner this afternoon?"

"Sure. What's Nanny cooking?"

Vicky relayed the question, smiling at her son. "Lamb. Sound good to you?"

"Yes, Mummy. I'll go and get ready." He got up from the table, hugging his mother before heading upstairs with a series of loud thumps and thuds.

"What time do you want us over?" She nodded. "Okay. We'll see you at one. Love you. Bye." Sitting back down at the table a few minutes later with a frothy coffee, Vicky slid the pad in front of her. Although crudely scribbled in various colours, Vicky could see the detail that her son had put into the drawing. She noticed what looked like swamps, with stubbly grass not far from the brown shack. She gazed at the two figures, facing away from her. "What made you dream about a place like this?" The kitchen was suddenly darkened as low clouds blocked out the sun. Vicky almost felt the temperature drop a few degrees, pulling her dressing gown tight around her neck to ward off the chill. *I need a hot shower*, she thought, following her son upstairs. The pad lay on the tabletop, immobile. An unseen puff of air from an unknown source gently lifted the top sheet of paper. The breeze suddenly increased, sending the pad skittering across the kitchen floor. It came to a stop next to the fridge, the drawing undamaged. The natural light in the kitchen was muted further as a mass of yellow mist appeared at the window. Another body of mist appeared from under the fridge, swirling and pulsing over the sheet of paper. Searching, hunting, and finding its prey.

* * *

"The rain has stopped," Bea said as she nudged Jake awake.

He looked around the shack, noting that it was still pitch-black outside. "How long have I been out?" He looked up at the woman from the straw mattress, noticing that Tamatan was still asleep on the table.

"Dunno. No clocks here, Jake. I slept next to you, with half an ear on the front door. I'm not sure what to do. Do we scarper and try and find Kaiden? Or wait here for him, in hope no one comes knocking? Fancy a drink?"

"Sure. What do you have?"

"Black coffee if you fancy?"

"How did you get coffee here?" Jake said sleepily.

"Bought it with me. I'm not living in this shit hole without a few comforts. I brought coffee, chocolate. Although that went by-the-by ages ago." Jake half smiled. "Sanitary stuff. Y'know. Women's things. Oh, and toothpaste. Don't want breath like a dunny eh."

"Good thinking. When we came through the doorway last time, we brought a shit load of stuff with us. It's still there, I think? Enough beer for a good piss up too."

"Damn. I could murder a cold one. Or even six cold ones."

Jake was about to reply when he noticed Tamatan sat looking at them both. "You're awake." He paused. "You okay?"

"Someone was watching us?"

"Who?" said Bea as he headed over to the far wall where the spear stood propped vertically.

Jake climbed to his feet, rubbing the back of his neck. "You look spooked."

"No. It's no one dangerous. It's a spirit. A ghost of sorts."

Bea turned to face the demon. "A ghost. What kind of ghost?"

"A boy. He was close by, high above the cabin. He's watching over us. He's from far away. I don't think he's lost. He's travelling."

"Travelling?" Jake said. "What do you mean?"

"He didn't speak to me, but I heard his thoughts. He was looking for a far-off cave. He said he'd had enough adventures for one night. Then, he was gone."

Tamatan looked at Jake, his red eyes glowing brightly in the darkened space. "He's from your land. His words were like your words."

Jake and Bea looked at each other, then back at the demon. The man leaned against the window, clearly taken aback. "What's the ghost of a little boy from our world doing way out here?"

"I do not know, Jake. All I know is that he sounded scared. Like something was following him. He seemed in a hurry to get away."

"What did he look like?" Bea was now intrigued.

"Very fair looking. Not that old, with sleeping clothes on."

"You mean pyjamas?" Jake said.

"Yes. I think."

"Well this is a welcome distraction to the bloodthirsty lunatics heading our way," Bea said, walking over to the fireplace. She stirred the dying embers, flaming motes erupting into the shack. A few well-placed logs were dropped into the fire, quickly crackling itself back to life. Bea reached for the black kettle next to the fireplace, hanging it on a black hook attached to the mantelpiece. The growing flames caressed the bottom of the kettle as the three continued their discussion.

"I'm at a loss as to what this means?" Jake said.

"Me too," Said Bea.

"It is indeed a strange occurrence. I have a feeling that he will be back. For what, I'm not sure."

The three lapsed into silence for a few moments, each lost to their own thoughts. The sizzle of water hitting the fireplace, stirred Bea from her daydream. "Okay. Who wants one?"

"Please," Jake said.

"I will join you in your refreshment," Tamatan said as Bea headed for the kettle. A few minutes later she handed two tin camping mugs to Jake and Tamatan. Jake took a sip, savouring the heady aroma. The demon sniffed at the brew, taking a tentative nip of the black liquid. He nodded to himself. "It has a nice taste. Thank you."

"If there are men heading our way, they may have sheltered from the storm," Bea stated. "But the rain's stopped. They may be on the move again."

"You may be right. What do you suggest?" Jake said, before taking another sip.

"We're not safe here. If they surround the place, there is no escape. They could even torch the cabin with us inside."

Jake's mind was cast back a few weeks. He'd been surrounded by a crazed gang, hell-bent on eating him. They'd torched the cabin he'd been holed up in. A cabin similar to the one he found himself in now. Only good fortune and a fast motorbike had saved him. He shook the memory from his mind, erasing the blood and gore that painted his memories. "So, where do we go? You said you wanted to wait for Kaiden to return?"

"I know I did. But things have changed. He may get back to find my head on the veranda. I know roughly which way he went. I say we head in that direction. What do you think?"

Jake paced the cabin, his footfalls heavy. His leg was throbbing again. He knew he needed holy water to douse the scar. He also knew he was a long way from anywhere that could supply him with it. "Let's do it. As nice and cosy as it is here, we may be sitting ducks."

"What are sitting ducks?" the demon asked as he sipped at his brew.

"It means we're a target," Bea said as she started her own pacing. "Let's get the hell out of here. We'll be safer out in the open. I know the path through the swamps. Let's finish these and make a move." Jake and the demon sipped at their drinks as the tall woman whirled around the cabin. A minute later, she placed a variety of weapons on the wooden table where Jake sat. "It's not much, but it is better than nothing." Jake watched intently as she pulled a small piece of white chalk from her pocket. She drew a compass in one corner, marking out the four directions. Underneath, she drew three stick figures and an arrow pointing west. "It's crude, but he should understand it if we miss him. Right. Let's move."

* * *

Tintagel

Kerry Hardman sat on a rock, looking north at the stunning Cornish coastline. The mild spring breeze ruffling her clothing and frizzy dark hair as she drank in the sight unfolding before her. Dark smudges underneath her eyes seemed to pale in the morning sunlight. The bad dreams were getting worse. From the moment she'd found a pair of ancient buttons, discarded in a bin, things had turned darker for Kerry. Finding out later that the buttons belonged to a vampire, her world began shifting on its axis. She'd dreamed of floating over far off lands, unseen monsters chasing her through darkened forests. Aside from the dreams, things had happened on a scale that would make one of her favourite video games seem tame. She'd been visited by something. Her mind was cast back a few weeks, as she remembered the foggy night when something or someone had appeared at her bedroom window. An episode that she still could not fully come to terms with. A pair of red eyes had pierced the fog, invading her home. Her screams had alerted her father, who'd burst into the room seconds later. Rationalising that zombie video games had fuelled her imagination, the episode was quickly forgotten about. By her father at least. Not by Kerry though. She knew what had visited her. *Vampires in Cornwall.* The more she'd thought it, the more it seemed outlandish and far-fetched. However, she knew it to be true. Her friend Jake had told her about a doorway in a forest to the north. A doorway leading to another world. A world where the impossible was possible. Where vampires, demons, and more, lurked under darkened skies. Kerry knew the layout of the land off by heart now, such was the vividness of her nightscapes. She knew that two giant forests lay next to each other, separated by a rutted track. The one forest fell away into a huge crater, the trees tightly packed. To the south of the forests lay a lonesome mountain, swathed in fog and cloud. She'd flown around it several times, dodging the lightning that flashed around its peak. To the east, the ground rose up into a massive ridge, splitting the land like a fractured spine. She'd yet to venture that far, staying around the forests and lakes in the centre of the land. When Kerry had woken from her dreams she'd walk around her house in a perpetual fog, until either breakfast, or her parents broke the spell. She was troubled that Jake was still not home. Nor was his father, who lived a few streets away. Their houses lay in darkness, seemingly abandoned. The village was talking too. She'd heard rumours. Neighbours talking about strange comings and goings. A stranger with long grey hair had been seen at Jake's house just before he'd gone missing. Jake's father, Douglas was also part of the rumour mill. Some were saying that the new resident of Tintagel, whose wife was swept out to sea in freak storms, had thrown himself off the nearby cliffs. Kerry knew it was idle gossip, but it still troubled her. The vibration in her pocket broke her from the dark thoughts invading her mind. She looked at the screen, noting that it was getting on for noon. The name Rick Stevenson presented itself to her, a green and red icon underneath, giving her a choice to talk or ignore. Her thumb hovered for a moment before she swiped the green icon. "Hello."

"Hello, Kerry. Rick Stevenson. Are you okay?"

"Err, yeah. I think so. Still having bad dreams. Are you both alright?" She shifted nervously, pushing her black-rimmed glasses up her nose.

A slight hesitation on the line told Kerry otherwise, "Not really. We're still trying to fathom out what you told us a few weeks ago. I've tried constantly to contact Dad and Jake, with no luck. Any news from your end?"

"No. The houses are empty. There has been an article in the local paper and a few signs posted on information boards throughout the village. People are talking too, which I suppose is good in a way."

"What makes you say that?" Rick asked, a little too abruptly.

"Even though it's gossip, the word is spreading. Someone somewhere may hear about it and may have some information."

"I suppose. Sorry for snapping."

"That's okay. You're under a lot right now. Is Marlies with you?"

"Yes. She's sat next to me on the sofa. She says hi."

"Hi back." Kerry was suddenly at a loss for words.

Rick sensed it from his sofa in Hamburg, Germany, where he lived with Marlies. "Look, Kerry. What you told us a few weeks ago has turned our world upside-down. While we're not discrediting what you said, the idea of vampires and other worlds is just too much to come to terms with."

"I know, Rick. And I totally understand. To be honest, I've had trouble coming to terms with it too. However, I've seen more than you guys have to convince me. I'm still having the dreams. Every night. I cannot seem to dream about anything else. And they only started when all this started."

"We believe you, Kerry. Really, we do. So, we've come to a decision. We're flying over on Friday. To Newquay. We're going to the doorway to see what happens."

"Why not fly closer? Newquay is a long way from Birmingham."

"We want you to come with us. After all, you probably know where this doorway is. We have no clue."

"Y-you want me to go with you?" she blurted.

There was a crackle on the line as a speakerphone was activated. "Hi, Kerry. It's Marlies. Yes. We need you to come with us. Is that okay?"

Kerry thought about it for a few seconds. "I guess so. I just never thought I'd ever actually go up there."

"Thank you, Kerry. It means a lot to us that you're willing to help." The woman's soft Belgian accent combined with the Cornish wind seemed to steady her heartbeat.

"Yes, thank you, Kerry. I'll text you our flight details. We should arrive Friday morning. If it's okay with you, we'll all drive up Friday evening. Then come home on Saturday."

"Fine. I will wait to hear from you on Friday."

"Thanks, Kerry. Speak to you soon." Rick said.

"Speak soon," added Marlies.

"Bye," Kerry replied, ending the call. Her brow felt almost as clammy as her hands as she replaced the mobile phone in her pocket. She looked out at the sea, trying to regain her composure. A thought suddenly occurred to her. *How will we be back Saturday if the doorway closes behind us? I need to think of something to tell Dad.* She hopped off the rock she was sat on, straightening her coat before heading back towards the village, butterflies dancing in her stomach as she went.

* * *

Hamburg

"I think you gave her a fright, Rick," Marlies said as she filled the kettle. The modern kitchen in which they stood was bathed in light from huge windows on the other side of the living space. Outside, the German city of Hamburg was steadily ticking away on a sunny Sunday morning.

"I know. This is all so crazy. I'm frightened myself, babe. Frightened on one hand that we won't find anything. But also frightened that we will find something." Rick was the pragmatic brother, dealing purely in facts and figures. He knew Jake was different. He'd often wondered if that was the reason why they were not close. They'd only spoken a handful of times over the last few years. Their lives taking different paths. When they'd met up it was stilted and awkward, mainly from Rick. He knew that. It was almost as if he had nothing to say to his older sibling. And for that, Rick was sorry. Especially now, when his brother was missing. His father too. Rick wanted nothing more than to be close to them once again.

Marlies walked across the tiled floor, her bare feet barely making a sound. She wrapped her arms around her man, nuzzling into his neck. He drank in the natural scent that mingled with her shampoo. Rick stroked her dark shoulder-length hair before holding her at arm's length. She smiled up at him, her milky smooth skin flawless in the natural light. He loved the gentle dusting of freckles that adorned her nose, planting a kiss on them. She grinned, her eyes warm and dark. "Whatever happens, I'll be holding your hand, babe." Marlies had been his rock over the last few months. When he'd heard the news that his mother had been killed in a freak accident, Marlies had been the one who'd been there for him. She'd telephoned her boss at her Cologne office, explaining that Rick had lost his mother and needed her support. Nothing was too much trouble for her. She was kind and thoughtful, putting others before herself. Rick loved that about her.

He smiled, kissing her gently on the lips. "I could not do this without you. I'll book the flights now." He walked over to the sofa, getting comfortable as Marlies prepared two coffees. Moments later, she placed a mug on a cork coaster next to him as he flicked through the internet on his tablet computer. "We can fly to Newquay at eleven am, landing at midday UK time. I'll hire a car too. Can you fly at that time?"

"Sure. Friday will be a quiet day in the office. I'll let Erik know that I'll be off."

Rick nodded, knowing that her manager, Erik Van Loon was more like a father figure than a boss. "Great. I've got a meeting Friday afternoon with Herman, but I'll re-schedule. You fancy lunch at the Rathaus?"

"Why not. My treat, babe."

"No. I'm treating you. Plus, I asked first."

Marlies climbed across the sofa, kissing Rick slowly. Portals to other worlds, flight tickets, and hotel reservations were momentarily forgotten as the young Belgian woman's tongue slid seductively into his mouth. He kissed her back, feeling the first stirrings of arousal. She broke the kiss, the disappointment evident on his face. "Go and get showered, Rick Stevenson. I will let you treat me to dinner. But when we get home, I'll treat you to dessert."

Nine

Kerry walked up the drive towards Jake and Katherine's house, the Atlantic Ocean behind her, shimmering in the spring sunlight. She knocked on the front door, waiting a minute for any signs of activity. Nothing. She stepped left, peering in through the lounge window. The downstairs of the house looked as deserted as the last time she'd visited. She wandered around to the carport, trying the kitchen door in the hope it would miraculously open for her. It was locked.

"Still no sign of them?" a voice said behind her. Kerry wheeled around to see a middle-aged woman with dark hair stood on the driveway in a floral dressing gown.

"No," Kerry said, the disappointment showing on her face.

The woman approached her, pulling her dressing gown tight as the breeze tried to expose her to the elements. "You're Kerry, aren't you?" The younger woman nodded. "My name's Linda. Do you have any idea where they've gone?"

Kerry shook her head. "No. I'm really worried. No sign of them." She omitted the fact that they could all be in a parallel dimension, filled with blood sucking fiends. She opted to play the dumb friend. "There is no sign of Jake's father either. I was going to pop round to try his house again on my way home."

"Such a strange business. Av you heard the rumours?" Her Cornish twang floated on the Atlantic breeze.

"No," Kerry said, playing dumb. "What's being said?"

"That Jake was seen coming and going in the middle of the night with an old chap with long grey hair. No one round ere fits that description. Except John who runs the youth club. And he's never met Jake. It's all very strange."

"Yes, it is," Kerry added, wanting to put an end to the conversation and get back to the sanctuary of her bedroom. "I'll head over to Doug's house and try there."

"Have you tried calling them?"

"A few times. It goes straight through to answerphone."

The older woman shook her head. "Well, I hope they all turn up soon. Don't seem right. Something queer is afoot if you ask me. I only hope the little girl is alright."

"Me too," Kerry added absently as the other woman turned and walked back down the driveway towards her house. "Me too," she repeated, feeling that it was a forlorn hope.

* * *

Worcestershire

Jasper flung himself onto the huge sofa, getting settled as the television across the room lit up. He clicked the remote control a few times, placing it on the coffee table when his program of choice appeared in front of him. His hand-held gaming device was next to him, in case he became bored of Ninja Turtles. In the kitchen, Vicky sat at a large oak table, a glass of red wine in front of her. Her father was standing over the sink, preparing the vegetables for his Sunday roast. Her mother, Karen, placed a tall glass of lager on the counter-top next to him.

"Here you go, chef! Get that down you."

"Thanks, love," he replied, wiping his hands on a tea towel. He picked up his glass, turning towards his wife and daughter. "Cheers."

"Cheers!" they replied as one, each taking a good glug of Pinot Noir. Mike downed a third of his drink, placing the glass back on the counter. He set about the veg once more, humming along to the background music coming from the radio.

Karen looked at her daughter, smiling. "You okay, love?"

"I think so, Mum. Had a rough night. I woke up a few times all disorientated. I felt across the bed for Steve, then realised that he wasn't there."

The older woman placed a manicured hand over her daughters. "Oh, love. You've not really had chance to deal with all this. Do you think you need to go and see someone?"

"I don't know, Mum. Truth is. It's been almost two months since the accident. Apart from the initial shock and pain, I've not thought about them as much as I thought I would. Does that sound bad?"

"No, love," Mike said. "People deal with it in different ways. Plus, you've got Jasper to look after. When my Dad died, I was looking after Mum, who was also sick. I never really grieved for Dad, until Mum died a few months later. Then I grieved for both of them at once. Knocked me about for a few months, didn't it, love?"

Karen nodded. "It did." She turned to her daughter. "So, don't feel bad about it. It may take a while to really hit home. And when it does, you can count on us to be there. Day or night."

Vicky squeezed her mother's hand, tears forming at the corner of her eyes. "Thanks, Mum. Thanks, Dad. I don't know what I'd do without you both."

"Well you don't have to worry about that," Karen said. "We'll be around for a while yet. Have you heard much from your sister?"

"Not really. The odd text here and there." The tension in the room suddenly ramped up a level.

Mike took a swig of his beer and turned to them. "Can we not, as a family, put our differences aside? Whatever happened before is in the past. Let's put a stake in the ground and move forward."

"I know, Dad. It's just been bad timing. The ruckus between Steve and Dave was only a few months ago. We'd not spoken after that, until the accident. I tell you what. I'll give her a call this week. Invite them over for lunch next weekend. How's that?"

"Okay, love. Don't invite us old farts this time. You guys need to have a good catch-up."

"I agree with your Father. You both need to build bridges. We need to go and visit Steve, Lucy and Brett anyway." The silence in the room was deafening as the three of them were suddenly lost in different thoughts. Karen started crying, her hands coming up to her face. "Why? Why did this have to happen? God, it's so bloody unfair?" Sobs took over her body as she buried her face in her hands.

Mike went to her, holding onto his wife tightly. His own tears ran down his cheeks, splashing the table top. "It's okay, love." He was going to speak again, his throat constricting. He tried in vain to swallow back his emotions.

Vicky, who had stood up to try and comfort her mother, crumbled to the kitchen floor, her back sliding down the cupboard door. She cried silently as she watched her parents cling to each other. Watching her father openly weep was a sight that she seldom saw. Her heart strained against her sternum as she watched her Father, her rock, cry in his wife's embrace. She tried to stand, to go to them. To share their pain, their embrace. However, her body would not comply. She was frozen on the kitchen floor like a statue. "How do we get through this?" They both turned to her, eyes red-rimmed, cheeks slick with tears.

Before either could say anything, a voice from the doorway made them all turn. "Mummy!" Jasper blurted. He slid across the floor, Vicky catching him, pulling the boy to her. His tears soaked into the material of her top as he wailed in her grip. "I miss them too, Mummy. I miss them all so much."

Mike and Karen were there in a flash, creating a mass embrace. Jasper's grandfather kissed his curls, closing his eyes tightly. "Don't cry, mate. We'll get through this. As a family. They would not want to see us like this." Vicky reached up, pulling Mike closer. For a moment, she was a little girl again, welcoming her Daddy's embrace. She inhaled his smell, loving his musky aftershave. She breathed it in as if the familiar scent would take away the pain. "Come on, Vicky. Let's get you off the floor," Mike said as he climbed to his feet. He lifted her upright, Jasper still in her embrace. The boy climbed down, his head hung towards the kitchen floor as he sniffed loudly.

Karen wiped her eyes, reaching for the kitchen towel. "Sorry, love. I started the waterworks and you all joined in." She laughed, the sound bouncing off the walls.

Vicky laughed too, hugging her mother. "What are we like?" They stood there, rocking gently.

Mike picked up Jasper, ruffling his hair. "Come on, mate, let's go and put something on the TV." He carried him out of the kitchen, leaving the vegetables and his beer unfinished.

The women parted, Karen ripping off a piece of kitchen towel. She handed it to Vicky who duly wiped her eyes for a few seconds, regaining some composure. "Thanks, Mum. I don't know what we'd do without you both?"

"It will get easier, love. I know that sounds silly at the moment. But it will. Small steps. We're here, whenever you need us."

"Thanks, Mum. I love you so much."

"I love you too, Vicky. More than you'll ever know."

The afternoon passed without any more tears. Mike and Jasper were inseparable, sitting on the sofa watching football. Even when dinner was served, they sat together. Karen and Vicky smiled at them, drinking in the love that was radiating from them. The dining room became a sanctuary, the outside world a grey and distant place. As the sun set over Worcestershire, Vicky strapped a sleepy Jasper into the rear seat of her car, letting his grandparents give him a farewell kiss and hug. They drove home in silence, climbing towards the summit of the Lickey Hills from the small town of Bromsgrove. By the time she opened the car door, Jasper was asleep, subconsciously clinging to Vicky as she took him into the cottage. She slipped his trainers off as they headed for the boy's bedroom. Pulling the duvet back, Vicky gently placed her son into bed, pulling his socks and joggers off gently. His snores were steady and quiet as Vicky headed over to the window to draw the curtains. As she was about to pull them together, something caught her eye. *Mrs Kirkby*, she thought as she saw her elderly neighbour stood at the bottom of the garden next to hers. The woman was standing, facing the fence that bordered the forest beyond. Vicky could see that she was swaying gently, a pink dressing gown the only thing protecting her against the oncoming chill. She stood watching the older woman for a minute, becoming concerned when Mrs Kirkby failed to move a muscle. Vicky looked back towards Jasper who was out like a light. *He'll be okay for a bit*, she thought as she drew his curtains, heading down into the kitchen.

"Mrs Kirkby," Vicky said as she climbed through the fence rails. "Are you okay?"

The older woman, who Vicky guessed was hovering around the seventy mark, stood rooted to the spot, her eyes glazed over. Closely cropped grey hair was being ruffled by a strengthening wind as the older woman continued to sway. At Vicky's touch, Mrs Kirkby came out of her trance, shaking the fug from her mind. "Vicky? What are you doing here," she said, confused.

"I was just putting Jasper to bed. I saw you out here in the garden. Is everything alright?"

The older woman looked at Vicky as her thoughts started filtering back to her. "I – I must have dozed off on the settee." She pulled her housecoat around her, suddenly feeling the chill in the air. A chill that seemed to settle over the garden. "I dreamed. Funny dreams. I can't quite remember them now. Where was it now?" she said as she looked down at her fluffy purple slippers.

"Let's get you inside, you must be getting cold out here," Vicky said as she guided Mrs Kirkby towards her house. Suddenly remembering Jasper, she guided the elderly woman towards the gate at the side of the kitchen, unlocking the bolt. The hinges protested in the wind as they crossed the driveway towards Vicky's gate. *Locked. Shit*, she thought. "Stay here for a minute," Vicky said, placing the woman against the rendered wall. She ran back through the garden, ducking under the fencing poles with ease. As she cleared her own fence a noise in the distance stopped her in her tracks. *What's that?* she thought as she strained to listen. It came again, a far-off drone, carrying on the wind. The fine hairs on her arms prickled to attention as the noise seemed to surround her. *What the fuck is going here?* Seconds later, she was unlocking her own gate, shepherding the older woman into her kitchen. The warm down-lighters bathed the room in a much-needed glow as Vicky flicked the kettle on. She seated Mrs Kirkby at the kitchen table, the woman resting her arms on the wooden top. She was muttering something unintelligible that Vicky could not quite make out. Two minutes later, she laid a mug of hot coffee in front of her, along with milk and sugar. "How do you take it, Mrs Kirkby?"

"Huh," she said, shaking her head.

"Your coffee. How do you take it?"

"Err, white with two please."

Vicky added a generous slug of milk along with two heaped spoons of sugar. The older woman took a sip, nodding in appreciation. "Thank you, dear."

"Are you okay now? What were you doing in the garden?"

"I don't rightly know. The last thing I remember was watching television on the settee. I'd had my dinner and then put something on to watch. An old movie I think. That's the last thing I remember."

Under good lighting, Vicky noticed the pallor of the older woman's skin. She'd known her for a while, liking the rosy complexion she carried with her. The Mrs Kirkby she looked at now had a waxy sheen about her. Leathery grey skin made Vicky's stomach tighten. "You don't look so good. Have you been feeling off-colour lately?"

"Well, funnily enough, I've not felt great over the last few days. I've been sleeping in too, which is not like me. Maybe I need to make an appointment at the doctor's tomorrow."

"Off colour? How so?" Vicky asked, becoming concerned about her neighbour's health.

"Not sick. I've not had a cold either. That flu jab I had last winter has kept that at bay, thankfully. I don't know. Just not myself really. I feel lethargic and woozy. I've been having strange dreams too. Since you found Gracie. Most nights I wake up in a sweat, unaware of where I am. Then I tend to sleep in late. Some morning's it well after nine. I'm normally up and about by seven. Strange," she said shaking her head.

"What are you dreaming about?"

"Not sure about today's dream. But over the last few days, I keep dreaming that I'm wandering through a huge forest. All the trees have been burnt. There are ghosts there too. No idea why I'm dreaming about this? I never watch scary movies and the only books I read are things like Ruth Rendell and Virginia Andrews. So why I'm dreaming about all this stuff is lost on me, Vicky?"

She reached across and squeezed Mrs Kirkby's hand, noticing how cool it felt. "Maybe a trip to the doctor's might be a good thing? They can check you over. You might have a kidney infection or something? Mum had one a few years ago and it sent her a bit peculiar for a few days."

"Maybe you're right," she said as she took a swig of her cooling coffee. The older woman coughed, bringing her hand up to her mouth. She coughed harder, trying to dislodge something in her throat.

"Are you okay?"

"I think so," she said clearing her throat. I think it went down the wrong way." Suddenly a sneeze erupted from Mrs Kirkby, startling Vicky. It happened again, louder than the first time.

"I'll get you a piece of kitchen towel," Vicky said as he got up from the chair. As she made her way over to the kettle the elderly woman sneezed a third time, tendrils of yellow vapour spraying from her nose. Vicky turned around as the mist dissipated in the atmosphere, lost to sight. "Here you go, Mrs Kirkby," she said handing her two pieces of quilted kitchen towel.

"Thank you, Vicky. And call me Maureen. Mrs Kirkby makes me sound like I'm still a school teacher."

"Sorry, Maureen," Vicky said, half smiling. She smiled back before blowing her nose loudly. The younger woman picked up her coffee cup, leaning against the kitchen counter as the older woman regained her composure. She took a sip of her coffee as Maureen's face took on a look of recognition.

"I remember the dream. I was walking at night. Near a marsh. Quite a spooky place if truth be told. There was a cabin up ahead which I was walking towards. There were people stood near it, facing away from me."

The sound of Vicky's coffee cup shattering on the kitchen floor caused Maureen to flinch in her chair. She looked at the younger woman, who had a look of disbelief etched across her dark features. Her mouth hanging open. *Jasper's drawing*!

Ten

They headed west on a lonely track. Jake let Bea lead the way, not knowing his bearings in the dark, foreign land. The swamps gave way to foothills, mountains looming up on their right in the distance. Jake looked at the dark forbidding peaks, his leg throbbing. "Does the sun ever come up around here?"

"Not seen it yet, and I've been here a while. Kaiden said that it does come up, but very seldom. Maybe it's like the Antarctic. Y'know, long winters and short summers."

Jake looked over at Tamatan, who was walking in silence. "Are you okay?"

"I am fine. I was just thinking about the boy. Why is he here, in this land?"

"Beats me," Jake said as he rubbed at his thigh. He looked to his left, seeing the outskirts of a forest on the horizon. "Nice place?"

"That's where Kaiden is. There is a track that winds through the forest. In there somewhere is a river. That's where the gold is."

"Have you not been there?" Jake asked.

"Nah. He said he'd not take me. It's a bit hairy out there. Gangs of marauding thugs lie in wait. He'd rather I was at the cabin."

"Is he not in danger, being out there on his own?"

Probably. But he can handle himself. I've given him a shotgun, which he's pretty handy with. Plus, he's a big fella. I'd not want to jump him in the dead of night. Except in the sack of course."

Jake chuckled, the joke lost on Tamatan, who continued to walk in silence. "So how far is the doorway?"

"It's a fair old yomp. At least three days until we reach it. There are places to stop off en-route though. Kaiden knows people here. They will put us up."

Jake suddenly lost his footing, landing hard on the rutted track. Tamatan was there in the blink of an eye. "Are you hurt?"

"No," Jake winced. Just the leg. It's getting worse."

"Your leg?" Bea asked. "What's up with it?" She handed him a plastic bottle containing brackish water.

He took a sip, nodding his thanks. "I was bitten. By a vampire. The one I told you about. Reggan. Since then, I've been applying holy water, which does work. However, I've been without any for a while. I only hope that whatever it is in my leg, is not spreading."

"Shit," Bea said. "There will be no holy water out here. We need to get you home. Before it gets worse." The moon came out from behind the clouds, lighting the land around them. Jake looked up at the strange blue orb, wondering how many different moons he would see in his lifetime. "See over there?" Bea said, pointing off to the right. "There's a track in the distance. That's the road we'll take. There is a place deep within the mountains where we can stay."

"What kind of place?" Tamatan asked. His voice low and monotone.

"It's called Kungback. Kinda like a saloon where people can stay and sleep. They have a barn out back. I've stayed there with Kaiden. The owner, Mimi will make us comfy. Although when you meet her, try not to stare?"

"Stare? At what?" Jake asked, suddenly curious.

"You'll see. Let's take a quick breather. There are some rocks up ahead. Let's rest our legs for a bit."

A few minutes later, they were sat on a series of square rocks. The giant stones were arranged in a tight circle, reminding Jake of stone structures from his land. He looked at the diminutive demon, noticing that the fire had left his eyes. "Tamatan. What's up? You've been quiet."

He looked up at Jake, his face full of sadness. "I'm thinking about Veltan and Jake. By now, they may know that I'm not coming back to them. I hope they have done as I asked. Or are at least planning the journey."

"What plans?" Bea asked.

"My friend, Sica, left me in Mantz Forest a moon's cycle ago. I gave instructions to return and wait for me. As you can see, I am not there, so Sica will return to the Unseen Land and tell my sister, Veltan. I have told her what to do if I fail to return. She is to take a journey to the interior, to the land of Marzalek. She will take our son with her. That way they will be safe. Safe from the monsters that may spill over into our land."

"Oh right. Sounds like you both need to get home. And quick."

"Yes, we both do. We have loved ones that are worried about us. And now you do too. I hope your man finds us," the demon said solemnly.

"Me too," added Bea as she wiped her mouth after a drink.

"Me three," said Jake. "Although, I hope he doesn't use his shotgun on us."

"Don't worry. If he finds us, he'll probably track us for a while. He'll see that you're not a danger to me. I just hope that whoever is following you does not show up at the cabin when he does. It could get messy. I don't want anything to happen to him."

Jake suddenly felt a heavy weight bear down on him. Their actions could put him in harm's way. He'd not considered that until that moment. "Let's just hope that we all make it to where we need to be. I'm tired of adventures. I want Katherine and Alicia back home, safe and well. I want you guys to find your loved ones and stay safe. I just feel it's going to be a long road ahead."

"Then let's get moving," Bea said standing up. I'm starting to feel tired. We need to at least find shelter, in case it chucks it down again." She grabbed her spear, settling it on her broad shoulder. "C'mon. Let's move."

* * *

The gang gathered outside the shelter, the hounds growling and baying at each other. A slap from Valkan across the head of the closest animal stopped the beasts from starting an all-out fight. He looked at his men. "Right. We've all had a good rest. If you need to shit, do it now. We will not stop until we can no longer run."

"We are ready," said one of his men.

"Remember. If we find them. No one touches them. Especially the hounds. The witch wants them intact and unharmed. Only Cranja and I will have any fun with them. Any other spoils we find along the way are yours. Let's go." The pack moved off into the night, heading west towards the swamp-lands and the mountains beyond.

Eleven

Karen knocked on the door on a blustery Monday morning. The weather had taken a turn for the worse, feeling more like winter than the beginning of spring. The door opened, warmth spilling out onto the front step.

"Hi, Mum. Thanks for popping round."

"That's okay, love," she said as she stepped into the hallway, removing her coat. She hung it on the bottom of the bannister before following her daughter into the kitchen. The warm lighting was a welcome refuge from the onslaught outside. "How was Jasper this morning?"

"Fine, I think. I dropped him at school and spoke to his teacher. She's going to keep an eye on him. Any problems and she said she'd call me straight away."

"That's good. So, are you going to fill me in?"

"Sure. Do you want a coffee?"

"Why not," Karen said enthusiastically.

A few minutes later they were sat at the kitchen table, Jasper's pad laid out in front of Karen. "He drew that yesterday," Vicky said. "He's been dreaming about it since he came out of hospital. What do you think?"

Karen looked at the pad, impressed with her grandson's drawing skills. She'd bowed out of her weekly yoga session when her daughter had telephoned her a few hours before. Looking at the pad, she was at a loss as what to add. "It just looks like a picture of a house with two people stood next to it. What's wrong with that?"

"It's just how he described it to me. That those two people are lost, far from home. He said he was floating above them, watching them."

"It's just a dream, love. He's a little boy with an active imagination. When you were a girl, you'd sit for hours doodling stuff. I wouldn't be too concerned."

"I wouldn't be overly concerned about just the drawing," Vicky said as she stirred her coffee with a spoon. "It's just the detail. And he knew the one person's name. Jake. However, that's not what's bothering me."

"So, what is?" her mother said as she tentatively blew on her steaming drink.

"When we got home last night, I spotted Mrs Kirkby stood at the bottom of her garden in her dressing gown. It was almost like she was in a trance, Mum."

"What?"

"That's what I thought when I saw her. Anyway, I brought her in here out of the cold. She was all confused and disorientated. It was then that she told me about her dreams. She described in detail the very picture you're looking at."

Karen looked down at the pad, stuck for words. The kitchen descended into silence as Vicky let the words sink in, the clock on the wall the only noise in the room. Seconds ticked by until Karen looked up at her daughter. "Coincidence?"

"Do you really believe that?"

"I'm not sure what to believe, love. I'm still trying to get my head around what you've just said."

"So am I. How could she know about this? She seemed different too. Her skin looked almost grey and her hands were cold. She looked like she'd aged ten years."

"Have you said anything to Jasper about his drawing?"

"No," Vicky said. "Like what?"

"I don't know, love. Has he had anymore dreams like this?"

"I've not asked him. Although, I really struggled to get him up this morning. Almost had to shake him awake. Come to think of it, he was a bit groggy, even when I dropped him at school."

Both women sat in quiet contemplation for a minute as the clouds descended over the land outside. Trees and bushes in the garden started swaying and rustling in the strengthening breeze. The sound of wooden chimes was carried on the wind, drifting in through the open window. The first patter of raindrops began to strike the patio, strengthening quickly, making Vicky and her mother look out into the garden. A thought occurred to Vicky as the window was pelted with rain and hail. "There was a strange noise last night too. When I was at the bottom of the garden with Mrs Kirkby. Like a far-off droning sound. Really freaked me out, Mum."

"You're giving me the willies, love. This is starting to sound like an episode of the *X-Files*."

"Sorry. Things just feel a bit weird at the moment. Jasper being found asleep up the Lickey Hills. The dead cat and birds in the garden. The drawing. And now, Mrs Kirkby's dreams. You have to admit, it's all very strange."

"I really don't know what to say, Vicky. Yes, it does sound strange. But I'm sure there is a rational explanation for all this." She shivered, crossing her arms. "It's cold today. I had to put a vest on." Vicky turned to the window, a strange noise catching her attention. One of the square pains began to splinter in its frame. Both women started to move towards the fracturing glass as a deep drone echoed through the kitchen. Then, the lights went out.

* * *

"I've never seen it go this dark since that storm back in '84." Karen looked out at the darkening scene, pulling her purple fleece jacket around her collar.

Vicky was a few feet away in the kitchen larder, her phone acting as a flashlight. "The fuse has tripped," she said before flicking the switch in the middle of the board. The down-lighters flickered back into life, cocooning them against the darkness that threatened from outside. "God, that really freaked me out, Mum," Vicky said. "What do you think caused the window to crack like that? And that sound. It was the same noise that I heard last night."

Karen looked at the pane that now contained a spidery pattern across its width. "Maybe a hail stone cracked it?" she said, her tone hollow and unconvincing. "The sound though, I have no idea. I'm at a loss for words, love."

Vicky also looked at the cracked glass, a chill snaking its way down her spine. "I'm not sure what to do, Mum?"

"What can you do? Yes, it all sounds very strange. But that's it. Could all be a coincidence? Although." She paused.

"Although what?"

"It's nothing. My overactive imagination is working overtime."

"Go on, Mum. What are you thinking?"

"I was just thinking about all the strange goings on around here lately. The murders up the Lickey Hills. I've lived around here all my life. There has never been anything like this before."

"You mean the guy killed down by the duck pond?"

"Well, yes. And there was the other guy, on Rose Hill last year. And the two people killed up on the Beacon Hill. Was that last year or the year before? Do you remember? You'd not moved in long."

"Yes. The prostitute and the taxi driver."

"That's it. So, what's that? Four people killed in the space of what, eighteen months? Plus, there are people who have gone missing as well."

"I suppose when you put it like that, yes, lots of bad stuff has happened around her lately."

Karen continued as something else came to her. "I saw on the news the other day that the local vicar in Rednal, along with a police officer have not been seen for weeks. One of the women from book club attends the church in Rednal. St Stephens it's called. She was telling me that he'd gone all peculiar over the last few months, hardly taking service. Then he found his wife dead in the back garden. Heart attack. Val said that he'd locked himself away in his vicarage, getting stuck into the bottle. And now he's vanished."

"And the policeman?"

"He's from Stirchley I think. Although, they said on the news that his car was found opposite the Hare and Hounds in Rednal. He's not been seen for weeks either."

"Sounds very strange, but what does this have to do with that?" she said pointing at the pad.

"Nothing. I just got a bit carried away, love. I think the lights going out did it. Strange though. All the things that have happened lately, don't you think?"

"I do, Mum. Maybe there are ghosts flying about the place." Vicky tried to smile, although it never reached her eyes.

"Oh God! Don't say that. I won't sleep tonight. I'll put the kettle on. More coffee is required."

Vicky watched as her mother busied herself at the kitchen counter, the sky outside gradually brightening. "What are you doing tonight?"

"Your Father's brought a shoulder of pork, which we're having later. Although he's probably sat watching TV if I know Mike. What about you?"

"I was going to pop into Bromsgrove at some point. I was thinking of getting Jasper a new school bag. But I might leave it, looking at the weather. There are a few things I can catch up on for work."

"Work? I thought you were not going back?"

"I'm not. Well, I don't think I will go back full time. But Sandra needs a few things doing. She emailed me last night, asking for a favour. I may just do a few bits and bobs for them, which suits me. If I don't do anything then I'll just get bored."

"You could join my book club?"

"Err, thanks, but no thanks. Maybe in twenty years or so."

Karen tutted, smiling at her daughter. She felt a swell of pride in her chest, causing tears to form at the corners of her eyes. The older woman swallowed them back as she placed two more mugs of coffee on the table top. "Well, I think it's a good thing you keeping your hand in with them. They have been good to you."

"They have. If all this had never happened I could have quite happily worked there forever."

Karen's phone started vibrating in her handbag on the kitchen counter. She stood up, the chair legs protesting on the floor tiles. She fished the phone out, looking at the screen. "It's your Father," she said as she answered the phone. "Hello, love. Are you missing me already?" She leaned against the counter as her husband replied. Vicky looked down at the pad, becoming lost in the drawing. "It's nothing really. Vicky just wanted to talk to me about something." She listened to her husband's reply. "Can I fill you in later, or do you need to know right now?" The older woman's eyes rolled up towards the ceiling. "Oh, alright then. Jasper's been having some strange dreams lately. He's drawn a picture of one of them, which spooked Vicky a bit." A short reply on the other end of the phone. "It's just a drawing, love, of two people next to a log cabin, with Jasper floating above them. You know he's got a good imagination though. The weird bit is, is that Vicky found her neighbour outside last night in a bit of a daze. She brought her into the kitchen to warm her up. It was then that her neighbour told her she'd also been having strange dreams, describing Jasper's drawing to a tee." Vicky could hear her Father's voice spilling from her Mother's phone. "I don't know, love. It's probably just a coincidence. That's it. Nothing to worry about. Oh, hang on. Vicky mentioned hearing a strange noise at the bottom of the garden. Like a droning sound. It's just happened again. We both heard it in the kitchen. I nearly piddled myself." As Karen listened to her husband's reply her face changed to one of disbelief.

"What's up, Mum?" Vicky said, noticing the older woman's expression.

"Hang on Vicky," she said. "Why didn't you say something, Mike?" Karen listened for a few seconds, drumming her manicured nails on the marble counter. "Fine. I'll let her know. I'll be back home in a bit." She nodded. "Okay, love. Ta-ra."

"What did he say, Mum?" Vicky said, a cold sensation settling over her.

"He said he's heard that noise too. The other day when he was playing football with Jasper. He thought it was a far-off train or something."

Goosebumps broke out over Vicky's arms, causing her to shiver involuntarily. "I don't like this. It's really weird."

"It's probably nothing, love. Maybe you heard a train like you Father did?"

"No, Mum. It was closer than that. It was there in the garden right next to me."

"It could have been anything. Don't let your imagination run away with you. You've got enough on your plate at the moment. Don't over analyse this too much. There's probably a rational explanation for all this?"

"Like what?"

"I don't know. Just keep an eye on Jasper. See if he has any more dreams like this. That's all you can do."

"And if he does?"

Her mother paused. "We'll fall off that bridge when we come to it."

* * *

He looked as his sons stood before him. Both were formidable. The one, Reggan towered over him, grey tusks pointing towards the sky. His monstrous face, grey and chilling. Yellow blank eyes stared back at the older one. His breathing ragged, spittle blowing from his mouth. He turned to his other son Korgan and smiled. He was impossibly beautiful. His white skin flawless. His dark hair slicked back. Keen yellow eyes smiled back at his father above a regal nose. Curved canines gently poked from his full mouth. Behind his one son, a grotesque figure stood, almost matching Reggan's height. The father did not know the henchman's name. He guessed he was new, not liking the feral look his face. Behind Korgan stood his friend and consort Elias. He smiled again. The tall vampire was Korgan's shield. His protector. He could feel the malice silently oozing from the brothers. Towards each other, and towards him from Reggan. He sensed danger. Imminent danger.

He was suddenly old. Weaker than before. His sons were with him again. The danger was with him again. Korgan and Elias were pinned against a wall by a multitude of Reggan's clan. The old vampire knew what was about to happen. He was about to be dethroned. The danger, the jealousy was a shawl that had settled over him like a cold mist. He was dragged through the crypt, down crudely carved red stone steps. Reggan led the way, the sword in his hand clanking on the hard floor. The king was dropped on the red stone, his tunic tearing.

Reggan towered over him, sword in hand. "Father," he rasped. "You have grown old, weak, and feckless. I will not stand by and watch as we starve. I will take your place as king of this land and the others that lie close. Your name, Virdelas, will always be remembered for cowardice and ill thought."

"Get on with it, you snivelling oaf! I only hope that Korgan does to you, what you are about to do to me." The king closed his eyes, welcoming the inevitable. His reign over the lands was at an end. He only hoped his elder son would survive. He felt no fear. No heartache. His heart had been a blackened lump in his chest since the dawn of ages. One day he would rise again. From the blackest of pits.

Maureen's eyes opened wide, the dream ending with the sharpest of pain. Yellow mist floated above her in the cold bedroom. She looked about feverishly, her skin clammy, almost slick. Her chest rose as she inhaled deeply, the thick fog sliding down her throat once more. The old woman sat up stiffly, grey light filtering in through the thick curtains. "Korgan," she said, her voice dark and distorted. "What happened to you, my Son?"

Twelve

Shetland

Katherine Bathurst stood on the stoop of her uncle's farmhouse looking out to sea. Her long brown hair was tied back in a pony, keeping it in place as the strong winds battered the peninsula. The spit of land, Shetland had been her home for a short time. It was named Shetland after her great grandfather, a man called George had lived out his days there with his family. He was from a far-off land called Scotland. Katherine knew his story well. She had heard countless times how a young George had been snatched from his world by a vampire, bringing him to her land. He'd escaped them though, making this spit of land on which she now stood his home. She'd arrived almost a moon's cycle before. Fleeing from another plane. A world full of evil and despair. Her uncle, Wilf had shepherded Katherine and Alicia back to his home. To relative safety. She felt that it had all been in vain though. Jake was not with her. He was trapped in that dark place, maybe injured, or worse. Katherine tried to block out the possibility that her man had been killed. She needed him to return, back to his woman and daughter. Alicia, lay sleeping in a stout wooden crib inside the farmhouse. Her gentle snores lost to the oncoming wind. The baby was in good hands though. Wilf was sat in a rocking chair on the other side of the door. His snores clearly recognisable over the wind. He had been an ever constant in her life. Protecting her from harm. Loving her like she was his own. Cedric, Katherine's father, had perished a few seasons before. Destroyed by a king. A vampire king. His brother Wilf had been there, barely escaping with his own life. Their world had been turned on its head when a young man had appeared in their land. A young man called Jake, from another place. Another world. He had fought with them, taking Katherine back to his world, where they had become one. They had settled to the south in a land called Cornwall. Katherine had fallen in love with that land. With its conveniences. With its fancy clothes and wondrous machines. It had not lasted though. The monsters had found them, snatching her and Alicia from Jake. He had followed, hunting them down across different planes until he'd found them. When he did, a skirmish had ensued. Jake's father, Douglas had also perished. Her eyes often prickled with tears when she thought of him. He'd been kind to her and she'd loved him for it. He was warm and cheeky, always ribbing her about something. When she thought that he had met his end in a foreign place, killed by his own wife, Katherine's heart screamed in pain. Alison, Jake's mother had also been snatched. But she had been turned by them. Elias, the head of the clan had chased them, hounded them, caused them untold grief and suffering. She only hoped that he too met his end out on that forsaken rock.

Katherine stepped off the porch, knowing that Alicia was safe in the farm-house. She pulled her woollen shawl around her shoulder as she took off across the green stubbly grass. The lump of rock on which she now lived was con-nected to the mainland by a long slither of land. The tide rose and fell, cutting them off for parts of the day. As she walked, Katherine felt the sun on her skin as it broke through the fast-moving clouds above. It lit the peninsular, bathing the scattering of stout wooden buildings in a yellow hue. Thick mist from the sea, sparkled in the sunlight, glistening in front of her as she walked. Katherine chatted to the villagers, asking how children and livestock were. She nodded at their replies, trying to concentrate on their lives instead of the plight she found herself in. She had a plan though. She knew there were doorways to the north. An expanse of swampland called Brynn-Halfsted was home to at least one such portal. She'd been reliably informed of this information by Zeebu and Zeeba when she'd arrived. They were elders in the next colony to theirs. A place called Fingles, that lay at the end of the track that connected them to the mainland. They were stunted people. Funny looking to her eyes, with long loping arms and small bodies. Her uncle had informed her that although small in stature, they were a hardy lot, who hunted the mutated Orgas that roamed the dark seas around them. They had agreed to take her to the north, to find a route that may lead to Jake. She couldn't sit idly by, hoping that one day, he showed up. She needed to take action. Katherine needed to find him. She only hoped that he was not alone, wherever he was. *Hopefully, Tamatan is with him, guiding him home, she thought.* Tamatan also needed to come home. Katherine knew that he had kin, who would also be worried about their loved one.

A young woman called to her as she meandered across the headland. "Katherine."

"Hi, Daria," Katherine said, changing course. The young woman approached Katherine, hands cupped under her considerable girth. "Don't bounce too hard. The baby might decide he wants to make an appearance right now. I can handle birthing animals. You might be a bit more troublesome."

The other woman laughed. She was roughly Katherine's age, with blonde hair that was at the mercy of the strong breeze. Her face was kind, slightly on the rounded side for her liking. But she was with child, and food was excuse enough to keep the unborn baby healthy. "No fear. I've still got half a moon cycle to go." Her expression suddenly became serious. "Any news on Jake?"

"Nothing at all. The plan I told you about. I'm going to do it soon. I'm going to ask Wilf to come with me."

"What about Alicia?"

"She will stay here. Old Jessie and Wilf have become quite close lately. I've seen the way she moons after him. I'm going to ask her to look after Alicia. She's had enough of the breast. When I'm gone she can try out good old cow's milk. I can trust Jessie. She will take good care of my baby girl."

"Yes. She's nice. Such a shame that her husband succumbed to the cold. But you're right. She does have a right soft spot for Wilf. Maybe we can have another Shetland wedding!"

"Uncle Wilf would spit his tea all over you if he heard that kind of talk. Let's keep that between us eh."

"It will go no further," Daria said, trying in vain to tuck her hair behind her ear. "When will you go?"

"Three days. The Finglers will take us north. They know the swamps and marshes better than anyone. At the far end of Brynn-Halfsted, on the fringes of Kloofbai, there is a doorway. To where we do not know. The Finglers have never used it but know where it is. They have met traders there over the ages, exchanging wares and so forth."

"So, what will you do when you get there?"

"We'll go through and see where we end up. Maybe we will find them. Or maybe someone on the other side may have seen them. I mean, a man and a demon should be easy to remember."

"You may be putting yourself in danger, Kath."

"Look around, Daria. There is danger everywhere. For most of our lives, we lived in a forest with monsters all around us. They took Alice from us. They killed my Father. They tried to kill me too. What's one more adventure? I need to find Jake. He's out there somewhere. If the doorway in Mantz Forest was still there, we could have used that. But it's not. It's buried under the ground."

"Just take care up there. Or wherever you end up. Yes, you need to find him. But you also have a daughter who needs you. She needs you more than you need Jake."

"I know. I've weighed things up with Wilf. He thinks I'm crazy for wanting to do it. But he'll always help me. And he loves Jake. Like the son he never had."

"Then go and find him. Bring him home."

"I will, Daria. I want my family whole again."

* * *

Tenta

Lenga's milky eyes opened as she heard a rap at the door. She coughed, spitting black phlegm onto the rough planked flooring. "Come," she rasped. A young woman entered, half dragging a youth behind her. "Ah, Brianna. Your tits are a welcome sight for my old eyes."

The young woman smiled, mainly out of fear. She looked down at her cleavage, wanting nothing more than to pull her woollen shawl around herself. The witch's stare felt like a cold mist, chilling her pale skin. She knew that folk liked to gawp at her prized assets. Her dark hair, pretty face, and straight teeth were almost unheard of on the island. It was only the fact that her father was the innkeeper and a cut-throated killer that kept her virtue intact. She ushered the youth forward. "What you asked for?"

"Nice. Come here, boy."

Brianna guided the youth towards Lenga, his eyes glazed over. "His name is Keto. He travelled here from afar, looking for work. Father tried him out for a couple of nights, but his only talent lies between his legs."

"Haha," chuckled Lenga as the boy came within arm's length. In one quick motion, she slit the drawstring on his trousers, letting them fall to his ankles. "My my," she said taking hold of him. "Come and stick that inside old Lenga. I need feeding. Brianna, you can watch."

The girl stood there motionless, the creaking of the bed and Lenga's grunting filling her ears. A few minutes later, the witch shoved the youth off her, pulling her long black skirts back into place. "That will keep me going until I have my next prize."

"Your next prize?" Brianna said.

"Have you not heard? The commotion a few days ago. That was caused by an Outlander. I've sent someone to bring him to me. I want his head to adorn my wall. But not before I've sampled his wares."

"Oh. I saw the fight outside the tavern. Many folk were killed. Father kept me inside."

"A wise man your father is. Anyway. We're gassing and gabbing and wasting time." The witch stood up slowly, her legs clamped together to hold in her prize. "Get up, boy," she said as a bony toe prodded his flank. "Brianna, take him over to the vat."

The young woman heaved the boy to his feet, trying not to look at his flaccid manhood that was coated in dark liquid. She looked into the large vat, its black surface churning with unseen creatures. "Now what?"

"Put him in," said the witch as she settled in her chair.

Keto's eyes suddenly cleared as he was lifted into the vat. "What's happening?" he blurted.

"You're about to find out," Lenga said, watching with interest. "Stand back girl. This could get messy." Brianna did as she was bid, watching in horror as several snakes climbed the boy's flesh, fastening their mouths onto his skin. A large red reptile forced its way between his lips, stifling his protests as a feeding frenzy began. Hundreds of sets of fangs attacked his skin, their venom melding into his bloodstream. His head thrashed from side to side as the tail of the red snake disappeared into his mouth. Brianna felt bile sting the back of her throat, swallowing it down as tears ran down her cheeks. The boy's cries died away as the venom took hold of him. His lifeless head lolled back on the lip on the vat, black liquid spilling onto the floor.

"What will happen to him now?" Brianna asked, her voice quivering.

"I'll leave it a day, then I'll cut him up and cook him. He will taste good. Almost as good as the Outlander will taste. But first I need something from him." Brianna froze on the spot as the witch's eyes turned black. Lenga held out a bony hand towards the vat, gnarled fingers curling and cracking. The red snake appeared from the corpse's mouth, flying across the cabin into the witch's grasp. Black, dead eyes looked at the old hag, searching for food. Lenga smiled before taking the head in her mouth, biting down hard. A sickening, crunching sound filled the cabin. Two more bites and the head came away, blood spewing onto the witch's face and neck.

Vomit hit the floorboards as Brianna's resolve collapsed. She fell to the floor, retching and crying. "Oh God," she blurted as she wiped at her mouth.

"You've seen enough," Lenga said as she finished eating the head. "Leave me to my feast, girl. Bring more, and I will reward you further. Now go!"

The door slammed shut as Lenga started consuming the remainder of the snake. The boy's essence fuelling her withered body. Giving her the strength she would need. For the journey ahead.

Thirteen

Worcestershire

Vicky heard the rap on the door as she stood in the kitchen, pondering lunch. The Tuesday morning had taken a turn for the worse weather wise, low clouds and mist blanketing the Lickey Hills. It felt more like late autumn than spring. Her dark socks made barely a whisper as she made her way along the hallway to the front door. As the door opened, a cool chill blew into the cottage. A man was stood on the step smiling at her. He was wearing a red jacket with dark trousers. His closely cropped grey hair was sprinkled with raindrops. His warm smile reaching his eyes, making Vicky smile back.

"Morning, Mrs Evans. Parcel for you."

"Morning, Ben," she said, accepting the small brown package. "How are you today?"

"Not too bad. Although the weather isn't helping much."

"I know. Feels more like November."

"You're not wrong there. I had to put a vest on this morning. And folk talk about global warming. It's all a con if you ask me." He looked to his left, his expression changing. "Have you seen much of Maureen?"

Suddenly stumped, Vicky tried to overthink the answer. "Err, yes. I saw her a few days ago. Why do you ask?"

"She's not been herself lately. I saw her yesterday. She looked very frail. Maybe she's coming down with something?"

"Maybe. She did seem a little off colour when I saw her at the weekend. She's normally very active. Maybe she needs to get checked over at the doctor's?"

"Maybe you're right. I've got a few letters for her. I'll give her a tinkle and see how she is."

"Good idea. Give her my best."

"I'll do that," Ben said as he turned to walk back down the driveway. "Be seeing you."

"Bye, Ben," Vicky said before closing the door. She stood in the hallway, inspecting the box in her hands, not liking the chill that floated around her ankles. The woman headed for the kitchen. A ham and pickle sandwich, her next task.

Ben made way across the driveway, looking between the two cottages for any signs of activity. Seeing none, he headed for the property's front door, pulling three envelopes from his postbag. He knocked on the door as his eyes scanned the remaining post tucked into the red plastic satchel. He felt the door move under his knuckles, looking up to see that it was open a fraction of an inch. His brow knotted as his fingers splayed across the door, pushing it open. "Hello," he called. "Maureen. It's Ben. Are you home?" The ticking of the wall clock seemed unnaturally loud in the dim hallway. He moved further inside, closing the front door with a click. Thick Paisley carpet along the hallway and up the stairs gave the cottage a muted feeling. The kitchen door up ahead was closed, as were the drapes in the hallway to his left. He shivered, placing his postbag on the carpet. The three envelopes were placed quietly on the telephone table underneath the window. A noise to his right startled him. He knew that the room behind the door was the cottage's lounge, where Mrs Kirkby would often sit with her crosswords and puzzle books. He knew the layout, sharing the odd cup of tea with her over the years he'd been on this particular round. He gently pushed the door open, not seeing the yellow mist that pulsed underneath the jamb. "Hello?" he said poking his head around the door. The lounge was in darkness, thick curtains to his right all but blocking out any daylight from outside. On the back wall of the lounge, a dark wooden bookcase stood. Its width taking up the whole wall. Mrs Kirkby stood there, facing away from him. His nose immediately picked up on the smell that hung over the room. It was the smell of death. His breath clouded in front of his face as he exhaled, the temperature in the lounge feeling more like a deep freeze to the ageing postman. He shivered, almost gagging on the cloying stench.

"Hello, Ben," her spidery voice said, barely reaching him.

"Are you okay, Maureen? Why are you stood in the darkness?" He stood there, unsure of what to do.

"I'm fine. Just getting a few things sorted. So many things to do. So little time."

"Are you sure you're alright?" Ben moved towards her, his rubber soles squeaking as he walked. He stood next to her, seeing that she was looking at a framed photograph. It was too dark for Ben to make out the contents in the gloomy confines of the lounge. She shifted slightly, noticing a presence next to her. The frame was placed back on the bookshelf, the woman's arms then dropping to her flanks. "Are you feeling unwell?" he asked tentatively.

"Just hungry. I've not eaten."

"Well let's get you into the kitchen and I can put some toast on for you." He reached around, turning her towards him. As she turned towards him, the man froze in horror.

"I don't want toast," she said. Their eyes met, only inches apart. His blue eyes opened wider as his bladder's contents emptied down his legs. Her eyes narrowed slightly as she smiled at him. They were keen and feral. Glowing yellow in the darkness. They had found what she wanted. The thing inside her, wanted it too.

* * *

"In bed, young man," Vicky said as she walked into Jasper's bedroom. She was dressed in a grey leopard print dressing gown, fluffy slippers, with a white towel wrapped around her head.

"Five more minutes, Mummy?"

"You said that ten minutes ago, Jaspy. Come on. Lights out, school tomorrow," she said as she picked up toys from the bedroom carpet.

"Oh okay," he said, feigning a small strop as he dipped under the covers.

Vicky bent over and kissed his curls, inhaling her son's fresh scent. "Night night, love. Sweet dreams."

"Night night, Mummy. Love you."

"Ditto," she said as she walked over to the light switch, flicking it. She smiled in the darkness before heading downstairs.

Jasper lay there, looking up at the ceiling. The room was not quite in total darkness. Light filtered in from the rear garden, making it easy for Jasper to look around him. He pulled the duvet up under his nose, getting himself comfortable. His mind wandered as sleep gradually took him. *Wednesday tomorrow. Library day. Need to remember to pack my books.* Random thoughts flooded his mind as his eyes suddenly became heavy. He liked library day. He liked the smell of books. He liked the window seat at the far corner of the long room. *Maybe Gemma Kings will sit with me like she did last week?* The last thoughts to cross his mind before he succumbed, were of a pretty blond girl with a toothy grin, smiling at him as he read his book. His eyelids fluttered closed. He was gone.

Jasper floated around the trees in his back garden, listening for sounds. It was deathly quiet. Unusually so. He didn't like it. He could feel something was not right. Propelling himself forward, Jasper steered himself towards the cottage next door. It was in darkness. Curiosity took hold as his nose pressed against the glass of the bedroom window. He could see Mrs Kirkby asleep on the bed. Her feet were hanging over the bottom of the divan, pointing towards him. Jasper watched silently as she slowly rose from her prone position. They locked eyes. The woman smiled, her yellow irises piercing the night. Blackness poured from her mouth, spewing across the bedroom towards the window. Jasper cried out, the noise silent. It had no force, or form. But he heard it in his ears. It rang in his head as he scooted back away from the cottage.

"Who are you? What do you want?" the distorted drone echoed from the darkness. Jasper turned and fled, slaloming between tall trees, heading towards his destination. A few minutes later he passed through the doorway, out of his world. Into the huge blackened forests that was called Amatoll. More trees fell behind him as he headed west towards another huge forest. This one was bigger, darker, and colder. He whistled through a tight gorge with a rambling stream, the dark waters passing beneath him. The gorge gave way to a thick blanket of trees. Even though Jasper was not physically there, he could almost feel the cold air penetrating his soft pyjamas. He rose up out of the forest, sailing over the dense canopy, continuing westwards towards the sea. His keen eyes picked out the glow in the distance, knowing that it was the doorway. Dropping through the thick foliage, Jasper floated next to a green doorway that lay lengthways on the forest floor. Around the doorway, the forest looked like it had been recently damaged. Like an explosion had rocked the ground underneath him. His feet touched the floor, not feeling the wet ground. To Jasper, it just tingled. He stood in a slight depression, slightly lower than the rest of the forest around him. The green doorway pulsed and throbbed in the darkness. Inviting him inside.

* * *

"Just up ahead," Bea said, pointing up the track into the inky night.

Jake could just about make out the twinkling lights further up the mountain track. "Great. I'm knackered." They had been walking for what seemed like weeks. In reality, it was just over two days. During that time, food and drink was scarce. Only the provisions in Bea's pack had kept them going. Tamatan had taken less than the two humans. He was stronger, not needing sustenance like they did.

"I'm with you, Jake. I need a proper meal and a soft bed. Hell, any kind of bed will do." The track grew ever steeper, the strength quickly draining from Jake. His leg was almost unbearable. It constantly pulsed and throbbed, making the journey a perpetual torment. Bea noticed him rubbing his thigh. "We need to get that seen to mate. Maybe someone up there can help?"

"Let's hope so. Will there be many people there?"

"Last time I was there it was packed. Lots of different types there too. It can get a bit feisty in there though. We'll have to be careful."

"Feisty?"

"Yeah. There was a big punch up. A few people were stabbed. Kaiden carried me out to the barn, locking us in one of the pens. It was quite a night."

"Great! Just what we need."

"We will be fine," Tamatan said. "I'm ready for anything. Anyone who tries to harm us, is harming my kin. I will not let anything stop me from finding them."

"Let's hope it doesn't come to that. I need a quiet night. No dramas," Bea said. A few minutes later they were resting against the front railings. The building was a low-slung affair, set at the side of the track. Tall, craggy cliffs stood to the front and rear, giving the setting a claustrophobic feeling. Horses stood a few feet away from the trio, heads bowed in a wooden trough filled with water.

Jake moved away from the railing, looking past the horses. "Is that where we are heading?"

"Yes. Further up the track. I'm pretty sure I can find it without Kaiden's help. In fact, I'm hoping he's not too far behind us. I really hope the drawing makes sense to him."

"Me too," Jake said as he turned towards the entrance. Above the doorway, painting in crude with lettering was the word.

KUNGSBACK

"Okay. Let's get some grub," Bea said as she headed towards the swing doors. Jake and Tamatan followed her, stepping into the saloon. Jake sized up the room as he stepped in. He guessed it to be roughly fifty feet wide and thirty feet from the door to the bar. Wooden stairs on the left, led up to a balcony with wooden doors evenly spaced. The space was almost deserted, save for a few folk sprinkled around the room, chatting and drinking. He relaxed slightly, not sensing any danger. He followed Bea and Tamatan towards the bar, his footsteps creaking on the wooden floor. A man stood behind the bar, facing away from them. "Hello," Bea said. "Can we get something to eat and maybe a room for the night?"

The man turned around and smiled at her. "Sure. I recognise you. Seen you here before I have." His voice was light and breezy, out of place in the dark saloon. "A while ago. You were with a big man, taller than the doorway."

"Yes. That's him," Bea breathed, clearly relieved at the innkeeper's response. Jake looked at him, sussing him out. He was slightly taller than Jake, with a round face. His thinning brown hair was unruly at best. He was thick-set, with bulging forearms and meaty hands. His kind features were just a ruse in Jake's opinion. He knew the innkeeper could handle himself if needed.

"My name's Matts," he said. "Welcome to Kungsback. Best food and drink for miles. Which is not saying much as there is nothing around us," he chuckled, rubbing his meaty paws on a dark apron.

"I'm Bea. This is Jake and Tamatan, friends of mine who are trying to get home. They've gotten a little lost."

He regarded them, his eyes lingering on the demon for a few seconds. "Not seen many of your type in these parts. Where are you from?"

"From beyond the Unseen Lands. A place called Marzalek."

"That's a new one on me. And you," he said as he nodded at Jake. "Where are you from?"

"A place called England. A long way from here."

"Never heard of that place either. Oh well, you're welcome in my humble home. Just don't go starting any fights. Or you'll have Mimi to deal with."

"Don't worry. All we want is a few mugs of ale, a steak and a bed," Bea said. She reached into her pack, pulling out a nugget of gold. She handed it to Matts. "Is this enough?"

He rolled the precious metal between his large fingers, liking how it shimmered in the candlelight. "This is way too much. How long are you staying for?"

"One night hopefully. I may pass by here on my way back, hopefully with Kaiden."

"This will keep you going for a moons cycle." He put the gold in his pocket before grabbing three large wooden mugs from the shelf. The innkeeper strode to the other end of the bar, where half a dozen large barrels were sat. He deftly filled the three mugs, walking back towards them as suds hit the floor beneath him. "Here you go. I'll get some food sent over to you." He looked up at the balcony. "JENNI," he yelled. "Get the griddle on. We have guests."

A door opened above them, out of sight. Loud footsteps echoed through the saloon as a young woman made her way down the rickety stairs. "How many, Pa?" she said as she crossed the room.

"Three. What have we got left?"

"Steak and tats." She walked behind the bar, standing next to her father. She matched his height, her dark hair cascading down her back and shoulder. Jake noticed a hoop that hung under her nose. The metal was black with a red gemstone set in the centre. It rocked back and forth as she moved. She had her father's features. A kind, pretty face, set below dark brows.

"That sounds fine by me," Bea said. She looked at the other two who nodded readily.

"Sit yourselves down somewhere. I'll bring it over to you soon." She kissed her father on the cheek before disappearing through a doorway next to barrels of ale.

Jake looked down into his mug, his throat suddenly screaming to be quenched. He raised the mug to his mouth, downing its contents in three giant glugs. He smacked his lips, "Boy I needed that. Can I have another please," extending his mug towards the innkeeper.

"Not a problem. Go and get settled. I'll bring it over to you." They found a table next to the flight of stairs, pulling chairs up before sitting down to wait for their food. Matts gave Jake a second mug, taking Bea's empty one back to be replenished. Tamatan sipped at his drink, apparently not as thirsty as his two companions.

Once the innkeeper had returned and left them, Bea addressed the others. "We'll bed down after we've eaten. Then we'll carry on after brekkie. If there are people on our tail, I don't want them finding us here. It could get messy. These are good folk. They do not deserve trouble."

"I agree," Jake said. "Let's just hope that no one is looking for us. And if they are out there, let's hope we've given them the slip."

"I'll drink to that," Bea said, clonking mugs with Jake. She looked at the diminutive demon, noticing a dark look on his face. "What's up with you?"

"He's back."

"Who's back?" Jake asked, his lips wet with ale.

"The boy. He's heading our way."

* * *

Jasper came across the barn. It lay below him under low cloud and mist. Something was wrong. A group of men and beasts stood around it, tossing flaming torched onto its roof. He watched in morbid fascination as the fire took hold, quickly engulfing the structure. He dropped down, trying to stay out of sight. He noticed a shape lay close to the front porch. Gliding closer, he saw that it was some kind of animal. It was not moving. It looked like a small horse, its legs twitching spasmodically in the long grass. Jasper could hear the men shouting, the beasts growling at whatever lay inside the cabin. The boy felt his stomach turn to ice. He hoped that Jake was not inside. He floated ever closer, thirty feet off the ground. The beasts sensed him, turning and baying at the unseen force. A giant of a man, grabbed them by their tufted necks, reigning them close to him. Jasper shrank back as the front door of the cabin burst open. The beasts flinched, spinning around as another giant leapt from the porch. One of the gang went down under one of his blows as the unknown man took off, striding away from the gang. His blond ponytail dancing behind him. Jasper rose up into the sky, slowly following as the man made a break for it. The gang followed, hounds released. The boy was amazed at how fast the man could run. Not even the beasts could keep up with him as his long strides ate up the pathway underneath him. He was heading towards far off mountains, looming high on the horizon. Who are you? Are you a friend of the others? Are you lost too? Jasper knew the mountains beyond. He knew where a doorway sat, high up in a craggy gorge. He made up his mind, speeding passed the running figure. After a minute he stopped and turned, relieved that the gang and hounds were falling back. He's so fast, he thought before turning and heading for the high peaks in the distance. Not knowing what he was he was looking for.

* * *

"How do you know?" Bea asked Tamatan, her face intrigued.

"I can feel him. He has a strong pull on me."

"Why is he here?" Jake asked as he took a swig of his ale.

"I'm not sure of such things, Jake. I have a feeling, but I cannot be certain."

"Go on," Bea said.

They paused as the innkeeper's daughter placed three wooden plates in front of them. Rudimentary cutlery clattered on the wooden top. "Sorry. I had my hands full. Enjoy the fayre."

"Thank you," Jake said, looking down at his food. He was suddenly hit by the aroma, his taste buds kicking into gear. "God, that smells good!"

"You're not wrong there," Bea said as she picked up an iron fork. Without saying another word, the three set about their plates. Even Tamatan, who was usually conservative in his eating habits, munched and chewed with vigour. His red eyes closed in glee as he gulped down the wholesome food. Jenni deposited a bowl filled with three large hunks of bread, still warm from the kitchen. They all used it to mop up the juices left behind from the meat and sauce. Sated, they sat looking around the bar, noticing the patrons who were scattered around them. They looked swarthy and menacing, beady eyes looking back at the trio.

Keen to break the glares, Bea looked at Tamatan. "So, why is he here?"

"I think he's here," he started, his eyes hooded as he stared at the table. "To guide us home."

* * *

Kaiden never slowed his pace as he ran, his loping strides eating up the track. He occasionally glanced behind, happy that the marauding gang were falling away in the distance. He had not shaken them though. The giant knew in his heart that they were just as fast as he. *They are waiting for me to tire,* he thought. *Then they'll set the hounds on me.* He'd only been in the cabin a short while when he knew something was wrong. The drawing on the table was barely digested when the first attack came. Dried blood still coated his knuckles from the impact. The man they'd sent in was dead before he'd hit the floor, his neck and face shattered from Kaiden's clubbing blow. Then the flames had come, forcing his hand. *Kungsback. That's where I'll find her. Whoever took her will die slowly.* He started to feel tired, his legs heavier than normal. He knew the land well, guessing that he could reach his destination faster than his woman. *Need to take a different route,* he thought. *Too exposed out here. If I stop, they will have me.* He looked to his right, dark foothills, giving way to craggy peaks beyond. He veered off the track, barely missing a beat. Kaiden knew a place where he could hole up to rest. The man knew the dangers too. *I've got to chance it. Hopefully the place will be deserted.* He steeled himself for the climb ahead, hoping that he would make it to Bea. In one piece. Hoping that his hideout's resident was away somewhere else. Or long dead.

* * *

Jasper flew on into the night. He knew that he'd have to head home soon. Time was getting on. His mind wandered as he went, almost missing the saloon underneath him as his thoughts drifted along with him. He dropped down lower into the gorge, the twinkling lights of the saloon strangely inviting to the boy. He scooted to the other side of the pathway, sheltered behind a large rock. The sheer cliffs rose above him, making Jasper feel very small and alone. His mind reached out, finding what he was looking for. He floated there, waiting.

* * *

The plates were taken away, their mugs replenished with another dark heady ale. The three sat there, almost relaxed. Conversation had died off as they became lost in thoughts of loved ones and far off lands. Suddenly, Tamatan sat bolt upright.

"What is it?" Jake asked.

"Outside. Now." He got up from his chair, drawing a few drunken glances from the other patrons. Bea and Jake followed him, slightly unnerved by the demon's actions. They came together at the bottom of the steps as a few droplets of rain began to fall into the gorge.

"What's up with you?" Bea asked as Tamatan began looking about feverishly.

"Over here," he exclaimed as he headed over towards a large rock that lay propped against the wall of the cliff. They followed as an unseen horse whinnied in the darkness. Tamatan stood looking at nothing, hands planted on his hips.

"You're freaking me out. What's wrong?" Jake said, rubbing his thigh.

"Can you not see him?" the demon asked.

Before they could answer, they noticed a dull glow in the darkness. To Jake, it looked like a bubble, hovering a few feet from the stone floor. Inside the bubble, Jake could just make out the shape of a boy. He strained to see, moving closer. "What the fuck?"

"Hello," Tamatan said. "We're not here to hurt you." He stood there, listening to words that Jake and Bea could not hear. "His name is Jasper. Hello, Jasper. I am Tamatan. This is Jake and Bea. Why are you here?"

Bea moved forward, touching the bubble. It gave off a resistance that she was not expecting. Kneeling down, she looked at the boy in the bubble. "He's like a hologram. But I can make out his face. He's a cute lad. Lovely hair too." She smiled. "Hello there, young man. You're a long way from home."

"He's from a place called Lickey," the little demon said as a gust of cold wind blew through the gorge.

"Jesus!" Jake exclaimed. "That's where I'm from. What is he doing here?"

Tamatan listened to the boy, rubbing his chin thoughtfully. "He knows we're lost. He wants to help us."

"Tell him I'm also from The Lickey's." Jake moved closer, getting a good look at the ethereal face in front of him. He smiled at the boy. "Hi there."

The bubble seemed to swell slightly, bumping against the rocks nearby. "He says that he knows a way home." Tamatan listened for a moment, his face turning grave. "There are people coming for us."

"What people?" Bea asked, suddenly on edge.

"A gang of men. They are heading our way. They are following a lone man. He is leading them to us. They are close to the cabin. Still a long way from us. But they are running."

"Kaiden?" Bea blurted. "They must be chasing him. I bet he saw the drawing and is heading our way. What shall we do?"

Tamatan looked at the boy, bowing his head. He listened intently for a minute. "He has to go back home now. He said he will return soon." The bubble rose into the air, heading away from them higher into the mountains. They stood there for a minute, digesting the message. "We must be ready."

"What can we do?" Bea asked, concern etched on her handsome face.

"We get help from inside," Tamatan said. "But not yet. First, we need to sleep."

Fourteen

Vicky gently nudged Jasper, trying to coax him from his slumbers. Wednesday's weather had followed on from Tuesday's, low clouds pressing close to the land. "Come on, Jaspy. It's time to get up for school." She watched him for a moment, the rise and fall of his chest steady. "Jasper. Come on, love. It's time to get up."

Another nudge, slightly more forceful stirred him. His eyes opened, lids slowly blinking. "Mummy?"

"Yes, love. Are you okay?"

"I don't feel very well. My tummy hurts," he lied.

"Oh no," his mother said, touching his brow. She was relieved to see that he wasn't running a temperature. "Do you want to stay home today? I can call the school and let them know."

"Yes, please, Mummy. Can I lie in bed for a bit? I'm really tired."

"Sure. I'll telephone the school. Do you want me to bring anything up for you?"

"Could I have some warm juice please, Mummy?"

"Okay. You lie there. I'll be back up in a minute." She leaned over, kissing his dark curls before heading downstairs.

Jasper lay there, staring up at the ceiling. His mind tried to piece together his dream. *Mrs Kirkby. What happened to her? Jake. He lives around here? I must tell Mummy this.*

A few minutes later, Vicky walked back into his room. A large beaker of juice in her hand. "Here you go. I've phoned the school. You can stay at home with me today."

"Thank you, Mummy," he said, taking a sip of the warm cordial. He thought for a moment, trying to find a way to start the conversation. "Mummy."

"Yes Jaspy," Vicky said, looking up from her phone.

"I had a dream last night. A really strange dream. I need to tell you about it."

Vicky placed the phone on the duvet, looking into the eyes of her youngest child. "Okay. What was the dream about?"

"I don't really know where to start. You remember my drawing?"

"Yes," Vicky said, a few hairs prickling to attention on her forearms.

"When I dream, I am flying through the Lickey's. There are doorways, Mummy. They take me to another place. I don't know why I'm dreaming about this. I found some people, Mummy. The people in the drawing. There is another one now too. There are Jake, Tamatan and Bea. They are lost."

"Lost. Where?"

"In this other place. I can go there through the doorways. But they cannot fly like I can."

"It's only a dream, Son. Are you sure you're okay?"

"I think so, Mummy. Since I came home from the hospital I've been dreaming about the same thing. I spoke to them last night. Jake is from Lickey too. He lives around here somewhere. I think he is trying to find the doorway that will bring him home."

"It's just a dream. It's not real, Jaspy."

"But it felt so real. And Mrs Kirkby was in my dream too. She was different. She scared me, Mummy."

"How did she scare you?" Vicky's stomach started churning.

"She looked like a monster. Her eyes were scary. She tried to get me to go into her house. I flew away, Mummy."

Vicky ruffled the top of his head. "Silly. There is no such thing as monsters. You've just gotten a very active imagination lately. Do you want to lie here for a bit while I carry on downstairs?"

"Okay. I'll be down in a bit."

Vicky walked downstairs, trying to recollect what she'd been doing before talking to her son. *Laundry.* She headed into the utility room, pouring detergent into the compartment on the washing machine. Starting the program, she walked back into the kitchen, her mind a maelstrom of thoughts. A tied-up bin liner in the corner of the kitchen, made Vicky unlatch the back door. Carrying the refuse sack in one hand, Vicky unlocked the back gate, walking between the cottages to where the bins stood. After depositing the bin bag, Vicky headed towards her neighbour's cottage. She gave two hard wraps on the wooden door, turning around to look at the other houses lay dotted along the quiet cul-de-sac. After a few seconds, she turned back towards the house, peering through the dappled glass on the front door. The hallway beyond was in darkness. Vicky could see that the kitchen and lounge doors were closed. She moved right, towards the lounge window. The curtains were drawn. *Strange*, she thought as she returned to the front door. Against her better judgement, she knelt down, opening the letter flap. She looked up the hallway and stairs, noticing a strange smell escaping into the blustery day. The house was still. Silent and dark. Vicky stood up, walking back around towards her rear gate. Before she went back inside, she tested the latch. It was locked. A sense of unease settled over her as she headed back into her kitchen. Making herself a cup of strong coffee, Vicky settled down at the kitchen table with her laptop. She knew that this would be a fruitless exercise. However, the conversation with her mother a few days before, coupled with Jasper's revelations, made her curious.

"Mummy. I'm going to have a shower," Jasper called from upstairs.

"Okay, love. Take a fresh mat and towel out of the airing cupboard."

"Okay," her son called back down.

She opened her internet browser, typing a question into the search engine. *Policeman killed in Birmingham.* Vicky took a sip of steaming coffee as the results loaded. She looked at the page, clicking on the second result, an article from a local paper. The headline read, *Policeman Murdered in Barnt Green.* Her finger clicked the mouse, loading the page. An image of a handsome man in police uniform unfolded on the screen. Vicky read the story, shaking her head as it recounted the brutal murder of Detective Sergeant Darren Harris by an unknown assailant. Reading on, her eyes settled on a name a few lines below.

Sergeant Harris had visited the Queen Victoria public house earlier in the evening with his brother-in-law Jake Stevenson. It is understood that Mr Stevenson, a former police officer gave chase, but was unable to apprehend the attacker. Police are calling for anyone who has information to come forward.

"This is all starting to sound like too much of a coincidence," Vicky said as she clicked the back button on the browser. She entered another question into the search engine. *Jake Stevenson Policeman Birmingham.* More results appeared on the screen. Vicky clicked on the top result, another article from a local paper. She scrolled down, reading about the deaths of Kate and Megan Stevenson at a nearby shopping mall. Tears formed at the corners of her eyes as she looked at a picture of a pretty young girl and an equally attractive woman.

She read the story, horrified as to the nature of their deaths at the hands of a hit-and-run motorist. She scrolled down further, as another picture came into view. "Jake," she said as she looked at a picture of a young man with dark hair. "Such a good-looking family," she said to herself, drawing comparisons with her own family and her own loss. She scrolled back to the top, noting the date was five years previous. Vicky clicked back to the home screen, logging into Facebook. His name was typed into the search bar, Vicky's heartbeat quickening somewhat. She scanned through the various Jake Stevenson's around the globe, disappointed that she couldn't find him. She typed in Darren Harris and clicked enter. After a few scroll-downs, Vicky found who she was looking for. A picture of the late Darren Harris smiled back at her. She clicked on his profile, another slurp of coffee needed. To her disappointment, his friends' list was private. Backing up, she clicked on his profile picture. It looked to Vicky like it had been taken on a stag party. Darren stood in the middle of a group of men, all holding large pints of lager. There were no comments, however, thirteen people had liked the photograph. She clicked again as a list of people appeared on the screen. Halfway down the screen was Jake Stevenson. "Bingo," she said as her cursor hovered over his face. Two seconds later his profile appeared on the screen. His friends' list was also private. "Typical policemen," she said to herself. Jake too had limited photographs, giving little away. She felt slightly deflated as she clicked the 'about' icon. Little information presented itself. Her quickened pulse was now steadying itself. The only point of interest was it stated that he lived in Cornwall.

"Finished, Mummy," Jake called down the stairs. "Can I have some toast please?"

"Okay, love. I'll bring some up in a minute." She looked back at the screen. *Cornwall. Why does he live there now? It's definitely the same guy from the newspaper.* The phone on the counter started ringing, pushing herself away from the table, Vicky picked up the handset, pressing the green button. "Hi, Dad. You okay?"

"Fine. Just checking on you? How are you both?"

"Jasper is not feeling great today. He has a sore tummy."

"Oh. Well, that's not good. Has he got diarrhoea?"

"No, Dad. Just a sore tummy. What are you up to?"

"I'm dropping your Mother at book club at eleven. Then I'll come home and potter in front of the television."

Vicky chuckled. "Don't let Mum hear you say that."

"She's in the shower, running up my water rates."

"Are you picking her up after?"

"Normally I would. But her friend is dropping her back."

"Oh. Which friend?"

"Val. The village gossip."

Another chuckle from Vicky. "Is she that bad?"

"Well put it this way. I'm glad we live five miles away from her. I couldn't have her popping round every hour with the latest goings-on."

A thought suddenly hit Vicky like a freight train. *Val. She's the one who mentioned the missing vicar.* An idea formed quickly in her head. A crazy thought, without reason or sense. "Dad. Can I ask a favour?" She began pacing the kitchen, her pulse quickening.

"Sure?"

"How long does book club last?"

"About an hour or so. Why?"

"Would you be able to pop round here after dropping her off? I have a few errands to run, and I can't really take Jasper as he's off school. I can pick Mum up on the way back and bring her here."

A brief pause on the other end of the line as her father thought about it. "Okay. I can do that. I'll see you both in a bit then."

"Thanks, Dad. You're a star."

"I know, love. Your mother tells me all the time. See you in a bit. Love you."

"Love you too, Dad." Vicky ended the call. She walked over to the counter, dropping two pieces of crusty bread into the toaster. *Vicky Evans. What are you getting yourself into?* she thought, a half-smile tugging at her lips.

* * *

Fingles

Katherine and Wilf dismounted the horses, tying them to a wooden rail that ran along the front of the largest building in Fingles. They had made the trip to the mainland quickly as the sea had receded, the horses spooked by the sound of the Orgas in the dark waters that lay on either side of them. Katherine arched her back, a satisfying click easing her stiff spine. She looked over towards her uncle, who was looking up and down the deserted street. Fingles was home to the Finglers. A stunted collection of individuals who made the harsh stretch of coastline their home. Wilf knew them well, as did Katherine, who had met them now on several occasions. The elders, Zeebu and Zeeba, had orchestrated the building of the new homes on Shetland a few seasons before. Wilf was indebted to them. However, they took it all in good spirits, happy to help out whenever they were called upon.

"Where are they, Uncle?" Katherine said, putting a pail of water down for the horses after their journey.

"Either in there," he said pointing into the saloon. "Or in their workshop. Come. Let's check the saloon first. I'm hungry."

They walked into the low-slung wooden structure, a strong smell of fish permeating through the musky air. A small woman appeared behind the bar. "Hail, Wilf of Shetland," she said beaming.

"Hail, Taniq. Where are the elders?"

The diminutive Fingler rubbed at her chin. Her long dark hair almost reaching the floor. Her face was kind and inquisitive. "They were here a short time ago. They have ordered breakfast. Shall I make up some more?"

"That would be most kind," Wilf said, drawing a smile from the woman. "I take it they are in their den?"

"Yes-yes. They are preparing for the journey. They have told us all about it. A trip to the north beckons. Such adventure. Such fun."

"Let's hope not too much fun," Wilf added.

Taniq looked at Katherine, smiling. "Hello again. I saw you last moon. I brought Orga meat to you."

"Hello," Katherine said smiling. "Yes. I remember it well. You really have been so kind to us."

"It's nothing really. A few steaks and skins. If we give more away, our bellies will be less tight."

Katherine and Wilf smiled as Zeebu and Zeeba entered through the swing doors. "Hail, Wilf and Katherine," they said in unison. "We are all set for the journey ahead. Our carts are fully laden."

"Excellent," Wilf said enthusiastically. "Shall we have some breakfast and set off?"

"Yes," they said. "A great plan."

A short while later, Taniq was clearing away crude crockery and goblets, tutting and fussing around the table. They waited until she had disappeared before Wilf addressed the elders. "How long to the doorway?"

"Two days. We must navigate the path through the swampland. Once across, it is a short hop to the place where the doorway appears."

"Hmm," Wilf said, eager to be on the move. "Well, shall we be on our way?"

"Yes," they said, once more in unison. "We will tether your horses to the cart and meet you outside."

They stood, thanking Taniq, who was cleaning behind the bar. The saloon was suddenly quiet, leaving Wilf and Katherine to their thoughts. The old man looked at his niece, a concerned look spreading over his grizzled features. "What if we cannot find him? It is not set in stone that we will, Kath."

"Then at least we've tried, Uncle. At least I will know that the doorway to the north is not where Jake is."

"But then what?"

"I've not thought that far ahead. The forest to the west is shut off for him. If he's going to find his way to me, he will do it through another doorway."

"Fair enough. You are a stubborn wench. So much of your mother was passed down to you."

Katherine stuck her tongue out at him, drawing a smile that transformed Wilf's face. "I am glad that I carry her traits, Uncle."

"So am I, Kath. Well, sometimes at least."

* * *

Kaiden's fingers were red raw as he climbed the last few feet of the ravine. He could still hear the gang behind him, the sounds of the hounds carrying to his ears. As he reached the summit, Kaiden took in his surroundings. His destination was still a considerable distance away. He knew that if he rested, he could make it there before the next day was at an end. Although, the sun would not rise and set on this land, giving him the indications he'd need. He would use his body-clock as an indicator, taking a quick rest before carrying on. Two large boulders stood at the edge of the drop. Kaiden walked over to them, hearing the barking and baying on the slopes below. He looked down the incline, seeing nothing. The moon above was shrouded in mist, blanketing the landscape in a black nothingness that stretched in all directions. He put his shoulder to the first boulder, his vision darkening further as he pushed the monolith forward. He felt it give slightly, slamming all his weight behind it. It toppled forward, bounding down the slope into the blackness of night. He heard the impact, an unseen howl reaching his ears. He ran to the second rock, his feet sliding on loose shale. After a few grunts and pushes, the second boulder headed ever downwards. More screams filtered up in the darkness. Screams of pain. *That should hold them off for a while,* he thought as he turned towards a narrow gorge. He could barely see the rocks ahead of him. However, Kaiden knew where the path led. He knew that he'd be able to find shelter for the coming hours. Whether or not he'd be alone was another matter.

Fifteen

A cool breeze hit Vicky as she climbed out of her car. The door half slammed itself, such was the force of the wind that was beginning to kick itself up around her. She walked briskly, pulling her jacket around her as she headed for the local hall. It was on the opposite side of the road to St Stephens Church. Vicky had observed the abandoned vicarage as she had approached in her car, noticing the pulled curtains and unruly lawn. Her brown boots skipped over unsteady paving slabs as she reached a small set of concrete steps at the side of the building. Taking two at a time with the use of the handrail, she found herself in front of a semi-glazed door. She peered inside, observing a dozen or so women, sat in a tight circle. Her mother's steely grey hair was easy to pick out, nodding up and down as she addressed the group of women. Vicky waited a minute, protected from the building storm by the enclosed doorway. Chairs slid back as women stood up, taking the blue plastic seating to a far corner of the hall. *Now or never*, she thought as she shouldered her way through the stiff door.

"Vicky?" Karen said, clearly surprised.

"Hi, Mum. You okay?" I was just passing, so I thought I'd pop in. Dad's at home with Jasper. He's a bit under the weather."

Karen's stony face dropped even further. "What's up with him?"

"Not sure. He slept like a log last night. I never heard a peep from him. This morning he was really sleepy. Said he had a tummy ache, so I've kept him home." Vicky smiled at the woman standing next to her mother. "Hello."

The other woman smiled back. "Hi. I'm Val," she said extending her hand. Vicky shook it briefly, feeling it was odd to shake hands in this manner. It felt very formal.

"Sorry, love," Karen began. "Yes. This is Val. You know, the one I told you about?"

Vicky feigned ignorance, trying to recollect where she'd heard the name. "When was that?"

"The other day," Karen said, slightly bewildered by her daughter's scatty memory. "Remember. The Vicar?"

"Oh yes. I remember now. I think," the younger woman said, pleased with her acting skills.

"Vicar? You mean Father Stephen?" Val said.

Gotcha, Vicky thought, knowing that her bait had been taken. "Was it Father Stephen, Mum?"

"Yes. Remember I told you that he'd gone missing, along with the policeman," Karen said. The hall was now empty, save for the three women. Glass rattled in tired old window frames as the rain started to fall outside.

Val looked over to the corner of the room. "Would anyone like a cuppa?"

"Oh I could murder a cup of tea," Vicky said enthusiastically.

Val made her way over the far corner with Karen, who gave her daughter a quizzical look. Vicky smiled at her mother, walking towards the small kitchenette.

A few minutes later, the three women were sat on plastic chairs as the rain beat down outside. No lights were on inside the hall, giving it a sombre feeling. Val took a sip of her drink, letting Vicky appraise her. She was roughly her mother's age. However, she didn't wear it as well. Her short brown hair was scruffy, the greys showing at the roots. Her ruddy features made her look a good few older than the mid-sixty mark. She was dressed conservatively, in dark trousers and a brown fleece. Vicky could smell a musty aroma oozing from the woman. Cheap perfume was the younger woman's guess.

"So. Tell Vicky what you told me about Father Stephen," Karen said as she tested her tea.

"Well, he started going a bit peculiar last year. There were rumours that he'd been hitting the booze. His recycling bin was always overflowing with empty bottles of Scotch. His wife, Denise, seemed to turn a blind eye. Shame. She was a lovely woman."

"Was?" Vicky said, casting her nets.

"It was tragic. He found her, dead on the back doorstep. Heart attack. Poor thing. Since then, he was seen less and less in church. Then all of a sudden, he's gone. No one's seen him in weeks."

"Where do you think he has gone?"

"No one has the foggiest," Val said. Although, there was the story on the news about a policeman, who had also vanished roughly about the same time. Strange business if you ask me. Been lots of weird things happening lately. I've lived in Rednal all my life. The last murder was in 1985. A man strangled his wife just up the road from here. Almost thirty years without any trouble. Then all of a sudden, half a dozen murders and disappearances in twelve months or so. Don't you think that's beyond a coincidence?"

Vicky looked at her mother. "It does sound very strange, Mum. What do you think?"

It hit Karen. Like a freight train. She knew why her daughter was really here. She was playing detective with her friend. She smiled inside. "It certainly does, love. Sounds like something from that *X-files* on the TV."

"I read something, not long after we'd moved in about a policeman being murdered in Barnt Green. Really shocked me, as we'd just moved into a new house, just a mile up the road." Vicky said, pushing her advantage.

"Darren Harris," Val said as she pulled an electronic cigarette from her bag. She looked at the women. "You don't mind if I have a puff, do you?" They shook their heads in unison. She took a deep drag, the tip of the cigarette glowing blue in the gloomy surroundings. The glow died away as Val exhaled a cloud of vapour into the air. "He was killed by an old man apparently. His brother-in-law, Jake Stevenson, who grew up down the road, tried to catch him."

"And did he?" Vicky said, her pulse quickening.

"No. He got away. How he did that, no one knows. According to the news, a man of a similar description was wanted for a murder in Cotteridge."

Vicky knew where Cotteridge was. A busy suburb a few miles to the north, that stretched towards the city centre. She never really ventured that way, preferring the rural surroundings of Worcestershire to the south. "How can an old man kill a young policeman, then escape without being caught?" Vicky said.

"According to the news, he was a giant of a man. Seven feet tall. He had a strange surname. Foreign he was. I forget the name now. My memory is not what it once was."

It seems pretty damn good to me, Vicky thought, trying not to laugh. "Do you know Jake Stevenson? The brother-in-law." She tried to keep her voice as neutral as possible.

"Yes. I knew his family too. They moved down to Cornwall last year. Tintagel, I think. Alison, Jake's mother died. Swept out to sea during a storm."

The hairs on Vicky's neck prickled to attention. "Wow. Something's not right. It's like something from a horror movie."

"I know," Val said, puffing away. "I never liked Alison. Proper old busybody. Her husband Doug was nice though. Jake too. Shame. He lost his family a few years before. Hit-and-run. Poor lad. He was a copper, like Darren."

Silence descended over the three women, each lost to their own thoughts as the weather outside deteriorated. Vicky was processing the information, realising that she may have only scratched the surface of something far bigger than she first thought. Her brain was trying to figure out how this was linked to her son. The dreams. The man called Jake, who was lost somewhere far away. It all sounded so far-fetched, yet something tugged at her instinct. Her limbic brain was yelling at her, enticing her to dig further. "Do you think it's all linked?" she said to Val.

"It could be," she said, puffing away once more. "It's funny how it all seems to centre around the Lickey's. The murders and the disappearances all take place up there? Or close by."

Karen, who had been sat listening, suddenly thought of something. "Why did Jake and his family all move down to Cornwall?"

"No one knows. He'd lost his family. Then he loses his brother-in-law. Maybe he needed a change of scenery."

"I suppose so," Karen said, seeing the logic in her friend's words.

"Karen tells me that your young lad had a funny episode recently?" Val said, taking Vicky by surprise.

"Err, yes. He did," Vicky said, looking at her mother.

"Sorry, love. Should I have kept it quiet?"

"It's okay, Mum," Vicky said. She looked at Val. "He's never done anything like this before. One of my neighbours found him, asleep up the Lickey's. Totally out of the blue. I take it you heard about what happened to Rick, Lucy and Brett?"

"Yes, I did. And I'm so sorry for your loss. Such a terrible tragedy."

Vicky's eyes filled with tears, threatening to spill down her cheeks. She composed herself, swallowing back her grief. "Thanks, Val. It's been pretty horrendous. On all of us. I think maybe that's why Jasper did what he did. He's never done anything like that before."

"Kids do funny things sometimes," Val said. "We all deal with grief in different ways. Maybe that's why he went sleep-walking."

"Hmm. Maybe," Vicky replied. Her mind wandered back to Jake. She needed to find him.

"We'd better get back," Karen said as she checked her watch. "Mike's probably filling Jasper full of sugar."

"Yes, I suppose you're right, Mum." Vicky drained her teacup, walking over to the kitchenette. The others followed her over.

"I'll tidy up, ladies. You two get yourselves home. Looks like the weather is not going to get much better today. And I was going to mow the lawn this afternoon."

Two minutes later, Karen and Vicky slammed the doors of the black SUV. They both shook themselves, smiling at each other. "Great weather, if you're a duck," Vicky said.

"So much for spring," Karen replied as the engine was started. "So. Are you going to tell me why you turned up here?"

"Jasper has been dreaming again. This Jake somehow has made it into his dreams?"

"What?"

"I know. Sounds bizarre. I did some digging this morning. Jasper told me that this Jake is lost somewhere. God knows where? I know it's only a dream, Mum. But something is not right here. All the murders. All taking place up the Lickey's. And now my son is dreaming about doorways to who knows where."

"Maybe he needs to see someone. A doctor perhaps?"

"Maybe. I might go with him. Before I start dreaming too."

* * *

Kaiden woke, a noise somewhere in the cave alerting him. The dying embers from his fire, barely illuminating the close confines. He scrambled about on the rocky floor, grabbing at some sticks and bones in his sore hands. A minute later, the fire had regained much of its previous strength. *Hungry. I need to get some food inside me. And quick*, he thought as another noise echoed through the cave. *What was that? I hope it's a stray animal. Maybe I can eat something after all.*

"There are no stray animals here," a voice said from the darkness.

The giant flinched, scrambling to his feet. "Who goes there? Show yourself." His heart was now hammering in his chest as a cold breeze blew in from the ravine outside.

"Why, I am the tenant here. And you have trespassed. A foolish move, traveller," the unseen foe replied. A male voice. Deep and distorted.

"Show yourself to me," Kaiden said as he looked around the cave for a weapon.

Shadows played across the floor to Kaiden's feet. He bunched his fists, ready for a skirmish. A figure emerged from the darkness. Kaiden could make out a cloaked form, shuffling towards him. As he approached, the temperature in the cave dropped considerably, fog erupting from the man's mouth as he breathed.

"Hello, Kaiden of Kloofbai. You are far from home. On a fool's errand."

"How do you know my name?"

"Why, I know lots of things. I know that you are hunting your woman. I know that you are being hunted. But you are a slippery one. You are cunning. Half of the pack following you, met their end when you sent the rocks down on top of them. A spark of ingenuity. I commend you."

"Who are you?"

"You know who I am. You knew my name before you scrambled up the slopes to take refuge in my sanctuary."

Kaiden could now make out blinking yellow eyes inside the hood. The figure was almost within touching distance. A cold settled over him as the unknown adversary approached. It made him shiver. He felt coldness seep into his bones. The figure uncovered his head, the firelight showing his features to Kaiden. "Alain," Kaiden said, his stomach turning to ice.

"You see. It was on the tip of your tongue."

Kaiden had heard accounts about the vampire of the high mountains. Scattered stories from travellers and traders. The tales were not happy ones. He knew at that moment, that survival was slim. "I never meant to trespass," he began. "Someone has taken my woman. She is deep inside the mountains. I must go to her before they harm her."

Alain shook his head. "No rush. Bea is not in danger. You however are. I have not fed for a moon's cycle. Your aroma intoxicates me." He took a step forward. His white face had a bluish tinge to it. Scarred features were partially hidden under wisps of white hair. He matched height with Kaiden, his cloaked shoulders as wide as a doorway.

"Stay back. Let's not do this."

"Why ever not? I am hungry. And you are healthy."

"Please. I have to find Bea. She needs me."

"Why should I spare you? Give me a reason to allow you on your way?"

"I have no reason. Apart from that, I have found someone. Someone I have grown to love. We have made plans to travel to her world. I beg you. Let me continue on my path."

Alain moved past Kaiden, sitting on a large boulder. His yellow eyes shimmering in the firelight. "I will make a pact with you, Kaiden of Kloofbai. Bring the marauders to my sanctuary. I will take them instead."

The big man nodded. "I can do that. Is that all you require?"

Alain shook his head slowly, his hair swishing to and fro, uncovering his features. "That is but a teaser of the work I need from you. I see all Kaiden. I know what is afoot."

"What?" Kaiden said, his heartbeat gradually returning to normal.

"The witch from Tenta sent those men. She is after the Outlander and the demon. They are far from home. Your woman is with them. The man, Jake is from her world. He and the demon are trying to get home."

"So, Bea is safe?"

"For now. The gang following you are out for the man and beast. Lenga, the witch will take their heads. However, she has other plans too. She is after the watcher."

"Watcher?"

"I've seen him. He comes and goes. A young boy, floating on the breeze. He too, from another world. I think he is trying to help them."

"Why?"

"Alas, that even Alain does not know. I do know that the man and demon came here from the world beyond ours. I hear things too. Stories of destroyed kings. Vampire kings."

"Korgan and Reggan."

"So, you are a knowledgeable man. Tell me of their story. Because I know, it is not yet fully told."

"They were feuding brothers, who waged an eternal war. They took the long sleep, their minions gathering food for them. They are both destroyed. Outlanders did for them."

"Yes, they did. Jake is one of them. Of that I am sure."

"So, why is he here?"

"All in good time. We are conversing, which is to my liking. I do not often get the chance for such things." Alain laughed, the noise distorted and dark. "I had heard a whisper on the wind that the brothers were no more. Do you know why they waged their war?"

"Rumours mainly. Folklore," Kaiden said.

"The brothers waged war because Reggan killed his own father. Korgan never forgave him, vowing to exact his revenge. It never came to pass. Now they are gone, but a spirit has stirred. I have felt it, even though it is many worlds away. Their father has woken from his slumbers. And he is searching for something."

"How do you know all this?"

"I know this," he paused. "Because he is my brother."

Sixteen

Worcestershire

"Hello," Vicky called.

"Upstairs," Jasper shouted back. The two women made their way up the staircase, turning right onto the landing. Pictures of happier times adorned the walls. Karen tried to avert her eyes, focusing on Jaspers open bedroom door. The scene that greeted them was one of sheer untidiness. Books and toys were scattered across the carpet, Mike was sat on the floor, stickers covering his face. "Hi, Mum," Jasper said. "My tummy is feeling a bit better." His cheeks flushed as he averted his gaze.

"It looks like you're on the road to recovery, young man." Vicky walked over, stooping to lift her son into her arms. "You carry on playing with Grandad. We'll go downstairs and put the kettle on."

Jasper hugged his mother, her eyes closing in delight. He nuzzled her neck, making her squirm. "Okay, Mummy. We'll be down in a bit."

"Just make sure that Grandad helps you tidy up, mister," Karen added before they headed downstairs. Giggles could be heard behind them as they made their way into the kitchen.

Ten minutes later, Vicky closed her laptop. "What do you think?"

"I've no idea, Vicky. It all sounds so unbelievable. This Jake now lives in Cornwall?"

"Yes."

"So why don't you contact him?"

"And say what? Hi. My son is dreaming about a man called Jake, lost in another world. Is it you? He'd think I was crazy, or he'd block me."

"Block you?"

"It's what people do on Facebook when a nutcase comes calling."

"Fair point. I don't know what else to say, love. What else can you do?"

"I don't know, Mum. Nothing I guess. Yes, it all looks very strange, but Jasper is fine, apart from the weird dreams. Maybe I should just leave it alone. Concentrate on getting ourselves back on track."

"I think that is all you can do, love. You've had a rough few months. This in a way, has been a bit of a distraction. Put it to bed, unless the dreams get worse. If they do, maybe look at getting him in at the doctors."

A knock at the door made both women turn towards the hallway. "Are you expecting a delivery?" Karen said, following Vicky towards the front door.

"Not that I'm aware of, Mum." She opened the front door to be greeted by two police officers. Two female police officers. "Hello," She said politely.

"Hello again. Mrs Evans, right?" the one officer said. "How is Jasper?"

"Err, he's fine," Vicky said, her stomach beginning to churn. "Do you need to see him?"

"No," the younger officer said. "We've had a missing person reported. Ben Waller. Do you know him, or have you seen him?"

"Ben. The Postman? Yes. I saw him yesterday."

"Did he seem alright? He never reported back to the sorting office and he's not been home. His wife contacted us late last night. A missing person report has been triggered as he's been missing for twenty-four hours now. We're knocking on doors, trying to find out if anyone has seen Mr Waller."

"He seemed fine. Really fine. We had a quick chat nothing important though. Then he carried on with his round."

Karen moved into the doorway, standing next to Vicky. "That's a few people who have gone missing recently. Strange isn't it?"

The officers, not wanting to be drawn into a conversation, looked at each other. "We're hoping that Mr Waller will turn up safe and well. If you hear anything or see anything, please contact us." The younger officer handed over a small card, which Vicky folded into her hand.

"Of course. I really hope he turns up. He's a sweet old man."

"We do too. Thank you, Mrs Evans," the older officer said. Vicky noticed the same dark smudges under her eyes that were there when they had visited her before. They moved away from the house, heading down the quiet cul-de-sac.

Vicky closed her door, following her mother towards the kitchen. "How strange. I hope he turns up okay."

Karen flicked the kettle on, looking out of the window into the leafy garden. "Maybe all this is not just a coincidence?"

"Really? You think this is linked to what we've been talking about?"

"I really don't know, Vicky. It's just odd. I try to rationalise it in my head. But somehow, I just can't."

"Why are so many people going missing?"

"God knows, love. It looks like it all started with this Jake. From what we know, all this started happening when the prostitute and the taxi driver died. Jake was involved soon after that. His friend died, he moved away. Other people have gone missing, including Father Stephen and a policeman. And now, a postman has vanished."

"Shall we tell Dad?"

Karen shook her head. "Best not to. Let's just keep this to ourselves for now. Keep an eye on Jasper and hope that the postman turns up."

"Okay. I guess that's all we can do. Now, how about that coffee?"

* * *

Tenta

Lenga lay there, her eyes flickering. On the floor next to her crib, another youth lay. Naked and headless, his blue skin covered in puncture marks. The floor writhed with reptiles, coiling around lifeless limbs. A larger snake pushed its head into the ragged stump where the head once sat. It slowly disappeared into the corpse, until its tail vanished from sight. Words started spilling from the witch's mouth, her eyeballs moving under weathered lids. "I feel younger. I am younger. My bones are not so brittle my beauties." She sat up, looking across the room at the young girl in the chair. Brianna stared back at her. Lifeless eyes, frozen in time peered past the witch. She was naked, her distended stomach roiling and moving. Lenga could see that something was trying to come out. The skin was stretching, unseen forces within trying to find their way out. The witch shuffled over, her bony fingers caressing the white skin. "There-there my pretty. Are you ready?" The witch's voice seemed to stir the movements, making them almost feverish. The skin stretched and distended to almost breaking point as Lenga watched on. In one quick movement, she slit the skin with a jagged fingernail. Blood and entrails splattered on the cabin floor, drawing a howl from the witch. She reached inside, pulling the creature from the cavity. Carrying it over to her crib, she cooed and made soothing noises to the blood covered mass. Reptilian eyes looked at her, a black tongue flicking between drawn lips. She ran her fingers over the scaly body, taking each limb in turn in her hands. "Such a lovely thing. Such a waste really. Oh well. Lenga needs her food," she said as she bit the new-born below the ear. Shrill cries rang out in the confines of the wooden shack as Lenga worried the baby's neck with her sharp teeth. Eventually, the cries subsided as the life-force was consumed by the witch. The discarded body hit the planked flooring as Lenga lay back. "I'm ready," she said as her skin began to fade. Her clothes became empty rags as she floated above her diminishing vessel. She passed through the timber structure, out into the dark night. The wind had picked up, propelling her towards another cabin. She headed upwards, looking down on the settlement of Tenta. *Right then, little boy. Let's see where you're hiding. I will find you. I have plans for you.*

* * *

Kaiden slid down the slope, his fingers screaming in pain as they clipped loose shale. His progress was halted by a large rock heading towards him. Strong thighs cushioned the blow as he came to an abrupt stop. He sat there, keen ears listening for signs of life. *They should be off to the left somewhere*, he thought as his eyes tried to pick out any shapes in the inky blackness of night. He picked up a small stone, hefting it into the darkness.

"Someone's out there," a voice called out. Scrambling footsteps could be heard, heading his way.

"What do you want with me?" Kaiden yelled, his voice edgy and stiff.

"Have at him, men. He's over by that rock."

He turned, digging his feet into the shale, his four limbs helping him escape the oncoming assault. "Leave me be," he called out. "You do not want to do this."

"After him, men. The one who catches him get first go at his backside." That was all the motivation Kaiden needed. His long legs powered up the scree towards the summit. Glancing back, he could almost make out the faces of two attackers. They looked menacing in the darkness. Big men, matching his size.

"Cranja. I've almost got him," A voice called as he cleared the summit, floundering on uneven ground. A figure hit Kaiden from behind, driving what little air from his lungs he still had. They rolled over, limbs entwined as others cleared the summit. Instinctively, Kaiden lashed out, striking the unknown foe across the bridge of his crooked nose. He felt the attacker's blood land on his face, spurring him to strike again. He did so, knocking the attacker into the night.

"Valkan," a voice said. Are you hurt?"

"He's busted my nose. Get him!" Renewed shouting carried to Kaiden's ears as he entered the gorge in front of him. He let them gain on him, ducking into a rocky recess that only he knew was there.

"In there, men. He's trapped."

As he entered the cave, Kaiden ducked into a gash in the rock, concealing him in the gloom. Figures rushed past him. He counted six of them as they headed into the main chamber. Squeezing back out, he listened as the footsteps came to a skidding halt.

"Welcome," a distorted voice said.

"Who are-" the voice was cut off abruptly before the screams and hollers started ringing out.

"It's a trap, men! Fall back."

Kaiden needed no further encouragement as he headed back out into the gorge. Cries of anguish and pain followed him into the night as he made his way towards the high mountains. Towards his woman and the two strangers. Strangers who were wanted, not only by a witch. But also, by a vampire.

Seventeen

Jake woke up, his head feeling foggy. "What happened?"

"You took a tumble," Bea said.

He tried to sit up, quickly realising that something was not right. "My head's pounding."

"You hit your head when you fell," Tamatan said from the corner of the dimly lit room. His red eyes, barely glowing.

"I don't feel well. I'm burning up."

Bea placed another damp rag on his head, pressing it down until rivulets of water ran down his face. "You've been out for several hours, Jake. We were walking back inside when you just went over. Do you remember?"

"No. I remember the boy. I remember him floating away. Then nothing."

"We've had to strip you off. You have quite a fever. The innkeeper is getting more water for you."

On cue, Matts and Jenni walked in through a wooden door. The innkeeper held a large bucket in his meaty paw. He placed it next to the bed, his face etched with concern. "We're asking around to see if there is a Shaman that can help."

"A Shaman," Jake said. "What for?"

"That," Matts replied, pointing at Jake's lower half.

With considerable effort, Jake propped himself on one elbow. The room seemed to swim for a moment before steadying. He looked at his thigh, the colour draining from his face. "Jesus!" The skin on his left leg had turned the colour of ash. Dark veins spreading from the puckered bite mark. Creeping slowly across his thigh.

"We need to get that sorted," Bea said, taking the rag from the mattress. She plunged it into the water, wringing it out and placing it over the wound.

Jake winced, his head swimming once more. He lay back, closing his eyes tightly. "What is happening?"

"It is taking hold of you, my friend," the demon exclaimed from his wooden seat. "When you were bitten, you thought you could control it. Maybe in your world, you could. But here, you cannot. We need to find someone who can control it for you."

"We've sent people out to the next settlement. I know there is someone who can help. We just need to find her."

"Who?" Jake said.

"A witch. She lives further up in the mountains."

"A witch? Aren't witches bad?"

"Not this one. She has helped us in the past. I know she will again. We just have to hope that she can be found. She travels here and there," Matts said.

"Drink this," Bea said, gently lifting Jake's head. The cool water ran over his lips and face, drenching the mattress underneath him.

"Your friends told us that you were bitten," Jenni said. She had moved to the far wall next to Tamatan. Her dark hair almost hiding her features. "Tell us exactly what happened to you? It may help us if we find her."

Jake focused, trying to drive the escalating fever from his thoughts. "I was bitten by a vampire, called Reggan. He was the brother of another vampire, called Korgan. I live in another world. Far from yours. Bea is from the same world. A few years ago, people where I live started vanishing. I accidently stumbled across it. It led me to the world beyond this one. I met people there who were in danger. They were being terrorised by a group of vampires. I helped. We killed almost all of them. I also met a woman called Katherine there. We got together and had a baby. They were snatched not long ago. I came back to find them and ended up here, with Tamatan."

"Sounds like you've been through much, my friend," Matts said sombrely. "I only hope you get to find your kin and make it back home."

* * *

Vicky's eyes flickered open. A noise in the cottage had woken her from a troubled sleep. "Jasper. Is that you?" Her brain was foggy, trying to focus. She climbed out of bed, casting the duvet aside. A noise from somewhere in the cottage made her start. Opening her bedroom door, she padded out onto the landing. The bathroom light was on. She heard coughs and moans coming from behind the door. "Jaspy?"

"In the bathroom, Mummy. I've been sick."

She opened the door, an acrid smell reaching her nose. "Oh no, Son," she said, kneeling beside him.

Jasper knelt over the toilet bowl, his face pale and clammy. He retched again, bringing up more vomit. Vicky steeled herself. She could deal with blood and had no trouble changing dirty nappies. Vomit was another level though. None of her children had been sickly. On the occasions where it had happened, her husband had taken over. Now she was alone, knowing that she had to deal with the situation the best she could. Vicky swallowed down the rising bile in her throat as her son started retching. She rubbed his back as he started to cry, his rear end rising into the air as his body tensed. After a minute, Jasper collapsed against the bath, his face a mess of vomit and tears. Vicky flushed the toilet, before picking her son up off the cool tiles. She walked with him in her arms, placing him gently into her bed. "Stay here, Son. I'll go and get a bucket from downstairs. Will you be okay?"

"I think so, Mummy," he said bravely. "I think it is all out. I hope."

She rubbed his damp curls. "Okay, love. Hang on." A minute later, they lay together in her bed, the lamp on the bedside table gently illuminating the room. "Maybe your sore tummy was a sign."

"I think so, Mummy. I was feeling better though. Can I stay off school tomorrow?"

"Yes, Son. I will keep you at home for the rest of the week. We don't want your friends catching your bug."

"Okay. Thanks, Mummy. I was dreaming again. A nasty dream. A witch was chasing me through the forest. She almost got me too, Mummy. I must have fallen out of bed. Then I was sick."

"Were you sick in your bedroom?" Vicky asked, dreading the answer.

"No, Mummy. I managed to get to the toilet."

"Okay. Well done." She thought for a moment, trying to make sense of what was happening. "It was only a dream you know."

"I know. I was going to try and find Jake again. When I got to the doorway, a witch was there. She said her name was Lenga. And that she wanted me to be her friend. I don't like talking to strangers, Mummy. They tell us that in school."

"I know they do. You did the right thing," Vicky said, realising that her words sounded stupid. *Running away from a witch is not what they teach you in school though!*

"She was horrid, Mummy. Her eyes were white, and her skin was grey. But I managed to get away. I came straight home."

"You did well. Maybe it's best that you don't go on anymore adventures, Jaspy. I don't want anything to happen to you."

"Okay. But Jake is still out there, Mummy. He needs my help."

"I'm sure Jake has other friends who can help him, Son."

"I know, Mummy. But I know the way home. No one else does. If I don't help him, he'll never get back."

"Don't worry about it tonight, love. You just get some rest. Okay?"

"Okay, Mummy."

Vicky leaned over, kissing her son on the cheek. She flicked off the lamp, the room suddenly darker. The light from the landing, provided the boy with some visibility. "If you need to be sick, use the bucket. Can you see it okay?"

"Yes, Mummy," Jasper said, suddenly sleepy.

Vicky lay there, a sense of disquiet running through her mind. *I think we need to see someone,* she thought, trying to empty her mind of witches and doorways.

Outside in the garden, Lenga walked through damp grass. Her skirts becoming sodden, her feet cold and wet. She looked up at the cottage, smiling. "You made it home to Momma. Maybe she will let you suckle on her titties tonight. But no matter. I have time. We shall meet again, Jasper, very soon. Then you can come home with me and suckle on mine." She moved into the bushes at the side of the garden, suddenly feeling like she was being watched. *Who goes there?* She thought.

"Leave him! I have plans for the boy."

Lenga spun around, coming face to face with an old woman. She was roughly the same height as the witch. Her eyes glowing yellow in the darkness. Her teeth grey and pointed. "Who are you?" the witch asked gruffly.

"I am Virdelas. And I know who you are, Lenga of Tenta. You are far from home. On a fool's errand. Go back to your snake pit. The boy is mine."

"Pah! He's no more yours than the old hag that you are hiding behind. I know of you. I know that your sons are no more. Leave this place. Go find a rock to crawl beneath."

A fist shot out, catching Lenga in the face. She staggered backwards, trying not to cry out in pain. "Is that the best you have to offer, old man?"

"That is the best this human can do. But I can do much more than that." Maureen shot forwards, hands ready to attack. They met thin air as Lenga vanished into the night. Yellow eyes looked around the darkness, trying to pick out the shape of the witch that was there a moment before. "Where are you?" the distorted voice said.

"Up here," Lenga called. Her physical form has dissipated, leaving nothing but a blurred outline that hung in a nearby tree.

"Stay away. Next time, I will leave this vessel and end you. Your powers mean nothing here, crone."

"You think so? old man," Lenga spat as she extended a bony finger towards Maureen.

The old lady crumpled to the ground, a ragged gasp escaping her lips. She struggled to a sitting position, her eyes scanning the trees. "I will be waiting next time witch. Next time. I will finish you. The boy is mine."

Lenga drifted through the forest, her mind a maelstrom of thoughts. *This has changed my plans. I want that boy. I need that boy. But he will make it tricky. But Lenga can be tricky too. I have lots of things up my sleeve, vampire. The next time I see you, we will be evenly matched.* She found a hollowed-out tree in the middle of a densely packed wood, settling down. To wait. For the coming night.

* * *

"He's still asleep, Mum," Vicky said, a cup of steaming coffee in one hand, her mobile in the other. She listened for a moment to her mother's reply. "Would you? That would be great. Sandra called earlier. She's asked me if I can pop in and see her. I think she has some projects to throw my way." Vicky listened to her mother's enthusiastic response, a half-smile tugging at her lips. "Thanks, Mum. I won't be out too long. I'll drop you back home afterwards. Do you need anything from the Co-op?" She took a sip of her coffee as her mother talked. "Okay. Great. See you in a little while. Love you." She swiped the screen to end the call, walking over to the kitchen window. The day was as dark as the last one, the oncoming summer showing no signs of making an early entrance. A knock at the door made Vicky start. She turned around, placing her coffee mug on the counter before heading towards the front of the cottage. She was greeted by a Postman. Another man. Asian. Roughly the same age as her. "Hello," Vicky said.

"Hi. I have a parcel for you."

"Oh. Thank you," she said as she took the brown jiffy bag. "Any news on Ben?"

"Who?"

"Ben. My regular postman. He's not been seen for a few days."

"No idea. They just asked me to fill in for a few days. My usual round is Stirchley."

"Oh. Okay. Never mind. Thanks anyway."

The postman crossed the driveway, heading for two large detached houses further down. Vicky looked at the cottage next door. *I wonder if Maureen is okay?* she thought. Latching the front door, Vicky walked over briskly as an oncoming wind buffeted her clothes. *Curtains are still pulled,* she thought. A sense of growing unease spreading through her body. Two hard knocks on the door were greeted with no activity from inside. Vicky bent down, opening the letterbox. "Mrs Kirkby? Maureen? Are you okay?" She was about to speak again, the words dying in her throat. Through the letterbox she spied an object in the hallway. It was almost out of sight, halfway into the lounge. It was a bag. A red postbag.

* * *

Kloofbai

The swampland eventually relented, giving the group an unrestricted march towards their destination. Wilf walked next to the solitary cart, its rear laden with provisions and weapons. "How much further?" he asked as the sun fell behind a bank of low cloud.

"Not much further, Wilf," they replied. "Can you see the gorge to the west?"

He looked to his left, spying the hunk of rock in the distance. "Yes. I can just about make it out."

"The lower the mountains, the closer we get. By the time the sun disappears, we'll be there. Shall we rest a while and take on some food?"

"Sounds like a good plan," Katherine said from the rear of the cart. She was lay on a pile of hessian sacks, her hands laced behind her dark locks. She'd been staring up at the sky since breakfast, her mind a maelstrom of turbulent thoughts. A flock of birds flew over them, heading north for the sea. She sat up in the cart, watching them until they disappeared on the horizon.

The cart came to a halt, the Finglers hopping down in the long grass. "We will make a fire. Wilf, can you carve some steaks for the spit. It won't take long to cook them."

"Aye. Shame we lost the other cart in the swamps. The mules too."

The Fingler's looked down at the grass. "Such a shame. Poor beasts. Breaking their legs like that gave us no choice."

Wilf nodded sombrely, remembering how easily Zeebu and Zeeba had snapped the mule's necks once they knew they were beyond hope. He'd have carved them up for the trip, rationalising that meat was useful. However, the diminutive folk in front of him only ate what came from the sea. "I'm going to take care of a few things first. Katherine, can you carve?"

"Yes," she said, opening a sack on the back of the cart. Pulling a knife from her boot, she quickly cut eight chunks of rubbery meat from the carcass of the dead Orga. She had to clutch it to her body, cursing to herself as her dress was smeared with oily remnants.

A few minutes later, Wilf returned to the side of the cart, tying his trousers up with his gnarled hands. The Finglers had erected a make-shift spit, eight steaks cooking just above the gathering flames. "Smells wonderful. I could eat a horse." His face dropped as the elders looked at him with disapproving eyes. They ate in silence, each of them contemplating the road ahead as the sun tracked its way across the sky, hidden behind low-slung clouds. As the last of the steaks were consumed, Zeebu packed away the spit and tools.

"Let us be on our way," the Finglers said. "We should make the sea before sundown. We know someone who will look after the beasts and cart while we're away."

"Who?" Wilf said, his curiosity piqued.

"An old friend of the Finglers. Carrie is her name. She has a farm next to the sea. Many travellers stay there."

"Can she be trusted?" the old man replied.

"Oh yes. Of course. She has known our kind for many moons. She will always help us. It is only a short walk from the farm. She will take us to the doorway herself."

"Then let us be on our way," Katherine said. "We have loved ones to find."

Eighteen

Vicky walked back into her kitchen, her head a turbulent collection of thoughts. *That's Ben's bag. What the hell is it doing there?* she thought as she pondered calling her mother. *She'll be here in a bit. No point calling her now.* She sat down at the kitchen table, swiping her phone's screen. Logging into Facebook once more, she quickly found Jake Stevenson. His profile was the same. No recent posts to report. However, Vicky knew that as they were not connected, she would only see limited information. She looked at his profile picture, studying his face. *Where are you Jake? How is all this possible?* The time at the top right of her screen told her that it was getting on for 11am. Her mind was working overtime, wondering whether to go with her gut instinct. She nodded to herself, pushing away from the table. Padding upstairs as quiet as she could, she headed for her son's bedroom. The bedroom was in darkness, the faint rise and fall of Jasper's chest enough to tell Vicky that she had time to check on her gut instinct. Sixty seconds later she was ducking between the fence poles at the rear of her neighbour's garden. The wind was picking up once more, buffeting and propelling her towards the rear of the building. A kitchen window and a patio door, which led to a small dining room greeted her as the first patter of raindrops fell from the sky. She looked into the kitchen, a dim interior staring back at her. No clues as to her neighbour's whereabouts could be gleaned from her vantage point. Hurrying over to the patio door, her heart increased in rhythm as she managed to slide it open silently. Vicky stepped inside, gently closing the door behind her. The wail of the strengthening wind was abruptly cut off as the door slid into place, the sound replaced by the ticking of the wall clock. It was then that Vicky was hit by a smell. A thick cloying stench of decay. Instinct made her pull her t-shirt over her nose, trying in vain to block out the dank aroma. "Mrs Kirkby?" She whispered, fearing the worst. No reply. Navigating the dark dining room, she headed into the hallway. Stairs on her right led to the upstairs of the property. The smell was more pungent here, almost making Vicky gag as she headed for the lounge. Faint light filtered in through the front door, the noise of the oncoming rain, hitting the glass panels. The red postbag was lay on the carpeted floor, leaning against the door jamb. Pushing open the lounge door quietly, Vicky poked her head into the compact room. A television was stood on a dark wooden unit to her right, thick curtains behind it pulled tightly shut. A fireplace in front of her led towards the back wall, where a large bookcase stood silently. Her eyes travelled to the floor, a rising scream locked in her throat when Vicky realised what she was looking at. "Ben," she said as she knelt next to her postman. He was lay face down, unmoving. Reaching over, she heaved him over onto his back. The body flopped lifelessly, empty eyes staring blankly towards the darkened ceiling. "Oh my God!" Vicky said, the noise loud in the confines of the lounge. Her hands came up to her face, trying to ward off the image in front of her. Tattered, ragged flesh underneath Ben's jawline was covered in blackened blood. The wound ran from one ear to the other. Tears fell freely from Vicky's eyes as she tried in vain to take in the scene in front of her. Her friendly postman lay beneath her. Or what was left of him. *Got to call the police*, Vicky thought before a noise above her made her start. She shot to her feet, banging into the bookcase next to her. Another noise filtered through the ceiling. A low sound, like dragging feet. She could almost see the sound as it moved across the ceiling above her. She moved forward, almost on autopilot as her feet carefully skirted the body. The noise came again, stopping Vicky in her tracks. "Maureen?" she called as she mounted the staircase. No reply. Twenty seconds later, Vicky stood at the door of the main bedroom. Three other doors on the landing hung in various states of openness. Only one was closed. The bottom of the door brushed against thick carpet as Vicky pushed against it. The stench came again, almost making her cry out. Clouds of breath formed in front of her face as her breathing increased, her heart hammering in her chest. "Maureen?"

"Come in, dear," a cracked distorted voice answered.

Vicky froze, a trickle of urine escaping her, wetting her denim-clad thigh. The dropping temperature seemed to envelope her, goosebumps erupting over her body. She gathered herself, tentatively edging into the bedroom. The pumps on her feet seeming to drag heavily across the carpet. The bed sat in the centre of the room, its metal headboard against the wall. A dressing table and a built-in wardrobe were situated on the other side. The layout was similar to Vicky's own bedroom. She wished that she was there now, tucked under a thick duvet. Safe and warm. She looked around the open door towards the window. More thick curtains hung, tightly closed to block out the light from the rear garden. Next to the window sat a small upholstered chair. Maureen sat in the chair, smiling at Vicky. "Oh my God! Maureen. What has happened to you?"

"Maureen is in here with me," the voice answered.

"What?" Vicky blurted. "W-what does that mean? She stammered, her voice faltering.

"She has plans for the boy. Your Son."

"Jasper?"

"Yes. She has travelled far. She wants him. I want him too."

"Who has travelled far?" Vicky said, the world seeming to tilt around her. She placed her hand on the bottom of the bed, cool metal the only thing in the room that felt real to her.

"Lenga. The Witch. She is here for Jasper. She has plans for him."

"Plans?"

"Yes, dear," Maureen replied, spittle oozing down her blood-caked chin. "Your boy knows where they are. He's watching over them, guiding them home." Ornaments on the dresser next to the window started to vibrate. Vicky looked over at them, an icy feeling seeping through her body as she noticed paintings on the wall starting to shake.

"He knows where who are?"

"The man and demon."

"Jake?"

"Is that his name? Yes. Jake. He killed my son, Korgan. Of that I am sure. He may have killed my other son too. Although, if he has, I bear him no ill will. But for Korgan, I want this Jake. He will pay."

Vicky started to shiver, the temperature in the room seemed barely above freezing point. Her breath was visible as she exhaled. "Did you kill Ben?"

"Ben?"

"The man downstairs."

"I was hungry. I'd not fed in a long time." Maureen rose out of her chair, seeming to float in the darkness. "Maybe I can feed again."

Vicky took a step towards the door, her stomach turning to stone. "What do you mean?"

"Come here, girl. I promise to make it quick. Come and bathe in the red waters."

Their eyes locked, Vicky suddenly relaxing. She let go of the bed, her arms hanging limply at her sides as the older woman approached. "Need to get back to Jasper," she said, her voice monotone.

"Jasper will join you very soon. Have no fear on that. I promise to take care of him. She will not have him." Maureen came within arm's length of the younger woman, baring her teeth. They were grey, pointed and sharp, slithers of flesh stuck between them.

Vicky took another step back, her feet sliding over the carpet. "Jasper," she breathed as her foot caught the leg of the double bed. She lost her footing, falling sideways towards the floor. As she looked up, Maureen made her move, flinging herself at her prey. On instinct, Vicky brought her arm up, an elbow catching Maureen in the throat. She screamed as Maureen started to bear down on top of her, teeth snapping together. "GET THE FUCK OFF ME!" she hollered, trying to push the pensioner away. In the back of her mind she heard a car pull up outside, a door banging shut before the vehicle drove off. "MUM. MUM HELP," she screamed as the weight on her arm became almost unbearable. The ornaments that were vibrating toppled from the dresser, thudding into the carpet. Paintings clattered to the floor, a sound of splintering glass carrying to Vicky's ears as she tried in vain to escape.

"Hold still, girl," Maureen spat. "You cannot escape. Just give yourself to me."

"MUM HELP!" she screamed again. Vicky knew that she was trapped. She felt that her strength was ebbing away, leaving her body forever. She thought of Jasper, lying only a few feet away. She could not die like this. Her son had already lost so much. She had to escape. As a teenager, Vicky had taken Aikido classes. Months of torment from the class bully had made her take up self-defence. She carried on with classes for a few years, enjoying the discipline and focus it gave her. The bullying had stopped when Vicky had propelled the girl across a packed classroom. The release had allowed her to continue with her exams, setting her on the path to college, university, and a flourishing career. Now as she lay on the carpet, her throat close to being torn out, something stirred in her memory. She shifted slightly on the floor, her arm dropping a few inches.

"That's it. Let Virdelas feed," the older woman cooed, sensing the battle was won.

Vicky raised her right leg underneath Maureen, pushing the arm lodged in her throat to the right. The older woman's momentum went with it as Vicky twisted her body. She fell to her left, striking her head on the side of the bed frame. Free of the hold, Vicky scrambled for the door, making it out onto the landing on all fours. Her feet found purchase in the carpet as she rounded the top of the stairs. Climbing to her feet, she had a split second to gather herself as Maureen careered towards her. Instinct took over again as Vicky allowed her adversary's momentum to be used against her. She feinted left as the older woman was about to plough into her. Maureen's face stuck the wall, a sickening crunch reaching Vicky's ears. The old woman staggered backwards, her heels snagging together. Then, she was tumbling down the stairs, landing in a heap on the hallway carpet. The bedroom door slammed shut, more pictures on the landing hitting the carpeted floor. Vicky slid down the wall, her hands coming up to her face. She sobbed uncontrollably, her body shaking. She suddenly remembered Jasper. *The witch has plans for him*, clearly echoing in her head. Staggering down the stairs, she kept her eye on her neighbour. Maureen was still, her neck twisted at an unnatural angle. Vicky had to get out of the house. She had to escape the pit of death that she now found herself in. She moved past Maureen on wobbly legs, almost ripping open the front door of the house.

"Vicky!" a female voice called out.

"Mum! Call the police."

The women collided together, arms wrapping around each other. "What's happened, love?"

"It's Maureen. She tried to fucking kill me! She killed Ben too. Call the police, Mum."

Another scream rang out, causing the women to flinch. They were still hanging on to each other, their embrace tightening. The noise was close by. It sounded in pain and scared.

Vicky looked at her mother, her flushed face draining. "Jasper!"

* * *

Kloofbai

Carrie addressed the group. She stood there, hands planted on her hips. Her shoulder length dark hair constantly ruffled by the northerly breeze. "I hope

116

you are all rested. It's only a short walk to the doorway. We will be there by the time the sun reaches the western sky."

They nodded in unison. "When will the doorway open?" Wilf asked.

"I've never been there when it does. I have been told that it opens when one day passes into the next."

"Midnight," Katherine replied, clearly eager to be moving.

"Yes. Midnight," Carrie replied, saying the word for the first time. "Let us be on our way."

"We will await your return," Zeeba and Zeebu said, standing shoulder to shoulder. "We hope you bring Jake back with you."

"Thank you, my friends. Make sure we have provisions for the return journey."

"Aye aye," they chirped as the first patter of rain fell from the sky.

Sometime later, the three headed down a steep pathway on the edge of sheer sea cliffs. "Mind your footing here. If you slip, you'll be fish food before the day is out," Carrie said.

"Hold on to the creepers, Kath," Wilf urged as spray from the roiling sea below covered them from head to foot.

"Good idea," Katherine said, shivering from dousing that had covered her. She felt it seep into her clothing, her skin breaking out in goosebumps.

After a few hundred yards, an opening in the cliff face presented itself as they rounded a corner. "Here we are," said Carrie, quickly hurrying into the dark void. "Let us make a fire."

A short time later, the threesome sat on the rough stone floor of the cave. The light from the flames bathed the cave in a shimmering glow. Katherine looked on in awe at the paintings that adorned the walls. Drawings of men with a variety of weapons, chased what looked like large beasts across the stone frieze. "Wow," was all she could think of saying.

"Impressive, aren't they?" Carrie responded. "The drawings have been here from the beginning of days. Before the trees stood and when the mountains were mere hills. Many a hunter and traveller have ventured here."

"Let us hope no one is waiting on the other side of the doorway when it opens. We must be ready," Wilf said as he reached for his axe.

"We should have no trouble from that quarter. I know many of the folk who travel this path. They will know my face sure enough. Unless we encounter monsters of course. Then I agree, we will need to be ready."

"Have you always lived here, Carrie?" Katherine asked, suddenly inquisitive.

"Most of my life yes. I grew up to the south, where the two great forest thin out into the grasslands. My parents had a small holding. We raised bison and elk, along with farming the land. Not that it yielded many crops. This land is not one for farming. A few tats and corn were our main harvest. Along with the meat of course. They were taken one night, by unknown giants from the west. I managed to hide out in the cellar when they attacked. They hung my Pa from a tree whilst they took turns in defiling my Ma. I found them the next morning. Ma lay dead in the grass, her head smashed like an earthenware jug. They took Pa's head. I never did find it."

"I give you my sorrow," Wilf said as he puffed sombrely on his wooden pipe.

"How awful," Katherine added, the words escaping her.

"It was a long time ago. Many seasons and moons have passed since then. I burned the farm to the ground before heading north. I knew my uncle lived in the settlement where I now live. He took me in, letting me work on his farm. When he passed a few seasons ago, I took over."

"Sounds like you have lost much, Carrie," Wilf said.

"Aye. But I don't dwell on such things. I have a good life out here. I have folk who now work for me. And travellers come and go, leaving me with their trinkets and wares. How about you? What is your tale? I only know what you told me when you arrived. What has brought you to my door?" Carrie opened a flask of ale, taking a swig before passing it to Wilf. He and Katherine had taken it in turn to unfold the story of their lives to the woman from the north. "Sounds like you have endured much. We are words on the same page, Katherine. We have lost so much. You too, Wilf. How you have lived through to this point is a blessing."

"I'd not call it a blessing," Wilf said, smiling at the woman. "But thank you. Our lives have been ruled for so long by the monsters that held sway over the lands. Even now that they are gone, their hardships are with us."

"Well. Let's cling to the hope that we find Jake. Let's find him and bring him home to his kin. He has a daughter that needs to be cared for and a woman that needs to be loved. I cannot think of a more noble cause."

"I'll drink to that," said Wilf as he placed the bottle to his lips, taking another long pull on the ale.

"I'll drink to it too," said Katherine. "As soon as my Uncle is finished."

* * *

"Wake up, Son," Vicky said as her nudges became more forceful. "Jasper. Wake up!" Her voice raising an octave as a growing desperation took hold.

"Come on, Jasper, you're scaring us," Karen said as she leaned over the bed. The boy lay there, his dark curls matted and slick to his head. His breathing was slowing, as was his heartbeat. When they had entered the room, Jasper was crying in his sleep. His piggy bank, hand-held console, along with other items were strewn across the room. The window was open an inch, rattling against its catch.

Karen walked over, closing it to. "What shall we do?"

"Call an ambulance, Mum."

Karen looked questioningly at her daughter, seeing the anguish in her eyes. "Okay, love."

"Call the police too. There are two dead people next door. They need to know."

"Okay," Karen said, almost on autopilot as she headed out of the room.

Vicky lifted her son into her arms, rocking him gently. Tears fell from her eyes, darkening his pyjamas. "Please wake up, Son. You're frightening Mummy." Her thoughts went to the two bodies that lay next door. *What the hell is going on here?*

Mike jumped out of his car, watching as the ambulance slowly pulled away from the house next to his daughter's. Another ambulance was parked directly outside his daughter's house, the blue lights fighting against the darkening skies. A police car was parked further down the driveway. He raced up the path, shouldering his way through the partially open door. "Vicky!"

"In here, Mike," his wife's voice called from the kitchen. He headed down the hallway, almost barging into the room at the rear of the cottage. Vicky was sat at the kitchen table, a tartan blanket draped over her shoulders. Her shaking hands were wrapped around a mug of coffee. Karen stood next to the sink, her face grey and drawn. Two male police officers were stood on the other side of the kitchen, one writing notes on a small pad.

"What the hell has happened?" he said, his already high blood pressure building to another level.

"Jasper won't wake up," his wife replied. They're taking him to hospital."

"What do you mean, he won't wake up?"

"We're not sure, love. Vicky has been attacked too. By her neighbour. Mrs Kirkby killed the postman, then she tried to kill Vicky."

"Fucking hell!"

"We cannot comment yet as to how the victim died, Mrs Tucker," the taller of the two officers said quickly.

"He was found in her lounge with his throat ripped out. Maureen then tried to do the same to my daughter. It doesn't take a detective to work it out."

Mike rounded the table, taking his wife in his arms. Her resolved crumbled, wracking sobs shaking her body. "It's okay, love. I'm here." He reached for his daughter, wrapping his other arm around her. She rose shakily to her feet, allowing her father to pull her towards him. Her body trembled as Mike buried his face in her hair. "Oh, Vicky. What the hell is going on here?"

"I don't know, Dad. I really don't know."

The kitchen door opened, a paramedic poking her head into the kitchen. "We're ready to take him now. Mum, are you coming with?"

"Yes," Vicky said. I just need to get my bag."

"I'll come in the ambulance with you, love," Karen said, wiping the tears from her face.

"We'll accompany you to the hospital, Mrs Evans," the taller officer said calmly. "We still have questions for you."

"Okay. I just need to be with my son."

"We understand," was the officer's reply.

"I'll follow in my car," Mike said, as tears spilled from his eyes. He left the kitchen, coming up short as he was met by a stretcher in the hallway. Another paramedic stood there, waiting for his colleague. Mike looked down at the stretcher, his resolve breaking when he saw his grandson lay there, covered in a red blanket. "Jasper," he blurted, rushing to his side. "What has happened to you?" he said, burying his face once more. He inhaled his grandson's scent, closing his red-rimmed eyes tightly.

"We'll take it from here," the female paramedic said. "They'll take good care of him, Mr Tucker. I'm sure he'll be fine." The reassurance sounded hollow and unconvincing as Mike moved to one side to allow the them to take his grandson out to the ambulance. His daughter shuffled past him, heading out into the oncoming rain.

"Come on, Mike. You lock up. We'll see you when we get there." She kissed his cheek, before following her daughter. He stood, rooted to the spot as the two officers followed the others outside. He left the house a minute later, closing and double locking the front door. The cottage was empty and silent, save for the ticking clock in the hallway. At the top of the stairs, tendrils of yellow mist appeared below one of the bedroom doors. They drifted down into the hallway, moving slowly around the house. Waiting for their master to return.

Nineteen

The rain had ceased when Rick and Marlies exited the small terminal at Newquay Airport. The balmy temperatures they had left behind in Hamburg were replaced by an icy breeze, blowing in from the Atlantic Ocean. They walked to a car lot, their luggage trundling behind them. "This is the one," Rick said as they stopped in front of a white saloon. He pressed the key fob, pleased when the lights on the car blinked to attention. A minute later, they were ensconced in a plush interior, the growing wind thankfully shut off.

"Have you got the address?" Marlies said as she struggled out of her tan coat.

"It's on my phone," Rick replied as he selected the cars built-in navigation. "There we go," he said seconds later. "It should only take an hour to get there. Let's hope the English weather is kind to us."

They drove in relative silence, Marlies looking out of the passenger window at the grey ocean. The midday Cornish traffic was light, allowing them an easy passage. They passed by Wadebridge, Padstow, and Port Isaac, before pulling off onto a smaller road that led to the sleepy village of Tintagel. Ten minutes after pulling off the main highway, they were driving into a public car park, opposite a collection of shops. "I'll text her," Marlies said, rummaging around in her handbag.

"Okay," Rick said, checking his own smartphone. He read through a few emails, deleting or replying curtly to banal requests from co-workers.

"She is on her way. There's a tea-room over there," she said pointing through the windscreen. "She will meet us there in five minutes."

"Okay. Let's move before the heavens open."

The bell chimed as the door opened, the small tea-room deserted. They walked to the counter as a tall woman came through an archway behind the counter. "Well good morning, if you can call it that."

Rick smiled thinly. "Hi. Can we order two regular coffee's please?"

"Sure. Anything else?" Her American accent seemed out of place in the Cornish surroundings.

"Could I have one of those pastries please?" Marlies said, pointing at the collection of cakes under the counter. "Rick, do you want a one?"

He bent down, eyes scouring the selection of treats on offer. "Could I have a Belgium bun please?"

"Not a problem," the woman said, placing her pad next to her crossword puzzle on the counter. "Two coffee's, one Belgium bun and one custard slice. Grab yourselves a seat and I'll bring it right over."

"Thank you," Marlies said, smiling at the other woman. She smiled back before heading back through the archway. They found a table, next to a fireplace. The small room's walls were adorned with paintings and small pallets with slogans like, *home is where the heart is*, and *follow your dreams*. "These are nice, Rick. Very rustic looking."

"Yes, they are," Rick said absently as he picked at a piece of loose skin on his thumb. The bell chimed once more as Kerry entered the establishment. She shook the rain from herself, wiping her black framed glasses on her black t-shirt.

They turned towards her, Marlies smiling, Rick nodding. "Hello, Kerry," the Belgian said as she walked over towards the door.

"Hi," Kerry replied, stiffening slightly as Marlies hugged her. The awkward nerd inside her didn't know how to react to the contact. She gave the other woman a brief squeeze before breaking pulling away. "How was your flight?"

"It was largely uneventful. So was the drive here. Your country is very pretty though."

"It can be, when it's not raining," Kerry said as she headed over to the table.

"Here you go," the tall woman said as she headed back through the archway. "Oh, hi," she said as she noticed Kerry. "You were here a few weeks ago, right?"

"Err, yes. I was," Kerry said shyly."

"What can I get you?"

"Could I have a coke please?"

"Sure. There is a cooler next to the counter. Help yourself if you want?"

"Thanks," Kerry said before selecting a bottle of *Pepsi* from the fridge.

They sat in silence as the American woman set down the drinks, coming back a few seconds later with two cakes on small china plates. "Can I get you anything else?" she said, directing her question at Kerry.

"I'm good thanks. This will be enough."

"Alright then. Enjoy," she said before walking back through the archway.

A silence descended over the three of them as they each thought how best to start the conversation. Kerry cracked open her drink, taking tentative sips as Marlies sugared her and Rick's coffees. Sensing an atmosphere, she decided to break the ice. "So, are you all set?"

"Yes. I have told my folks that I am staying at a friend's tonight. I've filled in my friend, having to tell a few white lies to get her on board."

"What did you tell her?" Marlies asked, trying to get a dialogue going.

"I've told her that I've got a date with a guy from Delabole. I've had to promise to give her all the juicy details when I get back. I'll make something up. It'll be fine."

"What's Delabole?" Marlies asked.

"It's a town not far away," Rick chipped in. He looked at Kerry. "Are you sure you're okay with this?"

"Yes. I have brought some stuff with me," she said looking at her pack on the floor."

"What kinds of things?" Rick asked.

"Stakes. Garlic. Crosses. We've all watched vampire movies, right?"

"I guess so," was Rick's absent reply. "Do you really believe that's actually true?"

"Yes. I told you about the incident in my bedroom. Jake, Katherine, Father Stephen and your Dad also believed in it."

"Crazy. I cannot believe this is happening," he said, lifting the mug to his lips.

"Let's keep an open mind, Rick," Marlies added, noticing the American woman eyeing them from her perch. What time shall we head off?"

"Well," Rick said, putting his mug down. "It's almost one now. It will take us a good four hours to get up there. Friday afternoon traffic. Then we need to find the doorway. I know the hills quite well, but they are big. We could be looking for hours."

"I know where the doorway is," Kerry said. "It's very clear in my head. There is a hotel at the foot of a forested hill. I don't know the name of it, as it's always dark. But the doorway is not far from the hotel. Only a few hundred yards or so, at the top of a big hill."

"I know where you mean. We can park at the hotel and walk up. We probably need a torch."

"I have one in my pack."

Rick smiled for what felt like the first time that day. "You've thought of everything, Kerry. We would not be able to do this without your help. Thank you."

"Yes, thank you," Marlies said, placing her manicured hand over Kerry's.

She didn't flinch this time. Instead, she grinned at them both, the smile transforming her face.

They finished their drinks and paid the tea room owner, thanking her. Minutes later, they were pulling out of Tintagel, heading north towards the motorway. Marlies sat in the back with Kerry, letting Rick navigate the way on his own. He was fine with that, a collection of thoughts and plans forming in his mind. He'd set his mind on proposing to Marlies as soon as they were back home. He knew that she was the one for him. Even his departed mother would have approved of the quietly spoken Belgian whom he had fallen in love with. He made a promise to himself to patch things up with his brother too, aiming to put the past few years behind them. Rick knew that Jake had been through so much. However, his blossoming career in Germany had taken him away from all the pain and loss. He'd hardly known his sister-in-law and niece, regretting it deeply. He would get to know his new woman and daughter. He silently nodded to himself as the rain beat against the windscreen in front of him.

Marlies chatted with Kerry on the plush rear leather seat. She told her about her upbringing in the Belgian town of Turnhout. How she'd graduated university, before moving into a role as a Packaging Technologist with a world leading company. She half expected Kerry to doze off, thinking that the shy girl from Cornwall would find the conversation boring. Marlies couldn't have been more wrong. Kerry listened to every word intently, amazed that so much effort and precision could go into a simple carton that held her breakfast cereal, or her perfume. She asked questions of the Belgian, wanting to know about the research and development of how they made smarter designs. It was then that Kerry let the cat out of the bag. Not only was she an avid gamer she also had a love of computer programming. The nerd in her was keen to hear how new designs came to fruition. How new products were sent to customers all over the world for them to test out. How the eight different colours used to finish the packaging, with a hot foil overlay to create prestige, premium effects.

"It all sounds so interesting, Marlies. It sounds like you have a fabulous life."

"It's hard work. Challenging sometimes too. But I would not change it for the world. We have made a nice life for ourselves in Hamburg. We work long hours, but that makes us appreciate the time that we spend together. Isn't that right, babe?"

"Absolutely. When all this is over with, Kerry, you'll have to visit."

"Really!" Kerry said, amazed by the invitation.

"Sure," said Rick, amazed that he'd just invited a relative stranger to stay with them. He felt good inside though. Whether it was the fact that he planned to propose to Marlies, or the fact that he was on a wild adventure, he knew not. And nor did he care. He suddenly felt care-free and younger than he had in recent times.

They hit the M5 north, heading into Bristol as the Friday rush hour finally caught up with them. Progress was painfully slow as they edged forward a car length at a time for what seemed like hours. Eventually, the traffic thinned, Rick pleased that they were moving again. After a break at the services, they finally pulled off the motorway. Ten minutes later, the car was gently bumping and rolling over an uneven car park. They came to a stop opposite a large hedgerow, a bouquet of flowers tied to the thick bushes. Climbing out of the car, they stretched in unison, Kerry walking over to the flowers. She looked at the card attached. "In loving memory of Jay. Gone, but not forgotten. Love Mum."

"Someone must have died here," Rick said as he scanned the car park. It was deserted. Low clouds, pressed against the Lickey Hills, making it seem later than early evening. "It's almost seven. Shall we take a look for the doorway now? If we find roughly where it is, we can grab some dinner, before coming back later."

"Sounds good to me, Rick," Marlies replied eagerly. "I am, how do you say? Famished?"

"Me too," Kerry said, walking back to the car to retrieve her torch.

They headed out of the car park along a gravel path. To the left beyond a wooden fence, lay a golf course. Trees lined the vast expanse of grass, another bouquet tied to one of the trunks. Marlies walked over, opening the card attached to the floral tribute. "Love you Son. Dad."

"Looks like a few people have died here recently," Kerry said. "I'm not sure I like that."

"Hmm," Rick said. "Let's not let our imaginations run riot. It's probably nothing."

Leaving the path, they crossed over another, looking up together at the steep forested slope in front of them. "Follow me," Kerry said, taking the lead. They used small pathways, crisscrossing the hill to reach the summit. At the top, they took stock of their surroundings, getting their collective breaths back. "That way," Kerry said breathlessly. "This looks very familiar. It's amazing that it looks exactly the same as it did in my dreams."

"Okay, lead on," Marlies said, a feeling of uncertainty creeping into her mind.

Like a homing pigeon, Kerry walked straight to a spot in the forest, a few hundred yards from where they'd crested the summit. She stood between two trees, looking at the bracken strewn ground. "I think this is it, guys."

"Are you sure?" Marlies said as she leant on another nearby tree.

"Yes. I am sure. This is where the doorway appears. I would bet my life on it."

"Let's hope you're right. Could you find your way back here later in the dark?" Rick said, a strange feeling washing over him too. Something felt wrong, although the reason eluded him.

"I think so."

"Okay. Let's go and grab a bite to eat. The Hare and Hounds is only a ten-minute walk away. We can come back later."

Marlies took his hand, squeezing it gently. "Let's go then. I need feeding. It could be a long night."

Kerry watched them walk off in the opposite direction to which they had arrived, following them after a few seconds. "You could be right, Marlies," she said under her breath as a wind blew through the forest.

Lenga appeared a few seconds later, watching the threesome walk off into the forest. She shuffled over to the doorway, her gnarled toes drawing a crude line between the two trees. The sun had almost set, the forest around her ever darkening in varying shades of green and brown. *They want to cross over into the other place. Why?* She'd felt the commotion in the far-off cottage earlier in the day. Lenga had watched from afar as giant beasts with flashing lights had appeared, taking the boy away with them. *It looks like the boy is lost to me. For now. But no matter. I have three more to have fun with. They will keep me entertained until the boy returns.* Her form faded away, leaving a mere apparition floating between the two trees. She glided up into the high branches. To wait for her quarry to return.

Twenty

Jake woke, his eyes slowly fluttering open. The room around him spun, the fever felt worse than before. "Tamatan? he croaked.

"I am here, Jake. We have news?"

"News? What news?"

"The witch is here," Bea said, placing another damp rag on Jake's burning skin. She lifted his head, pouring a few drops of water between his cracked lips. "She is in another room, preparing her things."

"What things?" Jake said in a confused tone.

"We do not know," Tamatan replied. "We will though. Soon enough."

Jake closed his eyes, drifting back into unconsciousness as the door opened. A figure appeared, dressed in a white cloak. Moving over to a side table, the figure removed her hood, looking at the sleeping man on the bed. Her hair was dark, eyes piercing grey. "We need to remove his clothing," she said. Placing her cloak on the table, she walked over to Jake, setting a white hand on his chest. "Hello, Jake. My name is Alana. I am here to help you. I only hope I am not too late," she said as she looked at the spreading infection on his thigh. The witch ran her hand over the mottled flesh, speaking unheard words to herself. "You are right. A powerful vampire did this. A king of vampires. It is taking hold, turning him."

"What can you do to help him?" Bea said, her voice edged with concern.

"I need to banish the infection. I have done this only once before."

"Did it work last time?"

"Yes. But alas, the woman passed shortly afterwards. Murdered by her own kin."

Bea looked at the woman stood in front of her. Her pretty face and long lashes didn't fit Bea's idea of what a witch should look like. She was attractive, her skin flawless, pale as virgin snow. A single gemstone hung from her neck on a dark chain. It shimmered in the torchlight, its edges glinting as she moved. "How do you get rid of the infection?"

"I have to end his life."

"What!" Bea said, taken aback.

"It has taken hold of him. There is no turning back for him now. If left, he will become one of them very soon. He needs to be purged before he can be healed."

"Just bring him back," Tamatan said quietly. "He has his own kin. An infant, who needs her father."

"I will do all I can. I give you my word." Alana glided over to the table once more, her long skirts flowing behind her. She picked up an amulet, copper in colour. It was spherical, markings and symbols adorning the reddish steel. A chain was attached to it, also copper in colour. She bent down, blowing into a hole in the top. More words came from her mouth before a puff of violet smoke puffed out of the small aperture. As it rose into the air, the witch blew it across the room towards Jake. "Dak-tak. Chenga-raas." The smoke found its mark, disappearing into Jake's open mouth. A singular shockwave like pulse rocked the room, startling Tamatan and Bea. "Leave us. I need to be alone with him when he passes. I will call on you all when I know."

They filed out of the room, Tamatan taking one last look at his human friend. "Please come back, Jake," He said, his red eyes burning brightly in the dim surroundings. The door closed, the latch dropping into place.

"Let it take you, Jake," she uttered, watching the rise and fall of his chest slow down until it was still. His head lolled to one side as his life ended. Alana nodded to herself, straddling his cooling body. She placed her hands on his lifeless chest and began humming to herself, rocking backwards and forwards. The torches dimmed until they were snuffed out, blue smoke wafting upwards towards the wooden ceiling. It pooled in the centre of the room above her, slowly turning in a circular motion, gaining pace until a funnel appeared above the witch. "Leave him," she commanded. "Leave him now." Furniture around the room started to move, the table shifting on the rough planks underneath. "Be gone, Reggan. Go back to the darkness." She placed her thumbs over Jake's eyes, her pendant touching his chest. She sat motionless, the bare skin of her thigh touching his. Alana could feel the flesh cool. She smiled to herself, starting to rock once more.

She would wait until the infection had left him before she went searching. For his soul.

* * *

Kloofbai

Carrying flaming torches, they moved quietly into the cave's interior. More paintings lined the walls, taking Katherine's eye off the pathway. A few times she lost her footing, helped back to her feet by her uncle. "Be careful, Kath. I'm buggered if I'm carrying you back to the farm if you break something."

"Sorry, Uncle. I wish I had a camera."

"Huh. What's that?"

"Oh. It's something they have in Jake's world. It takes pictures of things. Then you can look at them later. Or print them off to hang on your walls."

"That world has many wonders. Maybe one day I will return there."

"Let's hope so," she said.

"I think this is it," Carrie said, motioning with her torch. "Look."

Wilf and Katherine looked on as the cave came to an abrupt halt. A rectangular shape was carved into the rock, more depictions surrounding it. No animal pictures could be seen though. Different shapes and images were inscribed into the rocks. "Oh my," Katherine said, her mouth hanging open.

"Let us hope that we don't see any of them," Wilf added as he walked over to the doorway. He ran his finger over one of the paintings, a shiver running down his spine. "Vampires," he said quietly.

"We need to be on our guard," Carrie said, taking the pack off her back. Dropping to her knees, she pulled a crude axe from the holdall. She gripped the handle, liking the sturdy feeling it gave off.

Wilf and Katherine did the same, pulling stakes and crosses from their packs. "I guess we just wait," Wilf said as he looked for a place to sit.

"Aye," Carrie replied, following the older man's lead. Moments later, they were all sat a few feet away from the carved doorway, the tension in the cave almost audible. "It shouldn't be too long now."

"Let us hope the doorway has no surprises for us," Wilf said sombrely. "I'm getting too old for all these adventures. Promise me, Kath. If we get him back, that will be it?"

"You have my word, Uncle. I too am growing tired of this. I just want to raise a family and be happy and safe. Elias is gone. As too are Korgan and Reggan. Let us hope that no more monsters have their sights set on us."

"Hmm. Let's hope." They all looked towards the far wall. Waiting for the day to pass.

* * *

Their trip to the pub had been without incident. They'd found a table in the corner of the cosy lounge. Rick had taken care of the drinks, placing an order for three meals. Once the food had been polished off, they'd talked about various things. A few glasses of beer had lowered Rick's usual business-like demeanour. He told Kerry about their upbringing, a mere few hundred yards from where they were sat. Kerry listened intently, gaining more of an insight into the man that had vanished from her village.

They left the pub with just over an hour to spare, walking down a quiet side street so Rick could show Marlies and Kerry where he'd grown up. They stood under a street light, looking at the modest house as Rick recounted a few choice memories from his upbringing. They headed off once more, eventually walking back through a pitch-black forest, climbing higher with each step. They turned left at the top of the track, Kerry flicking on her torch to light the way to their destination. "Can you hear that?" she said quietly.

"Yes. It's music. Probably kids, drinking booze from the off-license. Let's hope they are not too close to where the doorway is," Rick said, slightly concerned.

As they walked on, the music faded until they could barely hear it. "Over here," Kerry said, playing her torch beam to her right. Leaving the track, they carefully trod over ferns and bracken until the two trees presented themselves.

"Okay," Rick said, finding a fallen log to sit on. "I guess we just wait."

Above them, Lenga floated out of the canopy, drifting a few hundred yards down the slope. Her form returned as she reached the forest floor. She could see the light further up the hill, moving to her right silently. Her bare feet made no sound as she made a wide circle of the threesome, coming to rest next to a large spruce. *Now then my beauties. Let us see what fun this night will bring,* her milky white eyes glowing in the darkness.

* * *

Many miles south of the Lickey Hills, Vicky sat on a hospital chair, her eyes red-rimmed and puffy. Jasper lay next to her, various tubes and wires attached to his small body. Karen sat on the other side of the bed, intermittently dosing. Vicky kept playing over the doctor's words in her head. *Coma. Not reacting to stimuli.* The doctor that had spoken to her a few hours before had a forlorn look on his face. The fact that he'd never seen anything like this before, shook Vicky to her core. She reached over, taking her son's hand in hers. "Wake up, little man. Mummy needs you home. Please, Jasper, wake up." She placed her head on the bed, crying quietly. Jasper lay there, unmoving. He could not hear his mother's pleas. He was far away. In another world, with a fallen king.

Twenty-One

A purge of wind skittered down the cave, snuffing out one of the torches. Carrie saw the flames extinguished, turning her body away from the howling gale that raced towards them. She shielded her torch from the brunt of the gust, her torch barely surviving. "I think it's about to happen," she said as she walked deeper into the cave.

"You're right," Katherine said. "Look."

A faint red outline appeared in the darkness, taking strength and shape. The doorway pulsed gently, illuminating the macabre paintings around it. "Let's move. We don't have much time," Wilf said as he scrambled to his feet. Walking over to Carrie, he relit the end of his torch, thankful that it took readily. He headed for the doorway, torch aloft, stake ready. "Keep close," were his last words before he disappeared from sight. Carrie followed quickly, feeling a slight resistance as she stepped into the void.

Katherine approached the doorway, the cave now in darkness. A deep drone rumbled in from the sea, making her start. She turned around, walking backwards until she could feel the portal vibrating against her back. "I'm coming, Jake," she said as she took a step backwards. Into, the unknown.

* * *

A wind kicked up along the hillside, bracken dancing around them on the forest floor. Rick's ear popped as a low hum settled on the hillside. "Jesus Christ!" he said as a faint blue outline began to appear between the two trees.

"Oh my God!" Marlies added, rising to her feet.

"Jake was right. It's all true," Kerry said as the doorway filled out, gently thrumming against the darkness.

They moved to within inches of the portal, Kerry reaching out towards it. "Careful," Rick said.

"It's warm. I can push against it. Jake said that it only stays open for a minute or so. Shall I go through?" Kerry asked, a feeling of excitement washing over her.

"No. If Jake's right, the doorway will close again. We'll be stuck on the other side for twenty-four hours. We've no idea what is through there. We need to think about this."

"We don't have time to think about it, Rick. Jake could be on the other side. He may need our help."

"I agree with Rick," Marlies said, running her hand across the blue edges. "We know it's real. If we are to do anything, we need to think about it first. We can always come back tomorrow, or at a later date when we have a plan."

Kerry looked at them both. "I thought we had a plan?"

"We haven't, Kerry," Rick replied. "Did any of us actually believe this would happen? I didn't, as much as I wanted to believe. We need to think about how we play this."

A noise in the forest made them all spin around. Out of the darkness, a figure approached. It appeared to be an old woman, dressed in grey rags. Her milky eyes sought them out. "You have found what you were looking for. And now I have found you."

"Who the hell are you?" Rick said, an incredulous look spreading over his face.

"I am Lenga. I am here for Jake too."

Marlies screamed, shaking her head in disbelief when the witch's eyes glowed white. Turning towards the doorway, she grabbed Rick's arm. "RUN!" she yelled. Before she looked to address Kerry, the girl from Cornwall disappeared through the portal, vanishing from sight.

"What do you mean you are here for Jake? He's my brother."

"Then I am here for you too. Your head will look good mounted on my wall."

"W-what?" Rick spluttered.

"Look," Marlies said, pointing towards the blue glow. "The doorway is fading, Rick."

Taking her cue, Lenga rushed them, gnarled fingers and ragged nails seeking flesh. Her index finger caught Rick just below the eye, splitting the skin.

"Get the fuck off me!" he hollered, shoving the old woman away from him.

Lenga lost her footing, tumbling over backwards, knocking the wind from her lungs. She scrambled around on the forest floor, eventually climbing to her feet. Her face dropped. The doorway had vanished, leaving only a darkened forest before her. "Oh, you are clever. You think you have escaped Lenga. But I have a surprise for you." Her form faded to almost nothing, just an ethereal shape remained, floating in the forest. Ahead, she could make out the doorway, glowing blue. The blurry outline crackled between trees that seemed to pulse and writhe. She drifted forward, passing through the doorway to the ancient forest beyond.

* * *

"Katherine! Are you alright?" Wilf said, looking at his niece sprawled on the rocky pathway.

"I'm fine. I think I lost my footing when I passed through." She climbed to her feet, aided by a strong hand from Wilf. "Thank you," she said, kissing him on the cheek.

Wilf smiled in the darkness, his face transformed for a moment. Shaking himself free, he quickly reverted back to his old gruff self, hiding his softer side. "Come on now. We've not got time for mooning about. Let's see where this path leads." The older man walked in front, the women behind him. He smiled again in the darkness, remembering a time when Katherine would plant kisses on his ruddy cheeks. *Always a sweetheart. Alice was too. Shame she was as scatty as a pack of geese.* His thoughts were interrupted as they came out of a tight ravine, into a wider mountain path. He held his torch aloft, trying to cast his light as far as he could. The others joined him, standing either side.

"Looks a bleak prospect ahead," Carrie said, looking at the dark mountains below them. She could make out a few lights further down the pathway. They looked a long way off. Pin-pricks of light against a dark canvas.

"I agree. Although I can just about make out something in the distance. Let's see if we have some luck in this forsaken place," Wilf said. He looked at his niece. "Stay close by. The ground underfoot is unsteady. We don't want to take a tumble out in these wilds."

"Okay, Uncle. I will be at your side." He nodded before setting off down the path, Katherine on his left arm.

Carrie walked on his right, her torch held in the crook of her arm, away from her face. "I've heard stories about this place. Travellers who pass through the farm tell of witches and vampires high up in the mountains. We must be on our guard."

"I've had enough of vampires to last me ten lifetimes," the older man said. "I thought we were shot of them. It looks like we were mistaken."

"Well," Carrie began. "It looks like there are many worlds that link to ours. Who knows what dwells there? Let us hope that our path is free of trouble. I have a farm to tend to. No vampires or witches need show themselves tonight."

They carried on in silence, each lost to their own thoughts. Animals could be heard on the horizon. Startled cries and howls that caused the three of them to consider turning back towards their homeland. "It sounds far away," Wilf said. "Keep an eye out though." They headed ever downwards, for what seemed like hours. As they came around a bend in the track, the first lights that they had previously seen presented itself to them.

"Not my ideal place to make a home," Katherine said as she eyed the small shack. It was single storey, a small porch at the front. An open doorway led into a dim interior, obscured by the darkness.

"A long way from home you are?" a croaky male voice said.

Wilf turned, holding his torch in front of him. "Who wants to know?" he barked aggressively.

On the porch, rocking back and forwards, a man sat watching them. "I didn't want to know. I was merely stating a fact. You're not from these lands."

They approached cautiously, their hands close to drawing on whatever weaponry was available. Wilf looked at the man. Or what was left of him. The figure in the chair was emaciated, to the point of being almost skeletal. Wisps of white hair hung from his head, his mouth a blackened maw. "Who are you?"

"Just an old relic, sat waiting for my granddaughter. Silas is my name. Who are you? And where do you hail from?"

The threesome relaxed slightly, sensing little threat from the ancient man. Katherine looked at his legs, noticing that one was missing below the knee. A stump hung in mid-air, rocking gently. She averted her eyes, addressing the man. "I am Katherine. This is my Uncle Wilf. And this is Carrie. A friend of ours. We are from the land beyond the doorway."

"Aah. I see. Well not really. I've not seen much more for many a season. My eyes gave up on me long ago. Tell me, what brings you to this hell-hole?"

Despite her surroundings, Katherine smiled. "Is it really that bad?"

The old man nodded, his hair tousling around his face. "Oh, it's much worse than Hell. At least Hell is warm. This place has never been warm. No sun kisses this land. We are forever in the shadows."

"We are looking for someone. They may have passed through these parts."

"Foolish they must be to loiter around here?"

"They are not here by choice. They came through another doorway in another place. They are trying to get home."

"Well don't hold out much hope for them, young lass. Not many folks traverse these lands with success. Only cut-throats and murderers manage to survive."

Katherine's shoulders sagged, the man's words deflating her resolve. "We cannot just give up on them."

"Nor should you. If there is a chance, there is a purpose."

She felt a tiny swell of hope return. "I will never give up hope." Changing the subject, Katherine's curiosity came to the fore. "How long have you lived here?"

"Oh, it's too long to count. More ages than I care to remember. It's been at least fifty seasons since my last tooth fell out. I'm a sad old wretch. It's only the love and help from my granddaughter that keeps me from keeling over. She will be back soon. I hope."

"Where is she?" Carrie said, also curious.

"A messenger came from Kungsback, which lies further down the mountain. Someone needed her help."

"Help?" Wilf said, his curiosity blossoming like the others. "What kind of help?"

"My granddaughter is a witch. But not a dark one. She is a white witch. Not many of her kind are left. A man is sick, almost at deaths gate. Evil has befallen him. She left in a hurry, gathering up her trinkets and fleeing without even making my supper."

"What kind of evil?" Katherine asked.

"The messenger said that he'd been bitten by a vampire. He was about to turn. Alana can help him though. I think."

"Oh God!" Katherine exclaimed. "Uncle. Jake's been bitten. It could be him that's sick." She turned to Silas, an expectant edge to her voice. "How far is it to this place?"

"Oh, not too far. If you hurry you should be there soon. Just don't stray from the path. Or you will never return to it."

"We give you our thanks, old-timer. We may pass by on our way back." Wilf said.

"Good luck with your search. Although I'm not sure that it is the man you are looking for. He was not alone y'see. He had others with him?"

"Who?" Wilf asked, his first footstep stalling.

"A strange beast. With flaming eyes."

"Tamatan," Katherine shouted, running off down the mountainside, Wilf and Carrie following in earnest.

* * *

"Oh my god, Rick! What the hell was that?" Marlies said.

"I don't know. But whatever it was, I think it's on the other side of the doorway."

A dark cloud passed by the group, knocking them to the ground. It flew off into the forest, a screeching wail echoing through the trees.

"JESUS!" Kerry screamed as she scrambled to her feet. Did you see that?"

"No. What was it?" Marlies said, tears and dark smudges covering her face.

"I – I don't know. It reminded me of my dreams."

"Shh," Rick said. "Listen." They stood frozen to the spot as the wails seemed to circle around them. They turned their heads, tracking the shrieks as they filtered through the trees.

"Look at the trees!" Kerry exclaimed. "They are all burnt. Like in my dreams."

The noise suddenly changed direction, heading towards them. "GET DOWN," Rick yelled as a black shadow passed over them, a gust of icy wind washing over the prone group. The shrieks died away again, hidden by the night. "We need to get out of here. Whatever the fuck it is, it's not friendly. Kerry. You know this forest better than us. Where do we go?"

"I don't know. There is an abandoned village close by. I'm not sure which way it is though."

"I don't care, Rick," Marlies said. "We need to move. Quickly."

They took off as screeches and wails circled them once more. The ground was uneven, making their escape difficult. Kerry went down first, then Marlies, tumbling over a tree stump. Rick helped them up, pulling them with him. Another noise echoed through the forest. Laughter. The noise started off light, dropping down until it was a dark guttural chuckle. They froze, their fear wrapping itself around them, paralysing them. They looked on in horror as the dark shape appeared before them. Its form changed and writhed until a figure stood a few feet in front of them. "Hello again. Why did you run? We were just getting to be friends."

"You!" Rick gasped, his bladder releasing itself involuntarily. Marlies was shaking uncontrollably, her mouth trying to form words that would not come.

"You are far from home, Rick. You are in Lenga's world now."

"Please. Just let us go. We didn't mean to come here?"

Lenga shook her head, slowly advancing on them. "It matters not why you are here. Or that you didn't mean to stray into this world. You are here now. And you will stay here."

"Let's just run," Kerry breathed, looking past the witch. She pulled at Marlies' arm, heading off across the forest. Rick followed, trying not to look back. More laughter echoed through the trees, hounding and harassing them as they ran blindly into the night. A few minutes later, they came to the remains of a collapsed gate. They could see blackened buildings in a large clearing.

Rick hopped over the gate, helping Marlies and Kerry. They stood looking at the remains of Heronveld, once a little community, now desolate and forgotten. "Over there," Rick said, pointing at one of the buildings. They followed on unsteady legs, their breathing ragged. A few seconds later, they reached the remains of a cabin. The charred frame barely standing. The roof had long since collapsed, falling into the main living area underneath.

"What now?" Kerry said, trying to regain her breath.

"I don't know. Whatever that was, it was evil. You said this place had vampires. Well, I think we've just met one. Kerry, your crosses. Get them out." Kerry dropped the pack from her shoulders, frantically rummaging around. She grabbed one, pulling it from the holdall. It immediately started glowing in her hand. "Fuck me!" Rick said, his jaw hanging open. "This is just." His voice trailed off as Kerry handed him the cross. He held it, feeling the heat radiating through his hand.

"We need to make a fire or something," Kerry said, pulling a lighter from her pack. She scurried along the remains of the porch, picking up scattered pieces of charred wood. Bringing them back to Marlies and Rick, she set about making a small fire. The forest bucked and roiled all around them. Blackened trees yawned and protested as an unseen entity echoed through Amatoll.

Marlies clung to Rick, closing her eyes tightly. "I want to go home, Rick. Please take me home."

He kissed the top of her head, his legs quivering at the sight of the forest around him. "We cannot get home until tomorrow night, babe. Don't worry. I'm not going to let anything happen to you. Or Kerry."

The flames took hold, bathing the porch in a yellow hue. "We need to find more wood to add to the fire," Kerry said. You two wait here. I will scout about. Keep an eye out."

"Kerry!" Marlies hissed as the younger woman hopped from the porch, heading for another dilapidated building. A screech shot across the clearing, knocking Kerry to the ground. "GET BACK HERE, KERRY," Marlies screamed as the forest lit up. White wisps emerged from the tree line, taking various shapes as they headed for the young woman.

Kerry stood up, holding the cross in her hand in front of her. It immediately glowed in her grip, the wraiths falling away, protesting as they did so. She turned to them, her face streaked black. "I'm okay. The cross seems to work on them. Try and find some more wood from over there."

"Sit down, babe. I will look inside. I promise I won't go far."

Marlies slid down the charred doorframe, pulling her knees up to her chest. "Hurry, Rick. The sooner we are home, the better."

Rick disappeared inside, the sound of creaking floorboards filtering through the doorway. A minute later, he returned with an armful of wood, placing it carefully on the small fire. It took readily, the flames lighting the porch and ground in front of them. "We can stay here until the sun comes up. Then we can decide what the hell we're going to do." Marlies just nodded, her eyes lost in the flames. Rick picked up the cross that was laying next to the fire. It immediately glowed in his hand. Shuffling next to Marlies, he sat cross-legged, the glowing crucifix pulsing gently.

Around them, the forest seemed to quieten, the shifting apparitions wrapping themselves around the trees at the edge of the clearing. Kerry headed back towards the fire, arms loaded with kindling of various shapes and sizes. She placed a few pieces on the fire, poking them into the gathering flames. Wiping her hands on her clothes, she sat down opposite the others. "That should keep going for a while. Hopefully until the sun comes up. Are you guys okay?"

"I don't know," said Marlies. "I really don't know what to think."

Rick put his hand on her shoulder. "I think we're all in the same boat, babe. The main thing is for all of us to get back home somehow. Kerry, do you think you'll be able to find the doorway tomorrow night?"

"I guess so," she said as she absently chewed at her thumb.

"Okay. Good. Now that we're stuck here, I think it's best that you tell us everything you know."

"I've already told you everything I know," she said nervously.

"I know. But to be honest, I've either forgotten it or dismissed it. Now that I know it's all true, I need to understand more about this place and what's been going on."

"Well, from what Jake and Katherine told me, there are lots of different worlds, joined together by doorways. Vampires have been travelling through them to our world, abducting various people over hundreds of years, so they can feed their master."

"Is this Korgan?" Marlies said quietly, her eyes scanning the forest.

"Yes. He and his brother Reggan, needed the blood to recover from a fight they'd had. It was centuries ago. Jake only found out about this when he stumbled across a murder close to where he lived. Once his friend, Daz I think," she said looking at Rick.

He nodded, knowing the tragic circumstances of his brother's friend's demise. "That's right."

Kerry continued. "Once his friend had been murdered, Jake ended up here. It was from there that he met Katherine, who lived in this village. There were more fights. Korgan and Reggan were both destroyed. That's when Katherine came to live in Cornwall. I think they thought they'd be safe there. Obviously not. The tall one, Elias, must have found them. He's the one who came to my window. And not long after that, your mother died."

Rick nodded, his face downcast. "Poor Mum."

"I know. I am so sorry for your loss," Kerry said. "I am pretty sure that Elias did something because not long after I met up with them all they all disappeared."

"Hmm," Rick said. "I only hope that Jake and Dad are okay. Katherine and the baby too."

"I hope so too," Kerry said. "I've thought about it every day since. I think that Jake and the rest of them are here somewhere. God only knows where though."

Rick looked up, staring straight ahead at the swaying forest. "Well as much as I want to find Jake and his family, we need to get back through that doorway at the first possible opportunity. Who knows what else is out there. I need to get you both back to safety."

Marlies interlaced her fingers into his, squeezing tightly. "You too, Rick. I need you home too."

Twenty-Two

Jake walked through the leafy forest, a gentle breeze ruffling the leaves above his head. Shafts of sunlight lit the forest floor in sporadic fashion. He knew the place well. He'd spent his whole life there, running, playing, hiding, and loving amongst the hills that surrounded him. He walked with a care-free loping stride, his wavy dark hair bouncing as he strode through the trees. Ahead, a woman and girl stood, hands intertwined.

"Hello, Jake," Katie said.

"Hello, Daddy," Megan said.

Jake looked at his wife and daughter, his face breaking into a serene smile. "Hello. Am I dreaming?"

"Yes, you are, love. We just wanted to say hello, and then goodbye."

"Jake's face dropped slightly. "Goodbye?"

"Yes, Daddy. You need to wake up." His daughter's voice was lyrical and clear.

He looked at Megan, noticing that she looked older. More mature than he remembered. "Why do I need to wake up, sweetie?"

"Because you are not ready to meet us again. One day you will, Daddy. We'll be waiting."

Jake closed his eyes, shaking his head. When his lids fluttered open, they were gone, replaced by a darkening forest of thick trees. Noises echoed through the confines, passing by him, making him turn around. Elias and Eddie stood before him, their eyes mocking him. "Stay with us, Jake. No need to go anywhere. We can take you," the giant commanded. His eyes burned crimson, reaching out to Jake.

"I'm not going anywhere with you," Jake stated flatly, readying himself for battle. In a blur of speed, they rushed him, knocking him to the ground. He closed his eyes tightly, his hands fighting off unseen attacks. A strong pair of hands grabbed

at his clothing, dragging him to his feet. He was shoved roughly against a fir tree, his eyes flying open in terror. He stared at the face in front of him, momentarily frozen. "Daz?"

"Go back, mate. It's not your time yet. You have a new family now. Go and find them. We'll all be waiting when the time is right."

Jake hugged him fiercely, feeling the bigger man's strength as he slowly squeezed the breath from Jake's lungs. He broke the hold, falling backwards over a tree root. His eyes closed once more, darkness consuming him as he fell ever downwards. Towards oblivion.

* * *

"Do you think it will work?" Bea said. She was sat in a wooden corridor with Tamatan, the uncomfortable bench creaking under their weight.

"It is hard to tell. I am sure that the witch will do all she can." Purple light spread from underneath the door. It seemed to pulse through the cracks in the wood, bathing the corridor in a violet hue. They could both hear a gentle hum coming from the room beyond. A soft lyrical tune that soothed their fears. "He has been through so much. He has lost more in one life than many have in a handful."

"I know he has," she replied, her thoughts drifting to her own life. Her upbringing in a small town, at the edge of another world, flashed before her. Kind but strict parents had steered her along the correct path, always ensuring that Bea had chosen the right fork in the road. She missed her family, hoping that one day soon, she'd be able to start a new family of her own. "I wonder where Kaiden is? I hope he didn't come a cropper with the fella's that are on your tail."

"If he's a capable as you say, I am sure that he is looking for you."

"Me too," Bea said, her mind wandering some more.

* * *

"Slow down, Kath," Wilf said as his heart pounded in his chest. They'd followed her down the rocky path, Carrie tumbling a few times as her footing became lost on loose pebbles.

Katherine came to a stop, finding a rock to sit on. A moment later, the other two collapsed next to her. "There it is, Uncle," she said pointing. "There is a building further down the slope."

Wilf looked in between ragged breaths. "So, it is. Let's get our strength back before we check it out. If Jake is there, I'm sure he's going anywhere for a good while."

Carrie pulled up her long skirts, examining the grazes on her knees. "I hope they have some salve that I can put on these," she said as her fingers gently pressed on the raw flesh. "I should have worn britches."

Wilf smiled, his heartbeat slowly returning to normal. He was about to speak when a movement behind Katherine caught his eye. She scrambled to his feet, a dagger in his gnarled hand. "Who goes there?" The women followed suit, clambering to their feet, weapons drawn.

A figure emerged from the gloom, approaching slowly. Their eyes took him in, noting with some trepidation the size of the stranger before them. He stood a full head taller than Wilf. Thickly muscled arms, hanging by his sides. "I am Kaiden. I am searching for my woman. She was taken by others."

"Well, we have not seen her. We are also searching for loved ones. They may have come through these parts." Wilf pointed to the saloon. "Over there. They may be a chance that someone there knows of their whereabouts."

"I mean you no foul. I only want to find Bea and get out of this land."

"Then we have a common purpose," Wilf said. "We need to find Jake and do the same."

"Jake?" Kaiden said, an alarming expression on his dark features.

"Yes, Jake," Katherine said. She looked at Kaiden, a knot forming in her stomach.

"Well, that complicates things. I am also looking for Jake. Alain, the vampire in the mountains wants him and the demon."

"Alain?" Wilf said, the grip on his dagger tightening.

"Yes. We've made a pact. He wants them, in return for Bea. I vowed to deliver them both to him."

"What!" Katherine blurted. "You cannot do this. I have to get him home. He has a daughter who needs her daddy back safe?"

"As I said, this complicates things. I had no idea others were looking for him. I was just told that this Jake destroyed some vampires and that a witch from another land is hunting him. It looks like there are a few who want him and this demon for what they have done."

"Jake is a good man," Wilf began. "He helped us rid our lands of these monsters. In doing so, Jake and Tamatan became lost to us. We are here to take them home. Are you here to stop us?"

Kaiden saw the dagger in the older man's hand. He also saw the steely determination in the eyes of the woman who sat opposite. He took in her features, seeing the anguish etched on her face. "I am at a loss. I think that Bea is in there," he said pointing. "If she is there, and Jake is there, then we may be able to make a run for the doorway together. I have no desire to return to this place"

The others relaxed slightly, but not totally. They still brandished their weapons, ready for anything unexpected. "How far is this Alain?" Wilf said.

"A good journey. I ran most of the way from his cave. He said that the vampires who were killed were his kin. He also said that a spirit has stirred. The fallen king who was Korgan and Reggan's father."

"Fuckenhell," Wilf said. "This is the last thing we needed to hear. But hear it we must. What else do you know?"

"There is a boy, floating on the wind. He has been trying to guide them here. Even the vampire does not know who he is, or why he is here."

"We need to move," Katherine said, climbing to her feet. "It looks like we're all in peril just by being here. I know Jake is in there. And if he is, then Tamatan and your woman are there too. Let's go get them and take them back to safety while we still can."

"But I have made a pact. Alain knows many things. He may even be able to hear our words right now. I am going back on the promise that I made him if I allow Jake to go free."

"If you try to take him, I will kill you myself," Katherine said, her voice flat and foreboding. "I do not care how big you are. My stake will find its mark I promise you that." She turned, walking stiffly towards the lights in the distance.

Wilf got to his feet, looking at the giant. "Heed those words, stranger. That woman has been through more than you will ever know. If you come between her and her man, I too will stick you like a wild boar." He turned, following his niece. Carrie took up the rear, not even looking at the giant, who stood on rubbery legs. His resolve and purpose crumbling around him.

* * *

Alain sat in his cave, the remains of the marauding gang littering the stone floor. A small fire in the corner of the cave, cast its glow across the crypt. Alain looked at the floor, his eyes closed. He could feel a presence close by. Something familiar. He could feel it pulling on him, like an invisible strand of silk was drawing something towards his cave. His thoughts had been with Kaiden, who he was tracking. The vampire knew that the giant was nearing his goal, Alain almost able to see what Kaiden was seeing. However, his thoughts had become clouded by this new entity that had appeared in the distance. His eyes flew open. "Virdelas! Is it really you I can feel? Come to your kin. Let us plot our future together."

* * *

Jasper floated through the forest, without purpose or thought. Virdelas floated next to him, his ethereal form complete. He drew the boy behind him, navigating the trees with ease. He felt a dark force to the east, knowing that it was probably the witch. He cast the thoughts from his mind as he felt another essence far away. He caught a whiff of it on the breeze, hardly perceptible at all. Once he'd caught it, he followed like a bloodhound, weaving through the packed forest of Mantz. Heading for a doorway, into another world.

* * *

Vicky woke up with a start. A constant beeping was the only noise in the small hospital room. Jasper lay next to her on the bed, the rise and fall of his chest the only indication he was still alive. Karen was asleep on the other side of the bed, arms folded in front of her. Her head in the crook of her elbow. "Please, Son," Vicky said. "Wake up. Mummy needs you to come home." She rubbed his hand, the skin feeling cool to Vicky. She looked at the clock on the wall, seeing that it was just past 1 am. Standing up, she walked over to the windows, parting the Venetian blinds. Rain pattered against the pane. A few lights below the window barely gave any clue as to the outside world. Vicky was not in the outside world. She was locked in a nightmare. A horrible dream, where her neighbour had just tried to kill her. A dream where her son would not wake up. Her wits-end was just around the corner. She was losing her resolve. Vicky could feel overwhelming emotions taking over her body. *I cannot lose him too. I have already lost the rest of my family. Please let Jasper be okay. Please, God. I beg you.* Walking away from the window with tears moistening her skin, Vicky climbed onto the end of the bed. Jasper's legs only reached halfway down the mattress, leaving an area where Vicky could curl up. She picked up a pillow that had been left on another plastic chair. As gently as she could, the woman got comfortable, curling up in a ball. Her eyes were on her son, watching for any movement. None came. He was still, the machines behind him, beeping away steadily. Vicky let her mind wander as sleep took hold of her quickly. *Why me? Why us?* Before she could think of an answer, she tumbled into the darkness. Finding some sanctuary.

* * *

Katherine burst through the front door into the saloon, Wilf and Carrie not far behind her. She spotted a large man, tending to a patron at the bar. She headed over, floorboards creaking under her boots. The man spotted her as his customer walked away, a large jug of ale in his mutilated hand. "Hello," the man said. "What can I get for you and your friends?"

"We are looking for someone. A man called Jake. Have you seen him?"

The man's jolly expression cooled somewhat as Wilf and Carrie stood next to Katherine, expectant expressions etched on their faces. "Who are you?"

"My name is Katherine. This is Wilf and Carrie. Have you seen him? You have, haven't you?"

Matts placed his towel on the bar, sighing. "Yes. He is out the back. How do you know him?"

"He's here, Uncle," Katherine said as she turned to Wilf, embracing him fiercely. Tears ran down her cheeks as the older man held her tightly. She looked at Matts, wiping her eyes with the back of her hand. "He's my man," she stated.

"Thank the gods that we've found him," Wilf said, cradling his niece's head. "I am lost for words."

Matts turned towards the door as Kaiden walked into the room, heads turning as the giant approached the bar. "Well?"

"He's here," Wilf said as he let go of his niece. He turned to the innkeeper. "Can we see him?"

"Come with me. But I urge you to be quiet and do as I say. The witch is with him." Before anyone could answer, Matts walked around the bar, heading for a door hidden in the corner of the room. Hinges protested as he held the door open for his new guests. He eyed Kaiden as the bigger man ducked through the doorway into a small corridor beyond. Matts led the way down the rickety passage, turning right into another part of the building.

"Bea!" Kaiden exclaimed as he rounded the corner.

"Oh, thank god you made it," the tall blonde woman said as she shouldered past the newcomers. She jumped into Kaiden's embrace, kissing him fiercely on the mouth. Their tears intermingled, sobs coming from Bea as she clung to her man.

"Hail, Wilf and Katherine," Tamatan said, shaking both their hands, clapping them on their backs.

"Am I glad to see you," Katherine said, hugging the demon tightly.

Tamatan's eyes shone a bright red, adding to the torchlight that adorned the walls. He broke the hold, salty tears being wiped away. "He is in there with the witch. We do not know what is happening? Or if the witch can save him?"

Katherine headed for the door, reaching out for the handle. "I need to see him," she said as she pushed her way into the room.

"No, Katherine," Tamatan urged. "We should not go in there."

"Come in," a soft female voice said to Katherine. "And close the door behind you."

She did as she was asked, closing the door quietly. She walked over to the bed at the far side of the room. A room that was bathed in a violet glow. The walls seem to pulse and move as the light played across the rough boards. "Jake," she whispered as she came to the bed. He was still, white skin bathed in purple.

"I am Alana," the woman said. "And you are the love that he has been waiting for."

Tears burst from Katherine's eyes at the witch's words. "Yes. I am his love. And he is mine." She looked at the witch who was sat atop of her man. Her white cloak covered most of her body. Her hair was dark and long, trailing down her chest. Small gemstones were tied into her locks, facets shimmering as they caught the hue from the crystal dangling from her neck. Her face was kind, her lips full, slightly upturned. "Can you save him?"

"I think it will be so. I had to end his life as the darkness had taken hold of him. In doing that, the infection has now left him. Jake is wandering through the void, trying to find his way back to me. I can see him, and I can feel him. You may be able to help. Please, take my hand."

Katherine took the proffered hand, liking the cool dry feel of the witch's skin. Their fingers entwined. "What happens now?"

"Do you trust me?"

"Yes, I do."

"Then come closer to me. I need more from you, as it will seep through me into him." Katherine moved closer until she was bent over Jake's inert form. "Trust me," the witch said as she let go of Katherine's hand, snaking her fingers through the woman's long hair, pulling her towards her. Alana kissed Katherine full on the lips, the other woman flinching at the contact. She was momentarily at a loss as how to react. She had never been kissed by a female before, yet it was not unpleasant. A warmth spread through her body, filling Katherine with a feeling of euphoria. It washed over her like the surf breaking on the shoreline. Her eyes closed as the witch held her. An image flashed through Katherine's mind. It was Jake, standing in a forest with another man. A man who looked familiar to her. Alana broke the kiss, her smoky eyes boring into Katherine's. "Place your hand on his chest," she said quietly.

"Okay," she replied, splaying her fingers over Jake's cool skin. She could feel no heartbeat, which dismayed her. The resolve and hope she carried started to slip away as she felt the lifeless corpse on the bed.

"Kiss me, Katherine. He needs to feel it." Their lips came together once more, the crystal dangling between them pulsing like a beacon.

She felt something echo through her palm. It came again, faint but noticeable. She broke the kiss, looking down at Jake. "I felt his heart."

"Yes, you did. He is coming back. You have found him, and he knows that you are here, searching."

Katherine wept openly, burying her face in the witch's hair. "Thank you," was all she could say.

Alana began to hum softly, her own tears falling freely. "You do not need to thank me. I am grateful for this. There is much darkness out there. Bringing someone back from the void fills Alana with joy."

Katherine pulled away slowly, smiling at the other woman. Alana smiled back, nodding her head before climbing off Jake, covering his nakedness with a thin sheet. She removed the crystal pendant from around her neck, placing it on his chest. "This is an Amertrine Stone. A stone of healing. A stone of the ages. They are very rare, mined from rocks in a far corner of the mountains by the dwellers in the darkness. My granddaddy wears one too. It keeps him alive, although his time grows short. But for Jake, it will be his companion. Once he comes back to us, he must wear this stone, or keep it close by. My essence is within it. It will keep him strong."

Katherine nodded, looking at the crystal on his chest. It was the size of her thumb, rectangular in shape with a pointed end that reminded her of the crude pencils that she'd used as a girl. She thought of her mother, who had schooled her at home before a tragic accident had ended her life, taking her away from Katherine and Alice. She shook the memory from her mind as her emotions began to rise. "How can I ever repay you?" she said as more tears spilt from her eyes.

"There is no payment needed. You have given thanks, which is enough. I will stay awhile until he wakes. Then I must take my leave, as old Silas will be grumbling that I've not made him his breakfast."

"Well, I am forever in your debt Alana. If ever there is anything that I can do, please find me. I am not that far away."

"I know. I have travelled to the land beyond the doorway. I have travelled far, spending time in the forests to the west. There was darkness there until recently. But now, another darkness has settled over the land. An ancient force has stirred. I have felt it. It came from another place. And it is out there somewhere."

"Jake helped us rid the land of these monsters. That's how he became lost. I just want him home. Alicia misses her Daddy."

"I can imagine. A child needs the love of its elders. Do you have far to travel?"

"Yes. It's at least a four-day walk back to my uncle's village. From there, when Jake is ready, we will travel back to his land. We have set up a home there. It is free from the evils of the other worlds. There are machines and wonders that you could only imagine, Alana. Things that have opened my eyes. It's where we belong."

"Then I pray that you make it home. When I have fed Silas, I will impart a spell to give you safe passage."

"Thank you."

"Katherine?" a faint voice croaked.

"Jake!" Katherine said, looking down at the bed.

He looked up at her, almost seeing her face for the first time. "You've found me."

"I have, babe," she replied, almost diving on top of him.

"I will fetch him some water. He will need to quench his thirst. I shall return."

The witch left the room, leaving Jake and Katherine on the bed. "Oh, Jake Stevenson. Don't ever leave me like that again. I am going to keep you on a leash from now on."

"I promise, babe. What has happened?"

"You were sick. Do you remember?"

"Vaguely. I remember that my leg was getting worse. I had a fever."

"Well you're cured," she said as she climbed off him, pulling back the thin sheet that covered his lower body.

Mustering as much strength as he could, Jake propped himself onto one elbow, looking down at his naked body. The angry scar on his leg was gone, the skin flawless. "Wow. How did she do that?"

"She's a witch. She knows such things. We are very lucky to have you back, babe. Wilf is with me."

"Wilf. Where is he?"

"Outside in the passageway. Others are with us too."

"Who?"

"A friend who helped us find our way here. And a giant, who is with the woman that brought you both here."

"Oh." Something suddenly occurred to Jake. "There are others following us. We are certain of that. The other witch has sent them to after us. To kill us both."

"Oh no!" Katherine said, her new-found happiness evaporating. "We need to get back to safety as soon as possible."

"I agree. Is there a doorway close by?"

"Yes. Higher up in the mountains. From there, it is a four-day walk back to Shetland. We will be safe there for a while until we are ready to return to Cornwall."

Jake looked at Katherine, his eyes suddenly sad. "I cannot believe Dad is gone, Kath. I've not really had time to think about it. Poor Dad."

"He was a wonderful man. I loved him with all my heart, Jake. And I'm sure that wherever he is, he is smiling down on us."

They embraced, clinging to each other. There love and pain becoming one again. The outside world forgotten, and the worlds beyond.

Twenty-Three

The sun rose over Amatoll forest, hidden behind thick cloud. The dying embers of the fire had burned through the blackened porch, falling to the hard earth below. Kerry added a few more planks and branches, dropping them through the gaping hole in the wooden boards. She turned to Rick and Marlies, who were curled up on the uneven planks. Exhaustion had finally won out, plunging them both into a fitful sleep. Kerry had also slept but woke when a bird had landed on the blackened rail next to her. After dropping the wood onto the remnants of the fire, she headed around the back of the cabin, relieving herself quickly. The young woman with dark unruly hair, walked around the clearing, the forest around her still and imposing. Her mind tried to take in the events of the night before, amazed that they had managed to survive. She walked past ruined cabins, looking for anything of use. Finding nothing, she headed over to the far end of the former village, spotting an opening in the trees. A single track wound its way through the forest, towards the plains beyond. *I know where this leads*, she thought as she remembered her vivid dreams. *The mountain is over there*, looking to her right. Her surroundings were quiet. No animals could be heard in the undergrowth below or branches above. *This place is a tomb*, she surmised before striding back to the others.

Rick was sat up when Kerry mounted the porch. "Hi," he said. "Are you okay?"

"I think so," replied Kerry as Marlies stirred from her slumbers. "I took a quick walk around the place. There is a track over there that leads out of the forest. If I remember rightly, the other forest is that way," she said pointing across the clearing. "There is a mountain in the opposite direction that I have seen in my dreams. Beyond that are just plains as far as the eye can see."

"Okay. We need to think about what we should do today. We have some food and drink, which we will have to ration." He looked down at his partner. "Hi, babe. You okay?"

"I think so," she said groggily. "I was hoping this was a dream that I was about to wake up from."

Kerry opened her pack, handing a bottle of water to Marlies. "Here. Have some of this."

"Thanks, Kerry," she said as she unscrewed the top. Taking a few sips, she passed it to Rick who did the same.

He gave it back to the girl from Cornwall, who after taking a sip, placed it in her pack, zipping it up. "I don't think we should just sit here all day. If that thing reappears, she will find us easily."

"Thing," Rick said. "Do we even know what it was?"

"I thought it was a vampire?" Marlies countered.

"I thought that at first too," Kerry said. "But the more I think about it, the more I think she wasn't."

"So, what do you think we're dealing with?" Rick asked heavily.

"I'm not sure. It looked more like a witch."

"I agree. She said her name was Lenga," Marlies said.

"Well whatever she is, we don't want to meet her again. She said she was here for Jake. How the fuck did my brother end up being chased by witches and vampires?"

"And where the hell is he?" Kerry said as she drew her knees up to her chest to fight off the chill of the morning air.

"I think we should take a walk," Marlies said. "Kerry is right. We shouldn't just sit here waiting for whatever that was to reappear. We might find somewhere else to hide out until tonight. What time is it anyway?"

Rick checked his Rolex. "7 am. We have a long day ahead of us. Okay. I need to take a quick pee. Then we can take a walk." He stood up, arching his back before heading around the rear of the dilapidated cabin. Marlies did the same, following his footsteps.

Kerry remained on the porch, her dark eyes scanning the forest around her. "Where are you, Jake? We could really do with your help right now."

* * *

"Do you think you're up for the journey?" Katherine asked.

"I feel okay. I'd rather be on the move than just sat here. Does the doorway open at midnight like the others?"

"Yes," Carrie said from the far corner of the room.

"Okay. Good. We can set off as soon as possible. What about you two?" Jake asked, looking at Kaiden and Bea.

"We're coming too," Kaiden said. "I'll not venture back to this place. The gold can stay here. I will not run the risk of meeting Alain again." In the hours that had followed Jake's reawakening, Kaiden had filled the group in on his meeting with the vampire from the mountains. They all now knew that Alain was related to Korgan, Reggan and Virdelas. They all knew that the vampire wanted to thwart the witch's plans, by taking Jake for his own. And they all knew that Alain wanted to avenge the death of Korgan. They were all in danger, subduing them somewhat.

The door opened, making them all turn. Jenni stood there smiling. "We've made you breakfast and some food for your journey."

Kaiden stood up from the chair, lifting Bea with him as if she weighed no more than a sack of feathers. "Lead on. I am hungry."

Two large tables had been pushed together, a selection of meats, vegetables, and bread covering most of the wooden tops. They all sat down, not waiting on ceremony. Kaiden set about a tray of steaks, using his hands to shovel chunks of meat into his mouth. Wilf did the same, placing a thick slice of meat between two dry hunks of freshly baked bread. Jugs of ale sat in the centre of the table, their dark liquid almost brimming over onto the dark stained wood. Jake feasted with them, feeling his shrunken stomach swell with each mouthful. He looked at Kaiden. "We're sorry if we gave you a fright when Bea left the shack."

"It is forgotten. Although at the time, I wanted to hunt you down. I thought you murderers. But then I had my own problems to deal with. The pack of brutes that were following you found me. I managed to make a run for it, heading high up into the mountains. That's where I met Alain. He did for them. So, we can relax on that front. The witch's plan looks to have gone awry."

"For now, at least," Tamatan said warily. "I do not think she will give up so easily."

"Tell me more about the boy?" Katherine said as she nibbled at a piece of bread.

"He is the watcher," Tamatan began. He is from Jake's world. He's out there somewhere. Where I do not know. His name is Jasper. He was trying to help us find our way home."

"Why would a young lad be this far from home? I know you said it was not a real boy. More like his spirit." Katherine said.

"I don't know, babe," Jake said as he poured himself a cup of ale. He wiped his lips, placing the clay mug in front of him. "Somehow, he has become involved in all this. I've no idea how he manages to do what he's doing. We just know that he was trying to help us. Let's hope nothing has happened to him."

They finished their breakfast in relative silence, each pondering the next few hours. Footsteps from the bar approached as Matts, Jenni, and a small woman headed towards them. "This should be enough to keep you going," the small woman said. She was old, small, and frail. Her darkened skin had a leathery look about it, making her look far older than her actual age. "I am Mimi. This is my lodge. I am sorry that I have not greeted you before. I had a few of my own things to take care of last night."

"We thank you for your hospitality," Wilf said warmly, noticing something odd about the little old lady. Katherine noticed it too, seeing that Mimi's head was shaped strangely.

She turned around, another face looking at the group. "I am Mama, but Mimi doesn't let me talk much. Do you Mimi?" She turned around once more, smiling. "Don't pay no mind to my sister. She is a pain in the hide most days."

"I am not," a croaky voice said.

"Hush, woman," Mimi said. "Sorry about that. You get used to it."

They all nodded, not knowing what to say as the old woman walked back to the bar. Carrie looked at Mama, her eyes fixated on her. "Don't stare, woman," Mama said. "It's not wise."

"Enough, Mama," Matts said, wringing his hands together nervously. He turned to them, trying his best to lighten the mood. "That should be enough we think. If you are ever unfortunate enough to visit these lands again, know that you are welcome here."

They all shook hands before heading out into the perpetual darkness. The first droplets of rain fell from the sky, a stiffening breeze blowing up the mountain towards them. "Let's be on our way," Kaiden said, shouldering Bea's pack. "If this gets worse we will have to take shelter somewhere." They headed up the rocky path. Kaiden and Bea took the lead, holding hands. Behind them, Jake and Katherine followed suit. Wilf and Carrie walked behind them, making polite chatter. Tamatan took up the rear, his red eyes scanning the dark slopes around them. He could not sense anything untoward, hoping that they had a clear path home. He missed his sister Veltan and their son Jake. Tamatan knew that he had many roads to travel before he was reunited with them once more. He only hoped he was not too late.

* * *

"Welcome, Brother. It has been countless moons since we were together," Alain said. He stood underneath a torch, looking across the cave at two floating apparitions. "Tell me, what do you have there?"

The reply echoed off the cave walls. It was a low voice, cracked and distorted. "I have a boy. He came from another place. The witch, Lenga wanted him. But I took him for myself. His body is back in the other realm. There was a battle. I managed to take the boy from the witch before heading into this world."

"What do you plan to do with him?" Alain said as he walked across the cave. Jasper hung a few feet off the ground, his face drawn and fearful. "What is your name?"

"Jasper," the boy replied. Not by voice. Their communication was on another level entirely.

"Welcome, Jasper. You are the watcher. I have seen you pass by, floating on the wind like a feather. You are indeed far from home. But not to worry. You are here now, with us. Virdelas. What are you planning?"

"Many things. There are scores to settle. This boy could help us achieve our aims."

Alain's mind suddenly plucked something out of the air. "He's betrayed me."

"Who," Virdelas' spirit asked.

"The giant. He is looking for his woman. There are others too. The man who killed your sons is with them. He was supposed to bring them back here. But he has cried foul. They are heading for the doorway." His yellow eyes burned in the darkness. Burning with hate and loathing. "Stay here. I have to stop this."

"Bring him back here, Alain. I will drain him. Maybe that will make me stronger. Maybe one day I will stand shoulder to shoulder with you once more."

"Hold that thought, Brother. Stay here with the watcher. I will bring as many back as I can. They will be easy prey for Alain."

Jasper felt despair wash over him as the vampire exited the cave. *Jake. If you can hear me, run. As fast as you can. He's going to hurt you.*

* * *

Sometime later, the group came across the battered log cabin at the side of the track. "This is where we met the witch's grandfather," Katherine said. "He was sat on the stoop."

"Maybe he went inside for his breakfast," Wilf said, noticing the front door hanging ajar. Clouds had moved down the mountain, blanketing the group in a fine mist, cutting visibility down to a few feet.

"There is something wrong," Tamatan said.

"What?" Jake said, eyeing the demon warily. His fingers reached for the stone hanging from his neck, liking the feeling it gave off. It felt warm and alive, gently pulsing against an old scar on his chest that bore the shape of a cross.

"There is a coldness in there."

The group looked at each other, the tension increasing ten-fold. Kaiden looked at the others. "Well let's not dwell here. How much further to the doorway?"

Wilf pointed up the mountain, aiming at a wall of impenetrable fog. "Not much further at all."

"Then let's be on our way," the giant said eagerly. "I yearn to feel some kind of sun on my skin."

"Maybe we should just check that they are okay?" Jake said, stepping towards the cabin. "I never really got a chance to thank her. We should at least take a look."

"I wouldn't," Kaiden said. "We have had good fortune by all coming together. Let us not undo all of that by taking risks."

"I'm sure everything is fine," Jake said, trying to sound positive. "I'll be back out in a minute." He looked at the demon. "Keep an eye on Katherine and the others." Tamatan nodded slowly.

"Hang on," Wilf said. "I'll come with you."

"Okay," Jake said.

"Have this," the older man said, handing Jake a stake. "Better to be on guard than have no guard."

Jake took the weapon, holding it in his left hand. They walked forward slowly, stepping onto the porch. Tired floorboards announced their arrival as they headed towards the front door. "I'll go first," Jake said, wishing that he had a torch. Wilf nodded, following closely behind. More squeaking rang out as the front door was pushed open. The two men stepped into a low-slung room, barely lit by a dying fire at the far end. A table sat in the centre, two chairs lying smashed on the floor next to it.

"Steady now, Jake. Tamatan may be right. I think trouble has passed by here."

Two doorways led from the main living area. One was open, the other closed. "Let's try that one first," Jake said, heading left around the table. He reached the door, lifting the latch carefully. He poked his head inside, relieved to see that it was just a small cupboard, filled with utensils. "All clear."

Wilf turned, walking over to the other doorway, cross held aloft. He shouldered his way through the door into a small bedroom with two cots on either wall. "It's empty," he said flatly. "No one is home."

A few minutes later they emerged into the ravine, thankful to be out in the open. Katherine looked at Jake. "Well?"

"Empty. No one's home."

"Strange. The old man could barely walk. Where would he have gone to so soon after we'd passed by?"

Jake considered her words for a moment before shrugging his shoulders. "Maybe they popped out to the shops?"

"Don't make sport with me, Jake Stevenson," Katherine said, a half-smile tugging at her lips.

"Sorry, babe. I was just trying to lighten the mood. Let's carry on towards the doorway." They all muttered their approval, heading away from the shack, climbing ever upwards towards their destination.

* * *

Jasper looked on in horror as Virdelas began consuming the old man that lay on the stone floor. He tried to cry out in pain but looked too weak to move. Jasper turned away, closing his eyes tightly as a muffled choking noise filled the cave. As the struggles died away, Jasper looked over at Virdelas' form. His outline was more pronounced, making it easier for the boy to see who he was sharing the dark confines with.

"Such a shame that I cannot have them both," Virdelas said. "But I will be patient. More is on its way."

Run Jake, the boy thought. *Get away from here.* His bubble sank to the floor, ethereal tears brimming in his eyes as he looked across the cave towards the other figure that lay there. He didn't know who it was. The figure was a stranger to him. But he knew that she was in grave danger. The unknown stranger lay there, seemingly asleep. Her white cloak laid out all around her.

* * *

They came across the remains of a burnt-out building. Next to it, a large lake brooded in the sullen daylight. "I wonder what this place used to be?" Marlies asked as she looked at the burnt-out shell?"

"Not sure," Rick said. "But I don't think they are open for lunch. Shame. I am starving."

"Look over here," Kerry said. She had walked away from the building, standing next to a large cart, laden with items. "There is some stuff here. Look," she said holding up an earthenware jug, listening to its contents as she tipped it upside-down. Kerry pulled out the cork with considerable effort as the others made their way over to her. She sniffed the contents, her nose wrinkling. "Smells like beer."

Rick held out his hand, taking the jug from the younger woman. He too sniffed at the contents, taking a tentative sip. "It is beer," he said before taking a larger swig. "Bloody hell! It's got a right kick to it."

"He handed it to Marlies, who took a long pull on the jug. "Not bad. Almost as good as our Belgian beer back home. Shall we sit down and take a rest?"

"Good idea. Kerry. Do you want some more?"

"No thanks. Not a fan of beer. I'll sort through this stuff to see what else is of interest."

Rick and Marlies took a jug each, walking towards the tree line. "Let's not sit here," Rick said, pointing to the remains of a man that sat propped against an old tree.

"Oh God!" Marlies replied, walking backwards away from the cadaver. They walked a hundred yards, following the tree line. The forest gave way to a small glade, a tinkling stream running through it.

"Kerry," Rick called. He waited for the dark-haired girl to turn around. "We're over here, okay."

"Okay," She replied before continuing her rummaging.

They got comfortable, Marlies sitting cross-legged on the cool grass. "We shouldn't have done this, Rick. I have an awful feeling that we may never return home."

"We'll get back home, babe. I promise. And I think we needed to do this, regardless of what has happened."

"Why?"

"Because my brother is out there somewhere. He could be dead for all I know. Dad too. I've been so wrapped up in my life in Germany, that I have taken my eye off what's important."

"How you do you mean?" Marlies enquired as she nursed the ale.

"I've been so career driven over the past few years. Since I left Uni, I've focused on me and me only. Looking back now, I can see just how fucking selfish that is. My brother lost his family and I hardly ever picked up the phone to him. Mum died, and I hardly ever rang Dad. I've been a colossal dick."

"No, babe. You have not. You've built a life for yourself with me."

"I know. And I love that life. And I love you. But I also have neglected my family back in the UK. That's going to change. I promise you. I want them to visit us. I want to show them what we've built."

"And you will. Now is not the time to feel guilty about the past. What we do tomorrow cannot change what happened yesterday."

"I love you. You always have a way of making me feel better about things. Will you marry me?"

Marlies looked at Rick, her eyes widening. "What?"

"Sorry, babe. That kinda slipped out." He placed his jug in the grass, shuffling over to her, taking her hands in his. "I was going to ask you to marry me when we got home. It's what I want more than anything in the world."

Tears erupted from the Belgian woman's eyes, cascading down her flawless skin. "Oh, Rick. Of course, I will marry you." She dropped her jug, the brown contents leaking into the grass. They embraced fiercely, lips colliding, tears mixing. After a minute, she pulled away, regarding him with red-rimmed eyes. "Just promise me one thing?"

"Anything, babe."

"Do this again, when we are all home. Hopefully with your family around you. They would love to see that."

"And if we never find them?"

She considered the question, her face clouded. "Then I will leave that to you. I am sure you will the right time and place."

He smiled at her, wiping away the tears. "I promise. And I will make you happy."

"You already do, Rick. More than I ever would have dreamed." They cuddled into each other, their eyes drifting over to the ruined building.

Minutes passed until Kerry headed over towards them, her arms full of differing objects. "I found some sweet water. And this lot too," she said, laying the items in front of them. "Two axes. A blanket. And what looks like some kind of ham, wrapped in cloth. I tried some. It's really good."

Rick unwrapped the rough hessian cloth from around the joint of meat, pulling a strip of meat from the leg. He popped it in his mouth, chewing it readily. He nodded his head, signalling for Marlies to try some. "It's good. Really good. It tastes like Serrano ham. It's been cured."

They sat in relative silence, taking it in turns to pull hunks of dried meat from the joint. The sun, hidden by clouds, tracked its path across the sky until the shadows started to lengthen. Rick stood, stretching his arms behind his neck. "We should make a move. Kerry, do you know where the doorway is from here?"

"Yes," she replied. "We can either cut through the forest or make our way back along the track to the abandoned village."

"What do you think, Rick?" Marlies said.

"I think it would be safer to go back the way we came. I don't fancy being in there," he said pointing into the dense forest. "Better to be out in the open."

"Okay," Kerry said. "Let's get going," stuffing the meat into her pack. They left the lake behind, ambling down the track that split Amatoll from Korgan's Vale. Heading south. In the distance, a lonely mountain guided them towards the turn-off. It sat there, forlorn and silent, swathed in grey cloud.

"I need a wee," Kerry said as they came to the path that led back to the ruined village.

"Okay," Rick said. "I could do with one too."

"I may as well join you," added Marlies. They dumped their belongings on the path, heading off in different directions. Marlies stayed close to Rick, Squatting next to a tree.

As Rick relieved himself, he looked into the forest in front of him. An icy sensation settled over him as he saw wisps of fog, trailing through the woodland.

They moved with purpose, circling tree stumps, wrapping themselves around branches as a faint drone rang through the forest. Finishing off, Rick walked back towards the track, looking over his shoulder. "You okay, babe?"

"Yeah," Marlies replied, pulling up her jeans. "Are you?"

"I think so. This place gives me more than the creeps. It's so eerie."

"I know it is. Remind me never to return." They came out of the tree line, spotting Kerry heading in the opposite direction.

"Okay," Rick said quietly. "Let's go find the doorway. I only hope we don't have company tonight. We need to have our eyes peeled at all times."

The village had not changed since they'd left. The clearing was growing darker as the sun began its descent towards the western horizon. A mist was spilling from the tree line, drifting aimlessly across the stubbly grass. They watched in silence, as the ground became hidden underneath a sea of grey. "Come on," Rick urged. "Let's get out of here." The trio picked up the pace, heading into the forest. They navigated trees, rises and depressions as Kerry led them towards the doorway.

"What time is it, Rick?" Marlies asked, her eyes flitting left and right.

"Almost 7 pm. We've got a long wait ahead of us, babe."

Marlies sighed, her shoulder dropping. *Please let us get home. Please God*, she thought as she walked towards her goal. Towards an unseen doorway that led back to her world.

* * *

"How much longer?" Bea asked.

"Not much longer," Carrie said as she added another log to the fire. The seven sat at the far end of the cave, well away from its entrance. Shadows flickered across the stone walls, as the group enjoyed the relative warmth of the small fire. Grey smoke pooled across the roof of the cave, gently wafting its way into the darkness beyond.

Jake looked at Tamatan. "What will you do when we pass through?"

The diminutive demon looked at his friend, his eyes shimmering. "I will make my way west, towards the great forests. Tamatan will move quickly as time is of the essence. I will find a way to get back to the Unseen Lands. I only hope that Veltan and Jake are waiting for me. I will find Sica. He will have news of my kin. If they have departed, I will follow them. The land of Marzalek is safe.

There we will live out our days. No more adventures for Tamatan. No more doorways or monsters. And you, Jake. What plans do you have?"

Jake looked at Katherine, who smiled back at him. Their eyes lingered, drinking in each other's features. "We've not discussed it yet," Jake said. "What do you think, babe?"

"Well," she began. "We will need to return to Shetland first. Alicia needs to see her Daddy. Then we need to think about the journey home. We will need supplies."

"That won't take too long," Wilf said, blowing a ring of smoke from his mouth. "We can rest up for a few days, while we figure out how to get back to your world, Jake."

"We?" Katherine asked quizzically.

"I'm getting old, Kath. Too old for this life. I want to come with you. I have grown too fond of my granddaughter to say farewell to her."

Jake and Katherine looked at the grizzled old man, smiling at him. "What about the villagers?" his niece asked.

"They will live out their days in peace. They are safe there. They have the sea. They have food and will be just fine without old Wilf. When we get back, we can elect a new elder. The folk will understand."

"We'd love you come with us, Wilf," Jake said warmly. "Dad's house is empty," he said, a sharp pang piercing his heart. "We will make it work somehow. I promise."

"I'll carry on as normal," Carrie added. "This adventure has given me my fill. I can return to my farm. That's all I need."

"And you guys?" Jake said, looking at Kaiden and Bea.

"I'm taking his hunk of love back to Tasmania. As you said, we'll make it work somehow."

"It looks like we all have a common purpose," Tamatan said. "Jake, you are my brother, bonded to my very existence. I never expected to follow your path. I am a demon, who has spent the centuries hounding folk like yourself. It was by chance that we came across each other. However, I would not have changed anything. We may never cross paths again. But I take you home in my heart. And you too, old man," he said looking at Wilf. "We too have endured so much. Go with them. Live out your days with the sun on your back and your kin close by."

"I give you my thanks," Wilf replied. "You do the same. Go and find your family and hold them close. We will do the same. Maybe one day we will meet again, under a different sky." An icy wind blew along the cave, buffeting the flames. They flickered and waned before returning to normal, the group around them feeling the change in temperature.

"A storm is coming," Kaiden said standing up as another torrent of wind enveloped them. "I will find some more firewood to add to the flame. We cannot lose that. Not tonight."

"I'll come with you," Bea said, dusting her backside as she stood up.

"Don't go too far. Remember, there is something out there looking for us," Wilf said between puffs.

"We'll not leave the cave. Alain could be out there. I'm not taking any chances."

"Take this," Wilf said, tossing the wooden cross over the flames. "If it glows, he's close by. Pray to your gods it does not."

"Thanks," Bea said, taking her man by the arm. They walked off into the cave, becoming lost in the gloom after a dozen steps. The others remained, moving closer to the fire. Hoping that the doorway would open soon.

"What happened after we were taken, Jake?" Katherine asked, trying to break the cloying silence.

"I got back home with Wilf to find Dad there alone. He explained what had happened. We grabbed supplies and drove north the next evening. We found Eddie and another vampire at the edge of the forest. We destroyed them, before finding Father Stephen a bit further on. You know the rest, babe."

"Poor Father Stephen. I wonder what happened to him?"

"Honestly. I think he must have died. He was already turning when we found him. He'd been force-fed Elias' blood. I only hope that Elias is also dead. If he's not, he will find us again one day."

"We will be ready if he shows his face again," Wilf replied. "I'll skewer that monster myself if he tries to hurt any of you." Jake nodded, knowing that the old man would lay his life on the line willingly to protect them.

Footsteps echoed through the cave as the giant returned, two pieces of driftwood in his hands. "Here," he said, snapping the dried wood into smaller pieces, adding them to the dying flames. "There is more at the entrance. We'll be back shortly."

Kaiden walked out of the cave, the wind battering him. Bea stood on the other side of the track, sheltered by two giant boulders. "Come on. We need to be quick," she said, unclipping her dungarees. They fell to the floor, Bea stepping out of them clumsily. She stood there in a dirty grey vest and underwear.

"It won't take long," Kaiden said, grabbing hold of Bea. He lifted her off the ground, pushing against the wet rocks. With his other hand, he unclipped his leggings, letting them slip to his ankles. The wooden cross lay a few feet away, forgotten for the moment.

Bea felt his hardness, her eyes widening. "I take it you're pleased to see me," she said before kissing him full on the mouth.

"I've missed you," Kaiden said as Bea wrapped her legs around him. He entered her, causing a gasp to escape her lips. Her arms wrapped themselves around his neck as she flung her head back, eyes closing in ecstasy as he bucked and pushed against her. Their movements matched the howling storm around them, their moans and grunts lost to the wind.

"Oww!" she exclaimed as she bumped her head off a sharp ledge of rock.

"What is wrong? Am I being too rough?" Kaiden said breathlessly.

"No, lover. I banged my head. Lie down. Let me get on top of you."

He smiled, falling to the floor quickly. "Quickly. They will be wondering where we have gotten to."

"It won't take long," she said as she straddled his huge body. She sank on top of him, slowly working his length inside her. "Oh, fuck me, babe. That's good. That's really fucking deep." She began gyrating her hips, then shifting position slightly to get into a rhythm. Bea placed her hands in Kaiden's flat stomach, lifting herself off his midriff then sinking down again.

"That is good," he said as he grabbed at her breasts, squeezing them roughly through the material of her top.

"Careful, lover," she breathed as she began to climb to her own summit. "I'm getting close. Are you?"

"Yes," he said as her movements became more urgent. Kaiden closed his eyes as animalistic sensation began coursing through his body. He was climbing ever higher, about to tumble into the void.

Bea felt him stiffen, her own muscles closing around him as the orgasm wracked her body. "Oh, baby! Kaiden. Oh my god, Kaiden! I'm-"

The giant was lost in the moment, his orgasm matching hers. He felt spatters of rain land on his upturned face, wiping them away with the back of his hand.

His eyes opened, not quite in focus. His large hand was still in front of his face as his sight sharpened. *Huh*, he thought, the back of his hand streaked in blood. Kaiden looked past his hand towards Bea who had ceased her movements. His brain didn't comprehend what his eyes were telling him for a few seconds. Bea was still on top of him. Most of her at least. Her head was a few feet to the left, a large bony fist holding it by its blonde hair.

"You betrayed Alain," the vampire said, his eyes burning yellow in the darkness.

Kaiden tried to mouth words that were locked in his throat. He looked at his woman, a glazed expression settling over her face. Her tongue lolled out of the side of her mouth as blood dripped from the base of her skull. Her now still body fell to one side, landing on the wet earth. "You bastard!" Kaiden yelled, scrambling to his feet. His leggings caught as he tried to advance on the vampire, sending him falling forward. Alain dropped the head, swatting the giant across the pathway. He landed in a heap, the wind knocked from his lungs. As he tried to pull his leggings up, large hands lifted him from the ground, smashing him into the rocks behind him. Stars burst through Kaiden's vision at the impact, all but knocking him unconscious. He hung in Alain's grip, the world around him growing dark.

"I hope she was worth it," the vampire hissed. "Go and find her, if you can." Kaiden tried to lift his head, his strength failing him. Bony fingers wrapped themselves around his huge neck, snapping it to one side. His life ended, as it was just about to begin. Alain discarding his body as footsteps echoed down the cave.

"JESUS," Jake yelled as he broke out of the cave. He saw Bea's headless body across the pathway, blood oozing from the ragged stump of her neck, coating the rocks. He looked left, seeing the giant lay on his side, his head at an awkward angle.

"You are Jake. Killer of vampires. I am Alain. Brother of Virdelas. You murdered my kin." Jake looked at the figure in front of him, his eyes widening. Alain smiled, baring his curved canines. They were grey and uneven, coated in blood.

"Get back," Wilf hollered, his cross coming to bear. It glowed in his fist, causing the vampire to fall back, hissing and cursing.

"Is that the best you have to offer, old man?" Alain goaded, his eyes boring into Wilf's. The others came out of the cave, stopping short when they saw the carnage in front of them. Carrie locked eyes with Alain, her expression becoming neutral. He smiled at her as she approached him, feet dragging across the stones.

"Get away, Carrie," Katherine shouted as she watched the woman walk towards the vampire. Alain swiped his ragged nails across her throat, a fine crimson mist covering his bluish skin.

A collective scream rang down the mountainside as the others saw Carrie fall to her knees. She toppled forward onto the wet earth, becoming still. Katherine raced back into the cave, shouting over her shoulder. "We need another cross, weapons too. Hold him there!"

Alain laughed, looking at the demon in front of him. "What is one of your kind doing travelling with menfolk? You betray your kin."

"You have already killed three," Tamatan said, eyes blazing. "If you touch the others I will end your dark days on this plane."

Katherine came out of the cave, cross held aloft. Alain fell back further, Tamatan wincing as two crosses burned close by. "Keep away. Or I will kill you myself," Katherine commanded.

"Stupid wench. Do you think that such fancies will put an end to Alain? I have lived a thousand lifetimes, putting pay to countless humans. What makes you think you are any different?"

Katherine rushed him, swatting his face with the burning cross. Alain screamed, his bluish skin puckering and hissing. The vampire had not noticed Wilf approach from the rear, his cross ready to strike. "We are different," he said as he pressed his cross into Alain's face. Flames burst from the wood, engulfing the vampires head. He fell back, pushing Wilf to the floor with a flailing arm, what little hair he had was singed to one side of his head. The others watched in frozen fascination as the monster propelled himself away from them down the mountain path, smoke and flames trailing in his wake.

Katherine ran to her uncle, falling to her knees. "Are you hurt?"

Wilf turned over on to his back, wincing. "My arm," he said through gritted teeth.

Jake and Tamatan were there a few seconds later, concern on their faces. The demon felt the injured limb, curses erupting from Wilf's mouth. "It is broken. Let us get you back into the cave. The doorway will open soon." As gently as they could, they lifted Wilf to his feet, shepherding him back to the darkened opening.

Jake looked at the fallen, his eyes brimming with tears. "I'm so sorry," he said, more to himself than the others.

"We need to get out of this place. Too many people have died here," Katherine said, her own tears falling freely. The light from the fire guided them back to the far end of the cave, the howling storm behind them lessening with every step.

"Sit down here, Wilf," Jake said, easing the older man down. He carefully rolled up the man's sleeve, looking for the injury. As he touched the upper arm, Wilf grunted, sweat peppering his brow.

"It's broken. Damn vampire!"

"It's not too serious," Jake said. "We can make a sling, which will support it. Once we get back home, we can get you some help."

"Don't fret, Jake. I've broken my other arm before. It healed well enough with a splint and some rest."

"Be that as it may, Uncle. But that was a hundred seasons or more in the past. You're older now. You need to make sure this heals."

"Stop fussing, Kath," Wilf said, a half smile on his grizzled face. Secretly, he loved the concern, although he'd never show it. "The Finglers will see to it. How much longer until that blasted door opens?"

"The time is fast approaching," Tamatan said. "We need to be on our guard though. The monster has departed, for now. He may return, with others. He too knows that we are trying to pass through. The crosses will help repel them if they decide to attack."

"Okay," Jake said, holding the cross in his hand. He saw the demon shy away from it slightly. "Sorry. I only thought that crucifixes worked on vampires?"

"They don't hurt me," the demon said. "It's more like a nasty itch that Tamatan cannot scratch. I will be fine. The cross is a symbol of light. It repels the darkness. I am from that darkness."

"I understand. Let's hope we can get rid of them soon," Jake said.

"And we will, as soon as we have passed through. I hope."

Later, they sat there next to the flames, thinking about fallen friends. "I cannot believe what just happened," Katherine said. "Such a waste of life."

"I know, babe," Jake replied. "I cannot believe it either. They were good people. They didn't deserve that."

"So, that vampire is the relation of Korgan and Reggan?" Wilf said as he looked into the flames.

"Yes," Tamatan said. "An old relic, who has revenge on his mind. Kaiden was to take us back to him. It looks like we are very much wanted. Not just by the witch."

"Well, we've almost made it, my friend," Jake said. "Once we're through the doorway, we should be able to get back home. Will you go back to your land straight away?"

"Yes. As soon as we pass through. You should be safe on the other side. If you ever need me, come and find me. But I pray you do not. As much as I love you all, I want to rest easy, knowing that you are all safe."

A wind kicked up outside, blowing through the cave. The flames were battered, dying down to almost nothing as a red glow appeared next to them. "Thank god for that," Jake said as he climbed to his feet. "Let's go."

Tamatan lifted Wilf to his feet, walking with him towards the crimson hue. One by one, they passed through the doorway. Out of the darkened world. One step closer to their destinations.

Twenty-Four

Rick looked at Marlies, concern etched on his face. "Are you okay?"

"I don't know, Rick. I feel sick. And my head hurts."

He touched her forehead, alarmed as the once flawless cool skin felt like it was on fire. "Kerry. Do you have the water?"

"Hang on," she replied, rummaging through her pack. She pulled it out, handing it to him quickly.

He unscrewed the lid, offering the drink to Marlies. She took it, her hands trembling. Greedily, she chugged at the water, downing the contents in mere seconds. "Is that better," Kerry asked as a wind started to whistle through Amatoll.

"RIIIIICK," she screamed, landing flat on her back, her eyes tightly closed.

"Babe!" he cried, lifting her head frantically. "What is it? What's wrong?"

Her screams died away, echoing through the forest. Screwed up eyes suddenly relaxed, her body becoming still as a blue glow appeared before them. "Come on, babe. The doorway is opening."

Marlies laughed, causing Rick and Kerry to flinch. It was a deep laugh, crackly and dark. "We don't need to hurry ourselves along just yet," she said. Rick's eyes widened as she spoke, knowing that it was not Marlies' voice. Her eyes opened, focusing on the man above her. White eyes, milky and cunning. "You're not going anywhere."

Rick shot to his feet, clattering into a nearby tree. Kerry scrambled backwards as Marlies rose to her feet. Her skin started turning grey, her dark locks following suit as her eyes sought out her prey. "Jesus," Rick said. "What the fuck have you done to her?"

"I took her," Lenga replied as she shuffled forward towards Rick. "She tasted sweet. As will you." Before Rick could comprehend what was about to happen, his former girlfriend rushed him, gouging a ragged nail into his eye. He cried out in anguish as he tumbled to the floor, the remnants of his girlfriend toppling with him. "Now you will come to me," she hissed as she planted her dark lips over his. Rick tried in vain to escape, his bowels voiding on the forest floor.

Kerry stood there, frozen in shock as Marlies covered Rick's body with her own. She knew that Marlies was gone. She knew there and then that Rick was gone too. Taken by the old crone who'd chased them through the forest the night before. She looked at the doorway, noticing that it was starting to blink against the darkness. "It's closing," she said to herself. Without thinking twice, Kerry grabbed her pack from the forest floor and took off towards the doorway, passing through without looking back. Rick's gargled screams were slowly diminishing as Lenga ended his life. His twitching body becoming still.

She stood, wiping spittle and blood from her lips. Marlies' face had been replaced by Lenga's, the skin puckered and sallow. "Where are you?" she asked, her eyes scanning the forest around her? "Oh. You are a clever child. You took the doorway, hoping to escape back to your plane. But it will not you any good. You will not escape Lenga for long," the witch said as she shuffled off through the forest, liking her new-found vessel.

* * *

Vicky woke, looking up at her son who lay sleeping. Her mother was still asleep, her head still in the crook of her elbow. "Wake up, Jaspy," she said, her mouth dry, eyes puffy and red-rimmed. Carefully, she climbed off the bed, walking over to a small table. She filled a plastic cup with water, drinking the contents quickly. Vicky checked her watch, *almost 2am.* The rhythmic pulsing of the hospital machines told her that Jasper was still with her. Her eyes sought out her leather bag, walking over to the window-sill to retrieve it. Vicky pulled out her phone, pressing the Facebook icon on the home screen. She typed in a name in the search bar, bringing up Jake's profile page. Nothing had changed on it. She scrolled down then back to the top, looking at the picture before her. *Help me Jake,* she thought as she clicked on the message icon, her fingers tapping on the screen rapidly as the machine's beeped beside her.

* * *

They made their way up the coastal path, the sea's fury battering the coast. After a while, the foursome came across a darkened farmhouse. "They should be asleep in the barn," Wilf said cradling his arm.

"What about the people at the farm? We must tell them that Carrie is not coming back," Katherine said.

"That is not wise," Tamatan said. "They may suspect foul play is at hand. I would simply slip away south with your companions. It's better that way."

Jake nodded. "It's not really a nice thing to do. But I agree. We've come this far, be a shame to get involved in a fight with the locals." He looked at the demon and smiled. "Is this where we say our goodbyes?"

"It is, Jake. A little piece of you will travel with me. A little piece of all of you. I will find my kin and live out my days, safe in the knowledge that you all made it home safe. I give thanks to you all." Before Jake could reply, Tamatan embraced him.

Jake returned the embrace, his eyes filling with tears. "Safe travels, my friend. I will always know that *Spring Heeled Jack* was actually a good person. Although, I'll never tell anyone. I would be arrested."

The demon pulled away, silvery tears sliding down his green skin. "Thank you, Jake. And thank you too Wilf and Katherine. Go in peace," he said, his eyes shining green in the darkness.

The older man clapped Tamatan on the shoulder. "Take the safe path, my friend. We endured much but have won through."

Katherine kissed him on the cheek, drawing a huge smile from the demon. His eyes lit up, casting a greenish glow across her face. "Go and find them, Tamatan. We will carry you in our hearts too."

"I will miss my friends," he said turning towards the darkened horizon. "Farewell."

Katherine snuggled into Jake as the demon trotted off, becoming swallowed by the night a few seconds later. "I will miss him," she said.

"I will too. I owe him my life," Jake replied.

"Do you think he will make it home?"

"Yeah. He's a wily old thing. If anyone can do it, he can." They turned towards the barn, walking slowly. Their footsteps ponderous and heavy. Wilf cradled his damaged arm, his mind in a different place. He was in Cornwall, walking along a coastal path with the Atlantic Ocean crashing below him.

Book II – The Watcher

Chapter Twenty-Five

Two months later
Cornwall

Jake pulled onto the drive, the warm sunny weather welcoming them home. They climbed out of the 4x4, stretching their collective backs. Katherine held Alicia close to her body, the child wriggling playfully. "We're home again, little one," she said, kissing her curls. "This time, we're here to stay."

"I'll drink to that," Jake said as he unlocked the front door. He put his shoulder to the door, pushing all the unopened mail across the hallway. He looked at the others. "Come on in."

A few minutes later, they were sat at the kitchen table as Jake emptied litres of sour milk into the sink. "We need to go to the shops, Jake," Katherine said. "Alicia will need nappies and wipes. Milk too. She needs that badly. I have none of my own to give her."

"I'll pop down to the shop. It should be open. I'll grab some milk and wipes. There should still be nappies upstairs. Is there anything else I should get?"

"Bread. Sausages. I'm really hungry," Katherine said as she tickled her daughter, drawing giggles from the infant on her knee.

"Okay. Wilf, anything for you?"

The older man looked at Jake and smiled. "Do you have any pipe-weed?"

Jake thought about it for a second. "They will have some, but no pipes. Not to worry. I'll buy you a pack of fags to keep you going. We can go shopping later, or even tomorrow, depending on how we feel. We will find you a good pipe."

"Thank you, Jake," Wilf said. He stood up, taking Alicia from Katherine's embrace. "Come to Grandpapa little on. He needs a' loving." The infant snuggled into her grandfather, burying her face in his neck, drawing a beaming smile from Wilf.

"I won't be a tick." He bent and kissed Katherine full on the lips before heading out of the kitchen door. Before Katherine could speak, the door opened again. Jake hurried in, pulling his mobile phone out of his jacket pocket. "Better charge this up. I'll check it when I get back," he said as he plugged it into a charging cable next to the toaster. He kissed Katherine again, drawing a low moan from her.

"Don't be long," she said breathlessly. He smiled, knowing what she meant. The kitchen door closed with a click, Jake walking down the driveway before turning left towards the high street. His stride once again, looping and carefree.

"What's that noise?" Wilf said as he looked around the kitchen.

"It's Jake's phone. He's been gone for a while. I am sure lots of people have been trying to get in touch with him. There will be many things ahead that he will have to sort out. Doug's house for one. I have no clue as to how he will explain that?"

Wilf nodded, not fully understanding the implications ahead. All he knew, was that they were safe. His villagers were safe. Shocked and alarmed at his departure, but safe. He would return one day, to check on them all. He cleared the memory from his mind, banishing the vision of crying friends and long goodbyes. His arm was almost back to normal too, save the odd twinge here and there. Zeebu and Zeeba had fixed it as soon as he'd hobbled into the darkened barn a few months before, placing it in a splint of wood and Orga skin. He looked at Katherine as he held his granddaughter. "I am sure he will put everything back in place."

"I know he will," she replied. "He will have to contact his brother to tell him the sad news of Doug's passing."

"Rather him than me," Wilf said as he peered out of the kitchen window, his eyes drinking in his new surroundings. His new world.

* * *

The front doorbell chimed as Vicky sat in her kitchen, her laptop staring back at her. She pushed back the chair, walking absently towards the front of the cottage. Daylight permeated in through the glass, bathing the quiet hallway in light. She never noticed it though as she opened the door. Two women stood on the doorstep, smiling back at her. They looked around the thirty mark both with dark, shoulder-length hair. The taller of the two wore black-rimmed spectacles. Both had kind faces, lightly tanned. "Mrs Evans?" the taller one said. Vicky could detect a Scottish accent, the voice calm and friendly.

"Yes," she replied, her monotone voice flat and uninspired.

"We're here to see Jasper," she replied. "How is he settling in?"

"There has been no change since he arrived this morning. But that's to be expected right?"

"I suppose so. But don't feel too despondent. "I'm Jennifer and this is Ashley," she said tilting her head towards her colleague.

"Hello, Mrs Evans. We will take good care of Jasper. We're here to take some of the burden off you."

"Well, I suppose you'd better come in. Would you like a cup of tea or coffee?"

"Sounds grand," Jennifer said. Ashley nodded readily too as Vicky moved aside to let them into the hallway.

A few minutes later, they were all settled around the table, sipping coffee. The summer rays cast shafts of lights across the kitchen, lightening the mood. Vicky decided to break the cloying silence. "So, what happens now?"

"We'll show you what you should be doing," Ashley said as she placed her mug down on the table-top. "We'll pay you regular visits to monitor Jasper too. Try to keep an open mind, Mrs Evans."

"Vicky," she replied, trying to smile.

"Okay. Vicky, it is then."

"We'll show you how to fit the nasogastric tube," Jennifer said. "We'll start him off with that. He's on a drip at the moment, right?"

"Yes," Vicky said as the room started to swim.

Jennifer sensed this, placing her hand over the other woman's. "Try not to get too overwhelmed. This is a standard procedure. If there is no change after six weeks, we will try another option to keep him artificially hydrated."

"Do you think he will come out of his coma?"

"It's hard to say," Ashley said. "We still don't fully understand comas. They are very unpredictable. He could wake up in an hour, a week, a year. We just need to make sure that he is in good shape when he does. Try to stay positive, Vicky," Ashley said, smiling at the other woman.

"I can't say that it will be easy. He's my little boy. I lost the rest of my family a few months ago in a car accident. Jasper is all I have left." Her resolve crumbled as she started to weep openly.

Jennifer placed her mug on the table, moving around the table to comfort Vicky. "Oh, how awful. We'll do all we can to make sure that Jasper wakes up. But it's out of our hands, for now, Mrs Evans. I mean, Vicky."

Vicky looked up at the nurse, her face streaked with tears. "Thank you. Just having you here to help means so much. I do not know what I would do otherwise."

"Don't mention it," the Scottish woman replied warmly. "It's what we do."

A few minutes later, the three women entered the bedroom, shafts of sunlight shining in through the open windows. Jasper lay in his bed, his chest rising and falling gently. A tube ran from his arm to a clear plastic bag attached to a machine. On the other side of the bed, a monitor beeped gently. Two wires trailed from it, attaching sensors to the sleeping child. The warm summer breeze invaded the room, gently ruffling Jasper's dark locks. He looked peaceful, ready to wake from his slumber at any moment.

"Okay," Jennifer said opening her bag. "We'll remove the drip, then show you how to fit the nasogastric tube. It's not terribly difficult, Vicky." She nodded a silent reply, her eyes transfixed on her son. She heard the instructions. Phrases like, *measure the tube from the tip of the nose to the ear* and *apply surgical tape to secure it,* were understood with nodded replies. She could feel an overwhelming surge of panic settle over her, unsure of how she would cope with the new turn of events that had changed the course of their lives. "Are you okay, Ashley?" Jennifer said looking at her colleague.

"I think so," she replied. "I just feel a bit warm." Ashley was about to say something else when a trickle of blood appeared from her nostril. "What the?" she replied before placing her hand to her face.

"Are you sure you're okay?" Jennifer said.

"Not sure. I feel a bit dizzy."

Vicky headed out of the room, returning a few seconds later with sheets of toilet paper. "Here you go. Use this."

"Thank you," was Ashley muffled reply as she sat on the edge of the bed, tilting her head back. She pressed the tissue to her nose with one hand, pinching the bridge of her nose with the other.

The other women looked at her, concern on their faces as a far-off drone echoed through the Lickey Hills beyond the window. "Do you want a glass of juice?" Vicky said, unsure of what to do.

"It's okay," Ashley replied as she removed the tissue. It was covered in bright red blood, her lower face smeared in crimson. "Can I use your bathroom to clean up?"

"Of course. It's at the end of the landing. Help yourself."

The nurse left the room, leaving Vicky and Jennifer lost for words for a moment. "Sorry about that," the Scottish women said as she turned towards the bed. "That's never happened to her before."

"It's okay. I get nosebleeds from time to time. Normally when the weather changes."

The nurse nodded, looking at Jasper's sleeping form. "Are you okay with everything we've explained?"

"I think so," Vicky replied. "When will you be back next?"

"A couple of days. We'll let you get into a bit routine. I was told that you are a stay-at-home mum. Is that right?"

"Yes. I have not worked since losing my family a few months ago. I may work in the future, although it will probably be from home."

"Well that's good," Jennifer replied. "You'll be able to keep a close eye on the wee man. I'll fit the tube now. You can see how I do it. Is that okay?"

"Sure," Vicky said as Ashley walked back into the bedroom. One of her nostrils had a plug of tissue inserted into it, hanging down towards her mouth.

"It's stopped. Sorry about that, Mrs Evans. It's never happened before."

"Why don't you go and pop the kettle on, Ash. We'll be down in a few minutes."

A few minutes later a tube ran from Jasper's nose to a clear bag, suspended above him on a chrome stand. They left the room, the door hanging ajar a few inches. A slither of yellow mist escaped the boy's nose, drifting aimlessly down the duvet. Ornaments on the nearby chest of drawers vibrated, moving a few inches across the whitened top. Pictures hanging from the walls rattled nervously as the room began to darken, the summer sun falling behind oncoming clouds. A few words came from the boy's mouth, barely audible. "Help me, Mummy," he said, tears forming at the corners of his closed eyes.

* * *

Alana woke, her eyes fluttering open slowly. She looked across the cave, the low torches barely lighting the dank cavern. "Jasper. Are you there?"

"Yes, Alana. I am," he replied.

Yellow mist swarmed around the cave, Virdelas moving across the cold stone floor. He moved quickly at the sound of the noise, covering Alana and Jasper in his form. "There is no need for words," Alain said. "You both need to save your strength. We have much to do."

Alana suddenly felt sleepy, her eyes becoming leaden. "What plan are you hatching?"

"All in good time, my white witch. We have roads to travel and friends to meet. Firstly, we will find the other witch. For she has much to answer. But let us not converse about such things. I must leave you soon. I have to secure us a means of carriage. I have paths to cross and places to see before we can begin our hunt."

"Hunt?" the witch said, becoming sleepier as the mist swirled around her. She looked at the vampire, her eyes locked on his grotesque features. One side of his face was scarred and puckered, his white wispy hair all but gone. It gave his head a lop-sided appearance.

"Yes. Virdelas has grown stronger. I have been bringing him provisions, as you can see." Husks littered the cave floor. Desiccated corpses of unfortunate travellers and wanderers lay strewn in the darkness. "He is almost ready to take a vessel. And I have someone in mind. I can see him now in my mind's eye. He is far away, but such trifles do not trouble me. He will be here soon enough."

Alana drifted off into the blackness of sleep, wondering what plans lay afoot. And what unfortunate soul was about to fall under the vampire's spell.

* * *

"Go and sit down in the lounge and check your phone, Jake. I will make you a mug of coffee and put the sausages on. Uncle looks quite happy with Alicia on his lap."

Jake smiled at Katherine as he unplugged the handset. It was a quarter charged, which would be enough for him to check it. "Thanks, babe," he said, putting the device in his pocket. He ruffled Alicia's hair as he walked past her, drawing a smile from the infant. Jake stopped in the doorway, looking at the older man. "If you're going to live here, Wilf, we need to get you new clothes and sort out that hair of yours?"

"What's wrong with my hair?" Wilf replied, his face dropping slightly.

"It's a bit long. Not many people around here have hair like that. You need to blend into your surroundings a bit. There is a barber shop in the village. A really good one too. They do hot towel shaves. We can get you a new wardrobe and a new look."

"I agree, Uncle," Katherine said. "You're not in Shetland now. You're in Cornwall. You need to look like one of the locals."

"I am in your hands. Whatever you think, I will do."

"Good," Katherine said, walking over to the counter. She began unpacking food as Jake walked into the lounge, flopping down on the settee. He got comfortable, swiping the screen of his phone. He had twelve answerphone messages and almost two hundred missed calls. He dialled his answerphone as a bin lorry ambled its way past the front window, men in brightly coloured vests following behind it.

Twenty minutes later, his cup empty, Jake walked back into the kitchen. The smell was intoxicating. Sausages sizzled gently in a large black pan next to a saucepan of bubbling plum tomatoes. Katherine was busy with plates and cutlery, busying herself in her favourite space. She looked up at him as slices of bread were laid out on a large chopping board. "All done?"

"Kinda. The phone needs more charge though. I've had several messages from Rick, asking me to call him immediately. I did so, but it went straight through to answerphone. I've left him a message. I'm sure he'll pick it up at some point. Apart from that, I've had lots of missed calls. Clients mainly. Although, I had a few from Kerry too. She's not left any messages though."

"Well, I hope Rick calls you back. He needs to know."

"I know, babe. I have the story all set out in my head. He's going to be devastated though."

"I know he will. But he will get over it in time. He has his woman with him. She will help bring him through this."

"I know, Kath. And I know we're not that close anymore, but I really feel for him. He's lost both his parents within a few months of each other."

"Try not to dwell on such things just yet. You need to eat. We all do, which reminds me, madam is due a feed. Could you take over while I take her upstairs with her milk?"

"Okay, babe. What are we having?"

"Sausages and tomato on toast."

"I can't think of anything better right now. You go and feed her, and I'll give you a shout when it's ready."

"Thanks, babe. I may as well give her a quick bath and put a proper nappy on her. Madam is a little bit ripe."

Jake chuckled. "I think we all are. I cannot wait to have a hot shower and a shave," he said, rubbing his new-found beard. "I'll turn the stove down. Take your time, babe."

"Come on, stinky-bear," Katherine said, holding out her arms. "Let's go and get you presentable once more." The infant smiled, relinquishing her hold on Wilf. They headed upstairs, muted footsteps filtering through the kitchen ceiling as Wilf and Jake smiled at each other.

"When will you speak to your kin?" Wilf said.

"As soon as he calls back. It's Thursday, so he's probably at work."

"Where does he live?"

"In Hamburg, Germany. It's another country. A few hours away from here."

"Oh," Wilf replied, looking out of the window.

"Are you hungry?"

"Famished."

"I'll do your sandwich now if you like?"

"Best thing I've heard today," Wilf replied enthusiastically.

Later, their bellies full, Jake scooped his keys from the kitchen window. "Gonna pop out. Are you guys okay here for a bit?"

"I think so," Katherine said. Alicia will be awake soon. Where are you going?"

"I'm going to pop round to Dad's house. I suppose I should really. Then I'll pop to Tesco to grab a few bit and bobs."

"Okay, babe. We'll be alright. Go and do what needs doing."

He bent down and kissed Katherine before heading for the kitchen door. "Love you."

"Love you too, Jake. Don't get into any trouble."

"I've had enough trouble to last me two lifetimes," he said grinning. He walked down the driveway, climbing into his 4x4. A few minutes later, he was pulling up outside his parent's house. He was pleased to see that someone had kept Doug's lawn neatly trimmed, making a mental note to thank his neighbours at some point. He approached the house slowly, rising emotion building within him. The house was still, as he made his way into the hallway. The small porch was littered with mail. *Something else I need to sort out*, he thought as he pushed the door closed behind him. He walked down the hallway, trying to avoid looking at the various pictures that littered the house. It was not the first time he'd done something similar. Years before, he'd walked through his own house after the loss of his wife and daughter, their smiles and love radiating through the empty family home. Now as he walked through his parent's house, he was faced with a similar dilemma. Jake walked into the kitchen, emptying mouldy milk containers into the sink and discarding blue bread into the kitchen bin. He busied himself for almost half an hour, tidying the house, trying not to let his grief overtake him. He'd lost both his parents in the matter of a few short months. Coupled with the loss of his wife, daughter and brother-in-law over the last few years. However, Jake hid the deep scars well, focusing on the here and now. The fact that he had died only a few weeks before, resurrected by a witch did not enter his mind. He was home, with his remaining loved ones. He was grateful for that. And he would make it count. *This won't be for nothing*, he thought to himself as he wheeled the large black bin to the bottom of the driveway. *I will make them happy guys. I just wish you were here to see it.*

His resolve almost crumbled when he played back the voicemail messages from Rick, knowing that a very difficult conversation was imminent. He pressed the delete button, erasing all the messages that had been left. Locking the house up, Jake climbed back into his 4x4 as the Cornish summer's morning turned into the afternoon. He pulled out of the cul-de-sac, turning towards the village high street. He was about to switch into second gear when a person on the pavement flagged him down. He buzzed down the passenger window, smiling. "Kerry, how are..." his words trailing off as he saw the look on his friend's face.

She yanked the door open, flinging herself at Jake. He returned the embrace, at a loss for words as the woman in his arms began to cry uncontrollably. "Oh, thank God you are back!"

"We just got back this morning."

"I have got stuff to tell you, Jake. Lots of stuff. Can we park somewhere and talk?"

"Sure." He performed a quick three-point-turn, heading back towards his house. At the end of his road, he steered left towards the imposing hotel on the headland. Parking the 4x4 a few hundred yards away. Cutting the engine, he followed Kerry out of the car towards a collection of boulders near to the cliffs. He noted the bedraggled look of the young woman, noticing that she had lost weight. Dark smudges lined her eyes, her complexion sallow.

"What happened to you?" she asked, fidgeting nervously.

Jake sat on one of the boulders, a resident of the peninsula since before time began. "Well. Where do I begin? Elias snatched Alicia and Katherine a few months ago."

"Oh, Shit! I knew something had happened."

"Well, the shit kinda hit the fan. I went back through the doorway with Dad and Wilf." Jake paused, composing himself. "Dad died. Father Stephen did too. Well, at least I think he did."

"I'm so sorry, Jake. Really, I am. Your Dad was so nice. I don't know what else to say?" Tears started welling up in Kerry's eyes. She wiped them away, sniffling.

"Thanks. That happened not long after we went through. I was stuck there for a while. Katherine and Wilf found me, bringing back through another doorway to their world. We spent some time there, mainly to recover. Then we set off home a few days ago."

"Well, I am so glad to see you. But I also have news."

"What's happened?"

"I'd say sit down, but you already are. A few weeks after you vanished, I met up with your brother and Marlies."

Jake's face changed, the surprise clear to see. "Where? Here?"

"Yes. They came looking for you both as they couldn't get hold of you. I told them everything, which freaked them out."

"Shit," Jake said, taken aback. "Rick's left me countless messages. I phoned him back earlier and left him one to let him know I am home. He'll probably call me later."

"I don't know how to say this, Jake, so I will just say it." She looked at the grass, readying herself before looking at him. "They are both dead."

"What?" Jake said shocked to his core. "No. Please tell me this isn't happening?" He shook his head, tears forming in his eyes.

Kerry reached across the rock, squeezing his hand. "I am so sorry, Jake. Truly sorry."

Jake sat there, staring out at the Atlantic as the news tried to sink itself in. He could not compute the news that he'd just heard. "How?" He started pacing in front of her as she began.

"After I told them what had been happening, they flew home to Germany. But we kept in touch. I think they were trying to come to terms with what I'd told them. Anyway, they came back a few weeks later, and the three of us went through the doorway together."

"What!"

"They insisted. I think they needed to see it for themselves. When we passed through we were attacked by something."

"Something? A vampire?"

"No. She looked like an old witch. Her name was Lenga. We managed to escape at first, hiding out in an abandoned village. The next night, we made our way back. That's when she attacked again. She killed them both. I managed to escape, running through the doorway. I had to phone my Dad, who came and got me. I had to make up a story, telling him I had been to a party in Birmingham and had been abandoned by my friends."

"Jesus! This just gets worse. Poor Rick and Marlies. People back in Germany will be asking questions. I am surprised no one has contacted me yet." He sat down, the news feeling surreal to him.

"She said she wanted you, Jake."

"The witch?" Kerry nodded. "Tamatan said that she would hunt us down. In the world where we got stuck, we were chased by a pack of lunatics. We got away though. But Tamatan said that this witch was after us."

"Well, I don't know what happened to her, Jake. She was also able to go through the doorway after it closes. I have replayed the scenes over and over in my head. I've been scared shitless, thinking that she'll turn up here somehow."

"I'm sure that won't happen. Although, I said that about Elias. This kinda changes things, Kerry."

"Why?"

"Because there is someone out there who wants to cause me harm. And that someone has already killed my brother and his girlfriend."

"So, what are you going to do? Go after her?"

"Fuck that! I barely made it out alive last time. In fact, I died whilst I was there. Another witch, called Alana brought me back to life."

"That's sick. You actually died?" Kerry suddenly appeared animated. "Did you see a white light? Or is it a white tunnel?"

"I don't remember. All I know is that I was sick one minute, cured the next."

"That's unbelievable, Jake."

"I know. I'm still coming to terms with it. The bite marks that I had on my leg have gone now. I am back to normal. I owe that witch my life."

"It sounds like you have been through hell?"

Jake sighed, his body suddenly feeling weary. "Yes, we have. I just hope it's all over now? Poor Rick and Marlies. They did not deserve that. Fuck!" He checked his watch. "I need to run a few errands. Then I'll head home and tell the others the news."

"Okay, Jake. I am so sorry for having to tell you all this."

He walked over to Kerry, placing his hand on her shoulder. "It's okay, Kerry. Thank you for letting me know. I am glad you managed to make it home. I just wish that you'd all made it."

"Me too," she said, standing up. "You know where I am if you need me."

"Cheers," he said as he fished his keys out of his pocket. "I will be in touch." They hugged briefly, the contact awkward and stilted. Jake climbed into his 4x4, watching as Kerry headed off down the road. *I'm so sorry Rick. I'm so sorry I got you involved in all this*, he thought as he gunned the ignition, pulling away from the hotel as dark clouds formed on the western horizon.

Twenty-Six

A few hours later, Jake pulled up onto his driveways as the first spots of rain began to fall. The summer's afternoon had darkened, a warm breeze blowing in from the sea. *Looks like thunder*, he thought as he pressed the key fob for his Nissan. It beeped twice as he headed towards the kitchen door, two shopping bags in his other hand. He entered the kitchen, heads turning as he did so.

"Hi, babe. Did you get everything?" Katherine said.

"Yeah." He placed the bags on the counter as the woman sauntered over to him, wrapping her arms around his neck. She kissed him longingly on the lips, the world around them falling away into the ether.

A cough from behind them broke their embrace. "Did you manage to find me a pipe?" Wilf asked. "These fag things are not what I am used to."

"Hang on," Jake said, rummaging through the bag. He pulled out a smaller bag, spilling the contents onto the counter. He walked over to Wilf, handing him a carved wooden pipe and a packet of *Golden Virginia*. "Here you go. Try this."

Wilf picked up the pipe, inspecting it with his rough hands. "Now this is what I am used to. And then some. I give thanks, Jake."

"Don't mention it," He replied as Katherine filled the kettle. "I have some more news. And it's not good news either." He sat down at the kitchen table heavily, elbows resting on the wooden top.

Katherine turned around, her face blank. "What is it?"

"I met Kerry earlier. It looks like quite a lot of bad stuff happened after you were snatched."

Wilf lit his pipe, sucking on it to draw the flame onto the tobacco. He inhaled deeply, savouring the aroma that was filling his lungs. He looked at Jake expectantly. "What stuff?"

"It looks like Rick and Marlies came here after we'd gone. They went through the doorway with Kerry."

"Oh my!" Katherine said, her tea-making duties momentarily forgotten. "Are they alright?"

Jake shook his head sadly. "No. They're both dead. Kerry barely made it home alive."

She hurried across the kitchen, bending down to hug him. "I'm so sorry, babe. I don't know what to say?"

"I am sorry, Jake. He was your kin. Too many folk have perished at the hands of these monsters."

"I'll be okay. It's just a lot to take in. First Mum, then Dad, now Rick and Marlies. It's never-ending."

"Well it's over now, Jake," Katherine said, rubbing his shoulder softly. "We made it home. There have been many losses along the way. But we can begin our lives again."

"I hope you're right, babe. Something Kerry said worries me though."

"What did she tell you?" Wilf said holding his new-found pipe.

"She said they were attacked by an old witch, called Lenga. That's the same witch that sent the pack of thugs after us after the doorway blew up. She told Rick that she wants me. And that she was there for me. If she's made it that far, she could find us here. Elias did."

"This is ill news. It seems that it is not over just yet," Wilf said as he puffed on his pipe, the smoke drifting across the kitchen.

"What can we do, Jake?" Katherine asked, clearly worried.

"I honestly don't know, babe. The last thing I want to do is head north, looking for trouble. We have Alicia to think about. But at the same time, I don't want to dismiss what Kerry told me. There is someone out there that wants my head on a spike. I hope that we are far enough away. But I want to be ready in case we're not. And then there is Rick and his girlfriend to think about. Someone will be looking for them. People will know that they flew to England. At some point, the police will be knocking on our door. And then we have Dad to think about. I will have that to sort out. I know we spoke about that in Shetland. I will have to speak to the police, telling them that he's gone missing. There may be lots of attention on us very soon." He was about to speak when the doorbell rang. They all looked towards the kitchen door, the tension in the room ramping up. "Wait here. I will go and see who it is." Jake walked from the kitchen, down the hallway to the front door. He could see a silhouette behind the dappled glass, red in colour. As the door opened, Jake relaxed inside.

"Hello, Jake," his neighbour Linda said. "We've been worried. Is everything okay?"

"Hi, Linda. Sorry, I never let you know we were going away. We've had a family bereavement up north. We've been up there for a few months, helping out with the arrangements. How are you?"

"We're both fine. We've not seen your Dad either. Did he go with you?"

Shit, Jake thought, his mind clicking into overdrive to keep up. "Yes. His sister died. Quite suddenly. We all went up and stayed there. Dad was devastated, as you can imagine. He came back a few weeks ago, but we've not heard from him. Have you not seen him?"

The woman's face clouded over. "No. I've not seen him. How awful. I am very sorry to hear your sad news. Is Katherine and Alicia okay?"

"They're fine. Alicia is upstairs asleep." Jake decided to press the improvised advantage before Linda could reply. "I will pop round to Dad's house in a bit. His phone is off, and I've been trying to call him. I hope he's okay. He took the news very badly."

"I can imagine," she replied. Her usual flirty way not evident. Instead, there was concern. "Especially so soon after your Mother passed."

The words stung Jake, tears threatening to rise to the surface. "I know. He's been through the mill lately. But I am sure he'll turn up."

"I hope he does." Curiosity rose to the surface, as something occurred to her. "The last time I saw you, you were with a man with long grey hair. Not seen him before?"

"Yes, you're right," he replied as a spidery thread of a story formed in his head. "That was my uncle. It's his wife who'd died. He came down after she'd had her stroke. Uncle Wilf wanted to tell Dad in person. We all travelled back up to Birmingham together the day after. She died the day after that."

"Oh, okay, she replied, appearing a little deflated. "Well as the little one is sleeping, I'll let you get back to it. If there is anything you need, just ring the doorbell."

"Thank you, Linda," Jake replied warmly. "Say hi to Barry for me."

"I will when he's woken up from his siesta. Be seeing you," she said as she turned from the doorway, heading down the path next to the driveway.

"Take care," Jake replied. He closed the door, leaning against the wall in the hallway, breathing out heavily.

"Babe?" Katherine called from the kitchen.

He headed back down the hallway, looking at the pensive faces that greeted him in the kitchen. "All sorted. It was Linda. I told her we've been up north. I also told her that Dad's sister had died, and that we've all been in Birmingham, sorting stuff out."

"Did your Father have a sister?" she replied, not recollecting her name being mentioned.

"He did. She died of cancer a few years ago."

"What's that?" Wilf said, packing his new pipe with more tobacco.

"It's a disease that affects lots of people. It kills lots of them too."

Wilf nodded sombrely. "Sounds bad. Pray I never get it."

"I hope you don't. Anyway, I told Linda that Wilf is my Uncle. She spotted him before we headed back through the doorway. I told Linda that he came down to give us the news and that we all travelled back together. It kind of fits. So, let's stick to that okay?"

"If you think it will work, I will stick to that," Katherine replied. Wilf merely nodded as he puffed on his pipe. His niece tapped him on the shoulder, shaking her head. "Uncle, if you insist on smoking that awful thing, you'll need to do it outside. I don't want Alicia breathing that in."

"Sorry, Kath. You're right. Best do this out in the fresh air. Can I just enjoy this last one?"

"Okay. Make it count," she said, kissing him on the cheek. "I'm going to check on the little one. She should be getting up soon. Why don't you two go and get your hair cut? You both look like you need it."

"Good idea," Jake replied. We have time if we leave now. You up for it, Wilf?"

"I will go along with your plan."

"Okay. We'll swing by Dad's house. We need to give you some clothes to wear before we go shopping. You cannot walk around like that. You look like something from *Lord of the Rings*."

"Huh?" the older man replied.

"Never mind. Just trust me. We need to make you look more like one of us."

"Then let us be on our travels," he said standing up from the table.

Twenty minutes later, they were heading for the main thoroughfare as holi-daymakers ambled in all directions. The sky had cleared once more, bathing Tintagel in warm sunshine. "It's just up ahead," Jake said. "They do a hot towel shave here. It's really good. If you'll trust me, I'll tell him what to give you. Are you okay with losing the long hair?"

"If I must. Truth be told, I only had it long because I could not be bothered to keep it in check. Maybe a change is needed."

They entered the barber shop, the bell signalling their arrival. A swarthy looking man in his mid-fifties appeared from a rear doorway. He smiled at Jake and Wilf, motioning for them to take a seat. "My friend," he said, his accent dark and smooth. "I have not seen you for a long time."

"Hi. I've been up north for a while. It looks like we turned up at the right time?"

"Yes. Very quiet. I sent Mehmet home for the day. What can I do for you both?"

"You can do my Uncle Wilf first. Could you cut his hair short all over, with a hot towel shave to finish? I'll have the same please."

"But of course. Please, take a seat." He looked at Wilf, smiling. "My friend," he said, holding his arm out towards a large black leather chair. Jake watched as Wilf carefully settled into the chair. A white plastic contraption stood next to him. The man flicked a switch at the back of it, powering it up. Jake knew that it was for the shave to come, as he regularly treated himself to a pamper-ing session on Katherine's orders. He knew that the older man would enjoy it. He pulled out his phone as passers-by walked on by, draped in lightly coloured towels and wetsuits. Jake swiped the screen, checking for messages. There were none, which pleased him. Navigating through the home screen, he clicked on the Facebook icon, passing the time whilst Wilf began his transformation. It asked him to log in, drawing a frown from Jake as he tried to remember his pass-word. He'd not used the application much over the years. It was something that had passed him by since he'd lost his wife and daughter. He tried to remember the last time he'd used it as he carefully typed his password. *Probably Christ-mas time,* he thought as his passcode was accepted, taking him to the home screen. The page told him that he had numerous notifications, messages, and friend requests. He pressed friend requests first, discounting them all. He then clicked notifications, scrolling through them with little or no interest. Bored of the notifications, he clicked on messages, scrolling down to the first unread one. He skim-read them all, offering him the chance to attend a Colmers Farm reunion or the chance of an intimate hook-up with a random woman whom he'd never heard of. The last message was sent almost three months previous from someone he'd never heard of. *Vicky Evans. Doesn't ring a bell.* He clicked on the message as the sound of snipping scissors filled the shop.

Hello, Jake. You do not know me. My name is Vicky. I don't know why I'm doing this, but I am at my wit's end and I don't know who else to turn to. I live in Lickey, not far from where you once lived. I know your story. I know some of what happened to you. And I am really sorry that you have endured such hardships. I lost almost all of my family in a car accident a few months ago, so I can relate to what you've been through. I only have my youngest son left. Jasper is eight years old, and he is my life. Strange things started happening a few weeks ago. Really strange. Things that I cannot explain. I type this message from Jasper's hospital bed. We don't know quite how it happened, but he is in a coma and has been for a few days. Before that, he kept telling me of strange dreams, of two people who were lost in a far-off place. I know this sounds bonkers, but he said it was you, Jake. He even drew pictures, describing in detail where you were. He said you were lost, trying to get home. Now he is sick, and I don't know what to do. I am really sorry to have bothered you, Jake, especially if you have no idea what I am talking about. But if by some miracle you do, please contact me.

Vicky.

Jake's mouth hung open, his eyes staring off into space. *Jasper. The Watcher.* He read the message again as Wilf's grey hair littered the tiled floor. By the time his hair had been finished, Jake had re-read the message a dozen times, a sinking feeling settling over him. "It can't be," he said quietly as he clicked on Vicky's profile. There was limited information on her feed, with only a few photographs on show. He clicked on a family picture, turning the screen horizontally to get a better view. His eyes fell on five people, closely packed together. Arms draped around each-others, the scene happy and loving. He looked at each family member, working out quickly the ones sadly departed. He zoomed in on Vicky, warm smiling eyes staring back at him. *Such a shame,* he thought as he moved his finger across the screen towards the youngest family member. Happy dark eyes smiled back at him, framed by dark locks and a creamy complexion that screamed vitality. *Fucking hell! That's him. Jasper!* Even though Jake had only seen a hologram of the boy, there was no mistaking the similarity. He backed out of Vicky's profile, locking the phone and placing it in his pocket as Wilf's haircut and shave were coming to their conclusion.

"What do you think?" the older man said, looking over at Jake. The ponytail was no more, Wilf's hair closely cropped and neat. His ruddy features pink and vibrant.

On any other occasion, Jake would have tried to crack a joke towards his friend. His face was still in shock mode though, his thoughts jumbled and whirling. "Huh. Oh. Yes, you look much better, Uncle."

Wilf picked up on Jake's expression, his brow knitting together. "Jake. Is everything fine with you?"

He quickly regained his composure, smiling back at Wilf. "Sure. You look forty seasons younger."

The barber's face registered confusion as Wilf grunted. "I just wish I felt it, Son."

Forty minutes later, Jake and Wilf were walking back down the High Street. "Fancy a quick pint?" Jake said as they approached the Ye Olde Malthouse Inn.

"Pint?" Wilf asked, confused at Jake's terminology.

"Beer. Ale," he replied pointing at the white-washed building on their right.

"Lead on. Best idea you've had today," he replied, rubbing his ruddy face.

Jake led the older man in through the main door, into a cosy lounge. Exposed beams and a quarry-tiled floor transported the men back to a bygone era. Wilf immediately voiced his approval as he approached the bar. "Nice place. I could get used to spending my time here."

"I'm sure you could," Jake replied as he rested his elbows on the dark wooden bar.

A woman came through a doorway, smiling at the men as she approached. They smiled back, Wilf more so than Jake. "Hello there," she said, her voice soft and friendly. "What can I get for you?"

"Two pints of Tribute please," Jake said.

"Coming right up," she said, selecting two pint glasses from underneath the bar.

"Nice place," Wilf said as he sat down on a bar stool.

"Thank you. I've not seen you in here before," she said. "I've seen you though," she said looking at Jake.

"I'm not from these parts," Wilf said. He appraised the woman on the other side of the bar, liking her attractive face and homely manner. He guessed her roughly at a hundred and fifty seasons. Her dark hair was pulled back in a ponytail, steel-rimmed spectacles sat on top of a lightly freckled nose. She was tall too, not far off Wilf's own height. *If I were a few seasons younger,* he thought as she placed the two drinks on the bar.

"What parts are you from then?" She said curiously.

"Shetland," Wilf replied, lifting the pint to his lips. He took a swig, nodding his approval. "That's some fine ale. We may be here for a while. My name is Wilf. This is Jake."

"Hello, Wilf and Jake. I'm Joanne. Nice to meet you," she said, a half-smile tugging at her lips. "Are you down for the holidays?"

Jake interjected smoothly before the older man made a hash of things. "I live in the village. Uncle Wilf is staying with us for the summer. I thought I would show him the sights."

"Well, I hope you enjoy your stay and I hope you'll venture in again at some point."

"I think that is inevitable," Jake said eyeing Wilf suspiciously.

"Okay. That will be £6.80 please," Joanne said.

Jake handed her a note from his wallet. "Have one yourself, Joanne."

"Why thank you." she beamed. "That's very nice of you." She walked to the till, ringing up the two drinks as the men looked on. A few coins were placed into a glass jar on the counter, Joanne handing Jake the remaining change. "Here you go," she said, smiling warmly. Jake nodded before she turned and walked back down the bar, towards an archway that led to the dining area. Wilf's eyes followed her, paying close attention to her figure-hugging jeans and vest.

"You sly old goat," Jake said. "We've only been in here five minutes and you're already making a play for the landlady."

"Your land has many fine women. If I am to stay here, I may snare one for my own."

"Well we have other things to talk about first," Jake said as he pulled his phone out of his pocket. He retrieved the message that he'd read in the barbers' shop, showing Wilf the screen.

"What is this, Jake?"

"A message."

"What kind of message?" Wilf said cautiously.

"In this world, people can send messages in many different ways. A woman sent me a message a while ago, asking for help."

"Go on," the older man said as he sipped at his pint.

"Her name is Vicky. Her son is sick. He's in a coma, which is when someone falls asleep for a long time. Sometimes they don't wake up at all. They can die. Sometimes they wake up after a certain period of time and recover."

"So, what does this have to do with you?"

"Do you remember what I told you about the boy? The one Tamatan called, the watcher?"

"Uhuh," Wilf said, recollecting Jake's words back in Kungsback. A young boy from his world had been trying to guide them back to the doorway in the mountains.

"Well, her son is the watcher. I have seen a picture of him. His name is Jasper. Just before I got sick, we saw this boy in the mountains. He told us that someone was hunting us. Then he vanished. We didn't see him again." Jake reached into his shirt, twirling the stone that hung there. The cool feeling it gave off comforted him as he rubbed it between his thumb and forefinger.

"So, what are you thinking Jake? You're not thinking about trying to go back are you?"

"I'm not sure, Wilf. When we arrived home, the last thing on my mind was doorways. I want to stop all this shit. I want to get back to a normal life with Katherine, Alicia, and you. But I cannot ignore what I have just found out."

"Katherine will not like this. She found you, dead on a bed. Do you really think that is going to let you go through all this again?"

"Probably not. But I have to tell her what's going on. She's a mother. She will be able to understand the grief this woman is feeling."

"I hope you are right. Anyway, enough talk of such things. My drink is nearly empty, as is yours. Shall we have another?"

Jake smiled, clapping the older man on the back. "Okay. I'll get them in. Just try to keep your urges in check before you get us thrown out."

On cue, the woman reappeared through the archway, walking over to them. "Same again, guys?"

"Wilf will never refuse ale. Especially served by someone like yourself," the older man said smiling.

"Aww, thank you," Joanne said, blushing slightly. Jake rolled his eyes, looking towards the ceiling as the pints were pulled. A minute later, they stood with their replenished glasses on the dark wooden counter.

"Cheers," Jake said holding his drink up.

"Cheers," the older man replied, clinking his glass with Jake's. They stood in silence for a few minutes as the world passed them by. The room was almost empty, save for a youth at the far end of the bar, content with emptying his pockets into the fruit machine next to a door that led to the toilets. "I think your mind is made up, Jake. You're going back, aren't you?"

"I don't know yet. I need to speak with Katherine first."

A rumble of thunder shuddered outside as a few spots of rain clattered against the old window panes. "It looks like a storm is coming. Better hope there is not one when you get home," Wilf said as he lifted the pint to his lips.

"Fingers crossed," Jake replied, his mind already wandering.

* * *

Tamatan had made his way slowly west, traversing the grassy plains next to the gorge that split the land like a crooked spine. He'd moved freely, not meeting too many folk as he made his way south towards the vast forests in the distance. The demon had sheltered there as a rainstorm had battered the land for many days, with Tamatan seeking refuge in an abandoned village at the edge of one of the forests. When the rain had relented, he'd walked through the trees to the doorway, dismayed when he'd found two backpacks on the forest floor. It was a bad omen he'd thought, wondering what poor souls had ventured to this haunted place. He'd taken a few provisions from the discarded packs, knowing they would give him strength for the journey ahead. Wisps of smoke, yellow in colour had followed him through Amatoll until he'd reached the western fringes. From there, Tamatan had taken the road through Monks Passage, heading towards Mantz Forest. The trees of Mantz were so densely packed, that it made progress slow, even for a demon such as he was. Two weeks later, Tamatan had emerged at the western edge of the forest, where the trees kissed the grey waters of the Western Sea. Using strength that few possessed, Tamatan dragged a dead tree trunk into the cold waters, using it as his raft. And so he began the next part of his journey home, paddling and steering the log towards the Unseen Lands over the bleak horizon.

Days later, under a leaden sky, he emerged from the frigid waters, shivering and bedraggled. The wind had blown him off course, setting him down on a deserted pebbly beach. He set off, towards the collection of buildings where he knew his friend Sica lived. After a while, kicking smooth stones with his green toes, he spotted the settlement. He saw the boat that had deposited him at Mantz Forest a few months before. Sure enough, his friend was walking up the crude jetty towards the haphazard cluster of wooden buildings that lined the shoreline. The inn was quiet, the traders and sailors not ready for their breakfasts. He waved a green hand, catching the man's attention. "Hail, Sica!"

"Tamatan?" the man exclaimed in shock. "Is it really you?" He swerved off the jetty, running clumsily over the loose shale. His belly bounded before him, barely kept in check by buckle and shirt. His sweaty bald pate, nodding back and forth as he ran. They came together, pats on the back and handshakes exchanging rapidly.

"It is indeed me. I have returned. I pray that I am not too late? Where are Veltan and Jake?"

Sica's face dropped, turning to look past the settlement to the beach beyond. "They have gone, as was planned. I took them to the lagoon a moon's cycle ago. They have taken the road into the interior. I dropped them there with provisions and they were ready for the hike. I am sorry my friend. Look at you! You must be wet through the skin. Come. I have warm blankets and food to eat." He led the demon back down the jetty, towards the fishing boat that plied the waters of The Unseen Lands. They hopped on board, Sica heading below decks. Tamatan sat on the wooden bench next to a crudely constructed stove. A few ashes still glowed against the sombre day, barely able to fight off the coming chill. The sailor returned, dropping an armful of kindling into its black metal interior. He used a skillet to stir the ashes, causing them to heat the chunks of wood readily. A minute later a small fire warmed the demon's hands as he rubbed them feverishly together next to it.

"I give thanks, Sica," he said as feeling started to return to his extremities. "Floating across the sea on a log is not something that I care to try again."

"I bet," he said as he hung strips of whale meat across the skillet on large skewers. The meat hissed and spat as the flames took hold, cooking the strips quickly. A tangy aroma floated to Tamatan's nose, his taste buds springing to life. "Here," Sica said, handing him a clay jug.

The demon nodded, pulling the cork from the neck of the jug, taking a few long gulps of the strong cyder inside. "I am starting to feel better. I will need to consume more before I set off."

"Are you to follow them?" the sailor asked curiously.

"Yes. At once. I will make my way through Pagbob. I know the land well, which will give Tamatan an advantage. I know where they will be heading. If I set a good pace, I will be returned to them soon."

They conversed for a while, Tamatan swapping damp blankets for dry ones, watching as Sica hung the sodden cloth over the galley entrance. The grey skies overhead pressed down upon the land, muting all sounds. It was deathly quiet, save for the odd bird that floated above the boat, looking for scraps. With his clothes dry, Tamatan looked at the sailor. "I must be on my way. I thank you for your kindness, Sica. If I am ever to pass by this way again, I will be sure to call upon you."

"I will keep a jug of cyder ready for your return," the portly man said as he headed for the galley. He returned a moment later, handing the demon a hessian haversack. "Take this. There are cured meats and cyder inside. They should keep you going for a good while yet."

Tamatan offered his green hand, which the sailor took readily. "Go in peace, Sica. I hope you live out your days sailing the calm seas."

"That I shall," was the man's reply as he smiled one last time at his friend.

He headed up the jetty as a few folk began emerging from the wooden buildings that dotted the shoreline. He paid them no heed, walking along the pebbly beach to his cabin. It was deserted. No signs of activity could be seen as the demon checked the small interior. *Clever*, he thought, seeing that Veltan had taken anything that could be used for their journey. The fishing spears were nowhere to be seen, giving Tamatan some comfort, knowing that they were as prepared as they could be. He walked out of the cabin, looking at the sea on last time before heading inland.

His keen vision cut through the thick misty soup that lay siege to Pagbob. The trees around him were stunted, twisted, and leafy. They were closely packed, a perpetual canopy of greenery dimming the forest floor. Strange four-legged beasts occasionally crossed Tamatan's path, grazing on the shrubs that grew out of the harsh soil. As they passed by him, the forest returned to silence, only the sound of his bare feet scuffing the ground could be heard. He walked until the hidden sun finally gave up its hold on the land. Tamatan sat down next to a tree, making himself comfortable as he opened his pack. True to his word, Sica had indeed given him many provisions to aid his strength on his long journey. He sipped at the cyder, biting chunks out of the plump whale meat as he regarded the darkening forest around him. At the bottom of the pack, a hessian blanket could be seen. He plucked it out, unravelling it as he sat cross-legged on the forest floor. A dagger fell from the shawl, landing next to his foot. Tamatan tested the blade, happy that it would come in handy if needed. Although, he knew the forest well enough. *I'll not encounter too many foes in this desolate place,* he thought as he finished his meal. Suddenly weary, the demon settled down on the ground. The blackness of sleep taking him quickly.

A noise woke him, close by in the forest. He fumbled around for his dagger, his eyes glowing red in the pre-morning light. "Who is there?" he said, his voice dry and crackly.

"Put down the knife. I mean you no harm, Tamatan." A figure appeared from behind a tree. She approached slowly and silently, her impish face smiling at him.

"Nini? Is that you?"

"Indeed, it is," she replied. The imp stood in front of the demon, her tiny feet kicking bracken across the ground. She was dressed in a simple shift, dark in colour. It matched her eyes and her hair, braided down her slender back with silvery ribbons adorning it. Her small face was perfectly formed, a small nose that was slightly upturned gave off a mischievous air. As she regarded him, Nini's eyes gave off a faint sparkle, making her face shimmer. "You are heading for Marzalek?"

"Yes, I am. How do you know this?"

"Because it is the land of your kin. The imps have heard ill tales from the east. Talk of dark creatures and witches. Pray they never venture to these lands."

"I pray that too. I have ventured to those lands. I have been helping an out-lander. A man called Jake. We became lost on another plane. There is indeed darkness there. And a witch called Lenga. We managed to make it back though. I have been travelling for a long time, in hope of finding my kin once more."

"And I'm sure you will. I have seen them."

"Really? Where?"

The imp sat down, crossing her white legs. "They came from the sea. Dropped by a boat. They skirted the forest and were headed for the high plateau. That was a while ago now. Many moons have risen since then."

"So, they are safe," Tamatan said, salty tears trickling down his green face. "I cannot tell you how relieved I am to hear that."

"I know they are safe. They will be almost at Marzalek by now. Only a short journey from Katarzin. They will be waiting for you when you get there."

"Thank you, Nini. That is a weight off Tamatan's shoulders. I will set off at once."

"I hope your travels run peacefully. I may cross paths with you very soon. I will be returning to the high plateau."

"What are you doing this far from home?"

The imp considered the question, smiling at the demon. "Why the ill news of course. There are many of us out here, scouring the forests. We have not seen any cause for concern and will return home soon. My brother, Tishak is close by. I can feel him," she said pointing off into the dense fog.

"Well, I wish you safe travels. If you do encounter anything, my advice would be to run in the opposite direction. Vampires and witches are not to be trifled with."

"Nor are imps. They would be wise to remember that." Moments later, the diminutive imp vanished into the thick soup that hung over the forest. Tamatan shouldered his sack after a quick drink of cyder. He carried a dried slice of meat as he headed further inland. Climbing, ever upward towards his kin.

Days later, tired and hungry, Tamatan walked through the land of Marzalek. He could make out the tall spires of Katarzin, shimmering in the early morning sun. He walked alongside the river, known to the people of Marzalek as Obtab. He let his eyes settle on the green waters as they flowed ever upwards towards the town ahead. Despite the hunger and fatigue, Tamatan quickened his step, a feeling of hope settling over him as he thought about his kin. He chatted with travellers as he drew ever closer to Katarzin, asking if they had seen his family. The answers were not encouraging, the traders and wanderers not coming across Veltan and Jake. He pushed on until at mid-morning, he walked through the high walls of the city. Demons and imps walked around him, unaware of his presence as they went about their day. The cobbled streets were framed by tall buildings made of grey stone. Many of the structures were adorned in violet creepers that clung to the facades, framing rectangular windows and doors. Flowers grew in window boxes, adding vibrant colours to the streets. His worries and concerns started ebbing away as a heady aroma filled his lungs. His bare feet brushed the cobbles as he turned into a side street off the main plaza, the demon's sense of direction taking him towards his goal. At the end of the passageway, he came to a squat building with twin red spires on top. The tiles of the roof glistened in the morning sunlight, casting its glow across the dim walkway. Tamatan rapped at the green wooden door, standing back a few paces, his hands wringing behind him in anticipation. The door opened, a figure emerging from the dark interior. "Tama? Is that really you?"

"Hello, Mama," Tamatan said, tears falling freely. He rushed forward, embracing the violet figure on the doorstep. She was dressed in white robes that fell to her feet. Her bare arms littered with markings. "I am home."

She pulled away, holding her son at arm's length. "How many moons has it been?" her red eyes blazed with glee, salty tears sliding down her magenta skin.

"Too many, Mama. I have much to tell you."

"To tell us. There are others waiting for you. Come."

Bikabak led her son inside, walking through a room that had creepers hanging from the dark beams that ran its length. A small window on the far wall, let the sun spill across the stone floor. It was just as he remembered it. A large stove sat on the other wall, black utensils hanging from its door. "Through here," she said, drawing Tamatan's eyes away from the welcoming sight. Through a narrow archway, Bikabak stood next to the stone wall, motioning with her hand. "Look who is home."

Veltan looked up from the straw mat, her eyes widening. "Tamatan!" Before he could answer, his sister was across the room, flinging herself into his arms. No words could be found by either of them as they embraced. Tears were all that was needed.

"Baba," Jake said from his mat, crawling over clumsily towards his parents.

Tamatan looked down, his face streaked with tears. "Come to Papa little one." He reached down, lifting the infant into his arms. Jake nuzzled his neck, wrapping chubby green arms around his father. They stood there for a long time, kissing and hugging as Bikabak watched on, tears falling from her ageing eyes. Tamatan played with his son's green horns that were sprouting from his skull, liking the furry tips. It drew giggles from the infant, who squealed with glee. "So big you have grown."

"He has, my love," Veltan purred. "Where have you been? You didn't come back."

"Why don't I prepare us some food," their mother said. "I am sure you are hungry, Tama?"

"I am, Mama."

She held out her arms. "Come to Nana, little one," she said, taking Jake into the other room. Tamatan and Veltan followed, watching as Bikabak placed the boy into a wooden pen, lined with furs. She handed him a piece of green fruit from the large table, Jake attacking it with glee. "Sit down you two. I will warm the water and chop some bread. It's fresh from the oven."

They pulled out chairs, sitting across the table from each other. Veltan looked at her brother, reaching across the table to hold his hands. "So, tell us your tale?"

"Where do I start?"

"The beginning is always a good place," Veltan replied, her face mirthful and inquisitive.

"Sica took me across the waters to the forest. I did indeed encounter vampires. They had taken Jake's kin for their own. They planned to turn them. We became engaged in a fracas, which led us through another doorway, to a world of dark chaos. Jake's kin did indeed escape, but Jake and I became trapped there."

Bikabak, stirred a pot on the stove, looking over at her son as he relayed his story. "Did Jake's kin make it to safety?"

"Yes, Mama. They were taken by their elder, back to their home. Jake and I had to flee the land where we had become stuck. A dark witch, who must be in cahoots with the vampires, sent a pack of her goons after us. But Tamatan and Jake were clever. We found help along the way, who took us high into the mountains, towards another doorway. The vampires eventually found us, but we won through. We lost friends along the way, Mama. It was a heavy price to pay. Good folk, who were just trying to help, perished at their hands. But the doorway was our solace. I left Jake and his kin and began to travel home. There is still darkness in that land. One that may seek them out. One that may seek me out too."

"You are far from harm's way here," Veltan said. "Whoever comes looking for you will have their hands full in Katarzin."

"Veltan told me of the vampires of which you speak. They got you to do their bidding?"

"Yes, Mama. They held Veltan, forcing me to travel to far off places to gather strength for their master. He is no more. Jake and his kin saw to that. But there is still evil out there. I have grown tired of this now Mama. I want to settle. I want to watch my boy grow and be with my kin."

"Then it shall be so," Bikabak said as she laid the table with their breakfast. Pots of jam and spreads were laid out alongside freshly baked bread and a large kettle, filled with sweet tea.

"I am thankful, Mama. I loved Jake like a brother. I wish him luck and love in his new life. And I hope that I never see him again."

"Why?" Veltan said.

"Because if I do, chances are, the darkness has found him once more." They sat for a long time, talking and laughing as the day wore on. Tamatan's smile hardly left his face as he drank in the sight of his family once more. He was safe. He was happy. His journey was at an end.

Twenty-Seven

Katherine looked at Jake as a squall of rain battered the kitchen window. "I cannot believe this!"

"Nor could I, babe. But I have shown you the proof. This woman needs my help."

"You're not going back, Jake. You can't. You barely made it back alive last time. You died. Next time, you may not be so fortunate."

"I know that. So, should I just ignore this?"

"I do not know the answer to that." They stood facing each other as Wilf's gentle snores drifted through from the lounge.

"This Jasper. Are you totally sure that he is this watcher?"

"Yes, I am. I saw him with my own eyes. It's the same boy that I showed you in the picture."

Katherine walked over to the sink, filling the kettle with water. Putting it on to boil, she walked over to the kitchen table, trying her best to smile at her daughter, who was laying in a baby bouncer. It was vibrating gently, the infant's feet raised to the ceiling as she smiled and cooed at her mother. "You ready for a feed, princess? Yes, you are aren't you," she said, tickling the outstretched foot. Her daughter giggled, pulling the foot away playfully. "Do you really want to risk all this? You know what we have all been through to get to this point, Jake."

"I know, Kath. But I cannot ignore this. She's a mother too. And her son needs help. I don't know if I can give her that help. But I think I should at least contact her, to see what she has to say."

"Fine," Katherine said as she scooped her daughter onto her lap. She arranged her skirt, flattening it before she tested the warm milk. Seconds later, Alicia was contently guzzling away, the world around her forgotten. "Make me a cup of tea, then do what you need to do. But I am warning you, Jake Stevenson. Do not do anything without speaking with me first. Promise?"

"I promise, babe."

Five minutes later, Jake settled on his bed, a mug of steaming tea next to him on the bedside table. He clicked into Facebook, selecting messages with his thumb. He reread the text, sending a brief reply before putting the phone on the soft duvet. He sipped at his tea as he gazed out of the window. Dark clouds were his vista. Low and foreboding. He sat, wondering just how he could be of help to the woman in the north. His thoughts drifted towards Jasper. *Where are you? And who are you with?*

* * *

Dark clouds gathered over the garden as the afternoon headed towards evening. Vicky stood up, placing her hands at the base of her spine, bending backwards. Next to her, a large plastic bucket sat on the neatly trimmed grass, half full of weeds and soil. She hefted the bucket by its twin handles, walking back towards the cottage. Emptying the contents into the garden bin, Vicky kicked off her pumps before heading into the kitchen. She flicked on the kettle, walking out of the kitchen into the hallway. Her bare feet barely made a sound as she climbed the stairs, heading towards Jasper's bedroom. She opened the door, tip-toeing over to her son who lay sleeping. A clear plastic tube ran from his nose to the bag positioned above him. The machine still beeped as constantly as ever, telling Vicky that nothing was out of the ordinary. And that nothing had changed. "Hello, Son. Are you going to wake up for Mummy today?" The request fell on deaf ears. She noticed that the room felt cool, even though summer was supposed to be in full swing. The window was still slightly open, a warm breeze blowing in. The coolness seemed to come from the room, not outside. *Strange. But what isn't strange anymore,* she thought, recollecting her altercation with her now dead neighbour. Opening the chest of drawers against the wall, Vicky took a fleece blanket out, unfurling it before placing it over her son's arms. She kissed the top of his head, drinking in his aroma. "There we go. Snug as a bug in a rug," she said, turning towards the door. Heading downstairs, Vicky remembered the kettle had just boiled, and that she was indeed thirsty after the gardening. She set to the task of tea making, unplugging her mobile phone and swiping the screen. Her thumb pressed the screen, selecting Facebook. There were numerous notification icons lit up, her thumb pressing the messages. The first message on the screen was from Jake Stevenson, causing Vicky to freeze with shock. She put the phone on the counter, pouring herself the tea, unsure of what the message would say. Milk was added to the tea, along with sugar as Vicky delayed reading the message for fear of bad news. Snatching the phone off the worktop, she sat down at the kitchen table with her tea. Vicky swiped the screen once more, pressing Jake's message. It was brief and to the point.

Hi Vicky
So sorry to hear about your son. I am the person you think I am. I have met
Jasper. I think it's better if we do this over the phone.
Jake

She blinked, reading the message over and over. Below was a mobile phone number. Holding her thumb on the message bubble she copied the text, pasting into her phone screen. Without thinking, she hit the green dial icon, her heart increasing its tempo. Vicky took a quick sip of tea, hearing the phone answer at the other end.

"Hello?"

"Hi. Is that Jake?"

A slight pause. "Yes. Is that Vicky?"

She breathed out. "Yes, it is. Sorry about the message. I am just glad that you knew what I was talking about. I am still trying to get my head around all this."

Another slight pause on the other end of the line. "That's okay, Vicky. Why don't we start at the beginning? Can you fill me in on what's been going on up there? Then I will fill you in on what I've been up to. It's probably better that way."

"Okay." She took a swig of her tea, swallowing it quickly. The burn at the back of her throat felt good. It felt real. "Well, I mentioned in my message that I recently lost most of my family in a car accident."

"Yes. I am so sorry to hear that."

"It's okay. I am slowly coming to terms with it. But I'm still not there yet." She liked that the man listened. He didn't compare his own loss with hers. It was a pet hate of Vicky's, with too many people quick to tell her of their own hardships. "Anyway, a few months ago, Jasper went sleepwalking. He'd never done anything like this before. A neighbour just happened to find him, up the Lickey's."

"Up the Lickey's?" Jake said with surprise.

"I know. Crazy right? He was okay though. They treated him at the Alex in Redditch. He came home a day or so later and seemed to be fine to begin with. Then he started telling me about these strange dreams that he'd been having. About two lost people in a faraway place."

"Hmm," Jake replied.

"Then things started taking a turn for the worse. And I mean really badly. My neighbour started feeling unwell, telling me of similar dreams. I'm not exactly sure what happened, but she killed our postman and tried to kill me too."

"What?"

"I know. Pretty hard to take in. I have thought about this over the last few weeks or so. I think Maureen was possessed by something. She looked different. Her skin turned grey and her voice was all crackly. The voice said its name was Virdelas, or Wirdelas. Something like that anyway."

"Shit. I know who that is. But please, keep going," Jake said, his own heart thumping rapidly.

"Okay. Anyway, she attacked me. I thought I was going to die. It was only by chance that I managed to escape. She fell down her stairs and broke her neck. About a minute later, Jasper started screaming in his bed. He'd been ill and was having a nap at the time. My mother called an ambulance and they took him to the hospital. The doctors say that he's in a coma. And they do not know why. He's here now, upstairs in his bed. I am watching over him, and the nurses visit every day or so." She finished the sentence, taking another swig of cooling tea.

"Sounds like you've been through hell, Vicky. I am so sorry to hear all this. I really am."

"It's okay," she replied quietly.

"Virdelas is related to someone I knew. Two brothers. He is their father."

"Who are they?"

"Okay. Are you sitting down?"

"Yes."

"A few years ago, I came across a series of unexplained abductions. At roughly the same time, two people were killed up the Lickey Hills."

"The prostitute and the taxi driver? I don't want to sound like a crazed stalker, but once all this started happening, a mutual friend from Rednal started filling in some gaps. She told me about the Vicar and your friend."

"Yes. My brother-in-law was involved with the case. He sent me to track down a crazy lead that we thought would go nowhere. I was a policeman back then. I quit the force though. That's why Daz sent me. I'm a Private Investigator now."

"Really?"

"Yes. Although, I've not really worked much lately. And I've probably lost some of my clients. Anyway, I discovered a link between the murders and the abductions. It led me to a doorway up the Lickey Hills. A doorway to another world. I know that sounds bonkers, but it's true. Tell me, whereabouts was Jasper found?"

"Above the golf course at the top of the hill. Why?"

"Because that's where the doorway is. I know this is a lot for you to take in, Vicky. But trust me, this is real. I've only just returned home today. I became lost in one of these worlds, chased by someone called Lenga."

"I know that name. Maureen mentioned something about a witch called Lenga. What the hell is happening here, Jake? I'm sorry to be so blunt. But after everything that has happened lately, this is one step too far. I don't know what to do."

"Let's take it one step at a time. There is more at play here. There were vampires too. I know. It sounds ridiculous. But it's true. I helped destroy quite a few of them. Now it seems that they want revenge."

"So where does Jasper fit into all this? Vampires. This is just, unbelievable!"

"When we were in the other world, Jasper came to us."

"Say that again. I missed that," Vicky said.

"I saw Jasper. Well, an apparition of him. He had his pyjamas on. I think he came to us while he was dreaming. He warned us about the gang that was chasing us. He also said there was another doorway, close to where we were staying. He was trying to help. Why he was there in the first place, god only knows? Perhaps being found asleep by the doorway affected him somehow. After all, we're talking about vampires, demons, and witches. Anything is possible."

"I suppose so. Hang on a minute, I'm going to send you a picture of his drawing. See what you think?"

"Okay," Jake said, switching to speakerphone. A few seconds later, his phone buzzed, signalling a message. "Okay. I've got the picture. Hang on." He pressed the attachment, the screen changing in front of his eyes. A crude pencil drawing appeared. Jake could see straight away that it was of Tamatan and him, right before they met Bea at the cabin. He looked at the screen for a few seconds before backing out of it, switching the speakerphone off. "That's me and Tamatan alright. It's a pretty accurate picture."

"Who?" Vicky asked.

"A demon, who you might know better as *Spring Heeled Jack*. He's was supposed to have terrorised London during the 19th Century. He was a local legend back then, but he does really exist. He's been helping me. And he's saved my life on numerous occasions. This leaves no doubt. Jasper was there. I saw him. He saw us. And I honestly think that somehow he has gotten lost too."

"So how do we get him back?" she said, a slight pinch of hope started to form inside her.

"I have to think about this, Vicky. It's not just as simple as me popping back through a doorway to look for him. People have died. Many people, yourself almost included. I said a few years ago, that I'd scratched the surface of something that wasn't meant to be scratched. Now I have seen more. There are many worlds out there, with things that you wouldn't believe to be true."

"Knowing that makes me want to go this fucking doorway myself and go look for him." She paused, her heart skipping along too quickly. Her anxiety levels rising. "Sorry. I'm just upset, and scared. I want my boy back. What you've just told me makes me think that I'll never get him back. That I'll have to switch off his life support one day and watch him slip away."

"Let's not go there just yet. Is he stable?"

"Yes."

"Okay. Let me talk with Katherine and Wilf and we'll decide what our options are."

"Is that your wife?"

"Kinda. My partner is what you'd call her I suppose. She is from the world next to this. We've not long had a little girl."

"What's her name?"

"Alicia. She was snatched, along with Kath. That's why I went back. To find them. I very nearly never made it back. That's why I need to speak to her. You understand, don't you?"

"Yes, I do, Jake. I totally understand. When can I call you back?"

"Can I call you in the morning? I need to sit down and talk to Katherine and Wilf first."

"Sure. I totally get that," she said, taking another sip of her tea. "I will speak to you tomorrow, Jake. Thank you."

"Try not to worry too much, Vicky. We'll figure something out. I'll speak to you tomorrow."

"Okay, bye for now."

"Bye," Jake said, ending the call.

Vicky drained the remainder of her mug, placing it next to her on the table. *What the hell am I getting into? Vampires? Other worlds? It's bonkers.* As strange as it all sounded to her logical mind, Vicky knew what she had seen. A murdered postman and a possessed neighbour told her that things were not as she had always thought. She started to feel a glimmer of hope spark deep within. *Maybe he can help,* she thought. She smiled, albeit briefly before she carried on with her chores.

* * *

The transport was very basic. A single horse and cart sat at the bottom of the dark scree slope. Mountains loomed over the land, low cloud drifting down the slopes towards them. Alain lifted Alana into the back of the cart, setting her down on a bed of straw. "I hope this is to your liking? The straw will disappear the longer we ride. The mule needs feeding after all."

She looked at him, her strength sapped. "Where are we going?"

"Witch hunting. I know of Tenta. She should be easy to find."

Alana's eyes closed, the vampires spell holding her in check. Next to her, Jasper lay. Virdelas covered the bubble in a yellow mist, settling over it until he was obscured from sight. Alain walked around the front of the cart, offering the black mule a hand full of straw. The beast snuffled it readily as the vampire climbed onto a single wooden bench. A quick snap of the reins and they were off, trundling across the grass to the roadway in the distance. Heading away from the mountains, towards a forlorn rock over the black horizon.

* * *

"I'm not saying that I am going back, babe," Jake said, the tension in the kitchen almost audible. "But I cannot ignore this."

Katherine looked out of the window, her hands on the counter top. "I cannot lose you again, Jake. You died. Remember that," she said turning towards him. Her eyes streaked with tears. "You died."

He rushed over to her, scooping Katherine into his arms. "Come on, Kath. I am not going to leave you," he said, enunciating every word fully. "I swear."

"Jake. I have lived my whole life surrounded by death. I lost Mother when I was young. Then Alice. Then Father. I could not cope if I lost you also. But I do understand. I am a mother. Alicia was snatched. And you came for me. Now another little boy needs help. I just wish that someone else could do what needs to be done. Not my Jake."

He kissed the top of her head, holding her against him. "Let's not get too carried away. I will call her tomorrow, then see how the land lies. If need be, I may travel up there to see her and Jasper. But I promise I will not go any further until I know what is going on. I will come back home first. I swear."

"Okay. I believe you, Jake. Do what needs to be done. But come home to us quickly."

Twenty-Eight

The apparition seeped out of the cave, the black sea coating the path that led to the settlement of Tenta. It drifted over loose, wet rocks until it came to the end of the pathway that connected with the clutch of buildings that sat on the forlorn peninsular. The apparition took shape as Lenga began walking towards her cabin. Gone was the ancient hag, who'd lived a thousand lifetimes. She walked on younger legs, her hair shorter, almost well-kept compared to that of her former vessel. Lenga pushed open the door to her cabin, kicking the slick reptiles out of her way. Her clothing was placed on the wooden chair in the corner of the room carefully. She waved her hand in front of her, the torches on the walls bursting into flame, bathing the shack in an orange glow. "I like these," she said, inspecting her breasts with smooth palms. Her fingers trailed down between her legs, liking the soft feel of her womanhood. "Lenga likes that too. It has been far too long since I had trinkets like this to enjoy." She climbed into the vat, the cool, slick liquid coming up to her neck. "It's good to be home, but things have moved on." She looked at the two empty spikes on her wall that sat between the half dozen others. Husks of dried out skulls stared into space. Empty eye sockets picked clean by a hungry bird, sat frozen in time. "Soon. Very soon I will have my heads. Lenga just needs to plan." She laughed as a snake wrapped itself around her thighs, rubbing its face between her legs. "I will have some fun before I take my leave of this place. I will find you, little one. And the others too. I may clear some of these old skulls away, making room for you all."

* * *

"Morning, Vicky," Ashley said as the woman opened the door. Summer was on hold as thunder rumbled over the land, flashes of lightning in the distance heading towards the cottage.

"Morning, Ashley. Come in. Would you like a drink?"

"I'd love a coffee," the nurse replied, running a hand through her dark hair. Once the door was closed, Ashley removed her Crocs, placing them on the front door mat. She padded behind Vicky towards the kitchen, her pink socks silent on the carpet. She wiped her uniform as she walked, subconsciously trying to remove the raindrops that were soaking into her blue tunic. "How is he?" she enquired as Vicky filled the kettle with cold water.

"No change. Everything's the same."

"Okay. Well, I'll pop up after my coffee and check him over." Vicky made the drinks while Ashley peered out through the kitchen window. "You have a lovely home. That garden is so pretty."

"Thank you," Vicky said handing the nurse her drink. "It's a really peaceful place. Well, it was until it all went downhill a few weeks ago."

"Yes. I saw it on the news. How awful."

"It has been. Not really sure how it all came about. I've spoken to the police a few times. But to be honest, the last few weeks have been such a blur. I've tried to focus purely on Jasper."

"Well, that's understandable. You certainly have had a tough time of it lately, Vicky. That's why we are here, to help. I am sure that the little man will recover."

"Do you really think so?" she said, a glimmer of hope surfacing.

"It's hard to say for sure. But I am hopeful. Many people slip into comas after strokes and trauma. Jasper has had a major trauma. It might be his body's way of healing."

"Well, I hope you're right, Ashley." Vicky looked at the other woman over the rim of her mug. "Do you live locally?"

"Yes, Bromsgrove. So, this is nice and easy for me. Only a ten-minute drive or so."

"Are you married?"

Ashley shook her head as she swallowed her coffee. "Not anymore. I was, but it didn't work out. Men huh! It's just me and Jeffrey now. Mum helps out a lot. She's got him today, which is good because child-minders don't do Saturdays."

"No, I suppose not," she replied, liking the dark-haired woman across the kitchen more and more. "It's just the two of us now too. Mum and Dad have been amazing. I think they are popping round later too." A thought suddenly occurred to Vicky. "Are you feeling better by the way? After the nosebleed?"

"Yes, thanks. No idea what happened there? It's a bit embarrassing really. And it's a good job I didn't bleed all over your lovely home."

"It's fine, Ashley. Sometimes things just happen I guess."

"You're not wrong there," she replied, placing her empty mug on the table. "Right, I suppose I'd better check on the little man. Do you want to come up or stay here?"

"I'll leave you to it. I have a few emails to catch up on."

"Okay. I'll be back down in a bit," Ashley said, picking her bag up off the kitchen floor.

As she made her way into the hallway, Vicky's phone started to vibrate. She looked at the screen. "Jake," she said, swiping the green icon to accept the call. "Hello."

"Morning, Vicky. Are you okay?"

"Not bad. The nurse is here, checking on Jasper. Are you all okay?"

"We're good. I spoke to Kath last night. She's not thrilled by the news. But she knows what you're going through. So, with that in mind, when can I pop up to see you both?"

"Really? You want to come up here?"

"Yes. I think that is a good place to start."

"Thank you. Anytime is good for me."

"Okay. Are you free today?"

"Err, sure. My parents are coming around in a bit. But we can work around that."

"Okay. It's almost 10 am. If I leave now I should be there in three hours. Does that work for you?"

"Are you sure this is okay? I don't want to cause trouble your end?"

"It's fine, Vicky. Katherine and Wilf understand. They're just settling back in, so me being gone for the day is not a problem."

"Okay, that's wonderful. I suppose I'd better give you my address."

"Okay. I have a pen and paper."

She relayed the address, her pulse quickening at the thought of seeing the one man that could help. "I hope you have a safe journey, Jake."

"Thanks. It should be okay. Saturday traffic should be light. I'll see you shortly"

"Okay. Bye."

"Bye," he replied before she ended the call.

Ashley headed upstairs as Vicky answered her phone in the kitchen. She heard her voice gradually fade away as she made her way into Jasper's bedroom. The curtains were partially drawn, the room dim and cool. Jasper lay in bed, wearing a pair of *X-Men* pyjamas. "Hello there, little man. It's Ashley. I'm just going to do a few checks on you. Nothing to worry about." The nurse set about her task, opening her bag and retrieving a thermometer. She placed the plastic end into the boy's ear, waiting for it to beep. Once it did, she checked the reading, making a note on the chart at the end of the bed. She checked the tube running from Jasper's nose, happy that all appeared to be as it should. A noise behind her, made the nurse turn around. A chest of drawers lay against the wall, a collection of action figures and other objects adorning the wooden top. One of the objects, a *Wolverine* action figure moved slightly, making the nurse flinch.

"Strange?" she said as she picked up the toy. It was cool to the touch, almost cold in her palm as she inspected it. Placing it back on the chest of drawers, Ashley looked at the other figures and clock that filled the space. *Hmm*, she thought before turning back to Jasper. To her right, the curtains ruffled as the wind outside increased in strength. *Must have been the wind*, she thought as she looked at a comfortable looking chair sat against the far wall. Without thinking, she walked over and sat down, her eyes playing over the boy's bedroom. A rumble of thunder echoed over the Lickey Hills outside, lightning flashing across the sky overhead. The room lightened for a split second, before returning to normal. She looked at the boy in the bed, the room seeming to darken at one end. Ashley suddenly felt sleepy, the long working hours seemingly catching up with her. She let her head loll back against the wall as the room darkened further. As her eyes closed, she did not notice twin wisps of yellow smoke exit the boy's nostrils, slowly making their way down the rumpled duvet cover towards her. *So tired*, she thought, falling quickly into the blackness of sleep as the mist climbed up her tunic, snaking its way into her mouth. Around her, the room started to vibrate, toys falling off the chest of drawers onto the carpet. More mist emerged from Jasper, pooling on the floor next to the bed. It gradually took shape, increasing in size as more thunder rumbled overhead. Ashley breathed steadily, her eyelids flickering as Virdelas floated before her. His shifting features smiling at the sleeping figure in front of him. He drifted forwards slowly as the room became colder, clouds of breath forming on the human's lips. A picture fell from the wall, the glass shattering onto the carpet as the entity swirled around the sleeping figure. It knew what it wanted. To take the human's life-force, back to the other plane where his brother, the witch and the boy made their way through the dark land.

Vicky put the phone down, walking into the small lounge to retrieve her laptop from the sofa. She got as comfortable as she could on the kitchen table, reminding herself that she needed a proper desk and chair at some point in the near future. A few clicks of the mouse and she was logged into her email, deleting the numerous junk items in her inbox. A tremor ran through the kitchen chair, her phone vibrating on the table top as a crack of thunder erupted outside. A few seconds later, lightning flickered across the sky. She looked up from her screen, turning her head towards the window as the rain hammered into it from the other side. *Good job I didn't hang the washing out*, she thought as she returned to her emails. Another noise came to her. Breaking glass, from somewhere inside the house. *What was that?* She headed into the hallway, looking up the stairs. The low clouds outside had subdued the landing above her, darkening it somewhat. "Ashley?" Vicky called out as she made her way towards Jasper's bedroom. Her hand hesitated on the handle for a split second as a cold gust of wind blew under the closed doorway. More noises from inside the bedroom stayed her fingers for another few seconds. She shook her head, opening the door slowly. She poked her head into the bedroom. And froze.

* * *

"I'll be back tonight," Jake said to Wilf and Katherine. They sat at the kitchen table, mugs of steaming coffee in front of them. "I shouldn't be too late."

"Okay, Jake," Katherine replied as she bounced Alicia on her knee.

He bent down, kissing the infant on the head. "Daddy back later, princess." She smiled at him, pink gums on display. He kissed her again on the cheek, holding her face in his hands. She giggled, lying back against her mother's chest.

"No adventures, Son," Wilf said as he filled his new pipe with tobacco.

"Promise. I'll be back tonight. Shall I stop in the village and get us some dinner on my way back?"

"That sounds good to me. What are you thinking? Fish and chips?"

"Could do. Or how about a Chinese? Wilf's not tried that."

She looked at her uncle who nodded his head. "Okay. Chinese it is. I'll have the spicy one again please."

"Singapore Chow Mein. No probs. I'll give you a call when I pass Bristol to let you know I'm close. Could you warm some plates in the oven, babe?"

"I will. Now come here and give me a kiss, Jake Stevenson. And promise me again. No crazy adventures."

He bent down, kissing her full on the mouth as Alicia grabbed at his dark jacket. Wilf rolled his eyes, walking over to the kitchen door, heading out into the carport. "I promise, babe. No adventures. No crazy stunts."

She pulled him closer, kissing him again. His eyes closed as her tongue found its way into his mouth. The world around them was forgotten for a moment, as they became one. Katherine let out a small moan as the kiss finally ended, her vision fuzzy as she opened her eyes. "If Wilf and Alicia were not here, I'd be taking you upstairs right now, Jake."

"Hold that thought. Maybe later I will let you do just that." He kissed her for a final time. The contact over too soon for her liking. "Love you, Kath."

"Love you too, Jake. Drive safely. Stay away from monsters."

"I will," he said, ruffling his daughter's curls as he turned towards the hallway. Seconds later, he pressed the fob on his key ring, the lights flashing on his Pathfinder. The sun had broken through the clouds, bathing the coastline in warm summer sun. Darker clouds out at sea were being blown away from them on an easterly breeze.

"Be careful up there," Wilf said.

"I will. Can you hold the fort here?"

"Fort?"

"Sorry. I mean can you make sure they are both okay?"

"I will," he said, puffing on his new pipe.

Jake clapped the older man on the shoulder. "Okay. I will see you later. Keep out of mischief." Wilf grunted, blowing smoke from his mouth. A few minutes later, Jake was pulling onto the main road, heading north with the Atlantic Ocean to his left. He mashed the accelerator, turning up the stereo as Fleetwood Mac sang about a Black Magic Woman. He felt good about the journey ahead, his fingers tapping on the steering wheel as he made his way north. Towards a young boy that needed his help.

* * *

"What the fuck!" Vicky said as she stood teetering at the entrance to the room. Ashley sat in front of her, seemingly asleep in Jasper's red chair. In front of her, a figure floated. It turned towards her, shifting and pulsing. She could make out a face as it moved towards the bed away from her. It smiled at Vicky, baring its teeth. "STAY AWAY FROM HIM!" she screamed, rushing towards the apparition, her fists clenched.

Ashley started in the chair, shaking her head. "Jeffrey. Is that you?" she said, slowly waking up. Her eyes took in the scene, widening when they locked onto the figure floating before her. "Oh my God!" she said as her bladder emptied itself.

Vicky swiped at the cloud, dissipating its form with her hand. "Get out!" she hissed. "Leave my Son alone, whatever the fuck you are!"

A deep laugh distorted and crackly filled the room. Goosebumps broke out over Vicky's arms as the figure mocked her. "Mine," it said, before losing its shape. It whirled around the room before the women, disappearing into Jasper's mouth.

"NOOOOOO!" she screamed, rushing towards her son. She fell on him, knocking the tube that ran from his arm to the apparatus next to the bed. It fell to the floor, clattering against the chest of drawers as Vicky held her son's face. "Jasper. Wake up," she said, tears falling onto his upturned face.

Ashley was there, stumbling clumsily across the bedroom. "What's happening, Vicky? What was that?"

"Jasper, please! Wake up, Son." It was a futile request. Jasper lay there, unmoved. His breathing was steady, the rise and fall of his chest the same as before.

A far-off drone drifted in through the windows, causing the nurse to shudder. "Vicky. Let me see to him," she said, gently moving the woman across the bed. Ashley picked up the drip bag, making sure that everything was connected as the other woman sobbed uncontrollably on the rumpled duvet. "He's fine. No change," she said nervously, her hands shaking. "What the hell just happened? What's going on here?"

"I don't know," Vicky replied, her face a mess of hair and tears. "Something bad has happened to him. He's not in a coma. Something has him. I don't know what it is. But it's taken my boy somewhere else. And they want to hurt him." She looked at her son's serene face and broke down once more, falling sideways onto the bed, head in hands.

Ashley stepped out of the front door, turning to look at the woman behind her. "I really don't know what to say, Vicky. I've only seen things like that in the movies. It's just." Her voice trailed off, Ashley unable to find the words needed.

"Please don't tell anyone about this just yet, Ashley. I have someone coming to see us today. He may be able to help."

"Who? A priest?"

Ashley's words hit Vicky like a sledgehammer. She'd watched movies like the *Exorcist* as a child, remembering the bone-chilling scenes vividly. "No. Just somebody who knows about this kind of thing."

"Oh, okay. Well, I will be back on Monday. Please take care. I am still trying to digest what I've just seen."

"I know it's a lot to take in. I wouldn't blame you if you never came back here. But please, don't say anything yet. The last thing I want is for Jasper to be taken away from me."

"Okay. I won't say anything. Yet. But please let me know what's going on? I am responsible for Jasper's care. He comes first." She turned, walking down the path on shaky legs as low cloud seemed to skim the tree-tops.

Vicky closed the door, walking back up to Jasper's bedroom. She flopped down on the bed, the beeping of the machine steady and calming. She closed her eyes, drifting off to sleep. Her dreams were plagued by unseen monsters, just out of sight. She saw what Jasper had seen before. Vast forests. A lone mountain swathed in fog. A burnt-out village, surrounded by writhing spirits. Next to her, Jasper slept peacefully. In his dreams, he was not far away from his mother. He bounced around on the back of a cart, under a dark sky. Heading towards an island on the horizon.

Vicky's eyes fluttered open. She blinked a few times, trying to focus on the ceiling above her. What had woken her? A noise came again, downstairs. *The door*, she thought as she looked at the clock. *Shit! How long did I sleep for?* Climbing off the bed, Vicky looked at her son. There was no change, her shoulders dropping. Ten seconds later, Vicky opened the front door, a warm gust of wind blowing in from outside.

"Mrs Evans?" Jake said.

"Err. Hi, Jake. Come in. Sorry. I look a state. It's been an eventful morning." She motioned him through to the kitchen. "Would you like a drink?"

"I'd love a coffee, please. I only stopped once on the way up. Fortunately, the traffic was light."

"That's good," she said as she put the kettle on, pulling mugs from the cupboard. She turned to look at him, trying to smile. She appraised him for a second, liking his friendly face and relaxed manner. "Something happened earlier."

"What?" Jake said, his expression changing.

"Well, the nurse was here, checking on Jasper. I was here in the kitchen while she went up to check on him. That's when it all kicked off."

"What happened?"

"I heard a noise. Like breaking glass, so I went upstairs to see what was going on. When I was walked into his room, Ashley was asleep in the chair, with this, I suppose you'd call it a ghost or something, hovering in front of her."

"Oh God!" Jake said, his face draining of colour.

"Tell me about it. I screamed and rushed towards it. It then disappeared into Jasper's mouth." She stopped talking, her voice threatening to crack. The kettle clicked, a good distraction for Vicky to compose herself for a few seconds, letting her anxiety diminish.

Jake stood there, watching the woman, trying to digest what she had told him. "I really don't know what to say about that. A coffee will help get my brain in gear."

She turned to him, seeing the crooked smile on his face. The laugh surprised her. It came out of her mouth, echoing around the kitchen. "Sorry, Jake. I don't know why I am laughing? There's not really much to laugh about at the moment?"

"It probably seems that way. But don't lose hope, Vicky."

"How do you take it?"

"Milk and two sugars please."

She handed him the mug, Jake nodding his thanks as he took a sip. "That's better. Right, I can handle anything now." He smiled again, relaxing the woman opposite some more.

"Why don't you sit down?" she said, pulling a chair out.

"Thank you," he replied as Vicky's phone started to buzz on the table-top.

"Hi, Mum. You both okay?" she said, listening to her mother's reply. "Could you pop round tomorrow instead? Sorry. The nurse is here at the moment, and I'm having a bit of a tidy around." Jake watched her as she listened to the voice on the end of the line. Vicky looked back at him, rolling her eyes for effect. "Okay. Well say hi to Dad for me and I'll call you in the morning, Mum. No really. It's fine. I have something in for my dinner. Okay. Love you. Bye."

"Mum's will never change."

"I know. She means well. They both do. They've been through all this with me. It's been really hard on them. To lose a son-in-law and two grandchildren in one go, then this." She stopped, letting the words sink in. "What about your parents, Jake? Do they know about all this?"

"They did," he said, trying to find the words to start the next sentence. "They were caught up in it too. I lost them both,"

"Oh no. I am so sorry."

"Thanks. I am still trying to come to terms with it myself. Mum vanished a few months ago from where we live in Tintagel. We thought she'd been swept out to sea during freak storms. However, we found out later that she had been turned. She killed Dad in front of me, before being swept out to sea."

Vicky reached across the table, placing her hand over his. "Sorry, Jake. I have unloaded all my problems onto you. I never thought about what you were going through?"

"It's okay," Jake said smiling. "I have had more time to get used to all this than you have. I miss them both terribly. And I'm so sad that I'll never see them again. They had only known Alicia for a few months. And they both adored her. Mum was lovely, but very hard work, as some mums are. Dad was great. A really genuine bloke. And on top of all that, I've just learned that my brother Rick has become involved in all this madness. It looks like he's dead too."

She let go, drawing her hand to her mouth in shock. "Oh, Jake." The light bulb above them flickered, her eyes looking upwards. She looked back at him, words forming on her lips. As Vicky was about to speak, the bulb exploded. They were showered in glass, the room plunging into darkness as objects around them started to move and shake.

Twenty-Nine

The table lurched across the kitchen, pushed by an unseen force. Wooden legs scraped loudly on the tiled floor before the table crashed into a cupboard door. "What's happening, Jake?" Vicky said as she backed herself into the corner of the kitchen worktop.

"Something's here with us," was all he could say as he saw the sky darken outside.

"Jasper," Vicky said, heading for the kitchen door. It slammed shut as she approached, a dining chair rattling into it from the centre of the room. It lodged itself under the handle, the wood creaking under the pressure. "Jake," she shouted. He was there in a split second, prizing the chair away from the handle. It skittered across the tiles as he tossed it to one side. Vicky heaved the door open, taking the stairs two at a time with Jake in pursuit. The door was flung open as they barged their way into the bedroom. The curtains blew inwards, a muggy breeze invading from outside. Jake looked through the window, his stomach tightening when he saw that it was almost pitch black. "Jasper," Vicky said. Jake looked over. The boy looked like he was sleeping peacefully. The machine behind him beeping rhythmically.

Jake walked over to the light switch, flicking it on. Nothing happened. "The fuse must have blown," he said. The darkness seemed to press down from the ceiling, cutting visibility to virtually nothing. Jake pulled his phone out, flicking on the flashlight. It lit up harshly, the LED glow aimed at the ceiling. He turned the phone towards Jasper, catching the figure that was floating next to him.

Vicky screamed, careening backwards into the wall. Jake held his ground, holding the phone towards the yellow apparition. "Who are you?"

The shape shifted, losing it form as it moved towards the wall away from Jasper. It solidified again, taking shape. It loomed over Jake, its head almost touching the ceiling. "You know who I am, Jake. I am the father of murdered sons."

"Virdelas?"

"Yes," it hissed.

Vicky walked around the bed, standing next to Jake. "What the hell do you want with my Son?"

"I am unsure. I want others first. The two witches will fall by my hand. Then the demon. Then this pathetic human in front of me."

"Is this because I killed your sons?"

"Yes," Virdelas said, his form roiling and shifting. "Although Reggan needed killing. But you took Korgan, and for that, you will pay."

"Your son was a monster. He'd terrorised people for centuries. He had to be stopped."

"And you did stop him, which means you are cunning. And you stopped Elias too. That in itself is impressive, Jake. It will make killing you all the better."

"So why don't you kill me now, and return the boy?"

"Because I cannot. Not just yet. I need to spill the blood of the witches. That will give me the strength I need to take a vessel. Then I will hunt down the demon. He has much to answer for. Then, I am coming for you and your kin."

"Leave my family out of this," Jake said as the darkness pulsed against the torch-light.

"No, human. You went after my kin. Now I will come after yours. You cannot hide. Alain and I will track you down and end you all."

Jake's flashlight timed out, plunging the room into darkness. He reached to his left, grabbing Vicky's shoulder as he reactivated the light. It came on, shining at the floor. He aimed it at the corner once more, only to find empty space. "He's gone," Jake said as the sky outside started to lighten.

"What can we do, Jake? He's never going to give Jasper up, is he?"

Jake looked at her as tears started spilling from her eyes. He moved forward, holding her to him. She closed her eyes, trying to shut off the outside world. A man's embrace was something that was sadly lacking from her life. She wanted nothing more than to stand there all day, feeling safe. "No, Vicky. He's not going to let him go."

Then the hug was broken, Vicky stepping back a few steps, feeling exposed "So, what can we do?"

"We need to finish this."

"But how?"

"Is Jasper okay. Just check on him. If we're going to talk, we need to do it outside, away from him."

Vicky nodded, checking her son. She fussed over him for a minute, making sure that all tubes and wires were connected properly. She then pulled the duvet up, kissing his lips before turning to Jake. "Okay. Let's go outside."

They walked down the front path, stopping next to a large tree on the pavement. Jake turned to Vicky, his face grave. "I need to go back and destroy them. You heard it yourself. He's going to hunt me down. And my family. Even in Cornwall, we are not safe. Elias proved that when he snatched them from me. And this Virdelas is not alone. He has his brother Alain to help him."

"So, what can we do?" she said as dark clouds passed over them. The wind rustled the tree's that lined the road, lowering the summer temperature somewhat.

"We? You're not thinking about coming with me, are you?"

"I don't know. I cannot expect you to do this alone, Jake. I am asking a lot. The least I can do is come with you."

Jake shook his head. "I cannot let you be put in harm's way, Vicky. And you have Jasper to look after. He needs you here."

"My parents can watch him. How long would it take to find Jasper?"

"Days, weeks, a month maybe. From what we've just heard, they are on their way to see the witch. She lives two worlds away. We'd have to travel firstly through Katherine's world, then through the second world."

"Is it far?"

"It's probably only thirty to forty miles or so. But to walk it would take a long time. The furthest world is permanently dark. There is no sun. Plus, there are mountains. Lots of climbing too. If only I had a bike or." He paused, the words stalling on his lips.

"Or what?"

He smiled, his face suddenly beaming. It was the best thing that Vicky had seen in a while. "My bike. I left it in Amatoll. When I passed through with Wilf and Dad I concealed it in the forest. I am betting that it's still there. How did

I not think of that before? I was in the forest a few days ago. It completely slipped my mind."

"Okay. So how long would it take on your bike?"

"A few days. I filled it up when we crossed over. I still have the key on my key ring," he said as he fished them out of his pocket. Jake smiled again. "I cannot believe I forgot my bike."

"You probably had other things on your mind."

"True. Like getting out of a world full of monsters with a young baby."

Vicky was thinking, her brain in overdrive. "So, let's say your bike is where you'd left it. You think you could be where Jasper is in a few days?"

"I think so. We are governed by the doorways. They open at midnight only. So, we'd pass through, go to the next doorway. Wait there until the next night. Pass through again. Ride to where the witch is, do what needs to be done, then come back. Four days minimum."

"Good. Then I am coming with you. I can ask my parents to stay over. I will make something up. They won't mind at all."

Jake's face dropped slightly. "I really don't want you to come with me, Vicky. I know you want to. But when you're on the other side, confronted with what I've seen, you may change your mind."

"Jake. I have lost almost everything that I love. My son is lost somewhere too. I really don't want to live if he never comes back to me. I am coming with you."

He saw the steel in her eyes, the fight draining from his body. "Okay. When do you want to do this?"

"As soon as you can. I know that you'll have to go home and talk to Katherine. She may not let you do this. I accept that. But if you don't go, I'll go alone. You can draw me a map."

"Let me get back to Cornwall. Let's see what Katherine and Wilf say. I know she won't like it, but we are all in danger now. I cannot let these bastards find us again. It has to end. Plus, there is Tamatan to think about. He is in danger too. And Virdelas mentioned the white witch. If that's who I think it is, he has Alana too. She saved my life. I owe her."

"Okay. You go and do what needs to be done. I do feel bad about this, Jake. I would like to talk to Katherine about it before she decides."

"Why?" Jake said, suddenly confused.

"Because I don't want her to think bad of me, Jake. I want to let her hear my voice. It may help."

"Okay. If you think it will help I will call you later when I get home."

Without thinking, she embraced him. Jake flinched for a second, before returning the hug. "It will all be okay, Vicky. I promise."

She broke away, flustered. "Sorry."

"No need to say sorry. I understand totally."

She smiled, her resolve strengthening. "I can see that. Thank you, Jake. Do you want another drink before you leave?"

"I'll be okay. I'll hit the road now. If I am lucky, I'll miss the traffic in Bristol. I think I've seen all I needed to see as well. You have a lovely son, Vicky. We're going to do everything we can to get him back."

"Thank you, Jake. I will call my parent's and ask them about maybe staying over for a few days."

"Good," he said as he turned towards the driveway. He climbed into his 4x4, buzzing the window down. "Oh. You'll need a crash helmet. Don't want you cracking your head on a rock."

"Okay. Good idea. I am sure I can pick one up tomorrow. Drive safe, Jake."

"I will. Will you be okay in there on your own?"

"I think so."

"Do you have a crucifix?"

"No why?"

"I would get one if you can. Just in case."

"Okay. I am sure I can pick one up on Amazon."

"Good." Jake looked up and down the tree-lined street. It was quiet. It looked safe. "Right, I'd better get going. I will text you later, Vicky. Any trouble let me know."

"I will. And thank you."

He smiled, reaching out of his 4x4, placing his hand on her shoulder. "Don't mention it. We will get through this. I promise." He slowly reversed out of the drive, leaving the woman standing on the tarmac.

Vicky waved as he headed off down the street, waiting until he was out of sight before she headed back inside to check once more on Jasper.

* * *

"He is with the boy and mother," Virdelas said, his voice barely audible over the sea breeze. "I am conversing with them both."

Alain let the words sink in as he tethered the mule to a wooden rail. "That is good news, Brother. It means that Jake will indeed come to us. The mother too. Or Maybe?"

His words ended as men jostled out of the building where they were stood. Alain pulled his hood over his head, turning away from the advancing party. He walked slowly, checking the load in the cart. Grabbing a blanket, the vampires placed it over his cargo, turning back towards the footsteps. "Who goes there?" a harsh voice said.

"Forgive me. I am a weary traveller. I am in need of rest and provisions."

"We don't want travellers here in Tenta. Too many outlanders have been here in recent times. Many people are dead. My daughter Brianna is missing. Untether your beast and leave."

"Surely you can see that I am no threat. I am an old man, who needs a bed for the night," Alain replied, his eyes hidden from the men around him.

"I'll ask you one last time. Leave!" The men huddled around them. Swarthy faces looking into the cart, fingers poised on the wooden boards. Many carried knives and sticks, ready for trouble.

One of the crew pulled at the blanket, uncovering Alana and Jasper. "Look at this," he said, his voice edgy. "A woman."

Karl, the innkeeper walked over to the cart, his eyes settling on the white witch. Before he could utter a word, a yellow cloud engulfed him. "It's a trap, men," he shouted as he fell to his knees, Virdelas smothering him.

"Kill them!" another hollered as knives and sticks were readied for battle.

Alain pulled his hood from his head, his yellow eyes glaring at them in the darkness. Canines bared. In a blur of movement, all six men fell to the ground, bones protruding from smashed limbs and necks. "They are all yours, Brother," he cooed as he looked up the main street of Tenta. He lifted Karl to his feet, slapping him across the face. Teeth skittered onto the muddy ground as blood seeped from the man's smashed lips. "Where is the witch, called Lenga?"

"Up the hill," he replied, his mouth a bloody mess.

"I thank you for your service," Alain replied as he pushed his fingers into the man's mouth. Karl gagged and retched as long bony fingers sought their way to the back of his throat. Vomit erupted from his mouth, covering the vampire's hand. He pulled his fingers upward, tearing the top of the man's head off, skin and bone ripping and splintering before the head hit the floor. Alain pressed his mouth into the ragged stump, gulping down the sour tasting blood before letting the man topple sideways. Sickening gurgles and cries were blown out to sea as Virdelas consumed the men's souls. They writhed in the mud as the yellow cloud drifted over them. Moments passed before the mist took shape next to his brother. Its outline more pronounced than before.

"I feel strong," Virdelas said, almost feeling the ground under his feet.

"You are almost back to full strength. We can find you a vessel soon. Very soon I hope." Alain lifted the witch out of the cart, tossing her sleeping form over his shoulder. "I can feel her. She is close by. I can feel something else too."

"What?" Virdelas said inquisitively.

"I'm not sure. But it feels familiar. Come. Let us explore this forsaken place and find the old hag."

Lenga stirred in her crib, something far off waking her from her cloudy dreams. She sat up slowly, rubbing her eyes. Snakes slid over the wooden floor as a stiff breeze blew in through the shutters. "They are close," she said, climbing to her feet. Shuffling across the floor, she grabbed a stick from the far side of the cabin. Her milky eyes looked towards the creaking door. Lenga was suddenly unsure of what to do. *Something is out there. And I think I know what it is*, she thought as she strode for the door. Prizing it open, the witch disappeared into the night.

They came across another cabin with a rickety porch. "Inside," Alain said heading for the door. He laid Alana in a dark corner, his keen eyes spying a torch on the wall. As he touched it, the torch burst into flame, bathing the cabin in a yellow hue. Virdelas hovered near the centre, Jasper suspended next to him. Two figures lay in the centre of the floor, one on top of the other.

"Look," Virdelas said.

Alain pushed the figure on top with his boot, the corpse falling sideward off the figure underneath. "Elias!" the vampire exclaimed. "So, this is where you met your end?" He looked at the other figure. It was a man, with a bushy beard and eye-glasses. His skin was grey, his eyes sunken. Alain noticed the large wound in his chest, the cavity black and desiccated, maggots crawling over the dead flesh. He knelt down next to the giant vampire, pulling the stake from his chest. It came away easily, clattering onto the floorboards. "Ten thousand moons you walked between worlds, only to be ended by a mere human." He looked over at Alana, noticing the gem that hung from her neck. Alain reached over, plucking the stone from the witch, holding it by the chain. "A healing stone," he said, liking the purple hue it gave off. He dropped it into the wound in Elias's chest, standing over the body. "I will return soon. Stay here with the others, Brother. I have an idea," he said before exiting the cabin. Elias lay there, unmoving as the stone pulsed in his chest. Jasper looked over, a sinking feeling settling in his stomach. *Please help us,* he thought.

"You are beyond help now, child," Virdelas said. You should accept that. No one is coming. You belong to us. You both do."

Tenta was quiet as Alain walked its winding streets and alleyways. He could feel the human's that lay in their cribs inside the buildings. He could hear their heartbeats, thumping loudly in their chests as he passed by doorways and windows. A plan was forming in his mind as he made his way ever-upwards towards the summit of the settlement. He turned onto a wider street, his feet coming to a stop. Ahead, a woman stood in strange clothing. Her milky eyes locked onto his. "Lenga," he breathed.

"I know you," she replied. "Although we have never met. But I know Alain when I see him. There are not many vampires that roam this place. I came across your brother in a far-off place. It did not go well."

"Well, you shall be meeting him again very soon. For we are here for you."

"Pah!" she spat. "What makes you think you I am not ready for you?"

Before he could reply, Lenga vanished into the night. Alain's yellow eyes scoured the street, finding nothing. As he turned, his senses were overcome with crippling pain, dropping him to his knees. Lenga was on him, fingers clawing at his face. "A vampire is no match for a witch. Did no one ever tell you that?" He reached for her, bony fingers grabbing at her clothing as sharp nails dug into his white flesh. He tossed her aside, coming to his feet, ready to strike. As he rushed her, she vanished once more, the vampire crashing into a building. Timber smashed and splintered as he came to on a kitchen floor. Alain heard noises close by. The inhabitants of the cabin being roused from their sleep by the commotion. He climbed to his feet unsteadily as Lenga rushed him, gouging at his face with ragged nails.

"I will end you, here and now," she spat as she straddled his inert form.

"You are mistaken," he spat as his large hands circled her throat, clamping down on her windpipe.

"Monsters!" a man shouted from the doorway. He stood there naked, his long arm reaching for a torch on the wall. The vampire released one hand from the witch's throat, a gnarled finger pointing across the room towards the man as his family appeared behind him. In a whoosh, they were all engulfed in flames, the children screaming in pain as their hair singed and skin blistered instantly. The mother screamed, trying in vain to quash the inferno that had consumed her children. It was in vain as they all crumpled to the floor, limbs kicking and thrashing about on the wooden floorboards. The screams died away as the fire started to spread, catching easily on the wooden structure and furniture.

Alain could feel the heat of the flames licking at his ankles as he struggled to fend off the witch. "You die," he hissed as his fingers renewed their assault on her throat.

"NOOOOOO," she screamed, a nail slicing into his cheek as her breath was slowly cut off. She could feel darkness surrounding her as the vampire underneath gained an advantage. As he tried to roll her off, she vanished once more, his fingers closing in on themselves. Alain scrambled to his feet, looking around the cabin that was quickly being engulfed by flames and smoke. Drunkenly, he staggered out into the street, suddenly knocked to the ground by an unseen force. Fingers dug into his throat from behind as Lenga continued the assault. She pinned his arms to the ground with her thighs, choking the life from him. He turned his head to the left, his vision darkening as he succumbed to the witch. As the life ebbed from him, Alain saw a pair of boots come into his vision, striding purposefully towards him. The fingers were ripped from his throat as he lay face down in the mud. "Get your filthy hands off me you..."

Her words trailed off, allowing Alain to turn over. He looked up, seeing a familiar figure holding Lenga by the throat. "Elias?" he said.

Elias looked down at Alain as he held the witch two feet off the ground. "I'm not Elias," he said. I am Virdelas." He backhanded Lenga across the face, knocking several of Marlies' well-kept teeth into the night.

She hollered in pain as blue lightning emitted from her finger-tips. She jabbed them into the vampire's face, forcing him to drop her. Lenga needed no instruction. She turned and fled, heading upwards towards the summit. Virdelas extended his hand, lifting his brother to his feet. "The witch and the boy are still sleeping. Let us finish the witch now."

"How did you do this?" Alain asked incredulously.

"The witch's stone. It healed the wound in Elias' chest. So, I took my opportunity and entered his vessel. I feel strong, Brother. If I can destroy the witch and consume her strength, then I will be stronger than I ever was."

"Let's finish this. I have a hold on the witch and you do on the boy. They will not go far. Come." They took off up the winding street, catching glimpses of their folly ahead. They quickened their pace, their huge strides making ground on Lenga. After a minute, she passed by the highest point in Tenta, scrabbling over rocks that led down to the black sea below. They crested the summit seconds later, spying a single-track road that led in the opposite direction from the road they'd arrived on. "She's heading for the road," Alain said. "Come, Brother."

"I'm with you. If I fall behind, keep going. I will catch up," Virdelas said, getting used to his new shell.

Ahead, Lenga tripped, gambolling down the wet slope until she lay floundering on the gravel roadway. Gingerly, she climbed to her feet, seeing the two giants advancing on her. Two pairs of eyes, burning into hers. One yellow, the other red. They were filled with hatred. She knew she was in peril. "DO YOUR WORST!" she screamed as they came within touching distance, stopping dead at her hollering. Blue flames emitted from her fingers, finding their target as she caught Alain in the chest. He fell over backwards, striking his head on the ground. Lenga's fingers sought out her next target, milky eyes hunting for the vampire she once knew as Elias. Before she could emit a charge, he crashed into her, driving the wind from her lungs. They both went down, rolling on the roadway as waves crashed next to them, engulfing the pair totally.

"Die, crone," Virdelas commanded as he pushed his thumbs into her white eyes, burying them to the knuckle.

"WAAAAA," she screamed as she heard each eyeball rupture with a sickening, squelching pop.

However, Virdelas was not finished. He removed his thumbs, pushing his index finger back into the bloody socket. Curling it inside her skull, he ripped the top of her nose off, another gargled scream coming from the witch underneath him. "Lenga, you die," he said as he bit her below the ear, pinning her hands to the ground. Virdelas lay on top, worrying her neck as he took her life-force. Blue sparks shot from her fingers, lighting the path and the sea beyond. Gradually, her struggles lessened until she lay still as another wave crashed over them.

"It is over," Alain said as he stood over Virdelas, hauling his kin to his feet.

They looked at each other breathlessly, a wry grin coming from Virdelas. "She was a tough old bitch. You would have struggled without me, Brother."

"You are right. She was strong and slippery. More than a match for most. How do you feel?"

"Strong. Ready for the next battle."

Alain noticed that Virdelas now stood a few inches over him, his frame broad and imposing. He clapped his brother on the shoulder, his yellow eyes glowing. "Then let us find our next battle. We have a demon and a man to kill. Let's head back and collect our friends from the cabin. Then we ride."

A while later, they opened the cabin door, ducking under the door frame to enter. In the centre of the room, Father Stephen's body lay, staring eternally at the ceiling. He was alone. The witch and the boy were nowhere to be seen. "They cannot have gone far," Alain said. "We will find them." As they stepped back onto the porch, readying their departure, they were greeted by a dozen flaming torches.

"Have at them," a man said as he stepped onto the porch, a large wooden cross held aloft. The vampires fell back into the cabin, slamming the door.

"Follow me," Alain said as he kicked a hole in the far wall.

Virdelas headed for the hole as a searing pain wracked his body. He turned, howling in pain as the ringleader was upon him. "Stay away," he shouted, his red eyes burning with fury.

"You killed our folk," the ringleader said, his long spear aimed at the vampire's chest. He lost his footing, falling backwards through the hole into a pair of strong arms.

"Come, Brother. Follow me." Virdelas needed no coaxing. They fled upwards, heading towards the spot where the witch lay dead. Shouts and curses followed them, glowing crosses propelling them upwards until they were floundering down wet rocks towards the sea. "Let them come," Alain said. "This path leads back towards town. We can make a break for it."

Virdelas pointed along the path as men started filing out of the settlement towards them. "Look, Brother. More of them."

Alain watched the other group of town folk, cursing at their bad luck. "They are trying to cut us off." A deep drone rumbled across the sea as large black shapes emerged from the frigid waters. "I have a plan, Brother. Stand behind me." Virdelas obeyed, as Alain stood in the centre of the path, his eyes seeking out the ringleader.

"You will pay for what you have done," the man shouted, trying to raise his voice over the crash of the sea. As he drew nearer, he locked eyes with the vampire, his cross and pike falling to the floor. The man smiled, walking towards the sea.

"Brynn. What are you doing?" another shouted as the ringleader stepped into the sea. Before anyone could speak, a dark shape plucked him from the shore, dragging him underneath the waves. The villagers screamed in horror, watching helplessly as their friend was taken by the Orga. Alain locked eyes with another, a large female with a shaved head. Moments later, she too was pulled from the path by a black behemoth.

"It's working," Virdelas said. He stepped forward, following his brother's lead. One by one, the attackers fell into the sea until only a few remained.

"They have us beat," one of the remaining party said. "Fall back." They turned, fleeing back towards Tenta, the brother's following. They picked them off with ease, draining them until half a dozen bodied littered the roadway.

"Now. Let's go and find the witch and the boy. They cannot be far away," Virdelas said.

They climbed the rocks, weaving their way back through Tenta as frightened inhabitants looked on through windows and doors. The brothers finally walked back to where they had tethered the cart. It was gone. "They have fled," Alain said, his voice thick with anger.

"Which way?" Virdelas replied.

"If I was to wager a bet, I'd say back the way we came."

"So, let us be after them. I can feel my hold on the boy slipping away the further he goes."

"We shall. But let's have some sport first. Lenga is gone. The humans are decimated. But a few remain. Let us feast before we hunt."

Virdelas smiled, turning back towards the settlement. "Why not. Lead on, Alain."

Away from the town, the cart lurched and bumped over the gravel path. Alana sat on the wooden bench, snapping the reigns feverishly. Next to her, Jasper bounced erratically, his face a mixture of horror and excitement. "Ya," she shouted as leather struck the beast's flank, urging it forward. "Just stay with me, little one," she said. "We need to be away from this place. We may have little time before they are on to us." Jasper said nothing. He just floated there, looking out towards the sea. Hoping, that they would find a way out of the forsaken land. Before the monsters came for them once more.

Thirty

Vicky sat in Jasper's chair, scrolling through her phone as her son lay motionless. The house had returned to normal after the incident a few hours previous. She had tidied the kitchen, replacing the furniture and restacking the shelves, where objects had moved and fallen. She sat, with a cup of coffee next to her, looking at Facebook as low cloud skimmed the trees outside. The machine beeped steadily, relaxing Vicky as she looked at her sister's photographs. A noise in the room made her look up from the screen. *What was that?* she thought as she scanned the bedroom. Jasper lay still, the rise and fall of his chest steady. Vicky was about to return to her phone when the duvet on the bed twitched.

"Jasper?" she said, standing up. He didn't answer. As she took a step forward, the bed cover moved again, uncovering the sleeping boy. *What the?* she thought again as it continued moving towards her until her son was totally uncovered. Vicky touched his foot, tickling the sole gently. "Jasper. Can you hear me?" she asked, her pulse quickening. No response. Gently, the woman covered her son over, tucking the duvet into the sides of the bed. Her hand moved towards his head, about to stroke his dark curls when Jasper bounced from the mattress. "God," she exclaimed as he landed back onto the bed, the machine next to him starting to beep quicker. Picking up her phone, she dialled Ashley's number, her fingers shaking.

"Hi Vicky," Ashley said.

"Ashley. Hi."

"Is everything okay?"

"I'm not sure. Jasper just moved. Well bounced actually. Plus, his duvet moved. Not a little bit. It rolled itself up on its own."

"Oh my god! That's just."

"Unbelievable," Vicky replied. Finding the nurse's word for her.

"Yes. I still don't know what to think about what happened earlier. It's just. Well. Weird?"

"I know. And I hope it's not scared you away. Would you be able to pop by? His machine is beeping faster now too."

"Okay. I am out with my family. But we are close by. I can swing past on our way to the bowling. Say, twenty minutes or so?"

"Perfect. I really appreciate your help."

"Don't mention it. I'll be there shortly."

"Okay. Bye."

"Bye for now," Ashley replied.

Vicky stood there, phone in hand, Facebook forgotten. *Should I call Jake?* she thought. *No. He's driving. I'll text later.* She walked over, picking up her tea before heading downstairs to wait for the nurse to arrive.

Fifteen minutes later, a car pulled up outside the cottage. Vicky walked down the path, smiling as Ashley climbed out of the car. "Thanks for coming."

"Don't mention it." She turned to the passenger windows. "That's Jeffrey," she said, pointing at the boy who peered out of the car window.

"Hello. I'm Vicky."

"This is my Mum, Rita. And my Cousin, Lizzy. We're heading out for an afternoon at Great Park. Bowling, then the movies."

"Sounds lovely. Hello," Vicky replied. Both women smiled back, saying their hellos. She could see the family resemblance. Her mother looked to be in her late forties, with an attractive face, framed by dark hair. Her cousin sat next to Jeffrey, with similar dark hair and black-rimmed glasses. Both women looked vaguely familiar to her.

"I won't be a tick," Ashley said to the others, following Vicky up the path towards the house. Once inside, they headed upstairs, both pulses quickening somewhat.

Vicky opened the door to the bedroom, walking in ahead of the nurse. "It's happened again," she said to Ashley.

"Oh my," the nurse replied as she saw the rumpled duvet cover that had collected at the boy's feet. She walked over, checking the tubes and wires carefully as Vicky watched on expectantly. After a minute, Ashley turned to her as she pulled the duvet back in place. "He seems fine. Yes, his heart rate is slightly elevated. But not worryingly so."

"So how do you explain the fact that he bounced off the mattress?"

"I have no idea, hun. I can see that the duvet has moved. And I believe you. After what I saw earlier, I think that anything is possible. Did your visitor come by?"

"Yes. And more weird stuff happened whilst he was here."

"Oh. Like what?"

"Can we keep this between us?"

"Of course. My lips are sealed."

"Someone or something has taken Jasper. I know that sounds ridiculous. But it's true. Everything that I thought to be true has been turned on its head over the last few weeks."

"I really don't know what to say, Vicky. It all sounds so far-fetched. But I know what I saw earlier. If what you say is true, maybe he's not in a coma. I just cannot get my head around it though."

"Well, hopefully Jake will be able to help. We're going to try to get him back"

"How?"

"Well. There's a doorway close by."

"Doorway?" Ashley replied blankly.

"Yes. To another world. Again, I am sorry if this is freaking you out. But I know it's true. I've seen too much to discount this, Ashley."

"Just be careful. I just cannot get my head around this."

"I promise I'll be careful. Jake will be back soon. We're going to try this."

Ashley looked down at Jasper, hoping somehow that the little boy was going to be alright. "Well, I'll be back on Monday. If you need me, call or text me."

"Thank you. And I am so sorry you've gotten involved in all this. As her words ended, the duvet moved once more, slipping from the bed onto the carpeted floor.

"Jesus!" the nurse exclaimed loudly. She looked at Vicky, taking the woman's hand in her own. Her complexion clammy, features stricken. "Just get him back. Whatever it takes."

* * *

Jake pulled onto his driveway at just after 6 pm. After leaving Vicky's house, he'd taken a tour of his old stomping grounds, driving through the suburbs of

Rednal and Barnt Green, before heading towards the motorway. He'd driven home at a leisurely pace, contemplating what to tell Katherine and Wilf about his visit to The Midlands. As he'd headed south, the clouds had parted, the land being basked in warm sunshine. The horrors he'd recently faced seemed to land on the motorway behind him as he edged every southward towards Cornwall. Jake knew though, that he had one more job to do. A final task, that may finish matters once and for all. He opened his car door, stretching his back before heading around the back of the 4x4.

The front door opened, Katherine appearing on the step, a tentative smile on her face. "Hi, babe. You okay?"

"Come here," Jake said as he wrapped his arms around her. He kissed her softly on the lips, drawing a sigh from Katherine. She broke the kiss, nuzzling his neck playfully. "Will you always welcome me home like that?" he said smiling.

"Always, Mr Stevenson." She looked at him. "So, what news?"

"Let's go inside before Linda comes out and starts flirting with me." They walked into the hallway, closing the door behind them. Jake kicked off his trainers, leaving them next to an oak telephone table near the foot of the stairs. He followed Katherine into the kitchen, smiling at Wilf and Alicia. "Hello, princess," he said, holding his arms out.

"Go to your Papa," the older man said, handing over his great niece. He stood up, walking over to the windowsill to retrieve his pipe and tobacco. "Come on then. Don't leave us with our blinkers closed. What news?"

Jake walked around the kitchen, bouncing his daughter on his hip whilst trying to find the right words to start. "Well. Things have happened."

"What kind of things?" Katherine said, taking Alicia from him. She walked over to the table, sitting down with the infant, an expectant look on her face.

"Okay. When I got there, things started happening. The furniture in the kitchen started to move on its own for a start."

"Fuckenhell," Wilf said as he opened the kitchen door. He lit his pipe, standing just outside of the house so the smoke blew away on the summer breeze.

"We headed upstairs to be greeted by an apparition."

"You mean a spirit?" Wilf said as he puffed away.

"Yes. It was Virdelas. The father of Korgan and Reggan. He is pissed at me for destroying them. He wants revenge. He said he is coming after us all. Tamatan too."

"They're never going to leave us be, Jake. They've already been here once, and we know the strife that caused. Do you think they will come here again?"

Jake sighed, his shoulders dropping. "Yes, I do. And I'm betting that two of them will come for us. His brother Alain is with him too."

"So, what do we do?" Wilf said.

"Jake's going after them. Aren't you, babe?"

"I don't think we have an option."

"I'll come with you," Wilf said without thinking.

"No, Wilf. You need to stay here with Kath and Alicia. If anything happens to me, at least I know that you are with them."

"Fair enough. When will you go?"

"Tomorrow, hopefully. I'd rather do this now, then wait for them to find us."

"What will you take with you?" Katherine asked.

"Well, I've taken guns before. But I think just stakes, crosses, and maybe some holy water. That's all I will need."

"When will you be back?" she asked, a sinking feeling spreading through her.

"Well, that's the thing. I left my bike there, last time. It should be where I left it. If it is, then we should be a lot quicker."

"We?" Katherine replied.

"Yes. Vicky is insisting that she comes with me. I said that if I was to go, I should do so alone. But she was adamant."

"Oh," Katherine said, not quite sure what her emotions were telling her.

Jake knelt beside her, taking her hand. "I promise I will be back. I lost you once. I won't let that happen again."

"No goodbyes. I won't do that, Jake. If you're going tomorrow, then let's enjoy ourselves tonight. We've hardly had the chance to do that recently."

"What are you thinking?"

"Let's take a walk into the village and find a place to eat. After all, you forgot to order Chinese food."

"Sorry, babe. That slipped my mind, Okay. I am easy. Whatever you guys fancy."

"Maybe we could visit the tavern with the nice innkeeper?" Wilf said eagerly.

"I think Wilf has his sights set on someone in the village," Jake said to Katherine, winking at her.

"Then I need to see this woman, Uncle. I need to see if you are good enough for her."

"Do you not mean if she is good enough for me?" Wilf said dryly.

"I know what I said, Uncle Wilf. Do not second guess a woman," she said smiling.

Thirty-One

Alana climbed to her feet slowly, an angry red welt appearing on her forehead. She touched it gently, pressing the swelling flesh at her hairline. "Well, that's the end of that plan," she said, looking at the smashed wheel of the cart. The mule had come free of its shackles, wandering over to a clump of dry grass to feed.

Jasper floated next to the witch, his eyes scanning the land around them. The cabin lay a few hundred feet behind them, dark slopes looming over them. "*I know the way home*," he projected, Alana hearing his thoughts. "*It is too far for us to walk though.*"

"I know, little one. We are indeed far from sanctuary." She looked around herself, an idea formulating in her thoughts. "I do have an idea. Are you ready?" The boy nodded readily as Alana extended her hand. The witch knelt next to Jasper, whispered words escaping her mouth as her fingers gently penetrated the bubble. They linked hands, Alana's form dissipating into an ethereal glow as the bubble consumed her. The orb swelled, until they were both suspended inside it. They looked at each other, smiling in the darkness. Jasper knew instinctively what to do, as he propelled them across the landscape towards the mountains in the distance.

A while later, they came across Alana's shack high up in the mountains. Low cloud had settled over the land, obscuring all around them. She gently tugged on his hand, making Jasper slow to a stop. More words escaped her mouth before she stepped out of the bubble that surrounded them. "Wait here, little one. I need to collect a few things before we carry on." Jasper nodded as the witch disappeared into the cabin, returning a few minutes later. He saw another pendant around her neck, a violet glow pulsing in the mist. An old haversack draped over her shoulder gently bounced against her hip as she hurried over to him. Moments later, they were linked once more, floating above the sodden pathway. "Right. Lead on, Jasper. Take us away from this land." He needed no further instruction as they headed into the cave, through the red doorway, into another world.

* * *

They came to a halt abruptly, their boots skidding to a stop on the pathway. The cart lay on its side, the occupants, nowhere to be seen. The vampires spotted the mule a few hundred yards away, nibbling on grass at the edge of the swamp. "They have fled, Brother," Alain said, his wispy white hair stuck to one side of his white skull.

"I cannot feel the boy. They must be far away. But how?"

"The witch is cunning. She may have cooked up an incantation. My guess is that are heading for the doorway in the mountains."

"Virdelas looked at his sibling, his red eyes burning. "Then let us follow. I know where the boy resides. It will take us a while to get there. But get there we shall."

They took off, their feet barely touching the land as they ran towards the high mountains on the blackened horizon. The vampires felt strong as they dashed across the land. The streets and homes of Tenta littered with their victims. They were not finished though. They had scores to settle. In a far-off place.

* * *

Vicky sat on the sofa, the television airing another program that she was trying to watch. A glass of wine sat perched on the coffee table in front of her. Condensation trickled down the glass and stem, collecting on the cork coaster on which it stood. She reached forward, lifting her Saturday night treat to her lips, the cool liquid relaxing her more and more with each sip. The glass replaced, Vicky placed her head back against the sofa cushions, letting the stresses and strains of the last few hours drain away slowly. She propped her legs on the table, flexing her toes as she tried to breathe deeply through her nose. Classical music floated around the room, adding to the calming atmosphere. The calmness ended as a double rap at the front door made her open her eyes. *What time is it?* she thought, looking at the clock on the mantelpiece. *Almost 10 pm.* She sat forward, taking a hearty glug of her wine before heading out into the hallway. Clicking on the outside light, Vicky opened the front door a few inches. Her brown eyes opened wide, fingers tightening on the door as a woman stood in front of her. She was dressed in a flowing white robe, her long brown hair cascading around an attractive face.

"Vicky?" she asked. Her voice was soft, without a trace of an accent.

"Can I help you?" Vicky replied cautiously.

"I think you can. My name is Alana."

"Err, hello. What can I do for you?"

"Can you not see him next to me?" she said, tilting her head to her left.

Puzzled, Vicky looked past the woman into the darkness. Nothing was there. Or so she thought at first. She could see a blurred image hovering on the garden path. "What the?" Her voice died in her throat as she saw the outline of a figure within the blurred image.

"We have travelled far. I have brought him back to you?"

"Who?"

"Jasper."

Hearing her son's name shocked the woman to her core. Her hand came up to her mouth as she exclaimed loudly. "What!"

The woman turned her head. "Jasper. Come forward," she said, stepping to one side.

Vicky watched, frozen to the spot as a blurred bubble floated towards the doorstep. She looked into the eyes of her son as he peered up at her. "Jasper! Is that really you," she said, her legs unsteady underneath her. Vicky stepped back a few paces, allowing the orb to enter the hallway. It bounced and vibrated against the carpet, the boy's face clear enough for Vicky to see properly. "Oh my god!" she said as tears spilled from her eyes. She remembered Jake's words, describing Jasper as an apparition.

Alana walked into the hallway, closing the door behind her. She looked down at the dark-haired woman who was sobbing openly. "Yes. It is he."

Vicky climbed to her feet unsteadily. "Quick. Follow me," she said, scrambling up the stairs towards the landing. They followed, walking into a darkened bedroom. A table lamp was flicked on, bathing the room in a mellow glow.

"He looks so peaceful," Alana said, looking down at the sleeping boy on the bed.

"Who are you?" Vicky said, still reeling from the shock a few moments before.

"I am Alana. I come from a land far from yours. I am a witch, but don't let that alarm you. Not all of us are bad. I met your Son a while ago. We've been travelling together. Shackled by two monsters. We managed to escape them. Your son led me here."

"Oh Jaspy. I don't know what to say."

"Then say nothing, my friend. Just sit a while." Vicky did as she was bid, walking over to the comfortable chair at the end of the bed. Alana took her son's hand, turning to the bubble that floated next to her. Vicky watched silently as the witch gently pushed her hand into the bubble, seeming to grasp a holographic hand. She looked at the ceiling, her eyes rolling back in her head. Vicky stared on in amazement as the woman uttered alien words that seemed to echo gently around the bedroom. Little by little, the bubble deflated, until it had vanished from sight, leaving the woman stood there, holding the boy's hand. Jasper shifted in his bed, his feet twitching underneath the duvet cover.

"Jasper?" Vicky said as she shot from the chair.

"Mummy," a voice replied as her son opened his eyes. She flew across the bed, burying her face in his neck, crying openly. Alana let go of his hand, stepping back against the wall as the mother and son were reunited.

The boy cried too, wrapping his arms around Vicky's neck. "I'm back, Mummy. I'm so glad to be home with you."

"Oh, love," she said, kissing his wet cheeks. "I've missed you so much. We've all been so worried."

"I know, Mummy. I was worried too. Worried that I would never see you again. Alana helped me."

Vicky looked at the woman, smiling at her. "I can never thank you enough," she said, tears still running down her cheeks.

"I need no thanks. Your son led me here, away from the vampire's that wanted to do us harm. I owe him my life. Many have fallen at their hands. Jasper and I were to be next."

"Oh no. that's terrible. Where are they now?"

"Far from here. We left them on the Island of Tenta. A dark place, where another witch dwelt. Lenga."

"I know that name. I also know what has been happening."

"How, Mummy?" Jasper said, trying to sit up in bed.

Vicky rearranged his pillows, ruffling his curls as she sat next to him. "Bad things have been happening here too. Someone who lives next door tried to kill me."

"Who, Mummy?"

"Maureen. Something happened to her. Someone took over her body. She turned evil. That's when I heard about Lenga. And others too."

"You are fortunate to still be with us," Alana said sombrely. Others were not so lucky."

"I'm just glad that it is over. Someone called Jake has been helping me. He was here earlier. We had planned to come and find Jasper."

"Jake," Alana said. "He was our ally. He was trying to get home to his loved ones. Did he succeed?"

"He did."

Alana smiled, drawing a smile from both mother and son. "He is indeed a fine man. When I met him, he was all but dead. However, the white magic brought him back from the darkness that had infected him."

"He is supposed to be coming back very soon. I guess I should call him." She looked at her son, hugging him tightly.

"Mummy. I'm hungry. Can I have some toast?"

Vicky smiled, kissing the top of his head. "I'm sure you are hungry," she said. You've not eaten anything in months."

Jasper reached up, pulling the tube from his nose. "Ugh. That's horrible, Mummy. Has that been in my nose the whole time?"

"Yes. It's been feeding you. It's called a drip."

"Well I think I would prefer toast, Mummy. The drip is not nice."

"Okay. Can you wait here for a minute? I will make you some toast."

"Thank you, Mummy. Could I have some juice too please?"

"Of course, love." She looked at Alana. "Can I get you anything?"

"That is very kind of you. Whatever you can spare will be more than enough."

Vicky hugged her son, rocking him gently in her arms. "Oh, Jaspy. Never leave me like that again," she said crying openly. Her tears were no longer sad. They were tiny droplets of joy. A few minutes later, the mother laid her son in bed, covering him over. "Okay. Stay here. I'll be back up in a minute." As she headed out of the bedroom, she turned towards the bed, drinking in the sight of her son. Vicky smiled as she watched the woman in white sit next to him, holding his hand lovingly. She left the bedroom, almost skipping down the stairs towards the kitchen.

* * *

"Is she okay?" Jake said as Katherine lifted the cover of the pram to check on their daughter.

"She's fine," Katherine replied. The three of them sat in a quiet corner of the public house as summer revellers started to leave the establishment.

A waitress walked over to the table, smiling at the group. "Was everything okay with your meals?" she enquired, her friendly Cornish twang drawing a smile for them.

"It was indeed fine fayre," Wilf said. "Fit for a king."

She grinned at the older man before clearing the plates away. As she walked off, Jake nudged his friend's arm. "Do you want another?"

"Why not. Shall I go and get them?"

"Well, I've seen you making eyes and the landlady all night Wilf. So, I will let you go and charm her some more. Babe. Would you like another cider?"

"Why not," she replied readily, downing the remainder of her pint glass.

Wilf walked over to the bar, leaving Katherine and Jake at the table. She entwined her fingers in his, pulling him towards her. She gently kissed his lips, her fingers melding into his dark hair. "What was that for?" he replied as goosebumps appeared on his forearms.

"Just because, Jake Stevenson. And because I love you."

"I love you too, babe."

"I know we said no goodbyes. But I am so worried about you leaving us again."

"It will all be okay. I'm coming back to you I promise." Jake looked over at Wilf, a smile spreading across his face. "Look at the old goat."

She looked over, seeing her uncle's attempts at flirting with the woman behind the bar. "I think he has a thing for the her. If only he was a few years younger."

"Oh, I dunno. She seems to be flirting back. Who knows, maybe he will find someone now?"

"I would like that. He's a good man, who's never had the love of a woman. It would make me happy beyond words if that happened now. And she does look nice."

"Well he seems to think so. I've never seen him like this."

"It makes me smile. Father would be scolding him right now. Telling him to stop acting like a goofy stable boy."

They watched as Wilf sauntered back over to them, his hands filled with glasses, his step that of a much younger man. "What is so funny?" he said, suddenly becoming the gruff old man they were used to.

"Are you planning on moving in here?" Jake said. "She seems quite taken with you."

"Nonsense. She is just being accommodating. Much better than the serving wenches at the Tackle Box Inn."

"Well I am a woman, Uncle. And a woman knows things. And I am telling you, she is not just being friendly. She has a soft spot for you, make no mistake."

Wilf sat down, grabbing his glass. "If you say so, Kath. She is a fair looking woman though. Nice way about her. And she has no man to warm her bed."

"How do you know that?" Jake asked, his curiosity piqued.

"She told me so. Her husband passed."

"Oh," Katherine said. "That is sad news."

"Hmm," Jake said as he sipped at his pint. "He can't have been that old?"

"She said he was much older than her."

"Oh right," Jake said. "Maybe she likes the older man?" He winked at Katherine, making her almost choke on her cider.

"I know when I am being made fun of, young Jake. You're not too big for a cuff around the ear."

"Sorry, Wilf. We're just having a laugh with you. It's nice to see you happy is all."

"Well I am. Finally. And I could get used to this ale."

"Play your cards right and you'll be having it for breakfast soon."

Wilf laughed. A hearty sound that made Katherine get up from her chair and hug him. "Bless you, Uncle. It's so nice to see you like this."

He embraced her back, tears forming at the corners of his eyes. "Now don't start getting all soppy on me, Kath. You'll start me off too."

They sat chatting as the world passed them by. When their glasses were empty, they gathered their belongings. They said their goodbyes to the patron, promising to return soon. She smiled back at them, her gaze resting on Wilf a moment longer than the others as they left the lounge. Outside, a balmy breeze accompanied them home. Wilf pushed Alicia happily, while Jake and Katherine ambled behind him arm in arm. Happy, safe, and slightly drunk.

Thirty-Two

They walked through Amatoll together as low mist clung to the forest floor. They had traversed the land of Elksberg, making their way from the sea in the north, to the vast forest that covered much of the western regions. "How far to the doorway?" Alain said.

"Not much further. It will not open for a while yet. Let us find the spot, then I will show you where we can settle."

"Korgan's Vale?"

"Yes, Brother. It is where my beloved son spent his days. It was a sanctuary to him whilst he took the long sleep. He should be here now in my place. Not ashes and dust. The human will pay."

"We must be careful, Virdelas. Put aside your want for revenge. This Jake has seen off many along the road. For a man, he is cunning and resourceful. We should be ready for anything."

"I know. He took my son's. He may have killed the vessel that I now dwell in. He has travelled far and wide, fighting off many foes. He also escaped the witch's thugs. Killing him will be most rewarding. But I will not draw it out. I will merely remove his head from his shoulders. Then kill his kin. Once they are gone, we shall return here."

"There is not much left here. The land is scant and forsaken."

"But we have doorways, Alain. My sons used them to their benefit. They may not be much to offer here, but we have time. And we have endless places to visit. The Vale will be our sanctuary."

"I hope you are right," Alain said, slowing down as his brother came to a halt between two trees.

"This is it. The doorway is here. I can feel it. We have time Brother. Let me show you where we can reside. Then we will come back when the doorway opens. And finish this." They headed through the forest at speed, weaving between the burnt trees, heading for their new home.

* * *

Vicky climbed into bed, an orange glow from the street light filtering in through the blinds. She pulled the duvet over her, which caused Jasper to stir next to her. The boy cuddled into his mother, a pyjama clad leg snaking around her own. She smiled in the darkness, draping an arm across her son. Vicky lay there, listening to her son's gently snores. *Thank god you're home, Jaspy. I'm never letting you out of my sight again.* The gentle snoring, coupled with the gentle rattling of the Venetian blinds, lulled Vicky into a deep and restful sleep.

In the bedroom next door, Alana lay staring at the ceiling. She liked the feel of the violet night dress that the other woman had given her. She climbed out of bed, her bare feet padding over to the window. *What a nice place this is. So different from my home. I may stay awhile, if they permit it.* A noise from behind made the witch look back at the bed. The clock next to Lucy's bed beeped, signalling that Saturday had now moved onto Sunday. However, Alana did not know that. There were many things in the room that made no sense to her. Like the large images that adorned the walls. Groups of young men, with very little in the way of clothing, huddled together, smiling faces looking out at her. Alana walked back to the bed, settling under the warm covers. Sleep took her quickly, which would lead to clouded dreams of darkened forests and strange doorways. Her breathing was steady, the rise and fall of her chest settled. Next to her skin, the magenta stone pulsed, warming her breast as she slept. She was at peace. For now.

* * *

Alain and Virdelas stood in the forest as the doorway vanished from sight. The Lickey Hills lay quiet, save for the noise of infrequent cars that passed a few hundred yards away. "They are close," Virdelas said. "I can smell them from here. The boy is lost to us for now. I have no hold over him. I am guessing that the witch had a hand in this."

"It matters little, Brother. We shall have them soon. Let us hunt."

"Not yet."

"Why ever not?" Alain said, feeling perplexed at his brother's stalling.

"Look up." They craned their necks, taking in the sight of the full moon above them. "There is no cloud, Brother. Half the night has already passed by. The sun will rise soon. And when it does, we will be in trouble. We must find a place to shelter. When the sun sets once more, we will have more time to find them, and kill them."

"You are wise, my, dear Virdelas. Let us find a place to wait. We do not know this land. It may be filled with dangers. We must be careful."

"I agree. Come. Let us forage." They made their way through the forested hill, vaulting a metal fence that led to thick plants and brambles. After a few minutes, they came across the old monastery, where others like them had sought solace. Virdelas led the way, Alain following silently, his eyes roving and searching as they made their way around to a small door at the back of the building. A wooden door opened stiffly, letting them into a musky storeroom. Closing the door behind them, they settled into a dark corner, surrounded by boxes and crates. "We will be safe enough here I think. When the sun kisses the horizon once more, we will make our move."

"Then let us get some rest. We have travelled far, and Alain grows tired." Their eyes closed, heads bowing as they slept. The inhabitants above them in the Monastery, having no clue that an ancient evil was close by. Waiting to cause chaos and destruction.

Thirty-Three

Jake woke early, a stiff breeze ruffling the curtains in the room. He looked over at Katherine, who slept peacefully beside him. He dressed quietly, slipping on a pair of shorts and a t-shirt before heading down into the kitchen. A few minutes later, Jake sat at the kitchen table, a mug of strong coffee in front of him. He scrolled through his phone, catching up on headlines from the news and sports. As he idly read the latest football scores, a message popped up on his screen. He read it quickly, before dialling a number from his contacts. "Hi, Vicky. Is everything okay?"

"Hi Jake," she replied. He could sense a change in her voice. "We've had a bit of an eventful night."

"Really? How so?"

"Well, I was at home last night when there was a knock at the door. I opened it to be greeted by a strange woman. Alana."

"Jesus!" Jake exclaimed, almost spilling his coffee. "You mean?"

"Yes. The same Alana that you know. She was with Jasper. Well, his spirit at least. At least I think that's what you'd call it. Anyway, he's okay. He's awake."

"Bloody hell! I don't know what to say."

"Nor me," she replied, her voice buoyant and chirpy. "I am just over the moon that he is back."

"Where are they now?"

"Upstairs asleep. Jasper came into my bed. It's the happiest I've been in ages."

"I bet." Jake paused, taking a sip of coffee. "So, I guess I don't need to come up today?"

"No. I guess you don't. But thank you anyway. I really appreciate everything that you have done for us."

252

"Think nothing of it. Jasper helped me get home. Without him, I may not have made it back. So, what are your plans now?"

"Well, I suppose I should call the hospital and let them know that he's out of his coma. But not today though. Today is our day."

"Well, I don't blame you. What about Alana?"

"I'm not really sure. What do you know about her?"

"Well, she lived in the place where we got lost. She is a witch. But not the scary kind. I owe her my life."

"Well, she seems lovely. Unusual but lovely. I'm not sure what she will do. She may want to head back home?"

"Err. I doubt that. Her only relative was killed recently. I'm pretty sure she has nothing to go back to."

"Oh well, I suppose we'll just go with the flow. She can stay here for as long as she wants. Not sure how I will explain it to my parents though."

An idea came to Jake as he listened, forming quickly in his mind. "I tell you what. Why don't I pop up anyway? I can bring Alana down here with us. After all, Dad's house is currently lying empty and I have no idea what I'm going to do with it. At some point, I'll have to let people know that he's gone missing or something."

"Oh. How will you manage that?"

"Not sure yet. Mum was reported missing a few months ago. She was declared dead shortly afterwards. The police said she'd been washed out to sea in the storms. I may be able to spin it that Dad never got over it and has gone AWOL."

"Do you think that will work?"

"I don't know. But I'll have to do something soon. But anyway. Alana could come down here for a while until we figure out what we're doing."

"Okay. That sounds good to me. When she gets up, I'll tell her what you've said. I hope she doesn't think I'm booting her out."

"She won't. So, what time shall I come up?"

"Whenever you want. There is no immediate rush."

"Okay. I will speak to Kath and Wilf, then send you a text."

"Good idea."

"And I am so happy that Jasper is back with you. I was ready to go and find him. Having him turn up like this great."

"God, you're not wrong there. And Katherine and Wilf will be happy that you're not going on any more adventures."

"True. I will tell them when they get up."

"I think I can hear movement upstairs. I'll go and see if someone's stirring."

"Okay. I will speak to you later, Vicky."

"You will. And thank you, Jake."

"Thank you too, Vicky. Have a good day."

"You too. Bye for now."

"Bye," Jake replied, ending the call. He sat at the table, a lopsided grin on his face. *Well done, Jasper. You made it,* he thought as he drained his mug. Placing it in the sink, he made Katherine a mug of tea, taking it upstairs to see if she was stirring too.

* * *

Vicky walked to the foot of the stairs as Jasper started descending them sleepily. "Hello, sleepy bear. Are you okay?"

"Yes, Mummy. I'm fine, but really hungry." She knelt on the second step, gathering her son into her embrace. "So, what would, Mr Sleepy Bear like for breakfast?"

"Could I have a bacon sandwich?"

"For you, anything," she replied as he cuddled her, wrapping his legs around her waist. She carried him into the kitchen, sitting him at the table. "Do you want a drink?"

"Please, Mummy. A milky tea please."

Vicky busied herself, flicking the kettle on before heading over to the fridge. She pulled out a pack of smoked bacon, piercing the film with a sharp knife. Jasper sat there silently, watching his mother prepare his breakfast. As he watched her, a thought came to him. "Mummy. Are Grandma and Grandad okay?"

"They're fine, Jaspy. They've just been really worried about you. We all have. I will call them in a bit. I'm sure that they will want to see you."

"I'd like that, Mummy. I have missed them so much."

"Aww. They will like to hear that. When we took you to the hospital, they were heartbroken. They've been worried sick."

"Well, I am better now. So, they don't need to worry anymore."

Vicky walked over to him, hugging him tightly. "No more worries. And no more dramas. We've had enough of that to last us a lifetime." She made his tea, placing it on a coaster for him while she cooked the bacon.

The kitchen door opened quietly, Alana poking her head through the opening. "Good morning."

"Hi. Did you sleep well?"

"As well as can be expected. Back home, I sleep on a straw mattress with animal furs. Your bed is much more to my liking."

"That's good. Would you like some breakfast?"

"Thank you. Whatever you can spare."

"Well, you sit down with the adventurer, and I'll cook you something."

"Thank you. Hello, little man. Are you feeling well?"

"Hello, Alana. I am, thank you. I slept with Mummy. Much better than bouncing around on the back of that horrible cart."

"Indeed, it is," she said, taking a place next to him at the table.

"Cart?" Vicky said as she placed three fresh rashers in the pan.

"Yes, Mummy. The vampires who took us put us in the back of a cart. They were going to kill the witch called Lenga. That's when we escaped."

"Oh. How did you manage that?" she replied, turning Jasper's bacon in the pan.

"They left us in a cabin, while they went to look for her. So, we escaped. If we had not, I think they were going to hurt us too."

"Well, they are gone now, love. And if they ever try to hurt you again, they will have me to answer to."

"Thank you, Mummy. You're the best."

Vicky turned to the stove as tears stung her eyes. Alana picked up on the woman's rising emotions, walking over to her. "You are safe now," she said, turning Vicky towards her.

Without thinking, Vicky embraced the witch, wrapping her arms around Alana's neck. "Thank you for saving him. I owe you everything."

Alana returned the hold. "You owe me nothing, Vicky. Your son helped me too. He is a very special little boy."

Vicky let go of the witch, smiling and wiping her eyes. "Yes. He sure is. Talking of special people, I spoke to Jake. He is coming up to see us."

"When?" Jasper said eagerly.

"Today I think. I need to message him back."

"Is Jake in good health?" the witch asked.

"He is. He asked about you, Alana. I told him you were well. In fact, we were wondering what your plans are now?"

The witch sat back down, arranging her nightgown as she got comfortable. "In truth, I have no plans. My kin is gone. My home was never really that. It was just a place where I resided."

"Well, you're more than welcome to stay here, Alana. However, Jake suggested that you travel back with him."

"Oh. Really? I do not know what to say. That is a very kind gesture from both of you. Does Jake live close by?"

"Not really. It's quite a long journey. Probably three or four hours by car."

"Car? What is a car?"

"Right. You're from another world. Okay. Well a car is something that you use to get about the place. Like a horse and cart. Only much faster."

"I see. Your world has many strange things in it. Even how you prepare food looks strange to me. But I cannot argue with how it smells. It is beyond words."

"Well, I only hope it tastes as good as it smells," Vicky said as she placed three well-cooked rashers of bacon on a slice of farmhouse bread. She added some brown sauce, placing another piece on top before slicing the sandwich in two. "Here you go, Mr Greedy Guts," she said as she placed the sandwich in front of her son.

"Thank you, Mummy," Jasper said, attacking his breakfast with gusto, brown sauce quickly becoming smeared across his face. He wiped at it with the back of his hand, licking it off greedily.

"Where are you table manners, young man?" she said smiling.

"Sorry," he said between mouthfuls. "It's so good, Mummy."

A few minutes later, Vicky handed the witch her sandwich, watching with interest as the strange woman polished it off quickly. "Thank you, Vicky. That was the finest thing I have ever tasted. Where I come from, food is scarce and very plain."

"Well I can do more if you like," Vicky said, placing a few rashers in the pan for herself.

"Thank you. I think that is enough for now." She sipped at her tea, liking the sweet taste it gave. "I have been thinking about what you said earlier. I think it would be a good idea if I travelled with Jake. You have just been reunited with your son. You need to be with each other, without a stranger getting in the way."

"Believe me, you're not in the way, Alana. You're welcome to stay as long as you like."

"I thank you for that. But I will go with Jake. I am sure I will see you both again."

Secretly relieved, Vicky smiled. "Of course, you will. You saved my son. I now consider you a friend for life."

The witch smiled, her face lighting up. "Really? I have never had a friend before. Only Silas, who was my kin. Where I am from, folk are as scarce as the food. And most of the folk I come across are not what you would call friendly."

"Well, I am glad you made it here. If you'd not turned up when you did, Jake and I would have been heading for your land." A thought occurred to Vicky as she looked at the other woman. "Could you stand up, please? I want to see how tall you are." Alana pushed back her chair standing in front of Vicky. "I'd say you're roughly the same size as me, although your figure is much nicer," she said, noticing the witch's curves. Her eyes were drawn to her cleavage, secretly envying the size and shape of the woman's breasts. "What is that?" she said looking at the pendant that sat in the middle of her chest.

"It's a healing stone. They are quite rare. I wear them all the time. They can come in most useful."

"It's so pretty," she said, gently taking the stone between her thumb and forefinger. Its purple edges shimmered under the down-lighters, gently pulsing in Vicky's grip." Wow. It feels like it's alive."

"It is, in essence. When you wear it, your lifeforce seeps into the stone. I have always worn stones like this. There are dark stones too. Ones that can be used for dark magic."

"Well, you will find our world very boring compared to where you come from. We have no witches or dark magic."

"That pleases me. I have had my fill of darkness and evil."

"Good. Anyway, I went off track slightly. I think you are about the same size as me. So, if it's okay with you, I'll give you some clothes. As beautiful as you are, flowing white robes might draw attention to you."

"I thank you for your kindness. I only wish that I could repay you somehow?"

Vicky looked at her son, smiling as she did so. "You brought my son home. It's me that will never be able to repay you."

Thirty-Four

Jake placed the mug on the bedside table, kissing Katherine on the lips gently. Her eyes opened slowly, a warm smile changing her features. "Hello, you," she said sleepily.

"Hi, babe. I brought you a cup of tea. Did you sleep well?" he said, walking around the bed before lying next to her.

"Yes. Alicia had me up during the night. But I am well-rested, thank you."

"I have just spoken to Vicky. Guess who is home?"

"What? Who?" Katherine said, sitting up in bed.

"Jasper."

"Oh my! How did that happen?"

"Alana and Jasper escaped from the vamps, and somehow made it back to Vicky's."

"That's unbelievable. I am lost for words."

"Well, there's a first."

She punched his arm playfully, picking up her tea. After taking a sip, she looked at Jake, her face expectant. "So, no more vampire hunts?"

"No. Although, I am driving up later. Just to see them. I may bring Alana back with me if that's okay with you?"

"Oh. I suppose so. Why?"

"Because she can't really go back. She may be in danger if she does. Vicky offered to put her up. However, we have two houses here, one of them empty. I thought that eventually, Wilf could take Dad's house. There would be room for Alana too until she knows exactly what she wants to do with herself."

"I suppose it makes sense. Uncle Wilf won't mind. We can ask him when he wakes up."

"Okay. So, it's all good. No more trips through doorways. No more vampires or witches. Well, one witch. A good one though."

Katherine placed her tea back on the bedside table, turning back to cuddle into her man. "What time will you leave?"

"Not sure yet. I'll text Vicky in a bit. I was thinking this afternoon, then driving back tonight with Alana."

"So, you have nowhere to go just yet?" she said, her hands sliding down the front of his t-shirt to his shorts.

Jake smiled, his arousal becoming evident. "What about Wilf?"

"Wilf could sleep through a stampede of bison. I need to feel what I have been missing."

"Your wish is my command," he replied as Katherine's hand slipped into his waistband.

* * *

"Hi, Mum. You both okay?" Vicky said as she sat on the sofa in her living room,

"Hi, love. We're fine. Your Father is cutting the grass. Keeps him out of mischief. How are things there?"

"Jasper woke up."

"W-what?" Karen stammered.

"He woke up last night. He's fine."

There was a pause on the line, Vicky could hear her mother running through her house. "MIKE. MIKE! Come here. I don't care. Inside now!"

Vicky smiled, picturing her father's face after being scolded by his wife. "Are you there?"

"Yes, love. Hang on. Your Father is coming." Vicky heard a crackle on the line as her mother switched on the speakerphone. "Can you hear us?"

"I can. Hello, Dad."

"Hello, love. What's up?"

"Jasper woke up last night, Dad. He's going to be okay." Vicky listened, tears rolling down her face as she heard her father break down on the other end of the line. She wiped her eyes, her parent's sobs coming through the phone clearly as their emotions soared.

"When was this?" Mike said, his voice faltering.

"About ten. I went up to him before I took a shower. His feet were moving," she lied, relaying the tale she had prepared in her head to her parents. "I sat with him, gently talking to him. Then all of a sudden, his eyes opened."

"Can we speak to him?" Karen said.

"Of course. Hang on." She walked into the kitchen, looking at Jasper and Alana. Vicky pressed the mute button, looking at her son. "Now remember. You know what to say. Okay? No talk of witches and vampires."

"Okay, Mummy." Alana sat next to him, looking curiously at the phone in the other woman's hand.

Vicky pressed the mute button again, then the speaker icon. "Are you there?"

"We are," they replied in unison.

She handed the phone to her son, taking her place at the table. "Hello?"

"Oh love. Oh, Jasper! Welcome back. We've been so worried about you." More sobs from Mike as he heard his grandson's voice again.

"I am fine, Grandma. Hello, Grandad. It's Jasper."

"Hello, sunshine," Mike said on the other end of the line. "We've missed you so much."

"I've missed you both too. When can I see you?"

"As soon as possible," Karen replied. "Vicky, can we pop round today?"

Vicky eased the phone out of her son's hand, composing herself. "Can we do it in the morning, Mum? The nurse is coming out to see him later. And to be honest, I'm shattered. I didn't sleep a wink last night," she lied once more. "I just lay watching Jasper sleep."

"Oh," her mother replied, slightly deflated. "I suppose so."

"Sorry, Mum. I look like hell, and I feel like crap. Jasper is still tired. I guess it will take him a bit of time to get back to normal."

"That's fine, love," Mike replied. "Whenever you're ready. We'll bring some cakes round to celebrate. Does that sound okay, Jasper?"

"Yes, please Grandad. Chocolate cake please," he said smiling.

More sobbing came through the phone, constricting Vicky's heart. She felt awful lying to them, delaying their reunion with Jasper. However, she knew it was the right thing to do. She had already lied to them over the phone. Having to do it again to explain why Alana was there, was one lie too far. She comforted herself, knowing that things would return back to normal tomorrow. Her parents would have their grandson back. It was a small price to pay for the greater good she thought. "We're going to have a bit of a nap now, guys.

When we wake up, I'll call you back, so you can have a good chin-wag with the man of the moment."

"Okay. That's fine, Vicky," Mike said.

"Yes. That's fine," Karen said, slightly cooler.

"Well, I will let you get back to your Sunday morning. I'll speak to you soon. Love you."

"We love you too. Both of you."

"Love you, Grandad. Love you, Grandma."

"Love you, Jasper," Mike said.

Karen tried to reply, her voice cracking as she broke down in her husband's arms. "Love you, Jasper," she croaked.

Vicky ended the call, wiping the tears from her eyes. She walked over to the counter, tearing off a piece of kitchen towel. Her tears wiped away, she looked at the clock on the microwave. "I'll call Jake back in a bit. See what time he's planning on coming up to see us. Does anyone want anything to eat or drink?"

"I am fine, thank you, Vicky," Alana replied.

"I'm good, Mummy," her son said. "I will make myself a juice in a bit."

Vicky looked at the witch, who sat there smiling back at her. "Why don't we get you kitted out in some Earth clothes?" she said clumsily. "As nice as you look in that nightgown, you might feel better once I've sorted you a few bits and pieces out."

"Thank you. That is most kind of you. I am afraid I have no way of compensating you for your garments."

"Don't be silly. It's no trouble. And while I think about it, I'll show you how to work the shower."

"Shower?" the witch said, a blank expression on her face.

"You've got so many new things to experience. I think you will like showers. I spend loads of time in ours. Come with me. We'll get you sorted out."

Alana followed Vicky out of the kitchen, up the carpeted staircase to the cottage's bathroom. It was a sizeable room, with slate grey floor and wall tiles. A toilet sat next to the door, with a white sink next to it, encased in a built-in unit. Above the sink, a large round mirror with LED lights dotted around its perimeter made a feature of the one wall. A white bath lay underneath obscured window on the far wall, a large shower cubicle a few feet away. "It's so shiny," Alana said, running her hand across the porcelain sink.

"We had the bathrooms redone a few years ago. Jasper mainly uses this one now. I have my own en-suite. Which is like a smaller version of this."

"Oh. I see," Alana said, not sure of what to say. "Is that what I think it is?" she said pointing at the pristine toilet.

"Yes. I take it the ones from your world are not like that?"

"You are correct. I won't share with you how we do things in my world. It's not pleasant."

"Well let me show you how to use the shower," she said walking over to the cubicle. Sliding the glass door open, Vicky flicked a chrome switch that was set into the tiling. The rose above her head sprang to life, cascading warm water into the cubicle.

"Praise the gods!" Alana said in awe. "I have never seen such a thing. It's truly amazing."

"I thought you'd like it. There are shower gels and shampoo there for you. I know it's a lot to take in. But it's very easy to use. You just open each bottle, pour some cream onto your hand and rub it into your body and hair. Then wash it off. You enjoy yourself. There are towels to use here. When you get out of the shower, wrap them around you. There is a brush to comb your hair, once it's dry. Oh, and if you need the toilet before you shower, just push that silver button when you're all done."

"What shall I do with my garment?" Alana asked.

"I'll wash it for you. You can take it down with you later."

"You are too kind," Alana said pulling the purple nightgown over her head. She handed it to Vicky, who stood there dumbstruck at the witch's nakedness. "What is wrong?" she said, completely unaware of the situation.

"Err. It's fine," Vicky said, trying to divert her eyes away from the witch's figure. Her eyes skirted over the other woman's pale skin, noting with envy the flawless complexion and toned muscles. She clawed her eyes back the witch's, smiling coyly. "People don't do that here really. I wouldn't do that at Jake's house. His woman might not like it."

"Oh. Sorry. I had no idea that I had done wrong." She turned, wrapping a towel around her body, covering up buoyant breasts and shapely hips. "I will remember not to uncover like that again."

Vicky smiled. "Believe me. If I had a figure like yours, I'd be proud to show it off." She left Alana to her own devices, smiling to herself as she crossed the landing to her own bedroom. Lying on the firm bed, she activated her phone, dialling Jake's number. "Hi, Jake," she said happily.

"Hi, Vicky. How's things there?" he replied.

"Good. Everything is just fine. I phoned my parent's. To say they're over the moon is an understatement."

"Ah. That's nice to hear. I bet they have been worried sick."

"They have. They wanted to come around straight away. I had to put them off though, which was hard."

"Because of Alana?"

"Yes. I'm not sure how I'd explain that one."

"True. Oh well, I'm sure they will see him tomorrow."

"They will. Are you still coming up today?"

"Yeah. Katherine wants to pop to Tesco's in a bit. We've not got much in, as you can imagine. Is it okay if I come up after that? Is about five-ish too late?"

"No. I think that should be fine. Are you sure you're okay to take Alana back with you?"

"Yes. We can figure everything out over the next few days, as to how we're all going to live. But you guys need family time. I think it's better this way."

"I know. She is lovely though. Unlike anyone I've ever met before."

"Well you don't get to meet many witches from parallel dimensions, do you?"

She laughed, the stresses and strains seeping into the mattress below her. "I guess not. Well, I will let you get ready for your trip to the shops, and I'll see you this afternoon."

"Okay. You have a good day."

"You too. Drive safe, Jake."

"Thanks. Bye for now."

"Bye," she said, ending the call. *What a lovely guy,* Vicky thought. *Not many like him around anymore. Nice looking too. Very nice looking.* She looked across the bed, where a picture of herself and her husband looked back at her. They were smiling and carefree, with palm trees behind them. "Sorry, Steve. I shouldn't have said that." She climbed off the bed, putting her phone in her back pocket before heading downstairs to check on Jasper.

* * *

Katherine stood on the doorstep. Her flowery dress being ruffled by the sea breeze. Alicia bounced happily on her hip, grabbing at her mother's buttons. "What time will you be home, babe?"

"I'd say about ten. Three hours each way. I'll probably stay for an hour or so."

"You should take some food with you?"

"I'm fine. I've just had a sandwich, and I'm sure Vicky will try and feed me something. I won't starve, promise."

"Good. We need to fatten you up. You've gotten so skinny lately."

"Well that's what happens when a good woman doesn't cook your tea every night," he said grinning.

"Well, when you get home, I will fatten you up, you can count on that, Jake Stevenson."

He walked over, kissing her hard on the mouth. A little moan escaped her lips, Katherine's neck flushing pink, despite the cooling winds. "And you can do that again when you get home, babe. I've missed those kisses."

"Deal. I hope you're ready. Bye princess," he said, kissing his daughter's chubby cheeks. She grinned at him, showing off pink gums as she tried to grab him. Jake scooped her into his arms, rocking her back and forth in the breeze. "You be a good little princess for your Mummy." She giggled as he tickled her pink toes, before handing her back to Katherine. A farewell kiss was planted on Katherine once more before he turned towards his dark Nissan.

"No adventures," Wilf said from the carport. He stood, leaning against the wall, pipe stuck firmly between his teeth.

"I promise. I'll be home later. You're in charge." Jake climbed into the truck, buzzing down his window as the older man approached.

"I think we both know who is in charge," he said, a wry smile etched on his face. Jake smiled as he backed out of the driveway, pulling away towards the end of the street until he disappeared from sight. Wilf walked over to Katherine, stroking Alicia's hair. "Don't worry yourself. He'll be home soon."

"I know, Uncle. I will always worry about him though."

"I know you will, Kath. He's your man."

"Yes, he is," she replied smiling. "My man."

Thirty-Five

Just over three and a half hours later, Jake pulled onto Vicky and Jasper's driveway. As he had crossed over into Worcestershire, dark clouds began looming on the northern horizon, signalling the onset of a downpour. Sure enough, it had only taken a few more miles before Jake's 4x4 had been pelted with rain and hail. The sky above had darkened considerably, making him flick his lights on. The rain had continued, not relenting an inch as he'd made his way through the winding lanes that border the Lickey Hills Country Park. Jake killed the engine, running up the driveway and rivers of rainwater splashed at his ankles. The rain had died away, a strong wind gusting down the quiet lane. As he went to knock the door, it opened, revealing Jasper on the other side. "Hi. How are you?" Jake said happily.

Jasper stepped forward, jumping into the man's arms. He hugged him tightly, causing Jake's throat to constrict with rising emotion. "I'm fine. It's so nice to see you again."

"You too. It's nice to see Jasper the boy, instead of Jasper the ghost." The boy smiled, liking the sound of the man's words.

"Hi," Vicky said as she made her way from the kitchen. She stepped out onto the path, giving Jake a hug.

Taken off guard slightly, he returned the hug with his free arm, awkwardly kissing Vicky on the cheek. She smiled, blushing slightly. "Hi, Vicky. Long-time-no-see."

"I know. It looks like you've brought the weather with you. Was it like this all the way here?"

"No. It's nice back home." He noticed Alana stood behind her, a warm smile on her face. "Hi."

"Hello again, Jake. We meet again. Under a different sky."

Jasper jumped down, allowing the witch to say her hellos. She walked forward, embracing him warmly. "I never got a chance to thank you, Alana," he said, as he gave her a squeeze.

"I give you my sorrow, Jake. I left soon after you had awoken. I needed to return home to give Silas some food. That's when the darkness came."

He let go of her, his face dropping slightly. "What happened?"

"Shall we go inside?" Vicky said. "It's getting a bit blustery out here."

"Good idea," Jake said, following the others inside. He closed the door, removing his trainers, placing them on the mat.

"Come through. The kettle has just boiled. I've not had chance to go shopping today, but I have some croissants if you would like one."

"Sounds good to me," he replied as they made their way into the kitchen.

Vicky fussed around the kettle, feeling slightly anxious as she pulled mugs from the cupboards. "Milk with two wasn't it?"

"Well remembered. Thank you, Vicky," he replied smiling evenly. Jake folded his arms as he leaned against a tall cupboard. "So, what happened to you, Alana?"

The witch took a breath, composing herself. "I left Kungsback shortly after you woke. I made my way back up the mountain to the cabin. Silas was there to greet me as ever, asking if I had seen the Outlanders. I took him inside, preparing some food. Then it all went black. The next thing I know, I was lying in a cold cave with Jasper. Silas was there too. The spirit consumed him before our eyes."

"I am so sorry," Jake replied sombrely.

"Thank you, Jake. In truth, Silas was not far from the end. But he did not deserve to meet his end like that."

"I feel responsible. After all, you were helping me. Maybe if that didn't happen, you would not have fallen foul of those b..." He stopped himself, aware that Jasper was sat there. "Monster's." Vicky smiled to herself as she stirred his coffee, liking the man more and more.

"Do not keep those troubles inside you, Jake. What is done is done. I am only thankful that we managed to escape them."

"How did you manage that?" he said as Vicky handed him a steaming mug. "Thank you," he said.

"You're welcome. Alana. Would you like another drink?"

"You're most kind. Yes please. That would be lovely." She looked back at Jake, her mind clicking back to the story. "They kept us in the cave for a while. Alain brought humans back for Virdelas to feast on. Then after a while, they loaded us both into a cart. The brothers had plans. The dark witch was to be first on their list. Then the demon. Then yourself. We travelled to Tenta, so they could destroy Lenga. That is when we made good our escape. I am not sure whether they made good on their promise. Or whether the witch did for them. She would not have gone to her grave lightly. We fled across the land, managing to cross over into Katherine's world. Jasper knew the way home. He is indeed a very brave and worthy young man. You should be proud, Vicky."

"Oh, I am. He's my world. I'm just going to make sure that he doesn't vanish into any other worlds though."

They all smiled at her words, the mood in the kitchen lightening. "Well I am glad you made it here," Jake said sincerely. "Let's hope that there are no more dramas or trouble around the corner. I am sure that we are safe now."

"Do you really think so?" Vicky said, concern appearing on her face.

"I hope so. I cannot say one hundred percent. But I am hoping that the brothers either met their match or are far enough away from here."

"Sorry to be negative. I really am. But what if they are not?"

"Then we will have to deal with that," Jake said. An edge of steel in his voice.

They moved into the lounge after the coffee and croissants had been polished off, talking about various subjects. Their plans for the next few months, in both The Midlands and Cornwall. As the sky started darkening further, Vicky noticed her son rubbing his eyes. "Are you getting tired, Jaspy?"

"No, Mummy. I am fine."

"Well, I think it's time that we took you up for a bath. Big day tomorrow. Grandma and Grandad are coming to see you. And I will have to phone Ashley, to tell her what has happened. I'm sure she will want to pay you a visit."

"Okay, Mummy. Five more minutes?"

"Okay. I'll pop upstairs. I have a bag for Alana that she needs to take with her."

"Thank you, Vicky," the witch replied warmly.

"Oh, it's fine really. Just a few things to make you feel more at home here." Vicky left the room, leaving the three of them sat looking at each other.

Jake pulled out his phone, dialling home. It rang a few times before he heard a familiar voice on the other end of the line. "Hi, babe. You all okay?"

"We're all fine. Is everything okay up there?"

"Fine. We'll be heading back in a few minutes. Should be home by about ten."

"Okay. Well, we'll wait up for you. I'm about to give Alicia a bath. Well, Wilf is. Although he doesn't know it yet."

Jake chuckled. "Tell him to go easy on her. Do you want me to bring anything in?"

"Just yourself. Is Alana okay?"

"Yes. She is fine. They all are. Vicky's just preparing her a bag to bring with her. Jasper is here with us. He's heading for a bath of his own," he said winking at the boy, making him smile.

"Okay. Well travel safely, and we will see you soon. Love you."

"Love you too, babe. Kiss my princess for me."

"Oh, I will. Bye, babe."

"Bye," he replied, ending the call. Jake stood up, sliding his phone into his pocket as footsteps sounded above them.

Vicky padded down the stairs, placing a sports bag, heaving with clothing and other items next to the front door. She walked into the lounge, smiling at the threesome. "Did you just phone home?"

"Yes. I told them that we are on our way shortly. I suppose we'd better make a move. Long drive ahead." The ceiling lights flickered, causing Jake to look up at them briefly.

"Okay, well it was lovely to see you again Jake. I cannot thank you enough for…" her words stopped at the lights went out, plunging the lounge into darkness.

Thirty-Six

Vicky looked at Jake in the darkness, a worried look on her face. "It did this recently. The lights in the kitchen popped off."

"Where is the fuse board?" Jake said.

"In the pantry off the kitchen. I'll show you." They walked through into the kitchen, Vicky heading over to a small cubby-hole in the corner of the room. She opened the door, motioning Jake over. "It's there. Above the highest shelf."

"Okay. I'll take a look." He walked over, dropping the plastic flap on the front of the fuse board. Upon inspection, he noticed one of the breakers had dropped into the off position. He reached up, pushing the switch with his finger. Nothing happened. "Are the lights in the lounge back on?"

"No."

"Mummy," Jasper said from the lounge. "Has Jake fixed it?"

"Not yet. He's taking a look at it now." Rain started pattering against the kitchen window. Vicky watched as the trees and bushes in the garden swayed back and forth under a stiffening breeze.

"Your fuse board isn't labelled. Does one switch power all the downstairs lights?"

"I'm not sure, why?"

"Try the kitchen light?" he replied, using the flashlight on his phone to light the small pantry.

A breeze blew through the kitchen, the utility door swinging on its hinges. "The back door must be open," Vicky said as she diverted her route from the switch on the wall. "Hang on Jake while I..."

"What was that?" Jake said, missing the end of the woman's sentence. He turned from the back of the cupboard, stepping out into the kitchen. Three sets of eyes looked back at him. One was Vicky's. The other sets of eyes were glowing yellow and red, reaching out to him across the kitchen.

"Reunited at last," Alain said, his long bony fingers wrapping themselves around Vicky's neck. She stood frozen to the spot, her face a mask of terror.

"Mummy. What's going on?" Jasper said as he walked from the lounge into the kitchen. He froze, his feet seemingly welded to the tiles as Alain smiled at him.

"The Watcher. I bid you a warm greeting."

Alana stepped into the kitchen, sliding gracefully past the young boy. "Leave this place. There is nothing here for you."

"Yes, there is," Virdelas replied. "There are scores to be settled and new friends to meet."

"Elias," Jake said, swaying on his feet. "I thought you were dead."

"Sorry for the confusion. But I am not Elias. He perished. A large man with dark hair and a hairy face did for him. I have taken his vessel. I am Virdelas. Father of Korgan and Reggan. Fallen brothers. Fallen kings. You saw to that. I am here to return the favour."

Jake was paralysed. He stood there, not knowing what to do. All he could think of was Katherine and Alicia. "I only did what needed to be done to get my loved ones back."

"And I commend your spirit. However, I cannot let that pass-by unpunished. I am here for you. And your kin. Where are they?"

Jake was lost for words. His mind could not compute what was happening. He was trying to think of a way out. But he was trapped. Boxed in by the two giant vampires that stood glaring at him. "My family are not here. They live far away."

"Then before I kill you, you will take me to them. I will enjoy ending your life before their eyes. They will watch you suffer as Korgan suffered at your hand. Then I will take your kin. We have plans for them."

"Leave my Mummy alone," Jasper cried, walking across to Alain. He tried to pull Vicky away from the towering vampire, tugging on her arm. Virdelas took a step forward, back-handing the boy across the kitchen. He landed in a crumpled heap on the floor, blood seeping from his mouth.

"JASPER!" Vicky screamed as she fought Alain's iron-like grip.

"Hush now. Your son just needed to learn some manners. You do not disobey a king." Alana gathered Jasper into her arms, her eyes burning into Virdelas'.

"Just leave them. Take me," Jake said. "You came here for me. I will come, just leave them alone. They are innocent in all this."

"We do not care, Jake," Alain said. "You will take us to your kin, right now. If you try to resist, I will rip the boy's limbs off one by one. Then his mother can watch him die slowly." Vicky wailed against him, struggling to break free.

Alain bent down, his canines touching the smooth skin of her neck. "Or I could just turn you right now. If that is your desire? Then we will watch while you turn your son. Is that what you would like?" Vicky never answered. The sharp teeth against her neck had stilled her movements, a dark patch appearing at the front of her jeans as her bladder emptied itself. The vampire looked at Jake, his eyes burning with hate. "Take us there, now."

"Okay," Jake said groggily. "It's a long journey though. My car is outside."

"Car?" Alain hissed.

"My car. It's what we use to travel here."

"Then lead on. But be warned. One wrong move and they all die. You'll die last. Painfully."

"MOVE!" Virdelas hollered, making Jake flinch. He walked drunkenly past Alana and Jasper, grabbing his car keys from the telephone table. "Bring him," Virdelas said to Alana, the witch complying without argument.

Outside, Jake unlocked the Nissan, turning towards the vampires. The sky had darkened further, the night coming on quicker than usual for the time of year. "It's a long journey. At least three hours."

"We don't measure time as you humans do. Just take us to your kin," Alain said. He let go of Vicky, who staggered around the front of the 4x4, climbing into the front passenger seat.

"Alana. You will need to ride in the boot. There is no room on the back seat for all of you."

"Just hurry up about it. My patience wears thin. The boy will ride with us. Do not try to be clever, Jake," Alain said. "I know you are cunning. Not this time though. This time, you do as we bid." Before he climbed into the car, he walked up the path, closing the front door as more rain started to fall. A few seconds later, he reversed out of the drive, heading towards the motorway. With no hope or clue as to how to survive the night.

The landscape was pelted with perpetual rain. *Typical weather. If only the clouds would break. It'd fry those bastards inside the car,* Jake thought. He pushed the 4x4 up to seventy miles-per-hour, his mind trying to think of some way out of the situation that they all found themselves in. *We've come too far to just die like this.* His thoughts went to his family, trying his best not to think about what would happen in a few short hours. *I could crash the car,* he thought. *We'd all die, but at least they would be safe down south.* He looked in the rear-view mirror, catching Jasper's eye. The boy looked back at him, his face streaked with tears. His mouth bloody where he'd been struck. *No. This is not going to go down like this. Think Jake, think.* As they passed the junction for Worcester, an idea formed in his mind. As carefully as Jake could, he pulled his phone out of his jeans pocket. Laying it on his lap, he slowly typed out a message, keeping his eyes on the road as much as possible. He hit send, nonchalantly slipping the phone back into his pocket. He looked to his left, looking at Vicky. She had seen what he'd just done, nodding at him before looking through the windscreen at the oncoming rain. *Please read that text,* he thought, as they headed towards the border with Gloucestershire.

* * *

Kerry sat cross-legged on her bed, her headset doing it best to stay on her head. Her unruly hair seemed to push against it as she attempted to kill her online buddy from California. Her thumbs worked the controller feverishly as she stared at the monitor in front of her. Outside, dark clouds pressed against the horizon as wind and rain battered the Cornish landscape. "Shit," she said as her friend from the other side of the planet took her characters head off with a well-timed swing of his sword. She dropped the controller in disgust, climbing off the bed. She headed for the kitchen, returning to her bedroom a few minutes later with a glass of coke and a pack of Jaffa Cakes. A message flashed up on the screen, her friend asking for a rematch. "You can just wait, Leon. Smug bastard," she said, taking a swig of coke. Less than a minute later, half a packet of Jaffa Cakes had been demolished. She reached for her controller, stalling as Kerry noticed a flashing notification light on her phone. Swiping the screen, she could see that she had received a text. She opened it, half looking at the monitor in front of her. Her eyes fell back to the phone, seeing a message from Jake Stevenson.

Kerry. We're in trouble. I'm on my way home from Birmingham. Vampires are with me. They are going to kill us. Warn Katherine and Wilf. Two hours till we get there. Please help.

Her mouth fell open, her eyes re-reading the message over and over again. "Fuck," she said, noting that the message had been sent an hour previously. She typed a quick reply, her shaky finger hitting the send button as she scrambled off the bed. Kerry slipped her trainers and tracksuit top on, running downstairs, phone in hand. "I'm just popping out. Be back later," she shouted to her parents as they sat watching Sunday night television. As the rain assaulted her, she pulled the hood over her head, running haphazardly through the streets of Tintagel towards Jake's house. A few minutes later, with little breath left inside her, Kerry banged on Jake's front door. As she waited, Kerry placed her hands on her knees, bending over to try to get her breath back. *God, I'm so unfit,* she thought as the front door opened.

"Kerry? Are you okay?" Katherine said.

"Can I come in?"

"Of course. Come in." Kerry walked into the lounge, nodding at Wilf who looked at the bedraggled woman in front of him.

"Kerry," he said, noting the look on her face. "What is it?"

Katherine walked in behind her, walking over to stand next to the fireplace. "Kerry?"

"I've just received a message from Jake. He's in trouble."

"What?" Katherine said. "What kind of message?" Kerry pulled out her phone, selecting her message folder. She looked at them both, her face stricken. Her voice was shaky as she read the message to Katherine and Wilf.

"Fuckenhell," said Wilf. "How long do we have?"

"He sent it over an hour ago, which means that you have maybe thirty minutes before they get here," Kerry replied.

"Oh no," Katherine said, sitting down heavily on the sofa, her head falling into her hands. "We're all going to die."

"No, we're not," Wilf said defiantly. "We know they are coming. We can prepare."

"How, Uncle?"

"Jake has stakes in the garage. Along with crosses. We can fend them off, then try to take them down."

"We cannot do that in this house. The neighbours will call the police. All hell will break loose," Katherine said. "Lawmen, Uncle. They will come in their numbers. They would uncover everything that we are trying to keep concealed from this world."

"So, where can we go? We need somewhere away from the rest of the folk. Somewhere that will give us a chance."

"Tintagel Castle," Kerry blurted. It's only a short walk from here. No one will be there in this weather. It will be deserted."

"What is it?" Wilf said.

"They are ancient ruins. Not far from here. A ten-minute walk tops."

"I've been there with Jake," Katherine said. "So, what do we do?"

"We go there now and make a stand," Wilf said, striding from the lounge. "Katherine, Kerry, come outside." They followed Wilf through the kitchen, out into the carport towards the side door that led into the garage.

Katherine flicked the light on, lighting the small space. "What do we have?"

Wilf walked over to the workbench, pulling a box from under the counter. He spilled the contents out, the wooden stakes and crosses clattering loudly. "We have this," he said, dividing the array of objects into three piles.

Kerry walked over to the counter, picking up a large stake in one hand, cross in the other. "Is that holy water?" she said, eyeing the small glass bottles.

"Yes," Katherine said. "Jake used them on his bite. He must have kept a few bottles spare, as he used to visit the church every week."

"So, this is what we have," Wilf said. "Is it enough?"

"It will have to be," Katherine replied. She looked at Kerry. "You must take Alicia to your home. We cannot risk having her close by."

"Why not," Kerry replied.

"Because she has the blood of Reggan in her veins. They will seek out her scent. I almost lost her last time. I will not put her in danger."

"Okay. I will take her to mine."

"Good," Wilf said. "We must be off. If they turn up with us here, it will all go to hell very quickly."

A few minutes later, they closed the front door behind them. "Okay," Kerry said. "I will wait for you to call me."

"Thank you, Kerry. If she wakes up, give her the bottle and try to settle her. There are nappies in the bag," she said. "I only hope that they see the note you've left them."

"I'm sure they will," she replied. Let's hope they follow us."

"Do you know where you're going?"

"Yes. We will telephone you soon."

Kerry walked over, hugging each of them in turn. "Good luck. I will make sure that Alicia is okay."

They both nodded, heading down the driveway, shouldering their packs. Kerry headed off in the other direction, gently nudging the pushchair forward, hoping that no one saw her walking a baby at that time of night. As she walked, she typed another message to Jake. Hoping that he read it in time.

Thirty-Seven

Jake had previously felt his phone vibrate in his pocket, opting not to read it as the rain battered the car. As he pulled off the main highway, he felt it vibrate again. He checked the rear-view mirror, happy that neither Virdelas nor Alain could see what he was doing. Lying the phone on his lap, Jake quickly read the messages, a swell of hope rising inside him. A few minutes later, the Nissan pulled up on Jake's driveway. He looked at the clock on the dashboard. 21:48. "Okay. We're here."

"Not tricks, Jake," Alain said, his voice dark and ominous. Jake climbed out of the car, opening the rear passenger door. Vicky did the same, the giant vampires climbing out.

"Mummy," Jasper said as he ran into his mother's embrace.

She knelt down, holding him. "Just be quiet, Jaspy. Do as Mummy tells you. Okay?"

"Okay, Mummy. I promise."

"Silence," Virdelas hissed. "Jake. The Witch."

He opened the boot, Alana climbing out stiffly. "Sorry about that, Alana."

"It is fine," she replied quietly.

Jake walked up to the house, glad that it was in darkness as the message had informed him. He unlocked the door, walking in. "Hello?" he called.

They filed in after him, Vicky closing the door behind them. "Where are they?" Vicky said, unsure what was going on.

"I'm not sure," Jake replied, flicking the hall light on. He walked through into the kitchen, turning the light on. Warm down-lighters gave the room a welcoming feel.

"Where are your kin?" Alain asked, grabbing Jake by the arm.

"They are not here," He replied sheepishly, seeing the note on the table. Jake picked it up, reading it to the others. "We're at Tintagel Castle. We'll be back later."

"What is this?" Virdelas said, grabbing Jake by the throat. He lifted him one-handed, the man's head thumping into the white ceiling. "Where are your kin?"

"They are at the castle," he spluttered, trying to breathe. "It's just a short walk from here. They must have spent the day there."

"Take us to this place. If you are tricking us, I will make sure they all die in front of you."

"This is no trick. Look," he said holding out the paper. "They are not here."

Virdelas swatted the paper from Jake's outstretched hand. "Don't offer me parchment. Take us to them. Now!" He let go of Jake, letting him fall to the floor. He lay there, gasping for breath, massaging his tender throat.

"We move. Now," Alain commanded, letting the man climb to his feet. He ushered them out of the house, leaving the front door ajar as they set off down the road. Towards their prize.

* * *

"Do you think they will come?" Wilf said as the wind battered the headland.

"I hope so, Uncle. I really do."

"Do you think we can take them?"

"Again, I hope so," she said, holding her weapons ready.

Wilf looked across the barren ground, liking the feel of his surroundings. They had walked down steep steps, crossing a large bridge on their way to where they now stood. Old stone ruins gently crumbled nearby, the sea winds gradually claiming them. "It feels like Shetland."

"Yes, it does, Uncle. Let us hope it is lucky like Shetland is."

A far-off noise made them both turn. "What was that?" Wilf said, his grip tightening on the cross.

The noise came again, slightly clearer. It was a voice. "It's Jake. He's calling us." Katherine was about to reply when Wilf grabbed her arm.

"No. Let's get ready first, Kath." They walked towards the sea, trying to find a good spot for a stand-off. An ancient ruin cut into the rock took Wilf's eye. "Here. This is as good a place as any for a scrap."

"Okay, Uncle." She turned back towards the mainland. "JAAAKE. OVER HERE," she shouted. They stood and watched for a few minutes, weapons ready, until a group appeared from the darkness. Light from the imposing hotel across the water offered Katherine and Wilf a degree of help in spotting the advancing group. "It's Jake," she said.

"Others too. Giants. Vampires. That must be the one that snapped my arm. There looks to a half dozen of them in total."

"Yes. Alana is with them. Along with the mother and boy. I have an ill feeling about this, Uncle."

"Hush now, Kath. Don't go getting the jitters. We need to be focused. Tuck your cross and stake into the back of your clothes. We need them to think we are without weapons."

Katherine did so, making sure that they were readily available. The pockets of her jeans contained two bottles of holy water, as did Wilf's. They were ready. "Uncle. If anything happens to me, promise that you'll take care of Jake and Alicia."

"Do not do that, Kath. We will win through."

A few minutes later, the group rounded the bend near to where Katherine and Wilf stood. Alain and Virdelas flanking them. Vicky and Jasper were in the middle of the group, holding hands. Alana walked next to them, dressed differently to how Wilf and Katherine remembered her. "Kath," Jake said.

"Jake," She replied. What's going on?"

"I remember you, old man," Alain said to Wilf. "You gave me this," he said, indicating his disfigured face.

"What do you want?" Wilf shouted across the headland.

"All of you," the vampire countered.

"That's never going to happen. Be off with you. We have endured enough from your kind."

Virdelas stepped forward, closing the gap between them. "My sons are dead because of your kind, human."

"And thank the gods for that," Wilf replied. "They've wreaked havoc over our lands for countless seasons. Their demise was a blessing."

"Reggan's maybe. But Korgan was a worthy king. He did not deserve to die at the hands of men. Jake will pay for killing him. You all will."

"It was I that killed Korgan. So, if you have a quarrel, it's with me."

Virdelas stepped closer, his eyes burning red with fury. "You did for my son?"

"Yes. And Jake did for Reggan. Not before the monster had taken a chunk out of him. It was an honest battle and Jake won through."

Virdelas looked at Jake, his expression changing. "You were bitten?"

"Yes," Jake replied.

"So why did you not turn?"

"He almost did," Alana replied. I brought him back from the darkness that had taken over his body. His family needed him. His daughter needed him."

"Daughter?" Virdelas exclaimed.

"Yes," Katherine said, realising that things had just become more complicated. She decided to take a risk "Our daughter has Reggan's blood running through her veins."

"Where is this child?" Alain commanded.

"Far from here. She is staying with friends. Elias came before. He snatched us away from Jake, taking us to the land where the witch dwelt."

"Lenga," Virdelas said. "So that's why Elias was there. He had plans for the child. As now do I. Take me to them."

"Never!" Katherine spat.

The giant vampire, covered the ground in a flash, grabbing Katherine by the throat. He lifted her easily, his teeth bared, ready to strike. "NOOOOOO," Jake screamed, running towards them. Alana broke with him, striding towards Katherine.

"You die, human," Virdelas hissed, grey canines pressing against the flesh of her neck as Katherine hung helplessly. Out of instinct, born out of pure survival, she reached around to her waistband, pulling the cross out of her jeans. Virdelas howled in pain, slamming the woman against the ground. She landed heavily in a crumpled heap, becoming still as Jake barrelled into Virdelas, bouncing off the vampire's flank, landing awkwardly at his feet.

The giant screamed in pain once more as Wilf strode forward, cross in one hand, holy water in the other. "Be gone," he commanded as the vampire gave ground back towards his brother.

Alana changed direction, heading over towards Katherine. Strong hands plucked her from the ground, turning her in mid-air. She looked into Alain's eyes, noticing Vicky and Jasper cowering on the floor behind him. Before she could struggle, Alain bit her below the ear, worrying her neck roughly. She tried to cry out in pain as she hung suspended above the ground. It was no use though as she felt her vision darkening.

"Now, you all die," Virdelas said, smiling as he saw the witch being drained.

"Not this night," Wilf said holding the holy water in his right hand. He took a step forward throwing it at Virdelas. His aim was true as the bottle smashed into the vampire's face, smoke and screams erupting into the night. Alain dropped the witch to the ground as his brother's cries pierced the darkness. Virdelas was on the ground, rolling on the stunted grass, swatting at his face. Wilf was on him in a flash, his movements that of a man half his age. Before Alain could interject, Wilf's stake pierced the vampire's chest, finding its mark.

"VIRDELAS!" Alain howled, rushing Wilf. The older man saw him coming, holding his cross aloft, forcing Alain to watch helplessly as his brother was destroyed before his eyes.

"Jake," Wilf shouted. "Catch," he said as he tossed a bottle of holy water towards him. He caught it one-handed, unscrewing the lid as he advanced on the remaining vampire. The older man plucked the stake from the vampire's chest as the already dead skin started to pucker and hiss.

"Now for you," Wilf said, the cross' force pummelling the remaining brother. He tried to scramble away, his feet skidding on the grass as Alain tried in vain to propel himself away from his attackers. Two soft hands came from behind, Alana's thumbs pressing into his eyes, bearing down with all her weight. Jake looked at her, blood smeared across her throat, dripping down her white skin. He acted instinctively, sitting down on Alain's chest. The vampire was trying to scream, his mouth wide open, exposing a mouth full of blackened teeth.

"This ends now," Jake said as he shoved the upturned bottle into the vampire's mouth, the contents emptying itself quickly. A shockwave erupted from Alain, knocking Jake and Alana backwards onto the grass. He tried to scream, the water scorching the insides of his mouth and throat.

A blinding light pushed against him as Wilf sat across his chest, pushing the cross into his face. "This is for every poor soul that you have terrorised," the older man said, slamming the stake into Alain's sternum. The vampire tried to move, but the fight had already gone out of him. He died quietly, his life-force ebbing away into the Cornish earth. His ageless reign came to an end with a whimper as flesh and bone crumpled and withered away to ash, blown across the headland by the stiff breeze.

Vicky and Jasper clung to each other on the floor, staring over at the carnage in front of them. "Is it over, Mummy?"

"I think so," Vicky replied, her body unable to move. They sat there, watching as Jake and Wilf looked at the witch.

"Alana. Are you hurt?"

She sat up stiffly, placing a blood-stained hand over the wound on her throat. "The darkness is taking hold of me. I must try and fight it," she said through tight lips. "Katherine. Go to Katherine," She said collapsing backwards onto the grass.

Jake and Wilf turned, hurrying over to the woman's inert form. "Babe," Jake said as he landed beside her, turning Katherine over. Lifeless eyes stared back at him, blankly peering into the night sky. "Katherine? He shook her gently, her head lolling to one side. Tears fell from his eyes, landing on her soft skin.

Wilf was beside him, taking her hand in his. "Katherine. Come on, girl. Wake up." He could see it was a forlorn hope. Both men knew that she was dead.

"No, babe, no," Jake said, lifting her into his arms. He sat there, rocking gently as he stroked her dark hair. He looked at Wilf who was sat next to him. "She's gone. Katherine's gone." Salty tears ran down the ruddy features of the older man, his resolve blowing away on the breeze. He wept, his hands covering his face.

Vicky knelt beside them, placing a hand on both their shoulders. "Oh, Jake," was all she could say as she wept with them. She cried for the woman. For Jake and Wilf too. Her body shuddering as sobs wracked it uncontrollably.

Jasper lifted Alana's head into his lap, looking down at the white witch. "Don't die. Please, Alana. Please don't die."

"I'm not sure I can fight it, little one. But I am trying to fend off the darkness that spreads within me." The boy noticed the pendant that lay across her chest. It was pulsing gently against the witch's pale skin. He took it in his hands, cuddling into Alana as she lay there on the grass.

Jake buried his face in Katherine's hair, holding her tightly. "I love you, Kath," he said as he started to feel her body cooling. "I will always love you." His voice faltered as he held her, not wanting to let her go.

Minutes seemed to pass, the headland silent, save for the sound of the waves lapping at the rocks below them. Jake felt a hand on his shoulder. He pulled his face away from the woman in his arms. Wilf looked at him, his face grave. "She's gone, Jake. Katherine is with her kin now. We need to go, back to your home."

"What about Kath?"

"We take her with us. We will lay her to rest. But not here. Come on, Son." Wilf stood, walking over to Jasper and Alana, leaving Jake and Vicky sat on the grass behind him. "You've been bitten?" Wilf said.

"Yes," the witch responded weakly. "I am trying to purge it from my essence."

"Can you do it?"

"Yes. I just need to fight it on my own."

"We need to move. Jake's home is not far. Can you walk?"

The witch nodded, letting the boy help her to her feet. "Will you help me, little one?"

"Yes, Alana. I will hold your hand." She smiled down at him in the darkness as she took a tentative step back the way they came.

"We will carry her together, Son. Let's get out of this place."

Jake merely nodded as he hefted Katherine's body into his arms, heading back to an empty house, with an even emptier heart.

Thirty-Eight

They sat in Jake's lounge, all of them silent. Vicky and Jasper huddled together on the sofa, the woman stroking her son's hair gently. Alana lay on the other sofa, soft cushions under her head. A fleece blanket covered her from the neck down. The witch lay still, holding the pendant under the blanket. She mouthed silent words, trying to bring herself back from the brink of darkness. Jake and Wilf walked into the lounge from the hallway. The younger man flopped down next to Jasper, his head in his hands. "We need Alicia back, Jake. Call your friend. I will boil some water."

Wilf headed out into the kitchen, as Jake pulled his phone out of his pocket. He dialled a number, dried tears streaked across his face. "Kerry. Hi. Is Alicia okay?" He listened to the response as fresh tears formed in the corners of his eyes. "Thank you. I will come around now. Bye." He hung up the phone. "She is fine. I'll go and bring her home."

Vicky looked up at Jake, her heart reaching out towards him. "I am so very sorry, Jake. I don't know what to say?"

"Nor do I, Vicky. I can't believe she's gone." He let the words hang in the air as he left the house, his feet dragging heavily.

Jasper walked into the kitchen, his mother following him. Wilf stood there, puffing on his pipe as the kettle started to boil. "Shall I make some tea?" Vicky said, her words sounding hollow and meaningless.

"Aye," replied Wilf. "You will probably make a better job of it than me." He shuffled over to the kitchen table, sitting down heavily. Wilf suddenly felt old. He sat, his pipe stuck between his lips, trying to come to terms with his loss.

"Do you take sugar?" Vicky asked from across the kitchen.

"Please. Jake normally makes it sweet for me. Vicky nodded, depositing three spoons from the earthenware jar.

"Jasper. Ask Alana if she wants a drink?"

"Okay, Mummy," he replied, walking into the lounge. She lay there, her skin pallid. "Alana. Mummy asked if you would like a drink?"

Her eyes opened, focusing on Jasper. "Just some cool water please."

He headed back to the kitchen, letting his mother know as she was busy stirring Wilf's tea. Vicky rooted through a few kitchen cupboards, finding a plastic sports bottle. She filled it with cold water, screwing the lid back on before handing it to her son. Jasper scooted back into the lounge offering the witch the bottle. Alana took a few pulls on the bottle, the water refreshing her. "Thank you, Jasper. Could you lie with me, please? You will give me added strength to fight the infection."

"Yes," he said, pulling the blanket back before snuggling down next to her. They fell asleep together quickly, the pendant glowing under the covers.

Vicky sat down next to Wilf, taking a sip of her tea. She looked at the old man, not really knowing what to say. "I am Vicky by the way."

He looked at her, smiling briefly. "Hello, Vicky. I am Wilf. If only we had met under happier circumstances."

"I know. And I'm so sorry for causing all this pain."

"It's not your fault. This story has rumbled on for a long time. Many have perished along the way. My brother and my two nieces have paid the price for where we are now. I only hope that it is over. I am getting too old. My heart has been broken too many times. Katherine was the daughter that I never had. I loved her every day of her life. She was strong and true. She loved Jake and the little one. And now they have to carry on without her."

"It will be really hard for you all. But you will make it. I know you will."

"Thank you. I know that you have endured similar pain. Time will heal old wounds." They sat there for a few minutes, sipping at their drinks until the front door opened. Wilf and Vicky walked through into the lounge, the woman seeing her son asleep with Alana on the sofa.

"She's asleep," Jake said. I'll take her upstairs and settle her down."

"Do you need any help?" Vicky said.

"I'll be okay. But thank you." He lifted the infant out of the pushchair, carrying her upstairs. Jake opened the door to the spare bedroom, walking over to the bed where Katherine lay. Her skin had taken on a waxy sheen, the light from the street lamp outside, giving her face an orangey glow. He sat next to her, Alicia looking at her sleeping mother.

"Ma-ma," she mouthed, making Jake hold her tight, his tears spilling down his cheeks.

"Your Mama will always love you, Alicia. So, will I." He leaned forward, kissing Katherine's lips. They were cool, the cold hand of death settling over her. Alicia reached out, a small hand patting her mother's face. Jake watched, his heart breaking as his daughter showed Katherine one last show of affection. He stood up, walking out of the room. His world falling apart around him.

* * *

The sun rose over Cornwall, the sky devoid of clouds. Jake and Wilf stood outside the kitchen door, the older man lighting his first pipe of the day. "What shall we do with Katherine?" Jake said. "We cannot bury her here. It's too complicated. The police will know that she didn't die of natural causes. It will cause a real shit storm."

"Then we take her back and lay her to rest at Shetland."

"Really?" Jake thought about it for a moment. "I suppose it makes sense. I still cannot believe she's gone." Tears started to form again, his emotions threatening to spill over.

The older man laid a weathered hand on his shoulder. "There will be time to grieve soon, Son. When we lay her to rest, we can say our goodbye's and shed out tears. Right now, we have things to do. You have a daughter that needs her father. Katherine loved us all. And she is somewhere better now, with her kin. We must carry on. It's what she would have wanted."

"I know you're right. I don't think last night has sunk in yet."

"And it won't. Not for a long time. But we need to plan. How do we get Katherine to Shetland?"

"My bike is still in Amatoll. We could use that to take her home."

"Good. Let's do that. Today. As much as I loved her, she will start to decay soon. We need to get her in the ground very soon."

"I know. I think I have an idea."

"Go on."

"I will ask Vicky if she could look after Alicia at her house for a few days. That way, we can both travel together."

"Makes sense. Let's ask her when she awakens."

"When who awakens?" a female voice behind them said. They turned, seeing Vicky stood at the kitchen door. Her dark hair was unruly. Her face drawn. Dark smudges sat underneath the woman's eyes, making her look closer to fifty than forty. Jake relayed their idea to her. "Of course. It's the least I can do."

"Thank you, Vicky. I will pack the boot of the car with her stuff after breakfast." Jake headed inside, leaving Vicky and Wilf to watch the sunrise, while he went upstairs to prepare Katherine. For her final journey.

Sometime later, Jake walked into the lounge, kneeling next to the sofa. Alana lay there, her skin pallid. "Alana. Are you awake?"

Her eyes opened, focusing on Jake. "I was just resting."

"How are you feeling?"

"I feel slightly stronger than last night. Having Jasper lie with me for a while really helped. So, did my stone," she said quietly.

"Good. I hope you can beat this. I really do. Listen. We have to go north later. We are taking Katherine home. We shall bury her at Shetland, where Wilf lived."

"That is a fitting end for her." She reached down, taking Jake's hand. "I give you my sorrow, Jake. She was beautiful. Inside and outside. And she died protecting the ones she loved. She was a queen amongst women."

Jake smiled, liking the kind words that the witch imparted to him. "Yes, she was. She was one of a kind. I will miss her so much." He felt his emotions surface again, changing tack. "Anyway, it's a long journey. Jasper and Vicky are going to look after Alicia while we're gone. It will probably take us four days to get there and back. Maybe longer. Are you going to come with us? Or would you rather stay here and rest?"

"I am quite weak. If you permit it, I will stay here and regain my strength."

"Okay," he said squeezing her hand. "There is plenty of food and drink here. Before we go, I will show how a few things work."

"Thank you, Jake." The witch sat up slowly, wrapping her arms around the man next to her. He returned the embrace, feeling slightly guilty. After a moment, she broke the hold, kissing Jake lightly on the cheek. "And you, are a king amongst men."

* * *

Two days later, under a different sky, the villagers of Shetland stood around the freshly dug grave. Jake and Wilf gently lowered Katherine's body into the ground, stepping back once they had done so. Wilf addressed his folk, his voice loud and commanding over the sea breeze. "We lay our Katherine to rest. She was a daughter of this land. She belonged here as much as the trees and the mountains. But she belonged in another place too. With the man stood next to me. She was strong and kind, a loving mother, partner and niece. Sleep well, Kath. We will carry you in our hearts from this day forward." The villagers bowed their heads, the women folk crying, the men forlorn and empty. People filed away, laying flowers at the graveside. Jake picked up Vicky's shovel, slowly filling in the hole in the ground. His tears mixed in with the soil, as he worked methodically. "I will fetch the sapling," Wilf said before heading off towards the main building.

"Okay," Jake replied, his brow slick with sweat.

The older man returned a few minutes later, laying the small tree next to the grave as Jake smoothed off the soil. "That is a nice gesture," he said.

"I think the tree will be a reminder of our Kath. When I saw it on the edge of Amatoll, I knew what needed doing." He dug a small hole, planting the sapling into the coarse soil. He pulled the soil around its base, patting it lovingly with his rough hands. "Sleep well, Kath. Give greetings to my kin. I will be there shortly." He stood up, looking at the younger man. "Come. Let's have a few mugs of ale before we travel back. I may return here one day. But for now, my heart needs to be close to Alicia. And I need a few jugs of ale if I am to be dragged across the land on that damn bike that Vicky gave me."

"I will go easy. We have plenty of time to get back to the doorway. I am glad you are coming back Wilf, although I thought you would stay here."

"Katherine will be here waiting for me when my time comes. But for now, I have a life to live. I want to feel the sun on my face and enjoy time with my kin. Come on. Let's toast our loved ones."

Thirty-Nine

Vicky opened the front door, smiling at the two men who stood there. "How did it go?"

"It went well," Jake replied.

"It was a fitting farewell," added Wilf.

"Well come in. I will put the kettle on. Are you hungry?"

"I could eat a horse," Jake said. Wilf nodded his agreement as the men stepped into the hallway, removing their footwear. "I've put your bike next to the garden gate. I will bring it around the back in a minute."

"Leave it there. I will sort it out in the morning. Did it work?"

"Yes. Although Wilf fell off a few times."

"That's the last time I ride something like that. I thank you for your kindness, Vicky, but I would rather ride a black unicorn than a contraption like that again."

"Well, I am glad that you are both back safely." They walked into the kitchen, Vicky flicking the kettle on before pulling a pack of sausage and bacon out of the fridge. "Is a fry up okay?"

"You read my mind," Jake said, leaning against the counter stiffly. "How's Alicia and Jasper?"

"Alicia is fine. She's asleep upstairs. Jasper's okay too. Still in shock, I guess. My parents came around earlier. They were so pleased to see him, but they could tell something wasn't quite right. And I had to explain that I was looking after Alicia for a friend. Mum tried to grill me on that."

"Oh. How did you get around that?" Jake said.

"I just managed it somehow. She will probably ask again. But I will handle it."

The men sat down, sipping tea while Vicky prepared them a late supper. "So, what are your plans now?"

"I don't know," Jake said. "I know that I have to report Dad missing. Then there is the small matter of trying to handle the fact that my brother and his girlfriend are missing, presumed dead. There may be a lot of eyes pointing in my direction. How about you?"

"You know. I have no idea either." She turned and smiled at Jake, returning her gaze to the frying pan to rustle the sausages. "Hopefully, life will return to normal. Jasper and I can try to move forward. It's been a hell of a year."

"It certainly has," Jake replied, his expression sombre, his heart aching for the woman who now lay a world away. Under a different sky.

The next morning, after a similar breakfast, Wilf and Jake were stood on the front step of the cottage. Jasper played in the garden, the warm summer sun piercing through the trees that lined the street. Vicky walked with them to the car, feeling slightly deflated. "I only wish this had a happier ending."

The men turned together. "We do too, Vicky. But we can't undo things now. We need to move on. We all do. You have Jasper. We have Alicia."

"I know. They both need us." She walked over to the Nissan, looking through the passenger window at the infant. "Safe travels, little one," she said, tickling Alicia's toes. She giggled at Vicky, displaying her pink gums. The woman turned, looking at Jake. "Keep in touch?" Her question was tinged with hope.

Jake walked over, giving the woman a hug. "Absolutely. I think we are now friends for life."

Tears welled up in the woman's eyes as she smiled at the dark-haired man. "I think so too. Thank you, Jake. You are a wonderful man."

Tears welled in Jake's eyes as he kissed the top of Vicky's head. "No. I'm just a regular guy, whose been caught up in a rollercoaster of events. But thank you. I'll let you know how Alana is. Hopefully, she is feeling better soon."

"I really hope so. I owe her everything. You as well," she said smiling, her face almost as radiant as it once was.

Wilf walked over, putting his arm around her shoulder. "You take care. He's a fine young man. You should be proud."

Her resolve melted, tears falling as she began to cry. "Sorry. I'm a mess."

Wilf held her, looking over at the boy. "Jasper. Come and say farewell."

He turned around, dropping his toy on the grass as he skipped over. "Bye, Jake. Bye, Wilf. Thank you for saving me. I am really sorry about what happened to Katherine. She was nice."

Jake extended his hand. "Yes, she was," was all Jake could manage on the subject. "Bye, Jasper. You take care of your Mummy. And no more adventures."

The boy jumped into his arms, burying his face in Jake's neck. "No more adventures. Unless you come with me."

Jake pulled back, smiling at the mischievous grin the boy held. "I'm getting too old for adventures. I need to take it easy."

"Farewell, young man," Wilf said, rustling the boy's curls. "Look out for your Ma. She's a good un."

"I know," he replied. "She's the best mummy ever." He reached out for Vicky, her welcoming arms gathering him. He sat on her hip, smiling as the two men and Alicia rolled out of the driveway. They all waved as the Nissan pulled away slowly, weaving its way slowly down High House Drive.

Vicky walked down to the roadway, watching the black car slowly dwindle until it was lost from sight. She looked at her son, half-smiling. "So, what shall we do today?"

I don't care, Mummy. As long as I'm with you, I don't care what I do." They walked back towards the cottage as the sun's rays dotted the grass.

"I don't care either, Jaspy," she said as she closed the front door, a crooked smile appearing on her face. "You're home now. And you're safe."

Forty

The Old Malthouse was not busy for a change. Wilf had liked the fact that as the weather grew colder, fewer revellers frequented his favourite watering hole. During the summer months, the bar area was crowded with youngsters, vying for position to be served. This was more to his liking. Half a dozen people sat around the room, as a roaring log fire dispersed its heat across the slate quarry tiles. He sat on his favourite stool, giving him a prime view of the snug bar. He liked how it looked and how it felt. It felt like home from home. Wilf sighed, his heart suddenly heavy.

"Hi, Wilf," a female voice said.

"Oh. Hi, Jo. Quiet in here today."

"It is. Which is not a bad thing sometimes. It gives me more time to do a few chores while I'm working." She smiled at him, her eyes meeting his for longer than with her usual punters. "The usual?"

"Thank you," he replied, his face neutral."

"Is everything alright, Wilf," she said as she selected a pint glass. "You seem a bit off. Sorry if I have spoken out-of-turn."

"No, it's fine, love," he replied. "I've just been doing a lot of thinking lately. Too many things buzzing around this old barrel," he said tapping himself on the head.

"Your niece?"

"Yes. Amongst other things." Wilf had told the woman about how Katherine had died a few months before. Jake had come up with a story to tell the innkeeper, knowing that the older man had become quite fond of her. They had omitted the truth, Wilf telling the woman that Katherine had died of a brain tumour. Jo had been shocked to her core, feelings of her late husband's untimely death resurfacing.

She handed him his pint, placing a smooth hand on his. "Like what?"

"I am returning home. I like it here. I really do. But I need to return to my village in Shetland."

The woman's face dropped. "Oh. When are you leaving?"

"Tomorrow. It's been on my mind for a long time. I feel now the time is right to head back home."

"But what about Alicia?"

"I will miss her. She brings me untold joy. Happiness that I never thought I would have at my time of life. But I miss Kath terribly. I want to visit her resting place and spend some time with her."

Jo looked at him, her face crestfallen. "I understand. I will miss you though. A lot."

He looked at her, not liking how her usually bright face had suddenly looked so sad. "I will miss you too, Jo. You have always been so friendly. I cannot think of many places where I would rather be than sat at this bar. And that's because you're here."

"I don't know what to say, Wilf. I'm quite shocked and saddened that you're leaving. I was kinda hoping that you would ask me out one day?"

"Ask you out? What does that mean?" he asked, slightly confused.

"Gosh, you really are from another planet. You know, ask me on a date?"

"I am lost, Jo. What's a date?"

Jo looked around at the other patrons, checking to see if they were being monitored by gossiping locals. No one was looking at them. The other customers were either reading newspapers or checking out social media on their smartphones. She leaned across the bar, pulling Wilf towards her. Their lips met, Jo's eyes closing. After the initial shock, Wilf's eyes closed too. They stood there, locked together, the rest of the world forgotten. Finally, Jo broke the kiss, stepping back a few paces. "Are you lost now?"

Wilf's eyes opened, his vision fuzzy around the edges. "I never expected that, Jo. I had no idea you thought of me that way. I'm an old man."

"You're not. And anyway, I prefer my men with a few grey hairs and plenty of miles on the clock."

He smiled, his face lighting up, making her smile back. "Well, I am at a loss. I thought I would just come in, drink a few ales and bid you farewell. This has addled my old brain."

"Has it changed your mind?"

"I will still return home tomorrow." He smiled at Jo, reaching for her. She came willingly, letting Wilf kiss her. "But I shall be back. If you'll wait for me."

"Of course, I will. Just don't forget about me, Wilf. And hurry back."

"How could I forget about you? I promise I will return. And I'll think of you every day until I do."

"Stay here a moment," she said, heading through to the lounge area. She reappeared a minute later, her face lightly flushed. "Louise is going to cover for a bit. Come. I want to show you something." Wilf stepped around the bar, following the woman through the archway that led to the lounge, turning right up a tight stairwell. They came out on a small landing with several doors, leading to the living quarters. Jo walked to the end of the corridor, opening a white wooden door.

He followed her into a spacious bedroom, a small window overlooking a rear courtyard that was growing ever darker as the sun dropped towards the horizon. "So, what do you want to show me?"

Jo walked over, kissing him slowly. Wilf wrapped his arms around her, letting her melt into him. She broke away, smiling at him. "I want to show you what you'll be missing. And I promise you, Wilf, you'll not forget this."

Epilogue

The sand felt cool as he buried his toes into it, sheltering them from the warm summer sun. He looked out across the beach, the Atlantic gently lapping at the shore a few hundred yards away. Jake rested his well-tanned arms on his knees, his face serene as he took in his vista. Locals and holidaymakers played and lounged about on Bude's vast beach. A Frisbee sailed through the air in front of him, as a wet Labrador chased it gamely.

"Daddy," a voice to his left called out.

He turned his head, seeing his daughter jogging towards him, ice-cream in hand. Her long limbs were tanned, in stark contrast to her white bikini and bonnet. "Hello princess. Is that Daddy's ice-cream?"

"No, Daddy. It not yours. It mine," she said indignantly. "Lana got your ice-cream."

Alicia sat down on the beach towel as a woman approached. She was dressed in an all-in-one white summer dress, her white bikini visible underneath. A large straw hat sheltered her pale skin from the summer rays, keeping Alana cooler. "And here is your ice-cream," she said, sitting down next to him. "I could really get used to these. Of all the wonders your world has to offer, ice-cream and chocolate are the most magical."

"Well I am glad that about that. Maybe you'll stick around?" Jake said, kissing her gently on the cheek. A tanned arm snaked around the witch's shoulder, drawing her towards him. "Did she behave herself?"

"She did. Although she does not like waiting for her treat. She is headstrong and feisty when she wants to be."

"Oh, I know. She is a right handful." He looked at his daughter as she happily licked at the vanilla cornet. Jake smiled, feeling at peace once more. The horrors of the past almost forgotten, but not quite. He licked his ice-cream, his fingers playing over Alana's cool skin. "We should head back soon. I've got to prepare the barbeque for tonight."

"That is fine. The sun is very hot today. My poor skin is not used to it."

"You'll get used to it. One day. Wilf has. He's got a proper tan going on."

"Yes, he has. He was destined to live out his days next to the ocean."

"I know. He's happy for the first time in a long time."

"Well, that's what the love of a good woman will do for you."

Jake smiled as he took another lick of his ice-cream. "I know, hun."

She snuggled into him, inhaling his scent. "I love you, Jake."

"I love you too, Alana," he said placing his hand on her perfectly formed tummy. "And I already love what we have made together. And I can't wait to meet them."

She turned towards him, hugging him tightly. Twin pendants came together as they embraced, shimmering as they collided. "Him, Jake," she said smiling. "I've already told you, countless times. It's a boy."

THE END

Dear reader,

We hope you enjoyed reading *The Witch and The Watcher*. Please take a moment to leave a review, even if it's a short one. Your opinion is important to us.

Discover more books by Phil Price at https://www.nextchapter.pub/authors/phil-price-horror-author-united-kingdom

Want to know when one of our books is free or discounted for Kindle? Join the newsletter at http://eepurl.com/bqqB3H

Best regards,

Phil Price and the Next Chapter Team

You could also like:

Watchers by S.T. Boston

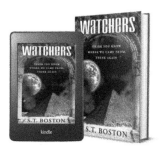

To read the first chapter for free, head to:
https://www.nextchapter.pub/books/watchers

Books by the Author

Unknown (The Forsaken Series Book 1)
The Turning (The Forsaken Series Book 2)
The Witch And The Watcher (The Forsaken Series Book 3)